✠✠✠✠✠✠✠✠✠✠✠✠✠✠✠✠✠✠✠✠✠

OBJECT: TO ROOK A KING

"Look at me!"

Jorian did, then tried to snatch his gaze away and found that he could not. The smith held up something in the palm of his hand. It glowed and sparkled with a myriad of rays. The very soul seemed to be drawn out of his body as he watched in stupefied fascination.

Closer and closer came the smith; brighter and more confusing came the sparkle of lights.

"Back!" said the smith. "Back! Another step!"

Dimly, Jorian heard the door clang and the lock stick. The dazzle faded, and he was in Zor's cage.

"Now," said Rhithlos, "since you have robbed me of Zor, you shall take his place."

By L. Sprague de Camp
Published by Ballantine Books:

The Goblin Tower

Volume One of **The Reluctant King**

L. Sprague de Camp

A Del Rey Book

BALLANTINE BOOKS • NEW YORK

A Del Rey Book
Published by Ballantine Books

Library of Congress Catalog Card Number: 83-90746

ISBN 0-345-29842-X

Manufactured in the United States of America

First Ballantine Books Edition: December 1983

Cover art by David B. Mattingly

To my fellow swashbuckler-in-phantasy, Lin Carter.

CONTENTS

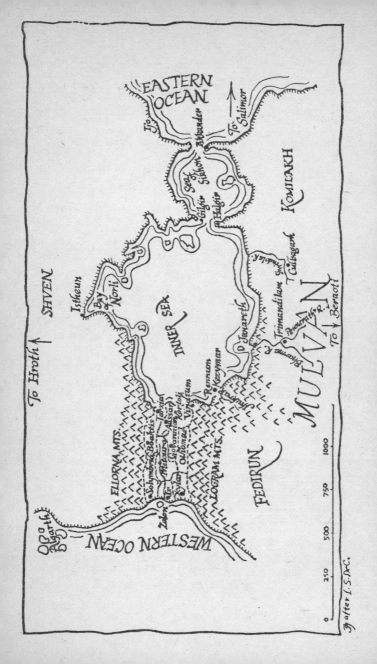

I

A LENGTH OF ROPE

"A CURIOUS CUSTOM," SAID THE BARBARIAN, "TO CUT off your king's head every five years. I wonder your throne finds any takers!"

On the scaffold, the headsman brushed a whetstone along the gleaming edge of his ax, dropped the stone into his pouch, squinted along the blade, and touched it here and there with his thumb. Those in the crowd below could not see his satisfied smile because of the black hood, which—save for the eye holes—covered his head. The ax was neither a woodcutter's tool nor a warrior's weapon. Whereas its helve, carven of good brown oak, was that of a normal ax, its blue steel head was unwontedly broad, like a butcher's cleaver.

The scaffold rose in the midst of the drill ground, outside of the walls of Xylar City near the South Gate. Here, nearly all the folk of the city were gathered, as well as hundreds from outlying towns and villages. Around the base of the scaffold, a battalion of pikemen in black mesh-mail over scarlet coats was ranked four deep, to make sure that no unauthorized person reached the scaffold during

1

the ceremony, and likewise that the victim did not escape. The two outer ranks faced outward and the two inner, inward.

Around the three sides of the scaffold, the notables of Xylar, in crimson and emerald and gold and white, sat on benches. Another rank of soldiers sundered the quality from the commonality. The latter, in brown and buff and black, stood in an expectant, amorphous mass, which filled the greater part of the field.

On the western side of the platform, this multitude surged against the inner ranks of soldiery. Here the throng consisted mainly of young men. Besides the hundreds of mechanics from the city and peasants from the farms, it included a sprinkling of the younger gentry. Hucksters wormed their way through this throng, selling cakes, sausages, fruits, sardines, wine, beer, cider, parasols, and good-luck charms. Outside the crowd of spectators, armored horsemen, with the scarlet hour-glass of Xylar on their white surcoats, patrolled the edge of the field.

Overhead, a white sun blazed in a cloudless sky. A puffy little wind ruffled the leaves of the oaks and poplars and gums that fenced the field. It fluttered the red-and-white pennants that streamed from the tops of the flagpoles at the corners of the scaffold. A few of the leaves of the gums had already turned from green to scarlet.

Seated among the notables, Chancellor Turonus answered the barbarian's question: "We have never had trouble in finding candidates, Prince Vilimir. Behold how they throng about the western side of the scaffold!"

"Will the head be thrown yonder?" asked Prince Vilimir around his forefinger, wherewith he was trying to pry loose a piece of roast from between his teeth. Although he was clean-shaven, Vilimir's long, light, gray-streaked hair, fur cap, fur jacket, and horsehide boots with the hair on gave him a shaggy look. His many massive ornaments of gold and silver tinkled when he moved. He had led the losing faction in an intertribal quarrel over who should be the next cham of the Gendings and hence was in exile. His rival, who was also his uncle, now ruled that fierce nomadic horde.

Turonus nodded. "Aye, and the catcher shall be our new king." He was stout and middle-aged, swathed in a voluminous azure cloak against the chill of the first cool

2

day of autumn. "The Chief Justice will cast the thing yonder. It is a rule that the king must let his hair grow long, to give the judge something to grasp. Once a king had his whole head shaven the night before the ceremony, and the executioner had to pierce the ears for a cord. Most embarrassing."

"By Greipnek's beard, an ungrateful wight!" said Vilimir, a wolfish grin splitting his lean, scarred face. "As if a lustrum of royal luxe were not enough...Be that not King Jorian now?" The Shvenish prince spoke Novarian with fair fluency, but with a northern accent that made "Jorian" into "Zhorian."

"Aye," said the Chancellor, as a little procession marched slowly through the lane kept open by soldiers between the South Gate and the scaffold.

"He took me hunting last month," said Vilimir. "He struck me as a man of spirit—for a sessor, that is." He used a word peculiar to the nomads of Shven, meaning a non-nomad or sedentary person. Among nomads, the word was a term of contempt, but the Chancellor saw fit to ignore this. The exile continued: "I also found him a great talker—too much so for his own good, methinks, but amusing to listen to."

The Chancellor nodded absently, for the procession had now come close enough to recognize faces. First came the royal band, playing a dirge. Then paced the white-bearded Chief Justice of Xylar in a long, black robe, with a golden chain about his neck. Four halberdiers, in the midst of whom towered the king, followed. All those near the lane through which the party proceeded, and many in other parts of the field, sank to one knee as the king passed them.

King Jorian was a tall, powerful young man with a ruddy skin, deep-set black eyes, and coarse black hair that hung to his shoulders. His face, otherwise shaven, bore a fierce mustache that swept out like the horns of a buffalo. A prominent scar crossed his nose—which had a small kink in it—and continued diagonally down across his left cheek. He was stripped to his slippers and a pair of short, silken breeches, and his wrists were bound behind his back. A crown—a slender band of gold with a dozen short, blunt, erect spikes—was secured to his head by a chin strap.

3

Prince Vilimir murmured: "I have never seen a crown with a—how do you say it—a strap of the chin."

"It is needed, to keep crown and head together during the casting of the Lot of Imbal," explained Turonus. "Once, years ago, the crown came off as the head was thrown. One man caught the crown, another the head, and each claimed the throne. A sanguinary civil war ensued."

After the soldiers came a small, lean, dark-brown man in a coarse brown robe, with a bulbous white turban on his head. His long, silky, white hair and beard blew about. A rope was wound around his waist, and he bore a kind of satchel by a strap over his shoulder.

"The king's spiritual adviser," said Chancellor Turonus. "It seems hardly meet that the king of Xylar be sent off by a heathen from Mulvan, rather than by one of our own holy priests. But Jorian insisted, and it seemed but just to grant his last request."

"Who—how did the king come to know the fellow?" asked Vilimir.

Turonus shrugged. "For the past year, he has entertained all sorts of queer persons at the palace. This mountebank—your pardon, the Holy Father Karadur—drifted in, doubtless having fled in disgrace from his own land after having been caught in some vile goëtic witchery."

Then came four beautiful young women, the king's wives. A fifth had given birth the day before and was judged not strong enough to attend the ceremony. The four present were gorgeous in silks and jewels and gold. After the wives came the shaven-headed, purple-robed high priest of Zevatas, the chief god of the Novarian pantheon; then a score of palace officials, and the ladies in waiting. Last of all came Kaeres the joiner, Xylar's leading director of funerals, and six cronies of the king carrying one of Kaeres' new coffins on their shoulders.

As the procession reached the foot of the scaffold, the band fell silent. After a low-voiced consultation, the Chief Justice mounted the steps of the scaffold, followed by two of the four halberdiers.

King Jorian kissed his four wives goodbye. They clung round his neck, weeping and covering his broad, heavy-featured face with kisses.

"Na, na," said Jorian in a heavy bass voice, with a rustic Kortolian accent. "Weep not, ma pretty lassies.

4

"The gods, who from their puerile pipes a billion
  bubbles blow,
Have blown us here. We waft and wobble, iridesce
  and glow,
Then burst; but from these pipes a billion bubbles
  more shall flow.

"Within the year, ye'll all have better husbands than I ever
was to you."

"We do not wish other husbands! We love only you!"
they wailed.

"But the weans needs must have stepfathers," he reminded them. "Now get 'along back to the palace, so as
not to see your lord's blood flow. You, too, Estrildis."

"Nay!" cried the wife addressed—though pretty, the
least beautiful of the four, stocky and blue-eyed. "I will
watch you to the end!"

"You shall do as I say," said Jorian gently but firmly.
"You shall go on your own feet, or I will have you carried.
Which shall it be?"

The two soldiers who had remained on the ground laid
gentle hands on the woman's arms, and she broke away
to run, weeping, after the others. Jorian called: "Farewell!"
and turned back to the scaffold.

As the king mounted the stairs, his gaze roved hither
and yon. He smiled and nodded as his eye caught those of
acquaintances in the crowd. To many, he seemed altogether too cheerful for a man about to lose his head.

As, with a steady step, Jorian reached the platform of
the scaffold, the two halberdiers who had preceded him
snapped to attention and brought their right fists up to
their chests, over their hearts, in salute. Behind him came
the Mulvanian holy man and the high priest of Zevatas.

On the far, western side of the platform, a few feet from
the edge, rose the block, freshly carved and shining with
new red paint. Between the flagpoles on the western side,
a length of netting, a yard high, was stretched to make
sure that the head should not roll off the platform.

Leaning on his ax, the headsman stood beside the block.
Like Jorian, he was stripped to breeks and shoes. Although
not so tall as the king, the executioner was longer of arm
and even more massive of torso. Despite the hood, Jorian
knew that his slayer was Uthar the butcher, who kept a

5

stall near the South Gate. Since Xylar was too small and orderly a city-state to support a full-time executioner, it hired Uthar from time to time for the task. Jorian had personally consulted the man before approving the choice.

"The great trick, Sire," Uthar had said, "be to let the weight of the ax do the work. Press not; give your whole attention to guiding the blade in its fall. A green headsman thinks he needs must help the blade; so he presses, and the stroke goes awry. The blade be heavy enough to sever any man's neck—even so mighty a one as Your Majesty's—if suffered to fall at its natural speed. I promise Your Majesty shan't feel a thing. Your soul will find itself in its next incarnation before you wite what has happened."

Jorian now approached the headsman with a grin on his face. "Hail, Master Uthar!" he cried in a hearty voice. "A lovely day, is it not? By Astis' ivory teats, if one must have one's head cut off, I can imagine no fairer day whereon to have the deed performed."

Uthar dropped to one knee. "You—Your Majesty—'tis a fine day, surely—Your Majesty will forgive me for any pain or inconvenience I cause him in the discharge of my duties?"

"Think nothing of it, old man! We all have our duties, and we all come to our destined ends. My pardon is yours, so long as your edge be keen and your arm be true. You promised that I should not feel a thing, remember? I shouldn't like you to have to strike twice, like a new recruit hacking at a pell."

Jorian turned to the Chief Justice. "Most eminent Judge Grallon, are you ready with your speech? Take a hint and make it not too long. Long speeches bore the hearer, be the speaker never so eloquent."

The Chief Justice looked uncertainly at Jorian, who indicated by a jerk of his head that he was to proceed. The magistrate pulled a scroll from his girdle and unrolled it. Holding the stick of the scroll in one hand and a reading glass in the other, he began to read. The wind whipped the dangling end of the scroll this way and that, hindering his task. Nevertheless, being familiar with the contents, he droned on.

Justice Grallon began with a résumé of Xylarian history. Imbal the lion god had established this polis many centuries before; he had also bestowed upon it its unique method of choosing a ruler. The magistrate spoke of famous kings of Xylar: of Pellitus the Wise, and Kadvan the Strong, and Rhuys the Ugly.

At last, Judge Grallon came down to the reign of Jorian. He praised Jorian's bravery. He narrated the battle of Dol, when Jorian had destroyed the horde of robbers that had infested the southern marches of the kingdom and had acquired the scar on his face.

"...and so," he concluded, "this glorious reign has now come to the end appointed for it by the gods. Today the crown of Xylar shall pass, by the Lot of Imbal, into those hands destined by the gods to receive it. And we have been a true and virtuous folk, these hands will be strong, just, and merciful; if not—not. The king will now receive his final consolation from his holy man."

Old Doctor Karadur had been unwrapping the rope from around his waist and coiling it in the center of the platform. From his satchel he produced a little folding brass stand, which he set down beside the rope. Out of the bag came a brazen dish, which he placed upon the stand. Out, too, came a compartmented pouch, whence he sprinkled various powders into the dish. He put away the pouch, took out flint and steel, and struck sparks into the dish.

There was a green flash and a puff of smoke, which the breeze whipped away. A many-hued little flame danced over the dish, sending up streamers of vapor. The high priest of Zevatas looked sourly on.

Karadur intoned a lengthy prayer of incantation—those listening could not tell which, since the holy man spoke Mulvani. On and on he went, until some of the spectators grew restless. True, they did not wish the ceremony over too soon, since it was the biggest event in their calendar. On the other hand, when it came to hearing the unintelligible chant of a scrawny old fakir and watching him bow his forehead to the platform, a little went a long way.

Then Karadur rose and embraced Jorian, who towered over him. The fire in the brazen dish blazed up and sent out a cloud of smoke, which made those on the platform cough and wipe their eyes. Thus they failed to see Karadur, at the moment when his arms were around Jorian's huge torso, slip a small knife into the hands of the king, which were bound behind him. Karadur whispered:

"How is your courage, my son?"

7

"Oozing away with every heartbeat. In sooth, I'm frightened witless."

"Face it down, boy! In boldness lies your only safety."

Next, the band played a hymn to Zevatas. The high priest, a gaunt, imposing figure in his purple robe, led the throng in singing the hymn, beating time with his staff of office.

Then the priest bowed his head and prayed that the lot of Jorian's successor should fall upon one worthy of the office. He prayed to the gods to look with favor upon Xylar; he prayed that, in smiting sinners, they would take care not to harm the far more numerous virtuous citizens. His prayer was as long as Karadur's. The head of the cult of the king of the gods could not let a foreign wizard go him one better.

At last the high priest finished. The Chief Justice read a proclamation that whereas, in accordance with Xylar's ancient customs, Jorian's reign had now come to an end, he willingly offered his head as the means whereby the next king should be chosen. Judge Grallon finished with a sweeping gesture towards the block, indicating that Jorian should now lay his head upon it.

"Will Your Majesty have a blindfold?" he asked.

"Nay," said Jorian, stepping towards the block, "I will face this with my eyes open, as I did the foes of Xylar."

"One moment, your honor," said Karadur in his nasal Mulvanian accent. "I must—ah—it was agreed that I should cast a final spell, to speed King Jorian's soul to the afterworld, without danger of its being trapped in another incarnation in this one."

"Well, get on with it," said the Chief Justice.

Karadur brought a little brass bell out of his satchel. "When I sound this, smite!" He poured more powders into his dish, which flamed and bubbled.

"Kneel, my royal son," said Karadur. "Fear nought."

The crowd surged forward expectantly. Fathers hoisted small children to their shoulders.

Jorian cast a thoughtful look at the old Mulvani. Then he knelt before the block and bowed his head until his throat rested across the narrow, flat place on top. His chin lay comfortably in the hollow that had been cut in the west side of the block. His eyes, swiveling sideways, kept Uthar the butcher in the periphery of his vision. Uthar,

8

bending over him, brushed Jorian's long, back hair forward to bare his nape.

Karadur uttered another incantation, gesturing with his skinny brown arms. This continued until Jorian's knees began to hurt from kneeling on the hard boards. Stepping back from the block, Uthar took a firm grip on the helve of the ax.

At last the Mulvani tinkled his bell. Jorian, straining to keep the headsman in sight without seeming to do so, felt rather than saw the ax swing up to the vertical. Then the bell tinkled again, meaning that the ax had started down.

Jorian's next action required exquisite timing, and he was not at all sure of success—even though Karadur and he had rehearsed for hours in his private gymnasium, with the old wizard wielding a broom instead of an ax. For one thing, Jorian was a little tired because four of his wives had insisted, the night before, on proof of his love for them.

As the ax descended, Jorian cast off the thongs that bound him, which throughout the ceremony he had been discreetly sawing through with the little knife. Simultaneously, he hurled his body to the left, falling on his side. Since the heavy ax had already begun its downward course, the burly headsman was neither quick enough of apprehension nor strong enough of arm to stop it in mid-career. It thudded into the block, sinking deeply into the red-painted wood.

In one swift movement, Jorian rolled to his feet and put the little knife between his teeth. Karadur cast something more into the dish, which flamed and smoked like a little volcano, sending up a swelling column of green smoke shot with red and purple. The wizard uttered a loud cry, flinging out his arms. Thereupon the coiled rope before him sprang erect, like some monstrous serpent. Its end shot up twenty feet or more, and the upper end disappeared into a kind of haze, as if it had pierced a hole in the sky. A tremendous cloud of smoke arose from the dish, obscuring the vision of those on the platform and hiding them from the spectators below. Some, supposing the king's head to have fallen already, set up a cry of "Red and white! Red and white!"

One long stride brought Jorian to the executioner. With the ax in his hands, Uthar the butcher would have been a formidable foe. But, despite his desperate tugs, the head of the ax remained firmly fixed in the block.

Jorian brought his left fist up in a long, swinging, ox-felling blow against the headsman's jaw. Uthar reeled back against the net and fell off the platform.

A cry from Karadur warned Jorian to turn. One of the mailed halberdiers was lunging towards him, thrusting with his weapon. With the leopard-quick timing that had once already saves his gore, Jorian caught the halberd below the head, just before the spearhead reached his skin. As he jerked the head of the weapon violently to the left, the soldier's lunge drove it past his body.

Seizing the haft with both hands and turning his back on the trooper, Jorian put the shaft on his shoulder and then bent his back, pulling the head of the halberd down. The halberdier, clinging to the shaft, found himself hoisted over Jorian's broad back and hurled head over heels off the platform, to fall with a clash of mail to the ground below.

Clutching the halberd, Jorian spun to face the remaining soldier, who stood coughing smoke. The Chief Justice and the high priest of Zevatas scrambled down the stair in such haste that the latter lost his footing and plunged to earth head-first, gravely injuring himself.

Whether for fear or for love of his former lord, the soldier hesitated, holding his halberd at port and neither swinging the ax head nor thrusting with the spear point. Having nothing personal against the man, Jorian reversed his weapon and jabbed the butt against the soldier's armored ribs. A ferocious push sent the trooper tumbling off the scaffold after his comrade.

Thus, twelve seconds after the headsman's blow, Jorian and Karadur found themselves the only persons on the platform. A vast murmur ran through the throng. The events on the scaffold had taken place so quickly and had been so obscured by smoke that nobody on the ground yet really grasped what had happened. It was plain, however, that the execution had not gone as planned. People jostled and shouted questions; the murmur rose to a roar. A sharp command rang out, and a squad of pikemen rushed towards the foot of the stair.

Jorian dropped his halberd and sprang to the rope. Not for nothing had he spent months practising climbing a rope hand over hand, until the muscles of his arms and hands were like steel. As he went up, the rope swayed gently but remained straight and taut. The platform sank beneath him. Somewhere a crossbow snapped, and Jorian heard the swishing hum of the quarrel as it sped past.

Below, the crowd was in a frenzied uproar. Soldiers scrambled up the stair. As they reached the top, Karadur, who had been performing another incantation, dropped spryly off the edge of the platform. Jorian had only a brief glimpse of the wizard; he saw, however, that as Karadur reached the ground his appearance changed. Instead of a deep-brown, white-haired Mulvanian holy man, he was now, to all appearances, a member of the lower Xylarian priesthood, clad in a neat black robe of good stuff. The crowd swallowed him up.

Again came the twang of a bowstring. The missile grazed Jorian's shoulder, raising a welt. The soldiers had reached the platform and were looking doubtfully at the lower end of the rope. The thought flashed across Jorian's racing mind that they would try either to pull it down or to climb up after him.

Sweat poured down his face and his massive, hairy torso as he mounted the last few feet of the rope. He reached the place where the rope turned hazy and disappeared. As his head came level with this terminus, he found that the rope remained as solid and clear as ever, while below him the scene became dim and hazy, as if seen through a gathering fog.

A final, heart-wrenching heave, and the scene below vanished. Around him, instead of empty air, stretched an utterly strange landscape. He lowered his feet and felt earth and grass beneath them.

For the moment, he had not time to examine his new surroundings. Karadur had repeatedly warned him of the importance of recovering the magical rope, the upper end of which still stuck up stiffly from the grass to nearly Jorian's own height. He seized the rope with both hands and pulled. Up it came, as if out of an invisible hole in the ground. As he pulled, the visible part of the rope lost its stiffness, drooped, and hung limply, like any other rope.

Then Jorian felt a check, as if someone below were holding the rope. One of the soldiers must have nerved himself to seize it as he saw it rising into the air. Since

11

the man was heavy, it was all that Jorian, still panting from his climb, could do to haul him up.

Then a better idea struck him. Rather than pull an armed foe up into this new world about him, he let the rope run loosely through his hands, dropping the man at the other end back on the scaffold. Very faintly, he heard a crash and a yell. Then he pulled quickly, hand over hand. This time the rope came up without resistance until it all lay in a heap on the grass before him.

Jorian drew his forearm across his forehead and sat down heavily. His heart still pounded from his exertions and from the excitement of this narrow escape. Now that he looked back, he could scarcely believe that he had survived.

Although Jorian was a young man of unusual size, strength, and agility, he entertained few illusions about the chances of a bound, unarmed man's escaping from the midst of his foes, even with the help of magical spells. Having practiced with arms for years and having fought in two real battles and several skirmishes, he knew the limitations of one man's powers. Moreover, spells were notoriously erratic and untrustworthy, and Jorian's break for life required perfect surprise, coördination and timing. Perhaps, he thought, Karadur's Mulvanian gods had helped after all.

He glanced swiftly about, thinking: So this is the afterworld, whither souls released from our own plane are sent for their next incarnations! He stood on a strip of artificially smooth grass, perhaps forty feet wide. The strip was bounded on either side by a broad strip of pavement, in turn about twenty feet in breadth.

More grass lay beyond these roadways. Beyond these lawns rose tree-covered hills, on some of which Jorian thought he discerned houses. The question struck him: Why should anybody in his right mind build two splendid roads side by side?

Then a swiftly rising, whirring, purring, swishing sound drew his attention. It reminded him unpleasantly of the sound of a crossbow bolt, but much louder. In a flash, his roving glance fixed itself upon the source of the sound.

Along one of the paved strips, an object was hurtling towards him. At first he thought it a monster of legend:

a low, humpbacked thing with a pair of great, glaring, glassy eyes in front. Below the eyes and just above the ground, a row of silvery fangs was bared in a fiendish grin.

Jorian's courage sank; but, as he backed away from the road, drawing the little knife and preparing to sell his life dearly, the thing whizzed by at incredible speed—a speed like that of a hawk swooping at its prey. As the object passed, Jorian saw that it had wheels; that it was, in fact, no monster but a vehicle. He glimpsed the head and shoulders of a man within, and then the carriage was gone with a diminishing whirr and sigh.

As Jorian, disconcerted, stood staring, another whirr behind him made him spin around. There went another vehicle—and yet another, a huge one with a towering, boxlike body and many wheels. In his own world, he was deemed a man of signal courage; but even the bravest loses his assurance in totally strange surroundings, where he knows not whence or in what guise danger may come.

Trapped between the two roads, Jorian wondered how he could ever escape to join Karadur. The roads extended in either direction as far as the eye could reach, neither converging nor diverging. It seemed as though he could walk along the grassy median strip for leagues in either direction without finding a safe means of exit.

After several more vehicles had passed, Jorian realized that one road was for eastbound traffic only and the other for westbound; and that, furthermore, the cars did not leave the pavement. So he was safe for the nonce. It might even be possible, by choosing a moment when no chariots were in sight, to dash across one of the roads to safety.

Jorian nerved himself to approach one of the paved strips. The road appeared to be made of some cement or stucco, with periodic narrow, black, transverse lines of a stuff resembling pitch. He jumped back as a huge vehicle roared past, buffeting him with the wind of its passage.

Jorian was appalled. He hoped that his soul would never have to live out an incarnation on this plane. One of those vehicles could squash him like a bug. How ironic to escape from the headsman's ax in his own world only to be run over in this! He wondered that anyone here survived long enough to become a driver of these chariots—unless the natives lived their entire lives in them, never setting foot on the ground. Perhaps they had no feet to set on the ground . . .

An approaching vehicle drew up and stopped with a thin, mouselike squeak. A door opened and a man got out. He had, Jorian saw, normal legs, encased in gray pantaloons that hung down to his shoes. He wore a hat with a broad, flat brim, and from a stout belt depended a small leather case. From this case projected the curved handle of some instrument, which Jorian guessed to be a carpenter's tool.

The man approached Jorian and spoke, but Jorian could make nothing of his words. Although he knew several languages, that of the man in the pantaloons were strange to him.

"I am Jorian of Ardamai, son of Evor the clockmaker," he said. This had been his name until that day, five years before, when he had innocently caught a human head hurtling through the air and found himself king of Xylar.

Staring intently at Jorian's golden crown, the man shook his head and said something else. Jorian repeated his statement in Mulvanian and in Shvenic. Looking blank, the man uttered more sounds.

Then another voice sounded; Jorian jumped, for he had not seen anyone else nearby. The voice, speaking unintelligible words in a squawking, metallic tone, seemed to come from the man's vehicle. The man smiled a forced smile of reassurance, and said something more to Jorian, and went back to his carriage, which soon roared off.

Jorian turned back to his rope and began to coil it around his waist. He recalled his instructions: Walk southeast one league, lower himself back to his own world, and await Karadur, if the holy man had not already reached the rendezvous.

But which way was southeast? Luckily the sky was clear, as it had been in Xylar. The execution had been timed for noon, and little time had elapsed since Jorian had placed his neck upon the block. Soon, however, the sun's motion would make it useless as a directional guide. He would have to risk crossing one of these roads despite the danger.

Looking along the nearest paved strip to make sure that no more vehicles approached, Jorian darted across. He continued to the edge of the lawnlike sward, where plants

14

grew more naturally. He broke off a stem of long field grass, found a patch of bare earth, and set the stem in it upright. Then, with the point of the little knife, he traced a line where the shadow of the grass stem fell. He drew a transverse line, then bisected the near left angle by still another line. That gave him his direction.

As he set out, Jorian paused now and then to cut a tree seedling and trim it to a wand two or three feet long. The first of these sticks he kept, cutting a notch in it every hundred steps. By thrusting the other sticks into the ground every fifty or hundred paces and backsighting, he kept in a fairly straight line. Every thousand steps, he checked his direction with the sun.

When he had cut fifty notches in his first wand, he halted in a gully between two wooded hillsides. Although he had seen houses in the distance, he was thankful that his march had not taken him close to any.

He counted the notches to make sure, unwound the rope from his waist, and took a turn with it around a tree. Then he uttered the Mulvanian incantation that Karadur had taught him:

> *Mansalmu darm rau antarau,*
> *Nodō zaro terakh hiā zor rau...*

He felt his feet sinking, as if the solid ground beneath him were turning to quicksand. Then it gave way, and Jorian fell. He fetched up with a jerk, hanging suspended by the rope between earth—his own earth—and the clear blue heavens.

Above him, the two strands of rope arose, diverging slightly, until they faded out a yard above his head. Below, he was disconcerted to see the dark, stagnant waters of the Marsh of Moru. Karadur had told him that their rendezvous would be near the swamp, but he had not expected to come out right over it. To the north rolled the fields and woodlots of Xylar. To the south rose the foothills of the mighty Lograms, and beyond them the snow-topped peaks of that range, which sundered the Novarian city-states from the tropical empire of Mulvan.

He thought of climbing back up and trying again from another tree but decided against it. He was not sure how long the "soft spot" that his spell had created between the two planes would remain soft. It could not do to have the earth solidify just as he was climbing through it. On the other hand, he was a good swimmer and did not fear the three-foot dwarf crocodiles found in Moru Marsh.

He lowered himself to where the ends of the rope dangled. If he had tied one end around the tree with an ordinary loop, the rope would have been long enough to reach the surface of his world. In that case, however, he would not have been able to recover the precious rope after his descent. Therefore he had applied the middle of the rope to the tree and let both ends hang down an equal distance.

The dark, odorous water lay about twenty feet beneath him. A look around showed no sign of the wizard. Here we go, Jorian thought, and released one end of the rope.

He struck with a tremendous splash. The rope poured down after him, striking the water in loops and coils. Taking one end of it in his teeth, Jorian struck out for the nearest shore.

This proved to be a floating bank of reeds. Jorian hauled himself out, brown water running off his shoulders. When he stood up, the surface beneath him quivered, gave, and sank in alarming fashion. The safest mode of progress, he decided, was on all fours. Trailing the rope, he crept towards higher ground, where willows and dark cypresses grew thickly. At last he felt firm soil beneath him and rose to his feet. A water weed trailed from one of the spikes of his crown.

"Karadur!" he called, pulling loose the weed and scraping the swamp water off his skin with his fingers.

He was not surprised when there was no reply. A league-long hike would be hard on the old fellow, and he might not arrive until nightfall. Since Jorian saw nothing else of a useful nature to do, he found a spot masked by ferns, took off his crown, stretched out, and was soon fast asleep.

The sun was farther down in the sky, although still far from the horizon, when a voice awakened Jorian. He sprang up to face Karadur, who stood before him in his normal guise, leaning on a staff and breathing heavily.

"Hail!" said Jorian. "How did you find me, old man?"

"You—ah—snored, O King—I mean, Master Jorian."

"Are we followed hither?"

16

"Nay, not so far as my arts reveal. Ah me, I am spent! Suffer me to rest." The wizard sank with a sigh into the ferns. "Not in years have I been so fordone. Working two spells at once wellnigh slew me, and this march through the forest has finished me off." He rested his head in his hands.

"Where have you hidden the gear?"

"Alack, I am too spent to think. How found you the afterworld?"

"Oi! Ghastly, from what little I saw," said Jorian. He described the double road of cement and the monstrous vehicles that whizzed along it. "By Thio's horns, life must be riskier there by far than in our own world, with all its wars, plagues, robbers, sorceries, and wild beasts! I'd rather take a chance on one of your Mulvanian hells, where one has to cope merely with a few nice, bloodthirsty demons."

"Saw you—met you any of the inhabitants?"

"Aye; a fellow whom I took to be a carpenter stopped his carriage and bespoke me, albeit neither could understand the other's lingo. He stared at me as the Xylarians would stare if a man-ape from Komilakh were to stroll amongst 'em." Jorian described the man.

Karadur gave a faint chuckle. "That was no carpenter but a peace officer—a man trained in the use of arms but employed solely against evildoers of his own nation instead of against a foreign foe. I believe some of your Novarian city-states posses corps of such stalwarts. It is a plane of great wealth and many curious devices, but I hope never to spend an incarnation there."

"Wherefore not?"

"Because it is a dimension of base materialism, wherein magic is so feeble as to be wellnigh useless; so what scope were there for an accomplished thaumaturge like myself? Those who pass for magicians on that plane, I am informed, are mostly fakers. Why, even the gods of that world are but debile wraiths, able to work but little weal or woe, beyond causing petty strokes of luck, upon those they love and hate."

"Have these folk no religion, then?"

"Aye, or say they do. They also patronize magicians—astrologers and necromancers and such. The reason is not that the gods and wizards of that plane can do them much good or ill, but that they come into incarnation there with

17

buried memories of their previous lives in this world, where such things in sooth are mighty and fell. But, on the whole, the folk of that dimension are blind in spiritual matters."

Jorian slapped a gnat. "Then I, having no more psychic powers than a head of cabbage, should do right well there."

"Not so, but far otherwise."

"Why?"

"Your strength and nimbleness—your strongest resources here—would avail you nought, because all tasks calling for such virtues in this world are there performed by soulless machines. What boots it if you can ride forty leagues between sunrise and sunset, when one of those mechanical cars you saw can cover thrice the distance in that time? Your strength were as useless as my moral purity and knowledge of spiritual forces."

"I'm not quite a halfwit, even though my thews be a trifle larger than most men's," said Jorian. "Natheless, belike you speak truth. In any case, old man, daylight will not last forever. So let us forth to find our cache, if you now be fit for walking."

"Aye, I am fit, albeit the prospect gives me no joy." With a groan, the wizard heaved himself to his feet and started poking in the nearest bushes with his staff, muttering:

"Now, let me see, where did I hide that accursed thing? Tsk, tsk. It was under the overhang of a boulder, I am sure, with a layer of leaves to conceal it..."

"No boulders here," said Jorian with a touch of impatience.

"True, true; methinks the place lay a furlong or so to the north, on higher ground. Let us look."

They moved off in the direction indicated and for the next two hours scoured the woods, looking for a boulder. Karadur mumbled:

"Let me see; let me see...It was a boulder of granite, with patches of moss, about as high as your shoulder, O Jorian...I am sure...I think..."

"Did you not blaze a nearby tree, or otherwise leave a marking to guide our search?"

"Let me think. Ah, yes, I marked three trees, on three sides of the cache. But there so cursed many trees..."

"Why not find it by divination?"

"Because my spiritual powers are spent for the nonce. We must use our material senses or none."

They went back to the swamp and started off in a slightly different direction. Insects danced in level spears of light, shining through the forest, when Jorian said:

"Is this one of your blazes?"

"Why, yes, it is!" said Karadur. "Now, let me see, where are the others ..."

"There are no more boulders here than there are fishes in the desert of Fedirun."

"Boulder? Boulder? Why—ah—I remember now! I left it not beneath a boulder at all, but under a tree trunk. There!"

Karadur pointed to a big trunk lying athwart the forest floor. In an instant they had scraped aside the concealing leaves and dragged out a canvas bag. Jorian let a hiss of annoyance escape through his teeth, for the wizard's vague ways often exasperated him. Still, he told himself, one should not be too critical of a man who has saved one's life.

As the sun set, Jorian arose. He was now clad like any forester, in coarse brown tunic and breeks, high laced boots in place of this tattered silken slippers, and sweat-stained green hat with a battered pheasant's feather stuck in the band. In his left hand he balanced a crossbow. A short, heavy, hunting falchion, better suited to gutting game and hacking brush than to swordplay hung at his girdle.

"What shall we do with this?" he said, holding up the crown of Xylar. "It would fetch a pretty stack of lions."

"Never, my boy!" said Karadur. "If aught would betray you, that surely would. Show it to any goldsmith or jeweler or money-changer within a hundred leagues, and with the speed of a pigeon's flight the news would fly to Xylar."

"Why not melt it down ourselves?"

"We have no furnace or crucible, and to seek to buy such things would direct suspicion upon us almost as surely as the crown itself. Besides, so ancient a golden artifact ought to have subsumed spiritual qualities from its surroundings, which could prove useful in making magic. It were a shame to destroy these qualities by melting."

"What, then?"

"Best we hide it here with your discarded garments. If

circumstance favor, you can recover these articles some day. Or, belike, you could compact with the Xylarians, your head for directions to find their crown. I thought you had money hidden on your person?"

"I have; one hundred golden lions, fresh from the royal mint, in this belt inside my breeches. Any more would have sunk me to the bottom of the Marsh of Moru. But one can always use a little more."

"But that is a sizeable fortune, my son! The gods grant that no robbers hear that you bear such wealth upon your person."

"Well, as things stand, there is no good place where I could bank the stuff for safekeeping."

"True. In any event, to seek additional gain from this crown were not worth the risk. And now I must trim your hair ere darkness fall. Sit here."

Jorian sat on the tree trunk while Karadur went over his head with scissors and comb. He repeatedly warned Jorian to stop talking, but the former king could not be stilled for long.

"It grieves me," said Jorian, "to have robbed my people—my people that was, I mean—of all their fun: the beheading, and the coronation, and the scattering of largesse, and the contests at running and shooting and wrastling and football and hockey, and the singing and dancing, and the feast."

"Followed, I doubt not, by a most wicked and sinful orgy of drunkenness and fornication," said Karadur, "so you may have accomplished some good despite yourself. You can always change your mind and go back." He worked around Jorian's right ear.

"Na, na. I'm satisfied with things as they are. And the gods must approve my course, or they'd not have let me travel so far along it, now would they?"

"Your argument were cogent if you assumed that the gods concerned themselves with single mortal beings—a point the philosophers have hotly disputed for thousands of years. Methinks the main factors in your escape were my thaumaturgy, reinforced by my moral purity; the favorable aspect of the planets; and your own strength and mettle. But he who seeks a single cause for an event would more easily trim a flea's whiskers. And, speaking of which, I must needs abate that monstrous mustache."

20

"You would jealously rob me of every vestige of my youthful beauty, you old villian!" grinned Jorian. "But the drowning man who seizes a log cannot be fussy about the quality of the wood. Proceed!"

The ex-king's flowing mane had now become a bristling brush, nowhere longer than a finger's breadth. Karadur trimmed the mustache closely, as he had the hair.

"Now," he said, "let beard and mustache grow out together, and none shall know you."

"Unless they noted my height, my weight, my voice, or the scar on my nose," said Jorian. "Can't you cast a spell to lend me the semblance of some slender, flaxen-haired stripling?"

"I could, had I not already cast two spells today. But it would accomplish nought, for such illusions last only an hour or two at most. You will meet none between here and the house of Rhithos the smith but an occasional hunter, charcoal-burner, or lonesome cotter. And what good would your disguise do then?"

"It might hinder them from putting the judiciary of Xylar on my track."

"Aye; but suppose you appeared as a stripling and then resumed your true shape before their very eyes? That, if aught, would arouse suspicion."

Jorian pulled a large, leathern wallet out of the canvas bag, and out of the wallet produced a loaf of bread and a piece of smoked venison. He ate heartily of both, while Karadur contented himself with a modest morsel of bread.

The wizard said: "You must bridle that voracious appetite, my boy."

"Me, voracious?" said Jorian with his mouth full. "By Franda's golden locks, this is but a snack for one of my poundage! Would you think to keep an elephant on one honey-bun a day?"

"Base material appetites were meant to be subdued; and, anyway, those victuals must needs last you until you reach the smith's abode, where they await your coming. Dig deeper and you shall find a sketch map, showing the trails thereunto."

"Good, albeit I already know the country hereabouts, from chasing brigands through it. Dol lies not a league hence."

Karadur continued: "They say Rhithos has a niece or

daughter, on whom rakish young oafs like you cast lustful eyes. Avert yours from her, for every sensual sin makes my magical tasks more difficult."

"Me, sensual?" said Jorian, raising an eyebrow. "With five ravishing young wives, what need have I for venery? Dip me in dung, but I shall enjoy a respite—although I shall miss the toddlers climbing all over me. But let us speak of this Rhithos the smith. What gives you such confidence that he'll not betray me to the Xylarians? A man could turn a pretty penny by putting them on my trail."

"Sirrah! No initiated member of the Forces of Progress would be so base as to betray the trust of another member!"

"Natheless, you once implied that this Rhithos belongs to the faction opposed to yours. And my five years as king, if it has taught me nought else, has taught me not to trust any man over much."

"True that he is of the Black Faction, or Benefactors, and so would keep the mighty powers of magic mewed up within our guild; whilst I, of the White Faction, or Altruists, would fain spread it abroad to aid the toiling masses. But, howsoever we quarrel amongst ourselves, we close ranks in dealing with the world outside our learned order, and I am as sure of Rhithos' honor as of my own."

"Judging from the names of your factions, you're all as pure as spring water. Still and all, from what I saw of men during my reign—"

Karadur laid a bony brown hand on Jorian's knee. "You trusted me perforce in the matter of saving your head, my boy. Trust me likewise in this."

"Oh, well, you know what you do," grumbled Jorian. "Holy Father, let me thank you now for saving my worthless head."

"You are welcome; but, as well you know, you shall yet earn that head."

Jorian grinned slyly. "What if I find a wizard to work a counter-spell, nullifying that which you and your fellow-sorcerers have so unscrupulously put upon me?"

"There is no such counter-spell. I warn you that the combination of our spell with that of some bungling outsider bids fair to be fatal. The geas was laid upon you by the leader of our faction, Vorko of Hendau, and can only be lifted by him.

"Now, forget not: One month from today, we meet at the—ah—the Silver Dragon of Othomae; then on to Trimandilam to fetch the Kist of Avlen; and lastly to the Concalve of my fellow-adepts in the Goblin Tower of Metouro. We must not tarry, for the Conclave meets in the Month of the Pike."

"That should give us ample time."

"Nay, but unforseen events oft spoil the most promising plans. First, howsomever, we must get to Othomae."

"Why shouldn't I wend thither with you, instead of wandering through the wildwood?"

"Because the Xylarians will be watching the roads for you, and you need time to let your whiskers grow. Rhithos knows of your coming, so you can tarry there for a few days to rest and replenish your provisions."

"I shall be there, if no calamity befall. If I be late, leave a message for me with the taverner, under a fictitious name."

Karadur: "A false name? Tsk tsk! Not ethical, my son."

"So? You forgot that, ere I was king of Xylar, I served a year in the Grand Bastard's foot guards. Many in Othomae will remember me if encouraged to do so."

"You need not fear. The Grand Duke and the Grand Bastard are both alike opposed to Xylar, because the land they rule is wedged betwixt your former kingdom and the Republic of Vindium, which has an alliance with Xylar against Othomae. The lords of Othomae would not turn you over the Xylarians."

"Perhaps not, but they might not be able to stop kidnappers from Xylar. The judiciary will stick at nought to complete their bloody ceremony. Besides, what's more unethical about a false name than about coercing me into stealing that damned trunk full of mouldering magical parchments from the king of Mulvan, as your Forces of Progress has done?"

"Why—ah—there are many differences..."

"Name one," said Jorian.

"That were easy—it is to say—oh, you are not spiritually advanced enough to understand. It is a matter of purity of motives—"

"I understand well enough that, if I'm caught between

23

here and Trimandilam because of some silly scruple of yours, you shall get no chest of wizardly screeds. A headless man makes a feckless burglar."

"Ah, well; your contention has a certain plausibility, although were I not so fatigued I could doubtless think of a counter-argument."

"What name will you adopt, if you can bring yourself to do anything so unethical?"

"I shall call myself—ah—Mabahandula."

"By Imbal's iron pizzle! That's a mouthful. But I suppose 'twere useless to feign yourself other than a Mulvani." Jorian repeated the name several times to memorize it.

Karadur winced. "Tsk, tsk. I would you did not blaspheme so freely, even in the names of your pretty local godlets. What shall your name be, if you arrive first?"

"Hmm—Nikko of Kortoli. I had an Uncle Nikko."

"Why not pass yourself off as a Zolonian? The isle of Zolon is farther away and hence safer."

"I have never been to Zolon and cannot feign their foul dialect. But I was reared in Kortoli, and a use the Kortolian country speech when a speak withouten thinking. How now, old kimmer, canst tha riddle me?"

"It is well. If I fail to appear at the Silver Dragon, inquire about the town for the wizardess Goania. She has custody of the instruments we shall need to liberate the Kist of Avlen from the wicked wight who now wrongfully holds it—the so-called King of Kings."

"Goania, said you? That I will. And you, my friend, do not in your absent way forget the name of the city and wander off to Govannian or Vindium and then wonder why I fail to join you."

"Never mind my absent way!" snapped the wizard. "Simply follow my injunctions and leave the rest to me. And guard that flapping tongue. On the scaffold, I thought your cheerful chatter had surely undone us. You had better drink nought but water, since wine and beer loosen your tongue at both ends."

"And if I wander about drinking strange waters, I shall come down with some fearful flux or fever and be wellnigh as useless to you as without my head."

"Well, at least measure your drinks; liquor and loquacity are your besetting weaknesses. And now, let us bow our heads in prayer to the true gods: the gods of Mulvan."

The wise man droned a prayer to Vurnu the Creator, Kradha the Preserver, and Ashaka the Destroyer. Then Jorian uttered a short prayer of his own to Thio, the Novarian forest god. He shook hands with Karadur, who said:

"Be wary and discreet; subdue the lusts of the flesh; seek moral perfection and spiritual enlightenment. All the true gods go with you, my son."

"I thank you, Father," said Jorian. "I'll be as discreet as a clam and as pure as a snowflake."

He strode off into the deepening gloom of the forest. Karadur, looking after him, began winding the magical rope around his waist. The song of nocturnal insects soared through the gathering darkness.

II

THE GRAND BASTARD'S SWORD

THE MONTH OF THE BEAR HAD BEGUN WHEN JORIAN reached the house of Rhithos the smith. In the foothills of the Lograms, all the leaves of the hardwoods had now turned to brown and scarlet and gold, while on the higher slopes the evergreens retained their somber, dark-green hue. Beyond these green-clad ridges looking black beneath the overcast, clouds half hid the white peaks of the central chain. A rain of red and yellow leaves, slanting down through the gray autumnal air and rocking and spinning in their fall like little boats on a stormy sea, drifted athwart the clearing where stood the house of Rhithos the smith.

The smith's house was larger and more substantial than one would expect for the dwelling of a solitary man. It had a first story of mortared stone and above it a half-story of logs, with a high-peaked roof. Besides the main house, a one-story extension or shed, at right angles to the main axis of the building, contained the smithy. Thence came the clang of hammer on anvil.

At the other end, against the house wall, stood a large wooden cage. Huddled in the cage was an ape-man from

26

the jungles of Komilakh, far to the southeast. Near the edge of the clearing rose the stone curbing of a well, whence a young woman was drawing water. As Jorian arrived with his crossbow on his shoulder, she had just raised a bucketful by the windlass and was resting the bucket on the curb preparatory to emptying it into the jar. Across the clearing from the well, a tethered ass was munching hay.

As Jorian started across the clearing, the girl gave a startled movement; water slopped out of the bucket. Jorian called:

"God den! Let me give you a hand with that, lass!"

"Who are you?" she said, still poised on the edge of flight.

"Jorian son of Evor. Is this the house of Rhithos the smith?"

"Aye. We've heard you were coming, but we expected you many days ago."

"I got lost in the damned woods," said Jorian. "With this blanket of cloud I could not find myself again. Hold the jar whilst I tip the bucket!"

As he poured the water, Jorian looked the girl over. She was tall—within a hand's breadth of his own height—and had a mane of black hair. Her features were a little too coarse and irregular to be called pretty, but she was still a striking, forceful-looking woman with fine gray eyes. She said, in a rather deep, harsh voice:

"No wonder you got lost! Rhithos maintains a confusion spell over all the land you can see from here, to keep hunters and woodsmen out."

"Why?"

"For the silvans. In return, they fetch us food."

"I thought I glimpsed a little fellow with long, hairy ears," said Jorian, carrying the jar towards the house in the girl's wake. The ape-man awoke and growled at Jorian, but a word from the girl quieted the creature.

"The spell was supposed to have been lifted to let you in," continued the girl. "But one cannot turn off a spell as neatly as snuffing a candle. You have nice manners at least, Master Jorian."

"Na, na; we former kings must keep up our good repute." Jorian broke into his rustic Kortolian accent. "And sin a be no king the now, a needs must swink for ma supper."

27

The girl opened the door to a large room. Scrolls, crucibles, and magical instruments were scattered about on tables, chairs, and benches. The house furnished solid rustic comfort, like the hunting lodge that Jorian had inherited from his predecessors as king of Xylar. The floor was of wooden planks. Weapons hung on the walls, skins of bears and other beasts carpeted the floor, and decorated cushions bestrewed the benches.

The girl led the way along a passage to the kitchen. Jorian staggered as he hoisted the jar to the counter beside the sink.

"What ails you?" asked Vanora sharply. "Tell me not that the weight of that jar has unmanned a strapping fellow like you!"

"No, my dear young lady. It's just that I haven't eaten in three days."

"Great Zevatas! We must remedy that." She rummaged in the bread box, the apple bin, and elsewhere.

"What shall I call you?" asked Jorian, setting down his crossbow and his pack. "It seems not meet to refer to one who has saved one's life as 'Ho, you!'"

"I haven't saved your life."

"You will have, when you get me something to eat. Well?"

"My name is Vanora." As Jorian looked a question, she added: "Vanora of Govannian, if you like."

"I thought I knew the accent. Is Rhithos your father or uncle?"

"He, a kinsman?" She gave a short, derisive laugh. "He is my master. Know that he bought me as a bonded maid-of-all-work in Govannian."

"How so?"

"I had stabbed my lover, the worthless vagabond. I know not why, but I always fall in love with drunken louts who mistreat me. Anyway, this oaf died, and they were going to chop off my head to teach me not to do it again. But in Govannian they let outsiders buy condemned criminals as slaves, provided they take them out of the country. If I returned to thither, they'd have my head yet."

"How does Rhithos entreat you?"

She set down on the counter a plate bearing a small loaf of bread, a slab of smoked meat, a wedge of cheese, and an apple. Standing close to him, she said: "He doesn't—

at least, not what you'd call 'entreat.' So long as I obey, he pays me no more heed than a stick of furniture—not even at bedtime, for he says his magical works require celibacy. Now he's in his smithy, fiddling with Daunas' new sword; won't put his head out of the shed until supper time."

She looked up at him from close by with half-opened lips and swayed so that her full breast rubbed gently against his arm. He could hear the faint whistle of her breathing. Then his eyes strayed to the laden platter.

"If you'll excuse me, Mistress Vanora," he said, reaching around her, "what I need right now is food, ere I drop dead of starvation. Where would you like me to eat it?"

"Food!" she snapped. "Sit at your little table. Here's some cider. Don't gulp it down; it has more power than you would think."

"I thank you, Mistress." Jorian bolted several large mouthfuls, then cleared his mouth long enough to say: "Do I understand that Rhithos is making a magical sword for the Grand Bastard?"

"I can't linger for light talk, Mister Jorian. I have work to do." She strode out of the kitchen, the heels of her boots banging.

Jorian looked after her with a smile curling his stubbly new beard. Now what, he thought, is she angry about? Is it what I suspect? He ate heartily, drank deeply, and wandered back into the cluttered living room. Here Rhithos the smith found him hours later, rolled up in a bearskin on the floor and snoring.

The faint sound of the opening door roused Jorian. As the smith entered his house, Jorian scrambled to his feet and bowed.

"Hail, Master Rhithos!" he said. "Your servant is humbly grateful for your hospitality."

The smith was shorter than Vanora, who entered after him; but he had the widest shoulders Jorian had ever seen. The huge hand on the end of his long arm had a grip that made even Jorian wince. The face under his tousled gray hair was seamed and wrinkled and brown, and out of it a pair of heavy-lidded, cold gray eyes looked without expression.

"Welcome to my house," rumbled Rhithos, "I regret

29

that your arrival was delayed by a trifling misfunction in one of my protective spells. Vanora tells me you arrived half-starved."

"True. I exhausted the provender I had with me and sought to kill some game to replace it. I'm not altogether incompetent with the crossbow; but not so much as a hare did I see."

"The silvans must have driven the beasts out of your way. They guard them from hunters—not for sentimental love of the creatures, but to hunt themselves. Sit down there, Master Jorian. For the evening you may take your ease, although tomorrow I shall find ways for you to earn your keep whilst you tarry here."

As Vanora poured wine, Rhithos continued: "Now tell me how you got into this strange predicament."

"It began five years ago," said Jorian, glad of a chance to talk after the long silence of the forest. "But I must go back further yet. My father was Evor the clockmaker, who passed his last years in Ardamai."

"Where is that?"

"A village of Kortoli, near the capital. He tried to apprentice me in the making of clepsydras. But my hands, while steady enough on bridle, sword, plow, or tiller, proved too big and clumsy for such fine work. I mastered the theory, but the practice eluded me. He gave up at last, albeit not before I had traveled with him to several of the Twelve Cities where he had contracts to install water clocks.

"Next, he apprenticed me to Fimbri the carpenter, in Ardamai. But after a month Fimbri sent me home with a bill for all the tools that I, not have yet learnt to control my strength, had broken.

"Then my father apprenticed me to Rubio, a merchant of Kortoli. This lasted a year, until one day I made a bad error in adding Rubio's accounts. Now Rubio was a bitter and hasty man, and things had lately gone badly for him. So he took his rage out on me, forgetting that in the year I had been with him I had grown from a stripling to a youth taller than he was. He laid into me with his walking stick, and I took it away and broke it over his head. It only stunned him; but I, thinking I had slain the man, fled back to Ardamai.

"My father hid me until it transpired that Rubio was

30

not seriously hurt. Then he got me into the house of a childless peasant, one Onnus. He told me that, if I moved my draughtsmen aright, I might inherit the farm, since widower Onnus had no known kin. But Onnus was a skinflint who would try to sell the squeal of a pig when he butchered it. He worked me sixteen hours a day and nearly starved me. At last, when he caught me sneaking off from work to spark a neighbor's girl, he laid into me with his horsewhip. Of course I had to take it away from him—"

"And flog him with it?" said Rhithos.

"No, sir, I did not. All I did was to throw him headfirst into his own dungheap, so hard he came out the other side, and went along home."

Warmed by the wine, Jorian became gay, speaking rapidly with animated gestures. "My poor father was in despair of finding a livelihood for me. My older brothers had grown up to be good, competent clockmakers, and my sisters were married off, but what to do with me? 'If you had two heads,' quoth he, 'we could charge admission to see you; but you're only a great, clumsy young lout, good only for clodhopping.' So we bethought us of Syballa, the local wise woman.

"The witch put herbs in her pot and powders in her fire, and there was a lot of smoke and flickering shadows with nothing visible to cast them. She went into a trance, muttering and mumbling. Then at last she said:

"'Jorian, my lad, meseems you're fit only to be either a king or a wandering adventurer.'

"'How so?' quoth I. 'All I want is to be a respectable craftsman, like my dear father, and make a decent living.'

"'Your trouble,' she went on, 'is that you are too good at too many things to push a plow handle or to sweep the streets of Kortoli City. Yet you are not so surpassingly good at any one thing that it is plainly the work wherefor the gods intended you. For such a one, if he be not born to wealth and rank, the only careers are those of adventurer and ruler. Betimes the one leads to the other.'

"'How about soldiering?' said I.

"'That is classed with adventuring.'

"'Then soldiering it shall be,' I said.

"My father sought to dissuade me, saying that I had too much brains for so routine a career, which would prove nine parts insufferable boredom to one part stark terror.

31

But I said my brain had so far availed me little and set out natheless. Kortoli rejected my application; I think Rubio must have put in a bad word for me.

"So I hiked to Othomae and joined the Grand Bastard's pikemen. For a year I marched back and forth on the drill ground while officers bawled: 'Slant *pikes*! Forward, *'arch*!' We had one battle, with a Free Company that thought to sack Othomae. But the Grand Bastard routed them with a charge of his newfangled lobster-plated knights on their great, puffing plowhorses, so that no foe came within bowshot of us foot. At the end of my enlistment I agreed with my father that the mercenary's life was not for me.

"When my time was up, I wandered into Xylar. I arrived on the day they were executing the king and choosing his successor. I suppose I had heard of this curious custom from my schoolmaster, years before; but I had never been to Xylar and hence had forgotten it. So, when a round, dark thing the size of a football came hurtling through the air at my face, I caught it. Then I found to my horror that I held a human head, freshly severed so that the blood ran up my arms. Ugh! And I learnt that I was the new king of Xylar.

"At first, I was in a daze as they clad me in shining raiment, plied me with delicious food and drink, and chose beautiful wives for me. But it did not take me long to learn what the catch was—that after five years I, too, should lose my head.

"Well, there are always more garments and food and drink and women to be had, but if a man loses his head he cannot grow another. After a year of going through the motions of kingship, as old Grallon and Turonus instructed me, I resolved to escape from this gin by fair means or foul.

"The first method I tried was simply to sneak out and run for it. But the Xylarians were used to this and easily caught me; a whole company of the army—the so-called Royal Guard—is made up of men expert with the net and the lariat, whose task it is to see that the king escape not. I tried to enlist confederates; they betrayed me. I tried to bribe my guards; they pocketed my money and betrayed me.

"The third year, I essayed to be so good a king that the Xylarians would relent and change their custom. I made many reforms. I studied the law and strove to see justice done. I studied finance and learnt to lower taxes without weakening the kingdom. I studied the military art and put down the brigands who had gathered around Dol and the pirates that had been raiding our coast. I don't mind admitting that battles fill me with trepidation—

"Who joys in the galloping destrier's gait?
　　Not I!
Who's happy to ride with a pot on his pate?
　　Not I!
Who loves to bear on his body the weight
Of iron apparel of mail or of plate,
And seek in a bloody encounter his fate?
　　Not I!

"Who yearns to thrust with the sword and the
　　spear?
　　Not I!
Or draw the goose-feathered shaft to the ear?
　　Not I!
Who's filled by the clatter of battle with fear,
Preferring a peaceable flagon of beer,
But lacks the astuteness to bolt for the rear?
　　'Tis I!

"But the thought of the ax dismayed me even more, so that I ended by making these evildoers fear me even more than I feared them."

"Whose verse did you quote?" asked Rhithos.

"A certain obscure poetaster, hight Jorian of Ardamai. But to continue: At the end of the year, all agreed that King Jorian, despite his youth, was the best ruler they had had in many a reign.

"But would the Xylarians change their stupid law? Not for anything. In fact, they posted extra guards to make sure that I did not escape. I couldn't go for a ride, to hunt or to chase bandits or just for pleasure, without a squad of lariat-men from the steppes of Shven surrounding me lest I make a break for freedom.

"For a time I was in despair. I abandoned myself to the pleasures of the flesh—to food, drink, women, and all-

33

night revels. Hence, by the end of my fourth year, I was a fat, flabby wreck.

"I caught cold that winter, and the cold grew into a fever that wellnigh slew me. Whilst I was raving in a delirium, a man appeared unto me in a vision. Sometimes he looked like my father, who had died that year. I had been sending my parents ample money for their comfort but durst not invite them to Xylar, lest I have a chance to escape but be unable to take it lest my parents be held as hostages for my return.

"Sometimes the man in the vision seemed to be one of the great gods: Heryx, or Psaan, or even old Zevatas himself. Whoever he was, he said: 'Jorian, lad, I am ashamed of thee, with all thy gifts of mind and body, giving up in the face of a little threat like the loss of thy head. Up and at them, boy! Thou mayst or mayst not escape if thou try, but thou wilt certainly not if thou try not. So what hast thou to lose?'

"When I got well, I took the vision's words to heart. I sent away all the women save my four legal wives, to whom I added a fifth of my own choice. I trained in the gymnasium and the tilt yard until I was more fit than ever. And I read everything in the royal library that might possibly help me to escape. I spent a year in training and study. And 'tis easier for an eel to play the bagpipes than for a man to train and study at the same time. When you train, you're too spent to study of evens; and when you study, you find you lack the requisite time for training. I could only do my best.

"Reasoning that, if the gods had in sooth condemned me to the life of a wandering adventurer, I had best be a good one, I studied whatever might be useful for that career. I learnt to speak Mulvani and Feridi and Shvenic. I practised not only with the conventional arms but also with the implements of men beyond the law: the sandbag, the knuckle duster, the strangler's cord, the poison ring, and so on. I hired Merlois the actor to teach me the arts of disguise, impersonation, and dialectical speech.

"During the last year of my reign, also, I gathered a squad of the most unsavory rogues in the Twelve Cities: a cutpurse, a swindler, a forger, a bandit, a founder of cults and secret societies, a smuggler, a blackmailer, and two burglars. I kept them in luxury whilst they taught me all their tricks. Now I can scale the front of a building, force a window, pick a lock, open a strongbox, and—if caught in the act—convince the householder that I am a good spirit sent by the gods to report on his conduct.

"As a result of these studies, I have become, one might say, a good second-rater in a variety of fields. Thus I am not so deadly a fencer as Tartonio, my former master-at-arms; nor so skilled a rider as Korkuin, my master of the horse; nor so adept a burglar as the master thief Enas; nor so learned in the law as Justice Grallon; nor so efficient an administrator as Chancellor Turonus; nor so fluent a linguist as Stimber, my librarian. But I can beat all of them *save* Tartonio with sword and buckler, and out-ride all *save* Korkuin, and speak more tongues than any *save* Stimber, and so on.

"Through my readings, I learnt of the Forces of Progress. One of my predecessors had closed the College of Magical Arts and banished all magicians from Xylar, and his successors had maintained this prohibition—"

"I know that," growled Rhithos. "Why think you I dwell up here in the wilds? To escape the net of laws and regulations that the Cities fling about the student of the higher wisdom. True, in none of the other Twelve Cities is the law so stringent as in Xylar; but in all of 'em are rules and licenses and inspectors to cope with. To the forty-nine Mulvanian hells with 'em! Go on."

Jorian: "Hence the only such practitioners in Xylar are mere witches and hedge-wizards—furtive lawbreakers, eking out a shadowy existence by amulets and potions and predictions, half of 'em fake. After I had tried several local witches of both sexes, with unpleasing results, I got in touch with Doctor Karadur, who came to Xylar as a holy man and as such beyond reach of our law. My escape from the scaffold was his doing."

"Karadur has his good points," said Rhithos. "Were it not for his foolish ideas and impractical ideals—"

A scratching at the door interrupted the smith. Vanora opened it, and in bounced an animal. With a start of surprise, Jorian saw that it was a squirrel the size of a dog, weighing over twenty pounds. Long, black, glossy fur covered the beast. It chirped at Rhithos, rubbed its head against his leg, and let him scratch it behind the ears, and trotted out to the kitchen.

"My familiar, Ixus," said Rhithos. "The body is that of the giant squirrel of Yelizova; the spirit, that of a minor demon from the Fourth Plane."

"Where is Yelizova?" asked Jorian.

"A land far to the south, beyond the equatorial jungles south of Mulvan. 'Tis only in recent years that daring mariners from Zolon have sailed thither and returned the tale to tell. Ixus cost me a pretty penny, I assure you. Some of my colleagues prefer that their familiars possess the bodies of beasts of the ape kind, because of their dexterity. I, however, demur. In the first place, these animals are delicate, easily destroyed by cold; in the second, being near kin to mankind, they have minds of their own and so often escape the control of the spirit." The smith spoke in a coldly controlled voice, without expression of face or of tone. Now he addressed himself to his dinner.

"You were saying about Karadur?" said Jorian.

"Only that he is full of ideals that, however appealing to the emotions, are impractical in the real world. The same applies to his faction."

"I heard there was a difference of opinion. Could you explain your point of view?"

"His faction, which call themselves the Altruists—"

"Or White Faction, do I understand?"

"*They* term themselves and us the White and Black Factions respectively; but we admit not the distinction. 'Tis but their own pejorious usage, to bias the case in their favor. To resume: these self-styled Altruists would fain release the secrets of the arcane arts to the vulgus, broadcast. Thus, they say, all mankind shall benefit from this knowledge. Every man shall have a warm back and a full belly; he shall enjoy a passionate youth, a teeming family, and a hale old age.

"Now, were all men as conscientious as we of the Forces of Progress, who must study many years and give up some of life's choicest pleasures to master our arts, who are straitly examined by the senior members ere being admitted to our fraternity, and who are bound by dreadful oaths to use our knowledge for the good of mankind— were all other men so sternly trained and strictly admitted to this arcanum, then might something be said for the Altruists' ideal.

"But as you have seen, Master Jorian, not all men are so minded. Some are stupid, some lazy, and some downright wicked. Most of 'em choose their own self-interest over that of the general; most of 'em elect the pleasure of the moment over what is good for them, and theirs in the long run. Loose this deadly knowledge on such a feckless rabble of fools, knaves, and lubbards? As well put a razor into the chubby fingers of a toddling wean! There are men who, possessing the fellest spells, would not scruple to use them to blast an entire city, if by so doing they could burke a single personal foe. Hence to this proposal are we Benefactors adamantinely opposed."

However emphatic his words, Rhithos never raised his voice, speaking in the same expressionless monotone. There seemed to be something mechanical about him, which reminded Jorian of the legend of the mechanical servant that Vaisus, the divine smith, had made for the other gods, and of the troubles that ensued when the clockwork man wanted to be ranked as a god, too.

"What of your current project?" he said as they finished their repast.

" 'Twill do no harm to tell you, since it will be finished in three days at most. It is the sword Randir, which I am forging for the Grand Bastard. When the spells that go into its tempering are complete, it will cut through ordinary armor like cheese.

"The trick, I may say, is to apply the spells during the tempering stage. Some apply them earlier, during the initial heating and forging. Most such spells, however, are wasted because the heating and pounding nullify them.

"But tell us of your escape. What price did Karadur exact? Despite his hypocritical piety, I know the old didderer would not work so taxing and risky a magical opus without a price."

"Oh, he said that your Forces of Progress demanded that I go to the capital of Mulvan and there seek out an ancient coffer called the Kist of Avlen, said to be filled with portentous spells from olden times. Karadur then wants me to lug this box back to the Goblin Tower of Metouro, where, I understand, your society is to hold a great Conclave."

"Aha! Now it comes out. If he told you that the order as a whole demanded this thing, he lied, or I should have heard of it ere now. It is his own faction, the so-called Altruists, who lust after this chest in order to force us Benefactors to accede to their mad proposals. How do they enforce this command?"

"By a geas that gives me a frightful headache and nightmares if I keep not on the road to Trimandilam. I have tested this spell and know that it works."

"I might have guessed. But continue, good sir, with the tale of your escape."

While telling of his abortive execution, Jorian silently cursed himself for a rattlepate. He had wrongly assumed that Rhithos was in on his project for the theft of the Kist of Avlen, or at least that there would be no harm in telling him about it. Now it transpired that Jorian had involved himself in strife between the two factions of the magicians' fraternity. Rhithos might well try to put sand in the works. Jorian's wine-loosened tongue had betrayed him, and not for the first time.

Jorian got what little comfort he could from the thought that his indiscretion was also partly Karadur's fault. The old wizard had managed to give Jorian the impression, without actually saying so, that his whole society was behind this raid and not merely his own faction. Jorian sighed at the thought that not even Karadur, despite his lofty talk of purity of morals and ethics, was himself not absolutely beyond all forms of perfidy and deception.

Rhithos listened without expression to the rest of Jorian's narrative. At last he said: "Bravely done, good my sir. Now let us to bed, for there will be plenty to do on the morrow."

Jorian spent most of the next day eating, resting, and taking a much-needed bath in Rhithos' wooden tub. He watched Rhithos holding the blade Randir by its tang wrapped in rags, for the hilt had not yet been attached. The smith repeatedly heated the blade to cherry-red. Then he laid it on the anvil and struck it, now here, now there, to take the least curvature or unevenness out of it.

A day later, Jorian had fully recovered. He helped Rhithos with the sword, holding with pincers the ends of the wires wound around the grip, polishing the blade and the silvered brass knuckle-guard, and otherwise helping to give Randir its final touches. He turned the crank of the grindstone as the smith administered the blade's preliminary sharpening.

The imp Ixus hopped about the smithy, fetching and carrying to Rhithos' orders. It chattered angrily at Jorian and bared its squirrel's chisel-teeth at his leg until a sharp word from the smith subdued it.

"He's jealous," said Rhithos. "You had better go out and help Vanora. I am about to put a minor spell on the hilt and prefer to do so alone."

Jorian spent some time in chopping wood, hauling water, kneading dough, and weeding the garden without winning more than a few curt words from the girl. He tried flattery and stories:

"Did you ever hear," he said, "about the great wrastle betwixt King Fusas of Kortoli and his twin brother Fusor? This king, you see, was a great athlete—almost as great as Kadvan the Strong in Xylar, with the additional advantage that they didn't amputate his head after five years. I have never heard of a headless athlete who was worth a piece of mouldy straw in a contest.

"Well, Fusas wanted to put on a grand celebration to mark the five-hundredth anniversary of the polis. Of course he cheated a little, for that there was a gap in this fine history, when for several years Ardyman the Terrible of Govannian united all the Twelve Cities under his rule; but the Kortolians thought it more seemly to ignore this break, and who shall blame them?

"Being himself a mighty man, King Fusas thought to please his folk by staging, at the climax of the celebration, an athletic contest between himself and another man. Now, the king's favorite sport was wrestling. But that presented a problem. For, you see, the king thought it bad for his royal dignity to be worsted in such a public contest. On the other hand, if his opponent were warned in advance to lose, the word might leak out, or the other man might too patently let himself be thrown. At best this would give a dull show, and at worst it might cause the king to be jeered, even worse for the royal dignity.

"Belike the king could match himself against a man so much smaller than himself that he were sure to win in any case. But again, the people would see their king fling-

ing a mere shrimp of an opponent about and would jeer
him.

"So King Fusas took counsel with his wise man, the
wizard Thorynx. And Thorynx reminded Fusas that he had
a twin brother, Fusor, living a quiet life in a small country
house in the hills of southern Kortoli—or as quiet a life
as one can lead when surrounded by spies and informers
watching for a chance to denounce one for plotting to seize
the throne from one's brother. Luckily for him, Fusor—
the younger of the twain by a quarter-hour—was of a
retiring disposition. He cared for little but fishing and so
never gave the informers any suspicious acts to report
upon.

"Now, said Thorynx, Fusor and Fusas were identical
twins and therefore a perfect match as wrastlers, albeit
Fusor might be in better physical trim as a result of the
simple outdoor life he led, not having papers to sign and
lawsuits to judge and banquets to eat and balls to keep
him up late. So let him be brought to Kortoli City and
there wrastle with Fusas at the climax of the festival. Both
would be clad identically, so that the viewers could not
distinguish them. Whichever won, it would be announced
that King Fusas was the winner, and who should gainsay
it? Then Fusor could be sent back to his country house
with a handsome gift to keep him quiet.

"And so it was done. Prince Fusor was fetched to Kortoli
City and lodged in the palace for a month preceding the
festival. And at the high point of the celebration, a grand
wrastle it was, with the king and his brother rolling over
and over on the mat in a tangle of limbs and grunting like
a pair of boars at the same trough. And at last one of the
twain pinned the other and was declared the winner. He
was also declared to be the king.

"But no sooner had they returned to the palace and
passed out of the view of the throngs than they burst into
a furious quarrel, with shaken fists and menaces. Each,
both winner and loser, claimed to be King Fusas and, since
they looked just alike and were clad in the same purple
loincloths, there was no easy way to tell which spake
sooth.

"First, the chancellor tried by questioning them separately about the affairs of the kingdom. But each claimant
readily answered the questions. It transpired that Fusor—

whichever of the twain he was—had made the most of his month's residence in the palace to familiarize himself with such matters, whilst his royal brother had been occupied with training in the gymnasium for the bout.

"Then the chancellor asked Thorynx if he had any ideas. 'Aye,' said Thorynx. 'I can settle the question. Give each claimant a sheet of reed paper and let him write an account of the last time he went in unto Queen Zeldé, with full particulars. Then show these two screeds to the Queen and let her say which is that of the true king.' For, unlike the southern tier of the Twelve Cities, the Kortolians do not allow even kings to take more than one lawful wife. It must be the Mulvanian influence that leads you southrons to permit such liberty.

"Anyway, so it was done. The Queen glanced over the two writings and forthwith declared that one was true and the other false. So the one she had declared the true king was restored to his crown and throne and dignities, whilst the other, still indignantly protesting his royalty, was beheaded for high treason.

"That had been the end of it, save that many years later, when the king had died and the aged Queen Zeldé was on her deathbed, she confessed that she had wantonly chosen the wrong screed—that penned by Prince Fusor and not that by King Fusas.

"'But grandmother!' cried the young princess to whom she made this avowal. 'Why did you ever do such a wicked thing?'

"'Because,' said Queen Mother Zeldé, 'I never liked that pig Fusas. His breath smelt bad, and when he made love he was always finished before I had even begun to warm up. I thought that by trading him for his brother I might get somebody more to my taste. But alas! Fusor proved identical with his brother in these as in other respects.' And so she died."

Vanora, however, remained scornful. "You're a fearful braggart, Master Jorian," she said at last. "I'll wager you cannot do one half the feats whereof you boast."

Jorian smiled ingratiatingly. "Well, any man would wish to put his best foot forward with an attractive girl, now wouldn't he?"

She snorted. "To what end? You are not even man

41

enough to enjoy the fruits of gallantry, unless you are first stoked with enough victuals to state a lion."

"I could show you—"

"Never mind, sirrah; you don't appeal to me."

"I am wounded unto death, as by one of the silvans' poisoned shafts!" cried Jorian, clasping his heart and pretending to faint. "What else would you like me to demonstrate?"

"That lock-picking skill, for example. See you the door of yonder cage?"

Jorian approached the cage. The ape-man, an exceptionally ugly one covered with short, grizzled hair, growled at him. Then, as Vanora came up to the bars, she extended a hand through them. The ape-man took the hand in his own and kissed it.

"A real gallant, this Komilakhian!" said Jorian, examining the lock. "What does Rhithos keep him for? He does not work the creature, as he does the squirrel, and the beast-man must be fed. What's the purpose?"

Vanora had been speaking to the ape-man in the latter's own clucking, hissing tongue. She said: "Rhithos means to use Zor here in the final stage of the making of the sword Randir. The concluding spell calls for thrusting the red-hot blade through the poor creature and leaving it there until it has cooled; then its edge is tested by striking off Zor's head. The spell should properly be performed with a human captive, but Rhithos assures me 'twill work as well with Zor, who is at least halfway to humanhood and is less likely to embroil us with vengeful kinfolk than would a man."

"The poor halfling! Zor seems to like you."

"More than that; he's in love with me."

"How do you know?"

"Look at him, stupid!"

"Oh, I see what you mean." Jorian fumbled in a small pouch, pinned to the inner side of his breeches, and brought out a short length of stout, bent wire. "I think this will take care of Zor's lock. Hold the cage door."

He inserted the wire into the lock, felt about, and twisted. The bolt clicked back.

"Beware!" said Jorian. "Zor might—"

Instead of helping Jorian to hold the cage door shut, Vanora stepped back and uttered a word in Zor's language.

With a roar, the ape-man hurled himself against the door. He was even heavier and stronger than Jorian, and the force of his impact was irresistible. Sent staggering back, Jorian caught his heel and sat down in the dirt, while the door flew open and Zor rushed out.

"Stop him!" cried Jorian, scrambling to his feet. But Vanora only stood with fists on hips, watching complacently as Zor raced off into the woods and vanished.

"You did that on purpose!" cried Jorian, scrambling up. "By Zevatas's brazen beard, why—"

"What's this?" barked the voice of the smith as Rhithos emerged from the smithy. "Great Zevatas, you've enlarged Zor! Are you mad, man? Why should you do this to me?"

"He was showing off his skill at picking locks," said Vanora.

"Why, you teat-sucking idiot—" raved the smith, shaking his fists. It was the first time that Jorian had seen the man express emotion of any kind.

"I like not to blame a woman, sir," said Jorian, "but your young lady here did suggest—"

"I did nought of the sort!" screamed Vanora, "'Twas your own self-conceit that drove you to the deed, despite my remonstrance—"

"Why, you little liar!" said Jorian. "Dip me in dung if I don't spank your—"

"You shall do nought of the sort, sirrah!" roared Rhithos. "Look at me!"

Jorian did, then belatedly tried to snatch his gaze away and found that he could not. The smith held up something in the palm of his hand—whether a gem, a mirror, or a magical light, Jorian could not tell. It glowed and sparkled with a myriad of rays. The very soul seemed to be drawn out of his body as he watched in stupefied fascination. A corner of his mind kept telling him to tear his gaze away, to resist, to strike down the smith and flee; but he could not.

Closer and closer came the smith; brighter and more confusing came the sparkle of lights. The world around Jorian seemed to fade and vanish, so that he stood in empty space, bathed in flickering, coruscating lights of all the known colors and some unknown ones.

"Hold still!" said the smith, his voice toneless again. Jorian found himself unable to move at all. He felt the smith's free hand searching his clothing. His dagger was taken, and his purse, and then the smith extracted the money belt and the little bag of pick-locks.

"Now back!" said the smith. "Back! Another step! And another!" He continued until he had Jorian backed through the door of the cage.

Dimly, Jorian heard the door clang and the lock click. The dazzle faded and he was in Zor's cage.

"Now," said Rhithos, "since you have robbed me of Zor, you shall take his place."

"Are you serious, Master Rhithos?" said Jorian.

"You shall see how serious I am. I shall be ready to cast the final spell tomorrow, and in that spell you shall play a vital role."

"You mean you intend to temper the blade by skewering me with it and testing it on my neck?"

"Certes. The poets will sing of this blade for centuries; so, if it's any comfort, know that you die in a noble cause."

"By Imbal's brazen balls, that's unreasonable! Whilst I own to some small blame in Zor's escape, no civilized man would deem my blunder capital offense."

"What are you or any other man to me? No more than insects to be trodden down when they cross my path. What is important is the perfection of my art."

"My friend," said Jorian in his most winning tone, "were you not better advised to send me to Komilakh to fetch you back another man-ape? You can assure my return by one of your spells, like that which Karadur's colleagues have laid upon me. Besides, how shall I seek the Kist of Avlen—"

"Your faction seeks to put this Kist to some foolish use, so better you did not live to carry out your quest. Besides, the next twenty-four hours are astrologically auspicious, and such a favorable conjunction will not recur for years." The smith turned to Vanora. "Meseems, girl, you've been talking too freely with our guest, or he'd not have known so much about the making of Randir. I shall have somewhat to say to you later. Meanwhile, back to your chores. Leave this lout to contemplate the fruits of his folly, for even this meager pleasure will not long remain him."

"Master Rhithos!" cried Jorian in desperation. "Faction or no faction, to slay the servant of a fellow member of your fraternity will bring troubles upon you. Karadur will avenge—"

The smith snorted, turned his broad back, and marched off to the smithy. Vanora disappeared. Overhead, the blanket of thick, gray cloud seemed to press closer than ever, and the clearing seemed darker than could even be explained by the heavy overcast. Bare branches stood up like withered black hands against the darkling sky.

Jorian felt a brooding tension, as he sometimes did before a heavy thunderstorm. He paced nervously about the cage, trying his muscles on the bars and hoisting himself up by the bars that formed the roof. He poked in vain at the lock with his thick, hairy fingers.

Later, when the light dimmed, Vanora passed the cage with a jar of water.

"Mistress Vanora!" called Jorian. "Don't I get anything more to eat?"

"To what end? Tomorrow you'll never need food again—at least, not on this plane of existence. Better to spend your time making peace with your gods and forget that bottomless pit of a belly."

She passed out of sight. Presently she was back, thrusting a loaf of bread and a crock of water through the bars.

"Quiet!" she whispered. "Rhithos would take it ill if he knew I wasted his victuals, as he'd say. As 'tis, he's like to stripe my back for telling you about the sword spell. He never remembers a favor or forgets an injury."

"An unlikeable wight. Can you get me out of here?"

"At eventide, when he's absorbed in his spells."

"I thought the final spell came tomorrow?"

"It does; this is but the penultimate cantrip."

The smith ate early and returned to his smithy, whence presently issued the sound of a drum and of Rhithos' voice raised in a chant. The shadows seemed to deepen about the shed even more swiftly than elsewhere. As full darkness fell, curious sounds came forth—croaks unlike any made by a human voice, and other noises unlike anything Jorian had ever heard. Now and then the voice of the smith rose in a shouted command. Strange lights of a ghastly bluish radiance flickered through the cracks between the boards of the shed. Jorian's skin tingled until he felt as if he could jump right out of it. He wanted to explode with tension.

Vanora, a blur in the darkness, reappeared at the bars of the cage. "T-take this!" she whispered, extending a trembling hand. "And drop it not, lest it be lost for aye in the mud."

It was the pick-lock with which Jorian had opened the cage door earlier. "You dropped it when Zor escaped," she said, "and Rhithos marked it not when he took the rest of your gear."

Jorian felt for the keyhole on the outer side of the lock plate and inserted the wire. His hand shook so that he could hardly find the hole. Manipulating the wire from inside the cage proved awkward, but after some fumbling the bolt clicked back. He put away the wire and opened the door. Another blue flash lit up the smithy.

"Here!" said Vanora, thrusting something cold into his hand. It was the hilt of his falchion. "You must slay Rhithos whilst he is sunken in his spell."

"Couldn't we just flee to Othomae? Your smith is no mean wizard, and I crave not to be turned into a spider."

"Faintheart! You're no gallant cavalier, ardent for a fight at whatever odds, but a common, calculating kern, weighing pros and contras as a moneychanger weighs out grains of gold dust."

"I've never claimed to be a gallant cavalier. These gambols affright me silly."

"Well, play the man for once! Rhithos will be weakened by his spell-casting."

"I still like it not; I do not enjoy killing people without necessity. Why can't we just flee through the woods?"

"Because the instant Rhithos learns of our escape, he'll cast a spell to fetch us back, or send his demons to herd us hither like sheep. And back we shall be forced if we're within five leagues of his house. Even if that fail, he's allied with the silvans, who at his command will fill us with their envenomed arrows. Since flight were fatal, there's nothing for it but to kill him, and that right speedily."

Jorian hefted the short, curved blade. "This is not an ideal utensil for the purpose, especially as he'll have that great brand Randir ready to hand. With this butcher's tool,

I shall need some defense for the left hand. Give me your cloak."

"You mean to get my one good garment all hacked and slashed in the fray? I will not! Oh, you villain!" she cried as Jorian shot out a long arm and wrenched the cloak from her shoulders. He whipped the garment around his left arm.

"Now *you* be quiet!" he whispered, as he glided towards the shed.

Rhithos had closed the shutters over the windows of the smithy. The louvers of these shutters were also closed, lying flat against one another like the feathers in a bird's wing. One louver, however, had been broken at one end and sagged from its socket at the other. Jorian put his eye to the narrow triangle of light.

Within, the anvil had been moved to one side. Where it had stood, near the forge, three pentacles had been drawn with charcoal: one large flanked by two small. Rhithos stood in one small pentacle, Ixus in the other. Six black candles, at the apices of the triangles of the main pentacle, shed a fitful light, to which a dull-red glow from the banked fire in the forge added but little. The sword Randir lay in the center of the large central pentacle.

In that circle, also, stood something else, although Jorian could not quite make it out. It was dark and wavering, like a misshapen cloud, man-high and man-wide but without any definite limbs or organs. A pallid glow, like a witch fire or a will-o'-the-wisp, flickered through the thing from time to time.

Rhithos was waving a sword and chanting. Ixus, facing him across the large circle, beat time with a wand.

"His back is to the door," breathed Vanora. "You can thrust it open and sink your blade in his back with one bound."

"What of that spirit in the pentacle?"

" 'Tis not yet wholly materialized; interrupt the cantrip and 'twill vanish. Come, one swift stab—"

"Not quite what a gallant cavalier would do, but— come on!" Jorian stepped to the door. "Does it squeak?"

"Nay. Hating rust, Rhithos keeps the hinges oiled."

"Then grasp the knob and open, gently."

She did as he bade. As the door swung silently open, Jorian took a short running step. One long bound would sink the falchion in Rhithos's back, to the left of the spine and below the shoulder blade...

But Jorian had forgotten Ixus, who stood facing the door. As Jorian started his spring, the familiar screeched and pointed. Without turning his head, the smith bounded to one side. As he did so, he kicked one of the six candles. The candlestick went clattering one way; the candle flew another and went out. The cloudy thing in the large pentacle vanished.

Jorian's rush carried him through the space where Rhithos had stood and across the main pentacle. He tripped over the sword Randir, staggered, and almost trod on Ixus, who dodged and went for Jorian with bared chisel-teeth.

Jorian struck at the hurtling, black, furry body just before the teeth reached his leg. The blow hurled the giant squirrel against the forge, where it lay, twitching and bleeding. The blow had cut it nearly in half.

Rhithos recovered from his leap. He stepped back to the main pentacle and snatched up the sword Randir. By the time Jorian had turned from his blow at the familiar, the smith was upon him, whirling the sword in great full-armed, figure-eight cuts.

Rhithos's wrinkled face was pale in the candle light and sparkled with drops of sweat. He moved heavily and breathed hard, for his sorcerous operation had taken its toll of his strength. Nevertheless, so vast had been that strength to begin with that Jorian found the man, even in his fatigued condition, all he could handle and a little more.

Since the smith's blade was nearly twice the length of the falchion, Jorian was tempted to fall back before the onslaught. But he knew that, if he did, the smith would soon corner him. Therefore he stood his ground, catching the blows alternately on the falchion and the rolled-up cloak.

At first the blows came so fast and furiously that Jorian had no time for a return cut or thrust. The smith seemed determined to squander his remaining strength in a whole-hog effort to beat down Jorian's defense by sheer weight of blade and fury of attack.

Soon, however, age and exhaustion slowed the smith's windmill assault. As he parried one slash with the cloak,

Jorian sent a forehand cut at Rhithos' chest. The tip of the falchion slit Rhithos' tunic and pinked the skin beneath.

Gasping, Rhithos fell back a pace. Now he fought more craftily, in proper fencing style, with his right foot forward and his left arm up and back. Since Jorian had to use his left hand, he employed the two-hand stance, facing directly forward with feet apart and knees slightly bent. The two were well matched. As they advanced, retreated, feinted, thrust, cut, and parried, they circled the main pentacle.

Jorian found that now he could fight an adequate defensive fight against Rhithos, but the other's length of blade kept him out of reach. When he tried to close, Rhithos's long blade licked out in a thrust at his exposed right arm. The point caught the fabric of Jorian's sleeve and tore a small rip in it. For an instant, Jorian felt the cold flat of the blade against his skin.

Around they went again. Both breathed in quick pants, watching each other's eyes. Jorian accidentally kicked over another candle, which also went out.

Now the smith seemed to have gotten his second wind, and it was Jorian who was beginning to tire. Again and again the smith sent thrusts and slashes at Jorian's right arm. Jorian avoided these attacks, but by narrower and narrower margins.

In the course of their circling, the smith once more had his back to the door. Vanora, who had been hovering in the background, stepped forward with the sword that Rhithos had been holding when first attacked, and which he had dropped. It was not a fighting weapon but a magical accessory—a straight, thirty-inch blade with little point and less edge, of well-polished soft iron, with a smooth ivory grip and a cross-guard in the form of a copper crescent. Practically speaking, it was useless for anything but spells and evocations.

Nonetheless, Vanora took the weapon in both hands and thrust the blunt point into Rhithos' back. The smith started, grunted, and half turned. Instantly Jorian closed with him. He whipped the tattered end of Vanora's cloak around the sword Randir, immobilizing it for an instant, and drove his falchion into Rhithos's chest. He jerked out the blade, thrust it into the smith's belly, withdrew it again, and slashed deeply into Rhithos' neck.

49

Like an aged oak, Rhithos swayed and crashed to the floor. Jorian stood over him, gasping for breath. When he could breathe normally, he took a rag from the pile that lay near the forge, wiped his blade, and sheathed it. He tossed the bloody rag on the banked forge fire, where it smoked, burst into flame, and was quickly consumed.

"By Imbal's bronzen arse, that was close," said Jorian. "Lucky for me he was already spent from his sorcery; I misdoubt I could have handled him fresh."

"Are you all right?" said Vanora.

"Aye. I'm relieved to see he has real blood inside him. From his cold, mechanical manner, I wondered if he'd prove to be full of cogwheels and pulleys, like one of my father's water clocks." He picked up Randir, squinted along the blade, and cut the air with it. It was a handsome, single-edged, cut-and-thrust sword with a basket hilt. "It won't have magical properties, since we broke into the spell. Still, a pretty blade. Do you suppose he has a scabbard for it?"

"He doesn't make his own scabbards but orders them from an armorer in Othomae. But one of those in the main hall might fit."

"I'll try them. Fit is important; nothing so embarrasses a hero as to confront a dragon or an ogre and find his sword firmly stuck in its scabbard. I do not suppose we need fear the law here?"

"Nay; there's none, save as each can make his own. Both Xylar and Othomae lay a claim to these hills, but they never send officers hither to sustain their claims or enforce their statutes."

With the toe of his boot, Jorian stirred the body of the giant squirrel. "I'm sorry to have slain his pet. It did but defend its master."

" 'Tis well you did, Master Jorian. Otherwise Ixus would have told the silvans, and they would have slaughtered us in reprisal for their ally's death. As it is, they will learn of Rhithos's demise soon enough."

"How?"

"By the nullification of the confusion spell, whereby he's kept woodsmen out of their territory. As soon as some hunter wanders into this demesne—and now is the hunting season—they'll come running to this house to learn what ails their sorcerer."

"Then we had best start for Othomae forthwith," he said.

"First we must gather our gear. I shall need a cloak; your set-to has reduced mine to tatters. One of the smith's will serve."

Taking three of the remaining candles, they returned to the house. Jorian said:

"I do not think it were well to start such a journey on empty stomachs. Can you whip up a meal whilst I collect my belongings?"

"All you think of is food!" said Vanora. "I could not down a crumb after all this excitement. But you shall have what you ask. Linger not over it, for despite the darkness we should put as much distance as we can betwixt ourselves and the house by dawn, when the silvans begin to stir." She busied herself with the fire and the pots.

"Do you know the trails hereabouts?" asked Jorian, watching her. "I have a map, but on such a starless night 'tis of little avail."

"I know the way to Othomae. We go thither every month to sell Rhithos's swords and other ironmongery, to take orders for more, and to purchase supplies."

"How do you carry the load?"

"The ass bears it. Here's your repast, Master Eat-all."

"Aren't you having anything?"

"Nay; I told you I couldn't. But now the damned tyrant is dead and good riddance, we need not drink cider." She poured a flagon of wine for Jorian and another for herself and drank hers greedily.

"If you so bitterly hated Rhithos," said Jorian, "how is it that you never fled from him?"

"I told you, he had spells for fetching back runaways."

"But if you set out directly the old spooker fell asleep some night, by dawn you'd be beyond the range of his spells. And you say you know the trails."

"I couldn't traverse these woods alone, at night."

"Why not? The leopard will not attack if you put up a bold front."

"I might meet a serpent."

"Oh, come! The serpents in these hills are neither ven-

51

omous, like those of the lowlands, nor huge, like those of the jungles of Mulvan, but small and harmless."

"Natheless, I have a deathly fear of all snakes." She gulped more wine. "Speak you no more of the matter; the mere thought of a serpent turns my veins to ice."

"Well then, shall we bury the smith?" asked Jorian.

"Indeed we must, and hide his grave, lest the silvans see his body lying in the smithy."

"Then we must needs do it tonight, albeit the scoundrel deserves it not."

"He was not a wholly wicked man, in the sense of doing that which he knew to be wrong." She hiccupped. "Though I hated his bowels, I would do him justice."

"He'd have murdered me for convenience in his sword-making, and if that be not a villain, I shudder to think of the crimes that would arouse your disapproval."

"Oh, people were nothing to him. All he cared for was his swordsmith's art. He had no lust for wealth, or power, or glory, or women; his consuming ambition was to be the greatest swordmaker of all time. This ambition drove him so hard that all other human feelings were squeezed out, save perhaps some small affection for Ixus the imp." She drank heavily again.

"Mistress!" said Jorian. "If you swill thus on an empty stomach, you'll be in no shape to march through the woods."

" 'Tis my affair, what I drink!" shouted Vanora. "Tend your business and I'll tend mine."

Jorian shrugged and addressed himself to his food. He did well by a rewarmed roast, another loaf of bread, half a cabbage, a fistful of onions, and an apple pie. He asked, "Why did you turn Zor loose?"

"For one, the creature loved me—and cursed few there have been who did. I include not all the lustful young men like yourself, who prate of love but only seek to sheathe their fleshy poniards. So it grieved me to see Rhithos sacrifice him to his mad ambition.

"For another, I—I took pleasure in thwarting Rhithos, to gratify my hatred. Lastly, because I wished to escape. Had Rhithos not died, I had spent my life here. He was as lively company as a granite boulder. The years of a wizard are not as those of a common man, and he might have survived me, old and shriveled. I durst not attack him myself, even in slumber, because the imp would have warned him; I durst not flee, for the reason I've given. So, thought I, I'll stir up strife betwixt these twain, and whichever win, I may escape in the confusion."

"You'd not have cared if I—a harmless stranger—had perished in this strife?"

"Oh, I hoped you'd conquer, if—if only because I should have gained no pleasure from your death. But if you'd lost," she shrugged, "that had been nought to me. What has the world of men done for me that I should bear them that all-embracing, indiscriminate love the priests of Astis counsel?" She gulped more wine.

"By Astis' ivory teats, you're frank, at least," he said, wiping his mouth. "I do not think we need wash these dishes, since we purpose to abandon the house. If you'll tell me where Rhithos keeps his shovel, I will bury him and his pet."

"On—on a peg to the right of the door of the smithy, ash— as you enter." Her voice had become blurred. "He wash a mos'—most particular man, with a peg for each tool, and woe betide the wretch who returned one to the wrong peg!"

"Good! Collect your dunnage whilst I perform this task." Carrying a candle, Jorian went out.

Half an hour later he returned, to find Vanora sprawled ungracefully on the floor, with her skirt up to her middle and an overturned flagon beside her. He spoke to her, nudged her, shook her, slapped her, and poured cold water on her face. Her only responses were a drunken mumble and a rasping snore.

"Damned fool woman," growled Jorian. "We're in such haste to flee the silvans, so you must needs get potulated!"

He stood scowling and thinking. He could not set forth without her, since he did not know the way. He could not carry her...

He gave up, stretched out on a bench, and pulled a bearskin over himself. The next thing he knew, dawn was graying the windows. He was being aroused by Vanora, who was showering moist, slobbery kisses upon him, breathing hard, and fumbling with his garments.

As the sun rose, they stepped out, closing the doors of

Rhithos' house and smithy. Jorian wore the sword Randir in a scabbard from Rhithos' living room. He also bore a dagger of Rhithos' make: a deadly affair, with a broad, cubit-long blade and a catch that prevented its coming out of its sheath unless one pressed a stud. The pommel was no gaudy gem but a simple ball of lead. When held by the sheathed blade, the weapon made a handy bludgeon in case one wished merely to stun a foe.

Jorian also carried his crossbow, and under his tunic he wore a vest of fine mesh mail, also looted from Rhithos' house. Feeling as if he could knock an elephant down with his fist, he expanded his huge chest and said:

"We shall have to take our chances with the silvans. Perhaps they won't soon discover Rhithos's disappearance. But I don't care." While loading provisions on Rhithos' ass, he burst into a threshing song in the Kortolian dialect.

"What are you singing about?" snapped Vanora. "You'll rouse every silvan within leagues, with that big bass voice."

"Just happy, that's all. Happy because a've found ma true love."

"Love!" she snorted.

"Couldn't you feel a little love for me? I'm head over heals in love with you, wench. And you did give me your all, as they say."

"Rubbish! The fact that I needed to be well futtered after long deprivation has nought to do with love."

"But, darling—"

"Darling me no darlings! I'm not the woman for you. I am just a drunken slut with a hot cleft, and forget it not."

"Oh," he said, his exalted mood punctured.

"Get me to a city and buy me some decent clothes, and then if you want to talk of love, I don't suppose I can stop you."

Jorian sighed, and his broad shoulders dropped. "You're nobody's sweet little innocent honey-bun, I will grant. I'm a bigger fool for loving you than Doctor Karadur was in trusting Rhithos. But there it is, damn it. Let's say a prayer to Thio and go."

III

THE SILVER DRAGON

Rhuys's tavern, the silver dragon, stood just off the main square of Othomae City, behind the Guildhall. The main taproom accommodated six tables, each flanked by a pair of benches, while to one side a pair of curtained alcoves served as private rooms for patrons of quality. Facing the entrance was Rhuys's bar: a counter with four large holes in the marble top, each closed by a circular wooden lid with a handle. Below each hole hung a cask of one of the cheaper beverages: beer, ale, white wine, and red wine, each with its own dipper. Choicer drinkables stood in a row in bottles on a shelf behind the taverner.

To the left of the bar, as one entered, was the door to the kitchen; Rhuys would have his wife cook dinner for patrons who ordered in advance. To the right were the stairs leading up to the dormitory and the three private bedrooms that the tavern rented. Rhuys himself occupied the fourth. Several oil lamps shed a soft yellow light about the room.

Although he bore the same name as a former king of Xylar, known as Rhuys the Ugly, Rhuys the taverner was not really ugly. He was a small, wiry, seedy-looking man, with thinning, graying hair and pouched eyes. He leant his elbows on the bar and watched his few customers. There were only five, for the morrow was a working day and few Othomaeans were out late that night. In addition, a huge, gross, porcine man sprawled in a corner.

The door opened, and Jorian and Vanora came in. Jorian, looking worn from his fiftnight's hike from Rhithos's house, approached the counter.

"Good even," he said. "I am Nikko of Kortoli. Has a Doctor Ma—Mabahandula left word for me?"

"Why, yes, so he has," said Rhuys. "He was in today, saying he'd be here right after the supper hour; but he has not come."

"Then we'll wait. We have given our ass in charge of your boy in the back."

"What will you have?"

"Ale for me." Jorian looked a question at Vanora, who said:

"Red wine for me."

"Have you aught to eat?" said Jorian. "We've come a long way."

"Plenty of bread, cheese, and apples. The fire is out, so we cannot cook a hot repast for you."

"Bread, cheese and apples will do fine." Jorian turned away to lead Vanora to one of the tables.

"Master Nikko!" called Rhuys. "Have you a permit to carry that hanger?" He indicated Jorian's sword, the hilt of which was now attached to the scabbard by a wire. The ends of the wire were crimped together by a small leaden seal bearing the two-headed eagle of Othomae.

"They gave me one at the city gate," said Jorian, waving a piece of reed paper. "I'm a traveler on his way to Vindium."

Of the other customers, two men were drinking and arguing in low tones. Jorian and Vanora leisurely ate and drank. Other customers came and went, but the pair in the corner continued their dispute.

Long after Jorian and Vanora had finished their supper, the other pair were still at it. One of these men raised his voice in anger. Presently he stood up, leaned over the bench, shook his fist, and shouted:

"You son of a eunuch, you will cheat me of my commission, will you? Any man who so entreats me has cause to rue his deed! I have warned you for the last time! Now will you pay me my share, or—"

"Futter you," said the seated man.

With a shrill squawk, the standing man hurled the contents of his mug in the other's face. Sputtering, the other man tried to rise and reach for his dagger, but his robe had become entangled with the bench. While he struggled and the standing man screamed threats and denunciations, the huge, stout man in the corner caught Rhuys's eye. Rhuys nodded. The stout man lumbered to his feet, took three steps, picked the standing man up bodily by the slack of his garments, strode to the door, and tossed the man into the street. Brushing his hands together, he returned to his seat without a word.

Vanora gave the stout man a long look as she said to Jorian: "I wonder they did not notice the Grand Bastard's name on your sw—"

"*Hush!* Don't mention that. When I get a chance, I'll have it filed off."

She waved to Rhuys to refill her glass, asking Jorian: "What is this title of Grand Bastard? It does not sound like a real title. I've heard of the Grand Duke and the Grand Bastard, but none has ever explained it to me. Which rules Othomae?"

"They are co-rulers. According to Othomaean custom, the eldest legitimate son of the late Grand Duke becomes the new Grand Duke and hereditary ruler of the kingdom in civil affairs, whilst the eldest illegitimate son of that same late Grand Duke becomes the Grand Bastard and hereditary commander-in-chief of the army. Since the Othomaeans set great store by legitimacy, the Grand Bastard knows that 'twould avail him nought to try to seize the civil power, for none would then obey him."

"What a curious way to run a country!"

"The Othomaeans set it up long ago, so that no one ruler should become too powerful and oppress his subjects. Now, Vanora, you are not going to get drunk again, I hope?"

"I'll drink what I please. How are you going to steal this Kist in Trimandilam?"

"That's for Karadur and me to decide when we get there. The plan for the nonce is for me to make up to the serpent princess."

"Serpent princess? What's that?"

"An immortal—or at least monstrously long-lived—being who is a luscious princess by day and a gigantic serpent by night. Karadur tells me she has the disconcerting habit of changing shape and devouring the poor wight who has just been making love to her, as I shall have to do."

She banged her mug on the table. "You mean, after giving me sweet talk of love all the way from Rhithos' house, you knew all the time you were going to try to seduce this—this snake-woman?"

"Please! I have no choice in the matter—"

"You're just another lying prick-hound! I should have known better than to listen to you. Farewell!" She started to rise.

"My dear girl, what in the name of Zevatas's horse is there to get so excited about? Surely you do not make an idol of chastity—"

Furiously, she replied: "I should not much have minded your futtering a proper human dame; but a *snake*! Ugh! Goodbye! That looks like the kind of man I understand!"

She staggered over to where the stout man sprawled and sat down beside him. The man's little, piggy eyes opened, and his thick lips wreathed themselves in a smile through his stubble. Jorian followed her, saying:

"Pray, Vanora, be reasonable!"

"Oh, hold your tongue! You bore me." She turned to the ejector. "What's your name, big man?"

"Huh? My name?"

"Aye, handsome! Your name."

"Boso son of Triis. Is this fellow bothering you?"

"He won't if he knows what is good for him."

"Who are you, fellow?" growled Boso at Jorian.

"Nikko of Kortoli, if it is any concern of yours. This young lady was with me, but she is her own woman. If she prefers you, I might question her taste but would not thwart her choice."

"Oh," grunted Boso, settling back in his corner once more. But Vanora burst out:

"He is not Nikko of Kortoli! He is Jorian son of Evor—"

"Wait!" said Boso, opening his eyes and jerking upright once more. "That makes me think of something. Let me see..." He peered up through narrowed lids. "Not Evor the clockmaker?"

"Aye; he's told me many a tale of his sire—"

With a roar, Boso heaved up out of his seat, stooping to fumble for the two-foot bludgeon that lay at his feet. "So you're the son of the man who cost me my livelihood!"

"What in the forty-nine Mulvanian hells do you mean?" said Jorian, stepping back and laying a hand on his hilt. When he tried to draw, he realized that he could not because of the peace wire threaded through the guard.

Boso bellowed: "I was chief gongringer of Othomae, and a damned good one! My helpers and I sounded the hours in the city hall tower and never missed a stroke. Twenty years ago—or was it ten? No matter—your perverted father sold a water clock to the town council, and there it stands in the tower, going *bong, bong* with its wheels and levers. Since then I've had to live by odd jobs, and life has been hell. I cannot beat your fornicating father to a pulp, but you'll do!"

"Boso!" said Rhuys sharply. "Behave yourself, you stupid lout, if you want your job!"

"Bugger you, boss," said Boso and went for Jorian with his club.

Unable to draw the sword Randir, Jorian had hoisted the baldric over his head and now gripped the hilt of the scabbarded blade in both hands. As Boso lumbered forward like an enraged behemoth on the banks of the Bharma, Jorian feinted at his head. As Boso raised the bludgeon to parry, Jorian poked him in the midriff with the chape on the end of the scabbard.

"*Oof!*" said Boso, doubling up and giving back a step.

Since Jorian and Boso were by far the two largest men in the room, the remaining customers crowded back to the walls to get out of the way. Cautiously, the two combatants advanced and retreated in the space between the two rows of tables, which was too narrow to permit them to circle. Every time Boso tried to close to bring his bludgeon into range, the threat of the scabbarded blade drove him back.

Boso made a determined lunge; Jorian whacked him above the ear. The blow knocked him sideways, but he recovered. His little eyes blazing with rage, he stepped forward and aimed a terrific forehand swing.

The bludgeon whispered through the air as Jorian jerked back; the end of the club missed his face by the thickness of a sheet of parchment. The force of the missed blow swung Boso halfway around. Before he could recover, Jorian stepped forward and to the left and brought his knee up hard against Boso's back, over his right kidney. As Boso staggered, clutching for support at a table top, Jorian, now behind him, slipped the loop of the baldric over Boso's head. He tightened the strap around the ejector's neck, twisting it with all the strength of his powerful hands.

Boso opened his mouth, but only a faint wheeze came forth. Eyes popping, he stamped and kicked and waved his arms, trying to reach the foe behind him. But his arms were too short and thick. He plunged and staggered about the confined space, dragging Jorian with him, but Jorian's grip never loosened.

Boso's struggles weakened as his face turned blue. He clutched the edge of a table, then slid to the floor.

The door flew open, and several people crowded in. One was Karadur, with his long, white beard and bulbous turban. With him was a tall, gray-haired woman in a shabby black gown. After them came a squad of the night watch: four men armed with halberds and an officer. The latter said, "Master Rhuys! We heard there was a disturbance. Who is that? What has befallen?"

"That is Boso, my ejector—my former ejector, that is. He picked a fight with this customer and got thrashed."

"Was he alone to blame?"

"As far as I could see, he was."

The officer turned to Jorian. "Are you fain to submit a complaint against this man?"

Vanora had pulled Boso's head up so that it lay in her lap, and she was trickling a little wine down his throat. Boso breathed in rasping gasps while his face returned to its normal hue. As Jorian hesitated, Karadur said:

"Do not—ah—send the fellow to prison, Jorian—"

"Nikko."

"Of course; how stupid of me! Do not send this poor fellow to prison. You have chastised him enough by strangling him nigh unto death."

"How do I know he'll not set upon me with that club as soon as he gets his breath back?"

"You must disarm him by your kindness. Remember,

60

the best way to destroy an enemy is to make him your friend."

"All very pretty. I suppose next you'll want me to find him another job."

"A splendid idea!" Karadur clapped his old hands together. To the officer he said: "I think, sir, you may leave us without a formal complaint." Then to Rhuys, "What is this man good for, save as an ejector?"

"For nought! He is too stupid," said the taverner. "If some big building construction were under way, he could carry a hod; but there is none just now."

The gray-haired woman spoke: "I can use one of thick thews but weak wits. Besides gardening and household tasks, he can protect me against those ignorant oafs who betimes raise the cry of 'witch!' against me, not withstanding that I am a fully licensed wizardess."

"I have not had the pleasure of meeting you, madam," said Jorian. "I am Nikko of Kortoli."

"And I, Goania daughter of Aristor." She leaned over and shook Boso's shoulder. "Get up, man!"

Boso and Vanora climbed unsteadily to their feet. Goania said sharply:

"Do you understand, Boso? You have lost your post here."

"Huh? You mean lost my job?" wheezed Boso.

"Certes. Will you work for me for what Master Rhuys paid you: sixpence a day and found?"

"Me work for you?"

"Aye. Must I repeat the terms?"

Boso ran a hand over his chin with a rasp of stubble. "Oh, I guess it's all right. But first, I'll just knock the pumpkin off this fornicating clockmaker, who goes around putting honest workmen out of their jobs."

"You shall do nothing of the sort! Sit down and calm yourself."

"Now, lady! I don't let no woman tell me—"

"I am not a lady; I am a wizardess who can turn you into a toad if you misbehave. And I say there shall be no more quarreling. We are all friends, henceforth."

"Him? Friend?"

"Verily. He could have sent you to prison but chose not to, thinking you more useful out than in."

Boso glowered at Jorian, spat on the floor, and mumbled

under his breath. But he let Vanora lead him over to the far side of the room, where the girl soothed and comforted him while he drank beer and fingered his sore neck.

Jorian, Karadur, and Goania sat in the opposite corner. Jorian asked Karadur, "Where in the forty-nine Mulvanian hells have you been, man? We have been here for hours."

"I obtained access to the Grand Ducal library," said Karadur, "and became so—ah—absorbed in reading that I forgot about time. But you look as if you had had a hard time of it, lad. You have lost weight—not that you could not afford to lose a little."

"I have had a hard time; had to kill Rhithos—"

With sharp exclamations, the other two bent closer. "Keep your voice down, Master Nikko," said Goania. "I know your true name but think it unwise to utter it here, unless you wish the taverner to set the Xylarians on your trail. Tell us how this calamity came to pass."

Jorian told his tale. "So we hiked to Othomae on the trails Vanora knows, and here we are. The ass is stabled in the rear."

"What sort of traveling companion did the lass make?" asked Goania.

"*Oi!*" Jorian rolled his eyes. "She once called herself a drunken slut with a hot cleft—begging your pardon, madam—and I fear she did but speak the truth. Since she makes no bones about her love of fornication, I besmirch no lady's name in telling you. Daily we quarreled and made up. Nightly she demanded that I dip my wick, and then she'd taunt me by boasting of some former lover who, she said, could stroke three to my one. When I was king, I flatter myself that I kept five wives happy; but now I could not satisfy one. She's careless with her contraceptive spells, too. Altogether—well, I own I am the world's greatest fool for falling in love with the drab, but there it is."

"She hardly sounds beguiling, from what you say," said Goania. "Why should you, who have known the pick of a kingdom, love so cross-grained a hussy?"

Jorian scratched his new beard. "A kind of painful pleasure. There's something about her—a blunt honesty, a forceful vigor, and an intelligence that, were it but cultivated, could hold its own with learned doctors...When in a good humor she can be more fun than a cage of monkeys. And when is love controlled by rational calculations? But the last few days have wellnigh cured me. I made a little verse about it, which she did not like at all:

"O lady fair,
    Why must you be
So sharp with me,
    When all can see
For you I care?

I'm not aware
    That nagging me
And ragging me
    Is how to be
My lady fair.

If handsome is
    As handsome does
(The saying was),
    Then cease to buzz
And sting and whiz.

Or else, beware!
    If like a flea
You pester me,
    You shall not be
My lady fair!"

"Only wellnigh cured, said you?"

"Just that. If she came hither now and pleaded and flattered, promising to be sweet and kind and to stay sober, and begging me to keep her with me throughout my journey, I should be her pliant slave again, though I knew her promises to be so much straw. Thank Zevatas, she seems to have found someone more to her taste."

Goania glanced towards the corner, where Boso and Vanora had fallen into drunken slumber, the girl's head on the man's shoulder. "O Karadur, you had better get the lad out of Othomae forthwith, ere the wench change her mind. Know you any member of our order in Vindium?"

"I stayed with Porrex on my way to Xylar, last year. A delightful colleague—so kind and considerate."

"He is also tricky; beware of him."

"Oh, I am sure so good a man is to be trusted, as far as

63

one can trust anyone in this wicked world. I had a chance of witnessing his kindness and generosity at first hand."

Jorian asked, "Why can't you perform a divination to find the results of our intercourse with Master Porrex?"

Goania shook her head. "The practice of magic introduces into the lifeline of the practitioner too many factors from other planes and dimensions. I can divine somewhat of the luck of a layman like yourself, Master Nikko, but not those of Doctors Karadur or Porrex."

"Well then," said Jorian eagerly, "tell me what lies before *me!*"

"Give me your hand. When and where were you born?"

"In Ardamai, Kortoli, on the fifteenth of the Month of the Lion, in the twelfth year of King Fealin the Second, about sunrise."

Goania examined Jorian's palm and thought silently for a moment. Then she held her goblet so that she could see the reflection of one of the lamps in the surface of the wine. With her other hand she made passes over the vessel, moving her fingers in complex patterns and softly whispering. At last she said:

"Beware of a bedroom window, a tinkling man, and a tiger-headed god."

"Is that all?"

"It is all I see at this time."

Familiar with the vagueness and ambiguity of oracles, Jorian did not press the wizardess for more detail. Karadur spoke, "And now, madam, or ever I forget, have you that which you promised me?"

Goania felt in her purse and brought out a small packet. "The Powder of Discord—pollen of the spotted fireweed, gathered when the Red Planet was in conjunction with the White in the Wolf. Blown into any group of men, it will cause them to bicker and fight."

"Gramercy, Mistress Goania. This may prove a mighty help in Trimandilam."

Jorian: "With the Xylarians hunting us, I would not try to walk to Vindium. We can afford horses, and we can lead the ass with our little baggage."

"No horse for me!" said Karadur. "A fall from so tall a beast would break my old bones like flowerpots. Get me another ass, instead."

"An ass would slow us."

"No more than the one you already have."

"So be it, then. When does the horse market open to-morrow?"

The folk of Vindium City observed their harvest festival, the Feast of Spooks, by dressing up as supernatural beings and dancing in their streets. Since the day was a holiday, masked Vindines began to appear in their costumes well before the early autumnal sunset. Before the dinner hour, they paraded the streets, admiring one another's costumes and trying to guess which notables were concealed by especially ornate and costly garb. The livelier events—the parade, the dancing and singing, and the costume contest—would come later.

Arriving at the West Gate while the sun was still a red ball over the tilled fields of Vindium behind them, Jorian and Karadur halted at the gate for questioning. Then they rode on into the city, Jorian on the elderly black he had bought in Othomae, Karadur riding an ass and leading another. The main street, Republic Avenue, sloped gently down from the West Gate to the waterfront. They passed the Senate House, the Magistracy, and other public buildings, wherein the austere plainness of the classical Novarian style was adulterated by a touch of florid, fanciful Mulvanian ornateness.

Porrex's dwelling, said Karadur, was near the waterfront, so thither they threaded their way through swarms of gods, demons, ghosts, ghouls, skeltons, witches, elves, trolls, werewolves, and vampires, and some clad as supernatural beings from Mulvanian legendry. Mulvanian influence showed in Vindium not only in the architecture and the costumes but also in the swarthiness of the people. When one reveler, dressed as the war god Heryx, hit Jorian's horse with a bladder on the end of a stick, Jorian had much ado to keep the beast under control.

They took a room near the waterfront, stabled their animals, and sought out the dwelling of Porrex the magician. Porrex lived in a rented room above a draper's shop.

"Come in, good my sirs, come in!" cried Porrex at the head of the stair. He was a short, round, bald man with blue eyes almost buried in fat. "Dear old Karadur! How good to see you again! And your companion—tell me not, let me guess—is Jorian son of Evor, former king of Xylar!

Come in, come in. Sit down. Let me fetch you a drop of beer; that is all I have in the place."

The room was small and sparsely furnished, with an unmade bed, a rickety chair, a table, and a small bookcase with a few tattered scrolls in the pigeonholes and a few dogeared codices on top. A couple of chests along the wall and a water-stained drawing of the god Psaan driving his chariot on the waves of the sea completed the meager appointments. A single candle inside a small lanthorn with glass windows shed a wan illumination. When silence fell, the patter of mice in their runs could be heard.

"My name, sir," said Jorian, "is Nikko of Kortoli. Who told you otherwise?"

"My dear sir, what good should I be as a diviner if I could not ascertain such simple facts? But, if you prefer to be known as Nikko, then Nikko you shall be." Porrex winked. "I grieve that I cannot receive you in a palace, with feasts and dancing girls; but my business affairs have not prospered of late as is their usual wont. Hence, I must retrench. This condition, I assure you, is only temporary; within a month I shall get some new clients, who will put me back among the rich. Meanwhile, I live as I can, not as I would. But tell me of your affairs. I take it that Master Nikko is fain to put a goodly distance between himself and Xylar?"

"Not exactly," said Karadur, sitting cross-legged on the bed. "Know you that project that we Altruists have mulled for several years?"

"You mean to lift the Kist of Avlen? Ah, now light dawns! You are on your way to Trimandilam, hoping with the help of this mighty youth to effect this righteous expropriation. Well, strength to your arms and stealth to your feet! You two have no engagements for dinner, have you?"

"Nay," said Karadur. "We hoped you would give us the pleasure—"

"Indeed, indeed I will! Would that I could entertain you in style, but at the moment my purse contains exactly one farthing. When my new contracts are signed next month, I shall repay you a hundredfold. Let us go to Cheuro's; there one need not order the meal in advance. What do you purpose to do for Mulvanian money?"

"How mean you?" asked Karadur.

"Oh, have you not heard? Since you left Mulvan, the Great King has promulgated new laws about money. Only Mulvanian coins may be accepted by his subjects. All foreigners entering the land are made to give up their foreign money and precious metal in exchange for coin of the realm. The rate of exchange, however, is murderous; the traveler loses half the value of his coins. If he fail to turn in all his foreign gold and silver and is later caught, he is put to death in various ingenious ways, whereof being trampled by the king's elephants is one of the simpler."

"That is a nuisance," said Karadur. "We had thought ourselves well provided, but if the King of Kings is going to rob us of half our funds—"

Porrex cocked his head and winked. "I might be able to help you in this matter. There are, naturally, those to whom an ounce of gold is an ounce of gold, and what matter if it bear the head of Shaju of Mulvan or Jorian of Xylar? Such persons smuggle foreign money into the empire and Mulvanian coins out—at the risk of their heads— to sell abroad at a premium. Or they coin Mulvanian coins—not base-metal counterfeits, but gold pieces— themselves. One can, with the right connections, buy enough of such coins, at a more favorable rate of exchange, to tide one through one's visit to mighty Mulvan."

"Do King Shaju's folk let one bring Mulvanian coins into the empire at face value?" asked Jorian.

"Indeed they do; for the endeavor of their government is to get all their coins into the empire and keep them there. In sooth, if their policy did not make such smuggling profitable, it would not occur in the first place. But Shaju's treasurer is obsessed with monetary theories, which he must put into effect willy-nilly, no matter if they cut athwart the grain of human nature. Wait here and help yourselves to the beer whilst I sally forth to see if the man I know can be found."

When Porrex had vanished, Karadur said, "Have you still your hundred Xylarian lions, my son? Methinks we should change them as Porrex proposes."

"All but two or three, spent on the road hither. But I prefer to confirm Doctor Porrex's statement before entrusting any money to him. I mean, his assertion about this new Mulvanian law."

"Oh, surely so kind a little man, and a member of my virtuous faction, were trustworthy—"

"Mayhap, but I still prefer to ask. Wait here."

Jorian in his turn went out. He soon returned, saying, "Your little butterball of a wizard is right. I spoke to several knowledgeable folk—taverners and the like—and they all confirmed what he said."

"I told you we could trust him. Here he comes now."

Porrex rëentered the room. "It is all arranged, gentles. My man awaits without. How much have you to exchange in gold or silver? Copper and bronze count not."

Jorian had ninety-seven lions and some silver; Karadur, much less gold but more silver. Porrex did some calculations on an abacus.

"I can get you forty-two-and-a-half Mulvanian crowns for that," he said. "That is deducting a mere sixth part for the broker's commission, compared to half at the border. If you will let me take this money downstairs; my man does not care to be seen..."

Karadur handed over his purse without demur, but Jorian held his. "You may change his money that way," said Jorian, "but I want to see your Mulvanian gold first."

"Oh, certes; it shall be as you say, dear lad. Wait." Out went Porrex again. This time he was gone somewhat longer. Karadur said:

"His gold speculator must be as suspicious of letting his money out of his hands as you are, Jorian."

"Better safe than sorry."

There was a clatter of feet on the stair, and Porrex came back in with another man. With a beaming smile, Porrex cried:

"Fortune is with us tonight! Let me present my dear old friend Laziendo. These are Doctor Karadur and Master Nikko, of whom I told you."

Laziendo was a rather small man, a little older than Jorian, bronzed and swarthy, with a sweeping mustache. He bowed formally to the travelers and gave them a charming smile.

"Master Laziendo is supercargo on one of Benniver Sons' ships," continued Porrex. "He sails tomorrow and was searching for somebody with whom to celebrate his last evening ashore. Now you need not buy my dinner; friend Laziendo insists upon treating us all."

"The pleasure will be all mine, fair sirs," murmured Laziendo.

"Now," said Porrex, "here is your gold, Doctor; and here is yours, Master Nikko. Count it. If you will now give me yours, O Nikko...Laziendo, old boy, would you be so good as to step out and hand this sack to him who waits in the shadow below? It were not well for me to climb these stairs so often. Good! Whilst he is out, gentles, I must find masks for us, lest we be pestered by drunken revelers for not being in costume."

Porrex rummaged in a chest and produced four devil masks with staring eyes and scowls and fangs. Jorian examined several square Mulvanian gold pieces, with the crowned head of Shaju or of his father on one side and an elephant trampling a tiger on the other. Then he took the mask that Porrex gave him and adjusted the string to fit his head. Laziendo returned, saying:

"It is done, fair sirs. Allow your servant to lead you to Cheuro's. We shan't need lights, the town being illuminated for the festival."

Located on Republic Avenue, Cheuro's was a much larger establishment then the Silver Dragon in Othomae. At the door, a one-legged beggar accosted the four. Porrex fumbled in his purse and handed the man one small copper coin. Karadur said:

"If that was your last farthing, O Porrex, what will you eat on after we have departed?"

Porrex shrugged. "I suppose I shall raise a loan on one of my remaining books, which my forthcoming new contracts will soon enable me to redeem. This way, gentles."

The main dining room had a clear space in the middle for entertainers. The dinner was excellent, the wine sound, and the naked dancing girls supple. As the table was cleared, Laziendo said:

"If we kill time here for another hour, our foreign guests will see the parade by merely stepping out the front door. It passes in front of Cheuro's. Stay, fair sirs, and try some more of Cheuro's liquors. Since Vindium is the busiest port on the Inner Sea, we get the best vintages from all over."

Porrex yawned. "You will excuse me, I pray, dear friends; the years have leached away my capacity for late hours. I am sure that Master Laziendo can show you the delights of our city. Good night."

When Porrex had gone, Jorian asked Laziendo, "We seek the road to Trimandilam, and you should be able to advise us of the best way thither."

Laziendo stroked his mustache and smiled. "Why, this is a stroke of good fortune! I sail tomorrow on the *Talaris*, a gaggle of slave girls for Rennum Kezymar and marble, copper, wool, and miscellaneous cargo for Janareth. The deck will be a thought crowded until we discharge the lassies at Rennum Kezymar, but I'm sure we can find room for you. From Janareth you can ascend the Bharma by river boat to the capital."

Jorian asked about fares and said: "What is this Rennum Kezymar, and why are you taking slave girls thither?"

"The name means 'Ax Castle' in the dialect of Janereth. It is a small island off the mouth of the Jhukna, ruled by Mulvan. A couple of centuries ago, the then King of Kings chose it as a home for retired executioners."

"What!"

"Aye, and with good reason. Be an executioner never so gentle and pleasant and virtuous in his private capacity, people still care not to befriend him. Hence the Great King found he had many headsmen, too old to swing the ax or knot the rope or turn the windlass of the rack, living in misery despite their pensions, because no man would treat with them. Betimes the locals would not even sell them food, so that they starved to death.

"Rennum Kezymar was then but a barren islet, good only for a winter pasture for the flocks of a few shepherds. It bore the ruins of an ancient castle, built many centuries back, in the time of the Three Kindgoms. The king had the castle rebuilt and gathered his executioners there, and there they have dwelt ever since."

"If they are old and retired, what need have they for young slave girls?" said Jorian. "As well go tilting with a lance of asparagus."

Laziendo shrugged. "To fetch and carry, peradventure. Some have wives, but of their own age. In any case, my duty is but to play sheep dog to these girls and deliver them to the destination averred in the manifest."

"What of the land route from Vindium to Trimandilam?"

Laziendo held up his hands. "Fair sirs! Although the map shows a road from here to Janareth along the coast, as a practical matter it's plain impossible."

"How so?"

"Because an easterly spur of the Lograms follows the coast for nigh a hundred leagues. The road is a mere track, winding up and down precipices, crossing swift mountain torrents like the Jhukna by swaying bridges of rope, and here and there ceasing entirely where a landslide has destroyed it. Besides which, the coastal country swarms with brigands and tigers. Nay, rather try to steal the emerald gold of Tarxia than essay this route!"

"Is not that coast under the rule of the mighty King of Kings, who maintains such fine roads and swift postal service?"

"Aye, but all these amenities you'll find in the interior, within a few score leagues of Trimandilam. The emperor neglects the borderlands—I think designedly, lest some invader take advantage of such improvements. In any case, better that you should go on my ship. This voyage is late in the season, but its very lateness, while it augments the danger of storms, lessens that of piracy."

"I thank you for your warning," said Jorian. "We may visit your ship early on the morrow to book passage. Tell us how to find her."

Laziendo gave directions and added: "Excuse me, fair sirs; all this wine necessitates a visit to the jakes. I shall return."

Jorian and Karadur sat over their flagons so long that sounds outside and the actions of Cheruro's other guests implied that the parade would soon begin. At last Jorian said:

"Is that fellow playing a jape on us? Wait here."

He went through the kitchen door, to be confronted by a fat cook.

"Aye," said the cook, "I saw such a man as you describe, a half-hour past. He went straight through and out the back, without stopping at the jakes. Why, is aught amiss?"

"No, nothing's wrong," said Jorian. He returned to their table, muttering: "The vermin has bilked us; slithered out and left us to pay the scot. Well, thank Zevatas we have the means."

"Speaking of which," said Karadur, "our host has in his eye the look of a man about to tender his bill."

Jorian pulled out his purse, which held a few of the Mulvanian crowns, the rest being stowed in his money belt. He shook out one and almost dropped it.

"By all the gods!" he whispered, eyes wide. "Look at this, O Karadur! Keep your voice down."

Jorian held out the object, which was no Mulvanian golden crown but a square of lead of the same approximate size. Hoping against hope, he dug into the purse and brought out several more coins—all of which turned out to be leaden slugs.

Karadur stared in horror, then frantically clawed at his own purse. His gold had likewise turned to leaden squares. His mouth sagged open.

"That's the bastard you wanted us to trust!" hissed Jorian furiously. "Goania warned us he was tricky; and now, by Imbal's brazen balls, you know what she meant! I could have lived comfortably on that pelf for years!"

Tears rolled down Karadur's wrinkled brown cheeks. "True. It is all my fault, my son. I knew of that deception spell, too. I am a useless old dodderer. Never will I trust a strange man again, however fair and upright he seem."

"Well, how in the forty-nine Mulvanian hells shall we get out of here? If we try to walk out, there will be a fracas, and the watch will pitch us into the Vindine jail, where the Xylarians will presently discover me and request extradition. And 'twere easier to make pies out of stones than to wheedle credit from this Cheuro."

"Go along, my son, and leave me to take the blame."

"Don't talk nonsense. I cannot assail the Mulvanian Empire singlehanded, so we must fight our way out together. Oh-oh, here comes Cheuro now." Jorian hastily swept up the slugs.

Cheuro leant his fists upon the table. "Have you gentlemen enjoyed your repast and entertainment?"

"We surely have, sir taverner," replied Jorian with a jovial grin. "I'm only sorry that our companions had to leave early. How much do we owe you?"

"Two marks and six. May I serve you a round on the house?"

"Delighted! Let me see, we should finish the evening with something special. Have you any of that liqueur they brew in Paalua, called *olikau?* Betimes we get it on the western coast."

Cheuro frowned. "I know the drink to which you refer, but I know not whether I have a bottle."

"Well, do us the kindness to make sure, whilst we reckon who owes what to whom."

When Cheuro had gone back to his bar, Jorian whispered; "What magic have you for us now? I've gained us a little time. How about an invisibility spell?"

"That calls for lengthy preparations, with far more apparatus than we have to hand. Furthermore, it does but make one's flesh and bone transparent, not one's raiment. Hence one must either go about nude—which the coolth of the present weather renders impractical—or present the arresting sight of a suit of garments walking about with no one inside it. Moreover, to see in this condition, one must exempt one's eyeballs from the spell. But let me think. Ah, I have it!"

Moving quickly, the old magician produced a wallet divided inside into many compartments. From several of these pockets he withdrew pinches of powder, which he sprinkled into his empty flagon. He stirred the powders with his finger and placed the mug on the floor between his feet.

"Be ready to cry 'Fire!'" he said.

"Hasten!" said Jorian. "Cheuro is coming back, and without his Paaluan liqueur."

Karadur mumbled as he raced through a spell, while the fingers of his two hands fluttered through figures on the table top, like the legs of a pair of agitated brown spiders. When Cheuro was halfway from the bar to their table, there was a hiss from the flagon. A tremendous cloud of thick, black smoke billowed up out of it, surging up against the underside of the table, spreading out in all directions, and hiding the table and the two travelers in its ever-widening billows.

"Fire!" cried Jorian.

There was a clatter of overturned benches and running feet, as the other customers stampeded towards the entrance. Jorian and Karadur snatched their masks and cloaks and joined the throng. Since smoke now filled the room, they waited until the jam at the door had cleared and so got through without being squeezed or trampled.

Outside, they lost themselves in the crowd, which had lined up along Republic Avenue to watch the parade. As they walked away from Cheuro's, they passed a fire company running the other way. In the lead came the fire engine, a wooden tub with handles at the corners and a large pump rising in the middle. Eight stalwarts carried the engine by its handles, and after them pelted the rest of the company, bearing buckets with which to fill the tub from the nearest fountain.

"Let's make for Porrex's room," said Jorian. "If I catch that knave, do you counter his spells whilst I turn him inside out."

Porrex's door stood open, and his room was dark and quiet. Jorian got out his flint and steel, struck sparks into tinder, and lighted a piece of taper. The light showed the room to be not only empty but also stripped. The bed, the bookcase, the chair, the table, and the chests had vanished. A mouse whisked out of sight.

"That's the spryest removal I have ever seen," said Jorian. "He's cleaned the place out."

"Not quite," said Karadur, grunting as he stooped to pick up the little glass-sided lanthorn. "They forgot this. Ah me! The candle seems to have burnt all the way down. With a proper candle, I might do something yet."

"Let me look in the cupboard," said Jorian, stamping on a roach as it raced across the floor. "Here we are, two usable candle stubs. What have you in mind, esteemed Doctor?"

"There is a spell, and I can remember it, which causes the light of a candle or similar source to pierce all disguises. Now leave me to my thoughts, my son."

Karadur took an eternity, it seemed to Jorian, to remember his spell and then to cast it, with a pentacle and chants and passes and powders burning in a broken saucer from the same cupboard. The candle flame in the lanthorn writhed and flickered as if blown upon by unseen lips, though no air stirred in the room. Faces seemed to form and dissolve in the smoke. Karadur, exhausted, had to rest for a time after the spell had been wound up.

"Now," said Karadur, picking up the lanthorn, "we shall see what we shall see."

* * *

Along Republic Avenue, the Vindines still stood deeply ranked, awaiting the parade; for this procession, like so many others, was late in starting. Wearing their demon masks, Jorian and Karadur walked slowly along the edge of the crowd. As Karadur held up the lanthorn, both peered at the faces of the crowd. Where the light of the candle fell, it seemed to Jorian as if the costumes and masks and false beards became almost transparent—mere smoky shadows of themselves, through which the Vindines' features stood out clearly.

They walked and walked, up one side of Republic Avenue westward and then down the other towards the harbor. Jorian looked at thousands of faces, but nowhere did he see that of Porrex or that of Laziendo. As they ambled towards the waterfront, Jorian heard band music, coming from the west and growing louder.

"Here they come," he said.

A group of men in the uniform of the Republican Guard, wearing shiny silvered breastplates and bearing halberds, walked down Republic Avenue, shouting to clear the street. Now and then they poked some laggard spectator with the butts of their weapons to hasten him.

As Karadur held up the lanthorn for another look at the crowd, Jorian's eye was caught by a little knot of men without masks or costumes—men in dark, plain garb, with a burly, self-confident bearing. One glanced at Jorian, stared, touched one of his companions, and spoke out of the side of his mouth. Recognizing the man, Jorian said in a low, tense voice:

"Karadur! See you those fellows in black? My Royal Guard. Their leader is a captain who twice caught me when I tried to flee Xylar. Across the street, quickly!"

Jorian plunged through the crowd, dragging Karadur after him. They came out on Republic Avenue in the midst of the guardsmen clearing the street. The band music grew louder, and over the heads of the guardsmen Jorian saw the leading units of the parade, with flags and silvered weapons.

Some guardsmen shouted angrily as Jorian and Karadur zigzagged through them and plunged into the packed mass of spectators on the other side. Jorian, being tall enough to see over the heads of most Vindines, looked back. The knot of men in black were pushing through the spectators on the far side. When they debouched on the avenue, however, they were blocked by a group of guardsmen. There was argument, lost in the growing noise. Arms waved; fists shook. The guardsmen roughly pushed the men in black back into the crowd and threatened them with their halberds. Then the parade arrived.

Gilt and tinsel flashed in the warm light of thousands of lamps, lanthorns, tapers, and torches. Bands brayed; soldiers tramped; pretty girls, riding on ornate floats, threw kisses to the crowd.

Jorian and Karadur did not wait to enjoy the spectacle. With a brief backward glance, they set off briskly down a side street. Karadur muttered:

"The parade will hold them up for a little while, at least. What I cannot understand is this: How did these men recognize us in our masks?"

"If you don't understand it, I do," said Jorian. "We forgot that the rays of this little magic lanthorn would have the same effect upon our own disguises as on others'."

"Ah me, I grow senile, not to have thought of that! But whither away, now? We are moneyless in a strange city, with your keepers searching for us."

"Let's find Laziendo's ship and hide in a nearby warehouse. If Laziendo appear, I shall know what to do. If he come not, we'll board the vessel, which is going our way."

Hours later, the parade had ended. The costume contest had been held, with prizes for the most beautiful, the most elaborate, the most humorous, and so forth. The soberer citizens had returned to their homes; the less sober raced and reeled the streets of Vindium City, yelling and singing. There was much hasty, hole-and-corner adultery, as husbands whose wives had grown fat and shrewish, and wives whose husbands neglected them for their trade or craft, sought excitement or comfort with strangers. As the lights of the city went out one by one, the late-rising crescent moon shed a wan illumination in their place. A fog crept softly up the streets from the harbor.

Jorian and Karadur huddled in a warehouse near the *Talaris'* dock. The warehouse was supposed to be guarded, but the watchman had left his post to join the revelry. Piles of bales and boxes bulked dimly in the darkness. Jorian whispered:

"That's what we get for trusting one of your fellow

spookers. I'll swear by Zevatas's brazen beard: It's the old fellows like you who are supposed to be cautious and crafty, whereas the young springalds like me are trusting and credulous and easily put upon. But here we seem to have the opposite."

"Could we not appeal the Vindine Senate to protect us from your Royal Guard?" replied Karadur. "Surely they do not wish harmless visitors kidnapped out of their proud city!"

"Not a chance! Othomae might have protected us, but Vindium is allied with Xylar; against Othomae, glad to turn us over. The Twelve Cities are forever forming and breaking these alliances, so that yesterday's implacable foe is today's staunch ally and contrariwise. Like one of those courtly dances, where you trade partners with every measure."

"You Novarians need an emperor to rule the turbulent lot of you, to stop you from wasting your energies in cutting one another's throats. We have a saying: Get three men from the Twelve Cities together and they will form four factions and fight it out to the death."

"Rabbits will chase wolves or ever the Novarians submit to such an overlord. Ardyman the Terrible once tried it, but he did not long abide. Besides, there are virtues in a group of squabbling little city-states, over against a big, monolithic empire like yours."

"To what advantage are your eternal, cruel and destructive internecine wars?"

"Well, each of the Twelve Cities is small enough so that a man feels that what he does matters. So our people take a lively interest in creative effort and in their respective governments. In Mulvan, the state is so huge and so rigidly organized that the individual feels lost and powerless. So you let Shaju and his like do as they please, be they never such idlers or debauchees or idiots or monsters. Now, in the Twelve Cities we have all kinds of governments—kingdoms, duchies, republics, theocracies, and so on—and if somebody invents a new and better one, all the others are eager to see how it works and whether they should consider imitating it."

"But if only there were a supreme ruler to stop your fighting and direct your energies into constructive channels—"

"Then we should soon be just like Mulvan, with the supreme ruler directing all these energies towards the enhancement of his own power and glory."

"But at least we have internal peace, which is no small boon."

"And what has Mulvan done with its internal peace? From all I hear, your customs and usages and beliefs are exactly the same as a thousand years ago. Why think you the Twelve Cities so easily routed the vast army that Shaju's sire, King Sirvasha, sent to conquer them? Because the Mulvanians still rely upon the weapons and tactics of the days of Ghish the Great. So our cavalry made mincemeat of your scythed chariots, whilst our archers swept your slingers and darters from the field. Compare unchanging Mulvan with the Twelve Cities; consider what in the last century we have accomplished in the arts and sciences, in literature and drama, in law and government, and you will see what I mean."

"All very well, if one deem such material things important," grumbled Karadur. "I suppose it is partly a matter of age. When I was young, such turbulence and change appealed to me, also; but now I find safety and stability fairer to contemplate. Mark my words, my son, some day one of the Twelve Cities will call in the hordes of Shven to help it against its neighbor, and soon you will find a Gending cham ruling all of Novaria. Such things have happened before."

"But at least—" Jorian broke off, listening. There were footsteps and a murmur of talk outside. Jorian pulled Karadur behind a pile of bales.

Two persons entered the warehouse. From their sizes, Jorian took them to be a man and a woman, although the predawn light was too dim to tell any more. The man was speaking:

"...here we are, fair mistress. Your servant will find you a comfortable bed amongst all these piles of cargo, I swear; for there is scant romance in doing it standing up ... Ah, here we are, my sweetling: a pile of new sacking, just the thing for—*unh*!"

The final grunt followed the thud of the leaden pommel of Jorian's dagger on the man's skull. The man fell heavily to the stone floor. The woman was drawing her dress off over her head and so could not see what had happened.

She completed her disrobing and stood for three heartbeats naked, holding the dress in her hands. The light was now strong enough for Jorian to perceive that she was a comely wench. A mask, which she had just dropped, lay at her feet.

Seeing her lover lying prone on the pave and Jorian's huge, shadowy form behind him, she uttered a thin little scream, fled out the door with her dress in her hands, and vanished into the fog. Jorian turned over the body and pulled off the mask.

"I was right," he said, squatting beside the body. "It was Master Laziendo, may dogs devour his vitals. I knew his voice. Let's hope the wench does not set the watch upon us."

"Is—is he dead?" quavered Karadur.

"No; his pate's only dented, not cracked, and his heart beats strongly." He looked up. "I have an idea that may save our hides. Can you sell a horse and a brace of asses?"

"I have never done horse trading, but I suppose I could."

"Then hie you to our room to fetch our gear and to the stable where our creatures dwell. Tell the stableman you wish to sell. It's early, but with luck he will know a couple of buyers ready for a quick bargain. The horse is worth at least two Mulvanian crowns or the equivalent, and the asses a quarter or a third as much apiece. Since it is a forced sale, you will have to take less, but at least do not accept the first offer."

"And you, my son?"

"I must bind and gag this rascal to keep him out of circulation until we have departed. When life stirs aboard the *Talaris*, I shall board the ship and see what my flapping tongue can do."

Two hours later, the risen sun was burning off the last wisps of fog, and Water Street was awakening. Carrying Jorian's pack and crossbow, Karadur shuffled across Water Street to the dock where the *Talaris* lay. The ship—a one-sticker of moderate size—was lively with longshoremen loading last-minute cargo, sailors handling ropes, and a dozen comely young slave girls chattering like a flock of starlings. Jorian stood at the rail, leaning on his elbows as if he had no cares. When Karadur climbed the companionway, Jorian helped him down, murmuring:

"How much did you get?"

"One crown, two and six for the lot."

"I could have done better, but we cannot be choosy. Let me present you. Captain Strasso, this is my friend, Doctor Karadur of Trimandilam, of whom I told you. Doctor, pay the captain ten marks for your passage and board to Janareth."

"Glad to have you aboard, sir," growled the captain. "Remember: no spitting, puking, or pissing from the weather rail! And no garbage on deck, either. I keep a clean ship. Get your girls out of the way, Master Maltho; we are about to shove off."

Later, when Vindium was small in the distance and the ship was heeling to the pressure of the wind on the striped triangular sail, Karadur and Jorian ate breakfast in the tiny cabin they occupied in the deckhouse aft. The cabin hummed with the splash, splash of the stem cutting waves, the gurgle of water against the hull, the creak of the ship's timbers, and the thrum of wind-quivered cordage. Karadur asked:

"What in the name of Vurnu's heaven have you done, my son?"

Jorian grinned. "I found paper and ink in the warehouseman's desk and persuaded Master Laziendo to pen a note to Captain Strasso, saying he'd broken an ankle during the Feast of Spooks, and would the captain please ship his friend Maltho of Kortoli—an experienced commercial man from the Western Ocean—in his place?"

"How could you compel him to do that?"

"There are ways." Jorian chuckled. "I also found nine of our missing Xylarian lions in his purse and repossessed them. Porrex must have given him ten for his part in the swindle, and he'd spent one on his lady love. Of course, he denied all, if not convincingly. What most infuriated him was my cutting his fine velvet mantle into strips to bind him. He didn't lack courage, for he called me all sorts of foul names with my dagger at his throat. But he wrote the note, which was the main thing.

"Captain Strasso didn't much like it, but he did not wish to lose a day's sail by going ashore to rout Benniver's Sons out of bed to demand another supercargo. And when Belius, the slave dealer, arrived with his twelve little lovelies, I signed for them without a qualm.

"Now, forget not my new name: Maltho of Kortoli. I thought Nikko and Jorian had worn out their usefulness. Which philosopher said: The best equipment for life is effrontery?"

"Were it not wiser to give your origin as some western land, like Ir? You claim you've sailed those waters."

"Not with my accent! I can ape some of the others with fair skill if I try; but that, methinks, were a little too much effrontery for our own good!"

IV

THE CASTLE OF THE AX

A COLD NORTH WIND FROM THE STEPPES OF SHVEN STIRRED the Inner Sea and swiftly bore the *Talaris* southeast. The coast was a thin black line on the southwestern horizon. The dragon-spine of the Lograms should have been visible above this dark streak, but a blanket of winter cloud concealed it.

On the ship, Jorian stood on the roof of the deckhouse with the captain and the two steersmen, one to each of the quarter rudders. Karadur was confined to his cabin and the slave girls to their tent by seasickness.

"You seem to have a good stomach for a blow," said Captain Strasso.

"I've seen worse on the Western Ocean," replied Jorian. "Why, one time when I was chasing pirates—ah—I mean, when pirates were chasing my ship—well, anyway, the sea made this one look like a millpond. This sea saved us, for it swamped the pirate galley, whilst we came through with nothing worse than some wreckage on deck."

"And I suppose, mighty Master Maltho, that you were not seasick?" said Strasso.

Jorian laughed. "Spare your sarcasms, friend. On the contrary. I was as sick as a dying dog. But I think great Psaan decided that I had had enough of this affliction for one life, because I've never been seasick since. How much farther south must we sail ere the weather warms?"

"Janareth is warmer—it never snows there—but you'll find no truly tropical clime until you cross the Lograms. On the hither side of those peaks, the summers are dry and the winters wet. On the farther side, they tell me, it is the opposite...There's one of your chickabiddies now, dragging herself to the rail as to the scaffold."

"I must below, to see how the wenches do."

Strasso leered. "And perchance to improve an idle hour in their embraces?"

"A good supercargo does not handle the merchandise more than he must to insure its safe delivery." Jorian lowered himself to the deck and accosted the girl. It was Mnevis, who by force of personality had become spokeswoman for the twelve. She looked bedraggled and woebegone, having lost weight from not being able to keep food down.

"Good Master Maltho," she said, "I fear some dreadful doom awaits us."

"Oh, come! Anyone feels thus after a bout of seasickness."

"Nay, 'tis not the sea I fear, but these fearsome men to whom we've been sold. Headsmen—ugh!" She shuddered. "I shall see their hands dripping blood whenever I look upon them."

"Executioners are just like other men, save that their bloody but necessary trade arouses prejudice in unthinking minds. And these men have quit their profession for peaceful retirement."

"Natheless, the thought of them gives me the horrors. Could we not prevail upon you to engineer our escape? Or at least, our sale to men of more normal bent. We have nought to bribe you with, save our poor bodies; but these have been thought not uncomely..."

"I'm sorry, Mnevis; impossible. I have promised to deliver you to Chairman Khuravela, of the retired headsmen of Rennum Kezymar, and delivered you shall be."

Later, Jorian said to Karadur: "You know, Doctor, never before have I thought of the problem that executioners face in everyday living; yet such people are necessary, just as are collectors of taxes and of offal—two other much maligned classes:

"Oh, I am a headsman; they blanch at my name;
I chop and I hang and I stretch and I maim;
But that I be shunned, it is really a shame—
   I'm a virtuous fellow at heart!

My tools are the ax and the rope and the rack;
I execute rogues with my head in a sack;
I swink at my trade and I've never been slack;
   It's a fearfully difficult art.

At home, I am good to my children and wife;
I pay all my taxes and keep out of strife—
The kindliest man that you've seen in your life!
   Oh, why must they set us apart?"

The morning after the *Talaris* left Vindium, gray clouds covered the sky and the shore. Captain Strasso, turning his sun stone this way and that to catch the gleam that betrayed the sun's direction, grumbled to Jorian, "If the weather worsen, we may have to lay up at Janareth for the winter, 'stead of returning to our home port. And then will Benniver's Sons give me a wigging! That's the way of it with shipowners. Take a chance, and they berate you for risking their priceless property; take not a chance, and they betongue you for wasting their precious time and costing them profits."

"Island ahead!" called the lookout.

Captain Strasso looked pleased. "After sailing all night by the feel of wind and wave, that's not a bad landfall, now is it?" To the helmsman: "A hair to starboard... Steady as you go." To Jorian again: "No proper harbor, but two anchorages, on the north and south sides of the island. At this season, ships use the south anchorage."

It was after noon when the *Talaris* dropped anchors in the small bay on the south side of Rennum Kezymar. The dinghy was lowered to transfer the slave girls ashore. With two sailors to row, Jorian, Karadur, and two of the girls went first. As they climbed out on the rickety little small-boat pier and the dinghy returned to the ship, a group of men approached from the shoreward end of the pier. They were brown-skinned, turbaned, and wrapped in many layers of wool and cotton, draped and tucked in various ways with loose ends fluttering in the wind.

The man in the lead was as tall as Jorian and much more massive—a mountain of muscle, now somewhat shrunken and sagging with age, with a big potbelly straining at his wrappings. Long, white hair hung down from under his turban, and a vast white beard covered his chest when the breeze did not blow it aside.

"Are you Chairman Khuravela, sir?" said Jorian in Mulvani.

"Aye." It was more a grunt than a word.

"Maltho of Kortoli, supercargo for Benniver's Sons. I have come to deliver the twelve slave girls you ordered from the dealer Belius in Vindium."

Another grunt.

"That is the second load, coming ashore now. One more trip will complete the task."

Grunt.

"My friend, the eminent Doctor Karadur."

Grunt.

This, thought Jorian, was becoming difficult. He continued to stand in the wind, trying to make conversation. But, what with his limited fluency in the language and the wooden unresponsiveness of the giant, he had little success. The other executioners—like their chief, big, burly men of advanced years—stood about silently, fidgeting and shifting their feet.

Jorian's gaze wandered from the sands of the shore, where clumps of sedge nodded in the wind, to the higher ground of the interior. The island bore no trees, only long grass, now dead and dried, and dark clumps of ilex and spreading holly. Around the castle on the highest point of the isle, cabbage patches added a touch of color to an otherwise sad, gray, washed-out landscape. The castle was gray against the darker gray of the overcast sky.

At last the dinghy arrived on its third shoreward journey. The rest of the slave girls climbed out on the pier.

"That is all," said Jorian.

Chairman Khuravela jerked his head. "Come."

They straggled up the slope to the castle. A few former headsmen were working in the cabbage patches. A dry ditch, half filled with rubbish and spanned by a lowered drawbridge, surrounded the castle.

The procession crossed the drawbridge, passed under the portcullis set in a vaulted archway with murder holes, traversed a short vestibule into which a gatehouse was built, and entered the main hall. Here, no artificial light relieved the dimness. Although the towers and walls had windows instead of arrow slits—the edifice not being now meant for serious defense—these windows were closed by sashes paned with oiled paper, and the gloomy day did not shed much light within. A pair of executioners sat over a game of draughts, ignoring the newcomers. On the other side of the hall, a huge bronze gong hung from a frame. Long tables stood against the walls.

When all were inside, Khuravela led the way to a big table with a massive oaken armchair at one end. He sat down heavily and said:

"Line them up."

Jorian did so. Khuravela counted them, wagging his thick forefinger and silently moving his lips. At last he said:

"They will do. Here is your money. At two hundred and forty silver marks apiece, the lot is worth ninety-six Mulvanian crowns at the current rate."

Khuravela spilled a heap of crowns, double-crowns, and five-crown and ten-crown pieces out on the table and counted out the amount. Jorian checked his addition and swept the heap of square golden coins into his own purse. Then he handed the chairman a receipt, saying:

"Sign here, pray."

"Oh, dung!" groaned the giant. "Fetch a pen. You two must witness my mark."

Khuravela made his mark, and Jorian and Karadur witnessed it. Khuravela said:

"Big feast this even. You and the doctor invited; so is your captain. Brother Chambra, send word to Strasso. Brother Tilakia, take the slaves away." He turned back to Jorian. "Time for our nap. Mehru can show you the castle. See you in three hours."

Khuravela heaved himself out of his chair and marched off into the shadowy corridors. The other Brothers wandered off until Jorian and Karadur were left with a single Brother. Karadur muttered in Novarian:

"O Jorian, I would fain not stay for this feast. Suffer me to return to the ship."

"What's the matter? Don't you want a real repast for a change?"

"It is not that. I feel an evil aura about this place."

"Nonsense! Forsooth, it's a gloomy old pile, but the dwellers therein seem normal enough."

"Nay, I have an astral sense about such things."

"Stay for a while, anyway. You can't leave me to face these fellows alone!"

The remaining executioner, Mehru, was a man of medium size and build. Unlike most of the rest, he was bareheaded and clean-shaven. Although gray showed in his topknot, he seemed younger than most of his retired colleagues. With a toothy grin, he said:

"If you gentlemen will come with me, I will show you the Castle of the Ax. You shall see sights you will long remember—momentoes of historic events which our mighty king—may he reign forever!—has graciously suffered us to bring hither upon our retirement."

"I do not think I wish to, thank you," said Karadur. "I am weary. Is there a place where I might lie down?"

"Surely: this chamber here. Make yourself at ease, Doctor, whilst I show Master Maltho around."

In contrast to Khuravela, Mehru proved a garrulous host. "If you look closely," he said, "you can see the difference in color between the lowest courses of this wall and those higher up. The lower courses are those of the original castle; the higher, those of the rebuilding under Cholanki the Third...This is our kitchen; those are the wives of the wedded Brothers, readying tonight's gorge..."

"Is one of them yours?" asked Jorian, looking at a dozen stout, middle-aged women.

"Me? Ha! Women mean nought to me. I was wedded to my art."

"Why did you leave it so young?"

"A soreness developed in my right shoulder joint, so that my hand was no longer so true as erstwhile. It still bothers me betimes in damp weather. I am good enough with rope and bowstring and chopper, but not with the two-handed sword. That polluted crowbar is the nemesis of every aging headsman."

"How so?"

"Know that amongst the Chosen of the Gods, each class has its appropriate form of execution, and the sword is deemed the only honorable instrument for royalty and nobility. For nobles the sword, for warriors the ax, for officials the bowstring, for merchants the noose, the artisans the stake, and so on—albeit special crimes sometimes incur special chastisements, such as trampling by an elephant.

"Well, one of the wives of King Shaju—may he reign forever!—had committed adultery with a nobleman, and it was decreed that both should die by my hand. This Lord Valshaka's head flew off as pretty as you please. But when I swung at the woman, a twinge in that cursed right shoulder caused the heavy sword to strike low, against her shoulder blades. As you can well perceive, all this did was to open a great gash across her back and hurl her prone upon the platform. My helpers dragged her, shrieking and bleeding, to her knees again and held her long enough for a second swing.

"This time, all went well. The head I presented to His Majesty—may he reign forever!—was the most perfect I ever saw—no biased cut, no ragged edges of skin. *Perfect.* But Shaju decreed that, in view of that one blunder, I had served out my time."

They had come out on the roof of one of the corner turrets. Mehru pointed: "That way lies the estuary of the Jhukna, a nest of pirates. In summer, we see their galleys swarming out as thick as water bugs when a trading fleet between Vindium and Janareth goes by. That is why Vindium now convoys these fleets with its war galleys."

"Why does not King Shaju build a fleet and help to put down the sea thieves? Why should the Novarian cities bear all the burden?"

Mehru stared. "My good man! A pious Mulvanian go to sea? Know you not that it entails a religious pollution, to be expiated by elaborate and costly ceremonies of purification?"

"You had to cross the sea to get here."

"Ah, but that was only once, and the burden was light. If I took to the sea for my livelihood, I should have to spend all my time ashore in purification. It is different with you barbarians."

"Doctor Karadur does not seem to mind."

"That is his affair. Mayhap he is religiously heterodox, or else his spells neutralize the polluting effects of sea travel. But let us go below, or ever I freeze to death."

"You Mulvanians are as sensitive to cold as tropic blooms," said Jorian, following Mehru down the winding stair. "The slightest draft, and you shiver and wilt. To me, that wind was only pleasantly cool."

"I will match you, then, against one of the Chosen of the Gods in the dank jungles of southern Mulvan, where the heat is such that no life but that of insects stirs abroad during the day. Now, where is that polluted key? Ah, here! This room holds the machine that works our drawbridge."

They looked into a room containing the mechanism of a large water clock. Water trickled from a spout into one of a circle of buckets affixed to the rim of a wheel. Jorian saw at once how the mechanism worked. When the bucket filled, the weight caused the wheel to rotate a few degrees until checked by an escapement. Then the next bucket filled, and so on.

"The used water runs into a barrel hung from the drawbridge mechanism," said Mehru. "At sunrise, the weight of the barrle, released, lowers the drawbridge—which, being counterweighted, takes little effort. When this barrel has descended, it empties, and the water flows into another, which raises the drawbridge. A clockmaster named Evor of Ardamai came by here some years ago, they tell me—"

"Why," burst out Jorian, he was my ff—" he checked himself. "I mean, he was a friend of my father. But go on."

Mehru gave Jorian a sharp look. "That is all. This man set up the mechanism, and ever since then it has raised and lowered the drawbridge. We need not turn a hand, save to pump water up into the tank in the room above. This we do by a treadwheel in the cellar."

"Can the bridge be sundered from the water clock, in case of emergencies?"

"Aye. The windlass in the gatehouse can be used to override the clock. But that happens seldom, for we have few visitors to Rennum Kezymar."

They descended another stair. Mehru unlocked another door, saying: "This chamber, Master Maltho, is our armory—but it is not an armory in the usual sense. It holds our choicest momentoes. Behold!"

"Good gods!" said Jorian, staring.

The momentoes were a collection of the instruments with which the headsmen carried out their duties. There were axes and blocks, swords, hangman's ropes, strangler's cords, and throat-cutter's hook-bladed knives. There were two complete racks and a cauldron for boiling oil. There were fetters and thongs and staves and scourges and branding irons. There were special instruments whose purpose was not at once apparent.

To one side, an elderly, whiskery Brother sat on a stool, lovingly whetting one of the axes with a faraway look in his eyes.

"How now, Brother Dhaong?" said Mehru. "Think you your edge will have the trueness tonight's contest demands?"

The ancient gave a dreamy smile and continued to brush the whetstone back and forth, *wheep-wheep*.

"What contest?" asked Jorian uncomfortably.

"You shall see," grinned Mehru. "Behold here, the very block whereon Genera Vijjayan's head was smitten off, after his revolt against King Sirvasha failed. Let me show you some of our more specialized instruments. This is a set of matched eye-gougers belonging to Brother Parhbai. This iron boot is very persuasive when placed in the fire with the suspect's leg inside it. This is an ingenious device for crushing a suspect's leg to a jelly. King Laditya employed it on a brother whom he suspected of plotting against him. Since then our kings have become more practical; they have all their brothers slain upon their accession."

"That sounds hard on the brothers."

"True, but it makes work for us. Now here is Brother Ghos's wheel, with the hammer for breaking prisoners on it. Here is a fine thumbscrew; see the gold and silver inlay on the steel...Brother Dhaong was one of the lucky ones in the draw; so was I. Hence we shall have a chance—but I must not spoil your pleasure by telling you now."

"I have seen enough, thank you," said Jorian. "Like Doctor Karadur, I crave rest."

"Oh, certes," said Mehru. "In that case, let us return to the main hall, where a chamber has been set aside for you."

* * *

Jorian was silent on his way back to the main hall. Mehru, still chattering pleasantly, showed him to the chamber whither Karadur had retired. Inside were two beds, on one of which the old wizard lay on his back, snoring.

Jorian closed the door and lay down on the other bed. He found, however, that he could not sleep. After a while he got up, went out, and did some exploring on his own. The castle was silent save for the sounds of cookery from the kitchen and the snores that issued from behind various doors.

Beside the stairs that led up from the main hall, a stair led down from it. Pursuing it, at the bottom Jorian found a long passage, lit by a single candle on a wall bracket, with rooms opening off from it. Some of these, to judge by the massive padlocks on their doors, seemed to be store-rooms for valuables. A couple were barred cells, and from one of these burst a chorus of familiar squeals. The cell contained the twelve slave girls.

"O Maltho! Master Maltho! Dear, kind Maltho!" they cried. "Why have they locked us up here? What do they with us? Can't you get us out?"

"Tell me what's happened," he said. All spoke at once, but the gist was that they had been taken directly to the cell from the main hall, given food and drink, and left in silence and solitude.

"I know not what these men intend," he said, "but I'll try to find out and, if it be evil, to thwart their plans. Be good girls!"

Jorian went back upstairs to the tower room that housed the clockwork. The locked door quickly yielded to one of his pick-locks. Thanking his gods that he was familiar with his father's mechanisms, he pulled out one of the keys that governed the raising of the drawbridge and inserted it into another hole. Then he returned to the chamber where Karadur slept and shook the wizard.

"Wake up!" he said. "I think you were right about your evil aura."

"Well?" said Karadur, yawning and rubbing his eyes.

"Unless I much mistake, these headsmen plan to stage a contest with their banquet this even, to exhibit their specialties in the practice of their calling."

"How mean you? To swing their axes and such-like to show they have not lost their form?"

"More than that. I think they plan to demonstrate their skills on those twelve slave girls we brought."

"You mean to chop and choke—Kradha preserve us! I will not stay here an instant longer to witness such wickedness!" Karadur began winding his turban, but so agitated was he that the thing repeatedly fell down in loops about his neck. "And you are he who has been talking about headsmen's being but human like all other men!"

"Now whither are you going so suddenly?" said Jorian. "If I am to rescue the lassies, I shall need your help."

"Rescue them? Are you mad, my son? How can one man rescue them from a castle full of these hulking brutes?"

"I know not, yet, but something may turn up. At least, I mean to see it through. I brought the girls hither."

"But—but—do not throw your life away!" Karadur clutched Jorian's huge hand, and tears ran down his wrinkled, brown cheeks into his silky white beard. "It will avail your lassies nought and ruin our chances of obtaining the Kist of Avlen!"

"If I perish, it matters not a whit to me what befalls the Kist of Avlen. If I succeed, I shall still be available for your bit of high-class burglary."

"But you have no true moral obligation! What are these wenches to you? Why risk your life for them?"

"Shame on you for talking like one of those selfish materialists you are always denouncing!"

"Never mind me. Give me a good reason for what you plan to attempt."

"Say it infuriates me to see the poor little harmless dears put to pain and death for frivolous reasons. I never allowed that sort of thing when I was king, and I won't begin now."

"But the women are the Brothers' lawful property, to rob them of which were theft and in itself a sin."

"Then I'm a sinner. Besides, they are Novarians and so, according to the philosopher Achaemo, should never have been held in servitude by other Novarians in the first place. Now calm yourself and help me to plan."

"I will not! I cannot!" chattered Karadur, making a sudden rush for the door. Jorian, being the quicker, got there first and set his broad back against the door.

"Coward!" he snarled. "With all your lofty talk of altruism and self-sacrifice and moral purity, you turn tail at the first chance to practice your preachments!"

"Nay, nay, my beloved son!" wailed Karadur. "I am no warrior, inured to bloodshed and deadly hazards! I am but a peaceful philosopher and student of the occult arts, long past the age of combat."

"Rubbish! I'm no warrior, either, but a common artisan masquerading as one. These adventures affright me half out of my wits. If I can face it, surely you can. You showed mettle enough at my execution in Xylar."

But Karadur only babbled: "Nay! Nay! Let me go, I say! If it be wrong of you to risk yourself uselessly, it were doubly wrong to involve me in your suicide!"

Karadur, thought Jorian, would be useless in his present panic. He said: "I'll make a compact with you. Let me see what magical properties you have with you, and tell me what each one does."

"Well," said Karadur, sinking down upon his bed and fumbling in his robe, "this phial contains the essence of covetousness; a drop in the soup of him to whom you would sell a thing, and your suit is two-thirds won. It requires no incantation and is very popular with horse traders. Next, I have here a ring with a beryl wherein is imprisoned the demon Gorax. When threatened by malevolent spirits, such as the swamp devils of Moru, you have but to utter the right incantation, and Gorax will come forth and put those beings to rout. Afterwards another spell will compel him to return to the ring. The cantrips, however, are long and difficult, and the commands to Gorax must be phrased with the nicest accuracy, since he is stupid even for a demon and can wreak grave havoc through misunderstanding. Now here..."

Eventually, Karadur came to a packet of powder. "This is the Powder of Discord, which I obtained from Goania in Othomae. But—ah—you may not have it, because we shall need it in Trimandilam."

"It's just what I need," said Jorian. "For the others, I can see no use in my present plight. But your Powder of Discord would, methinks, serve very neatly here."

"No, no! I have told you why I cannot—"

"No powder, no escape. I'll hold you here until dinnertime. Then the drawbridge will be up, and you'll not be able to leave."

"But—but if you plan to abide beyond that time, how shall *you* escape?"

"Leave that to me. You may go when you give me the powder, not before—what's that?"

A hollow, metallic boom resounded through the edifice. Karadur squeaked: "That is the gong that summons the Brothers to meat! Let me go at once!"

Jorian held out his hand. Muttering something that— had he not known Karadur's stern views on blasphemy— Jorian would have suspected of being a Mulvani curse, the wizard put the packet into Jorian's hand. Saying: "Tell Strasso to send his dinghy in close to shore to await me." Jorian opened the door.

The lamps in the main hall had been lit, and a fire crackled in the fireplace. Some of the Brothers, yawning and stretching, were drifting into the hall, where tables had been pulled out from the walls. Prominent among them was the gigantic chairman. As Jorian and Karadur emerged from their chamber, Khuravela caught Jorian's eye and beckoned.

"Doctor Karadur is unwell," said Jorian smoothly. "He begs to return to the ship, where his medicines are."

Khuravela grunted. "If he will, he will. Your captain, also, sent word he could not attend. Hmph. Too many think themselves better than their origins."

While Karadur scuttled out, Jorian accepted a flagon of spiced wine and answered questions about the news from the Twelve Cities of Novaria. He was tempted to give a thrilling account of the escape of the king of Xylar but suppressed the urge.

When the chairman took his seat, the other Brothers sat down also. They seemed a taciturn lot, communicating in grunts. Jorian, however, found himself next to a tall, lean, skull-faced man with a fondness for gossip. The latter whispered:

"See how Mehru strives to bait the chairman, and how Khuravela ignores him. Mehru is ambitious to become chairman in the other's room. He is eternally buzzing about our ears, saying that Khuravela is but an old, dead oak— impressive to look at, but without sap in its bark. And, in truth, none knows if any thoughts do stir behind our chairman's noble brow, for he goes for days on end without uttering a word. On the other hand, see you Brother Ghos, he of the purple turban? He heads a third faction..."

The tale of the endless bickering and intrigues of this ingrown little world became boring at last. Jorian finished a plain but plentiful repast in a silence unusual for him.

When the women had taken away the plates, wiped the tables, and poured fresh mugs of beer, a buzz of talk arose. Chairman Khuravela, in his armchair, made a sign. Several Brothers rose and left the hall. Presently two came back, one balancing a red-painted headsman's block on his brawny shoulder while the other bore an ax. Another man returned with a coil of rope, with a noose on its end, over his arm. He climbed on a table and tossed the noose end of the rope over a beam. Jorian said to his neighbor:

"Tell me, sir: Are the Brothers about to demonstrate their skills?"

"Why, of course!" said the skull-faced man. "Methought you knew."

"Using those slave girls as subjects?"

"Certes! We cannot practice on free men like yourself; that were a crime. Do you think us murderers?"

"Is this a contest?"

"Aye; the other Brothers will judge the skill and dexterity displayed in each execution. Thank the true gods of Mulvan, it is the first break in the maddening boredom of life here in many a moon."

"Why does not everybody take a turn?"

"The Brothers refused to vote money for a larger number of slaves; a matter of internal politics. Khuravela ordered the largest number for which funds were to hand, and we cast lots to see which amongst us should be chosen to take part in the contest."

Two men staggered into the hall, bearing a rack from the armory. Jorian stood up and watched Khurevela. When the latter glanced in his direction, Jorian caught his eye and called:

"Master Chairman, may I speak?"

"Speak!" growled Khuravela. "Silence, pigs."

"Gentlemen!" said Jorian. "Permit me to thank you from the bottom of my heart for the sumptuous repast and the delicious potations you have served me. In fact, I am so full I can scarcely stand. Though I live to be as old as the eldest amongst you, I shall always remember this even as one of the high spots of my life—"

"If he have aught to say, I wish he would say it," growled a Brother to his neighbor. Jorian heard it but continued:

"And so, to make a very meager and inadequate repayment for this delightful entertainment, I should like to tell you a story."

The Brothers straightened up. The boredom vanished from their faces, and their eyes shone with new interest. Jorian stepped out into the clear space, in the midst of the tables.

"This story," he said, "is called the Tale of the Teeth of Gimnor. Many centuries ago, it is said that there reigned in Kortoli a small but lively and quick-witted king named Fusinian, sometimes called Fusinian the Fox. The son of Filoman the Well-Meaning, he came to the throne quite young and wedded the daughter of the High Admiral of Zolon. If you know not, Zolon is an isle in the Western Ocean, off the far coast of Novaria, and Zolon counts as one of the Twelve Cities. Being an island, it is a maritime power; and being a maritime power, it is ruled by a High Admiral. Therefore, it was a suitable match for the king of Kortoli.

"This maid, who hight Thanuda, was divinely tall and famous for her beauty. King Fusinian fell in love with her picture and dispatched his chamberlain to sue for her hand. She made no objections, despite the fact that she was the taller of the two. They were wed with all the usual pomp and settled down to such happiness as is granted to royalty, who marry for reasons of statecraft.

"Soon thereafter, war broke out betwixt Kortoli and its northern neighbor Aussar. It was some footling squabble over a bit of territory, and as usual, between them the two combatants had soon spent blood and treasure worth a hundredfold as much as the land. And in these struggles, Aussar, which began the hostilities, had the better of it. First the Aussarians drove the Kortolians out of the disputed area. Then, when Fusinian counterattacked, they routed him in two great battles. Fusinian's sire, Filoman the Well-Meaning, had been full of humane ideas about reducing the army and spending the money thus saved to uplift the masses, so that Kortoli had fallen behind the other Twelve Cities in the arts of war.

"Had Fusinian been older and craftier, he might have yielded to Aussar at the outset and used the time thus gained to strengthen his army, eventually to take the land back. But, being young and ardent and full of romantical notions of honor, he plunged into a war to which his forces were not equal. So he was beaten three times running. And then word came that the Aussarians meant to invade Kortoli proper, to get rid of Fusinian and put some puppet on his throne.

"In desperation, Fusinian went with a small escort to a witch named Gloé, who dwelt in the rugged hills that sunder Kortoli from its southern neighbor Vindium. The witch harkened to his plea for succor and said:

"'As a patriotic Kortolian, I will of course help Your Majesty to my utmost. Howsomever, there is the matter of my license.'

"'Eh? What is this?' said the king. 'My kingdom totters on the brink of ruin, and you babble of licenses?'

"'It is no mean matter, sire,' replied Gloé. 'Know that I am no illicit practitioner of magic through choice. Thrice I have applied to your Bureau of Commerce and Licenses, and thrice they have turned me down. They demand a diploma from the Lyceum of Metouro or other institution of higher learning, or that I pass an examination, or take a refresher course, or some other nonsense of this sort, when I have been successfully healing the sick, summoning spirits, finding lost articles, and foreseeing the future for sixty years!'

"'But what has all that to do with the peril of Kortoli?' asked the king.

"'Because the efficacy of magic depends upon the state of mind of the magician. Did I but know that you would summarily command your finicking clerks to issue me a proper license as wizardess forthwith, the relief to me would enhance my chance of success.'

"The king frowned. 'I like not to interfere in the orderly processes of administration, nor yet to urge partiality upon my officials,' he said. 'But in this extreme, I suppose I must swallow my scruples. Very well, if your spell work, you shall have your license, though you know not a zoömorph from a zodiac. Pray, madam, proceed.'

"So the witch went into a trance and writhed and mumbled and spoke in strange voices, and shadows flickered about her cave without material objects to cast them, and strange, dissolving faces appeared in mid-air, and the king was seized by freezing cold, whether from some being from outer space or from simple fright is not known. When the king had stopped shivering and the shadows had gone away, the witch said:

"'Know, O King, that you must slay the dragon Grimnor, who sleeps under a mountain nine leagues hence. Then you must take out every one of this dragon's teeth. On a night of a full moon, you must sow these teeth on a plowed field, and there shall spring up from these teeth that which will enable you to vanquish Aussar.'

"So King Fusinian journeyed westward, following Gloé's directions, until he came to the mountain. The dragon lay snoring in a cave, which opened into a ravine at the root of the mountain. Fusinian feared that neither his arrows nor his lance nor his sword would pierce the dragon's scales—which are, as everyone knows, so hard that they make excellent mail, provided that one can obtain a dragon's hide to begin with—especially since Fusinian stood only three finger-breadths above five feet. At last Fusinian and his men found a boulder of the right size and drove an iron spike into it, and to this spike they belayed a long rope. Then they balanced this boulder precariously over the mouth of Grimnor's cave.

"Then Fusinian went to the mouth of the cave and shouted a challenge to Grimnor. And the dragon awoke and came looping and hissing out of the cave. Fusinian ran back before him, and when he saw that the head and a few feet of the neck were out of the cave, he jerked the rope. Down came the boulder, with a snapping of draconic skull bones. The thrashing and writhing of that beast were fearful; they shook the mountain and brought down a small landslide. But at length Grimnor lay still and dead.

"Fusinian discovered that the dragon had forty-seven teeth in each side of each jaw, making a total of one hundred and eighty-eight. He had thoughtfully brought along the royal dentist, who extracted these teeth. Fusinian put the teeth in a bag and, on the night of the next full moon, he sowed these teeth on plowed field. He sowed and sowed, thus."

Jorian strode about the hall, making sowing gestures. Actually, he was tossing into the air above the heads of the diners pinches of the Powder of Discord, the packet of which he concealed in his left hand. He continued:

"Just as Gloé had predicted, the points of spears could presently be discerned, sticking up through the soil and shining in the moonlight. And then came the crests of helms, and soon there stood up, in the moonlight, one hundred and eighty-eight giants, eight feet tall and armed to the teeth.

" 'We are the Teeth of Grimnor,' said the tallest of the giants in a voice of thunder. 'What would you of us, little man?'

"Clenching his jaw to keep his teeth from chattering, Fusinian said: 'Your task, O Teeth, is to vanquish the armies of Aussar, which are overrunning my fair kingdom.'

" 'Harkening and obedience,' thundered the giant who had spoken. And off they marched towards the Aussarian border, so fast that they soon left King Fusinian and his escort behind. So Fusinian returned to Kortoli City to see how things fared there. And when he arrived, he found that the Teeth were there ahead of him. They had routed the Aussarians so utterly that those who escaped the carnage ran all the way back to Aussar City before stopping to draw breath. For it transpired the Teeth had hides of such toughness that the blows of swords and the thrusts of spears were no more to them than the scratches of a kitten are to one of us.

"Well, a pair of the giants at the West Gate admitted King Fusinian and his escort. But when Fusinian got to the palace, he was taken aback to find the biggest of the Teeth sitting on his throne—or rather, on a table top laid across the arms of his throne, for the throne itself was too small to accommodate that monstrous arse.

" 'What,' quoth he, 'in all the heavens and hells are you doing in my chair?'

" 'I am not in it, I am on it,' said the Tooth. 'And as for what I am doing, we have decided to run your kingdom for ourselves. This is but natural, since we are so much stronger than you that it were ridiculous for us to take orders from you. Besides, only thus can we assure ourselves enough to eat, for our appetites are to yours like those of tigers to those of titmice. I have taken your queen for my concubine, and now I shall make you my body slave—'

"But Fusinian, with that quickness of wit that long served him so well, raced out of the throne room, dodged a giant or two who tried to snatch him up, vaulted on his horse, and spurred like a madman for the gate. He was out and on his way ere the Teeth could prepare themselves to stop him. They set out a pursuit; but, although they could run as fast afoot as Fusinian's horse could gallop, he knew the country better than they. By weaving back and forth like a fox dodging the hounds, he got over the border to Govannian.

"Fusinian had been on good terms with the Hereditary Usurper of Govannian until the latter refused to aid him against Aussar, as he had once promised to do. Fusinian's news, however, was ominous enought to patch up the quarrel. No fool, the Hereditary Usurper raised an army to scotch the Teeth before they decided to annex his realm as well as Kortoli.

"Fusinian meanwhile went from one to another of the Twelve Cities with his story. In most of them he got contingents for the army of liberation, although the Syndics of Ir demurred on the ground that it would cost too much, and the Senate of Vindium debated endlessly without deciding aught, and the Tyrant of Boaktis declared it was all a hoax by Fusinian to subvert his own enlightened and progressive rule and restore the reactionary exploiters.

"At length an army, with contingents from all the remaining Twelve Cities—even from Aussar—gathered on the border of Govannian and marched into Kortoli. But alas! The army halted in dismay when the forces of the Teeth approached them. Some of the Teeth were riding on mammoths, which they had bought from the cham of the Gendings, in Shven. The beasts had been towed down the coast on rafts. Other Teeth fought on foot as officers of platoons of Kortalians, whom by terror they had trained to obey their slightest command.

"Fusinian was not altogether unprepared for such a reception. Knowing the might of the giants, he had constructed a battery of the largest wheeled catapults that anybody had built up to that time. The catapults went off with great bangs, hurling sixty-pound balls of stone.

Some missed and some plowed into the hapless Korto-lians, but one came straight at one of the Teeth. The Tooth leisurely caught it, as one catches a handball, and threw it back as accurately as it had been shot at him and with somewhat greater force. For it struck the He-reditary Usurper of Govannian, where he sat his horse in the midst of his host, and took off his helmet with the head inside it.

"After that, there was not much of a battle. The mam-moths on the wings closed in, and Fusinian's mighty array dissolved into a mass of shrieking fugitives, among whom the Teeth amused themselves by striding and riding and smashing people like so many bugs with their ten-foot clubs.

"For some months, little was heard of Fusinian save rumors of his appearing and vanishing like a ghost along the borders of Kortoli. At length he sought the cave of Gloé the witch.

" 'Well, King,' she said, stirring her cauldron, 'How about my license?'

" 'Bugger your license madam!' quoth he. 'That cure you gave me was worse than the disease.'

" 'That was your fault, laddie,' she said. 'When you gave the Teeth their orders, you forgot to tell them to vanish or to turn back into dragon's teeth after they had routed the Aussarians. As it was, they were free of all obligation as soon as they had carried out your complete command.'

" 'How in the forty-nine Mulvanian hells was I to know that?' he yelled. 'You never told me!'

" 'Why should I?' said she. 'Knowing you for a king and a smart one at that, I assumed you would have the com-mon sense to do so without my telling you.' And they fell to shouting and shaking fists at each other in most un-kingly wise until they ran out of breath.

" 'Well, let us forget what has been said and be practi-cal,' said Gloé. 'You want more help, yea?'

"Fusinian muttered something about damned women who can never give precise directions, but aloud he said: 'Yea, but Zevatas help us if it avail us no better than the last time! These creatures are eating my kingdom bare, not to mention niggling the wives of all the leading men, including mine.'

" 'Their voracity is explained by their draconic origin,'

101

quoth Gloé. 'Now, I know a spell to call an army of aërial demons from the Sixth Plane. It is a spell of the utmost difficulty and danger. It also requires human sacrifice. Whom are you prepared to dispense with?'

"The king looked at his escort, and each member of the escort looked as if his keenest wish were to become invisible. But one man spoke up at last, saying 'Take me, O King. The physician assures me that, with my leaky heart, I have not long to live anyway.'

"'Nobly spoken!' cried Fusinian. 'You shall have a monument when I have reconquered my kingdom.' And in a good sooth, this monument was duly erected and stands in Kortoli City even yet. 'So, madam.'

"'Just a moment, sire,' said Gloé. 'I need something for myself as well, to put me in the right mood to cast an effective spell.'

"'Here we go again,' said the king. 'What is it this time?'

"'I want not only a proper license as wizardess, but also to be made your court magician.'

"They argued, but in the end Fusinian gave in, not having much choice in the matter. So the spell was cast. The moon turned to blood, and the earth shook, the forests were filled with weird wailings, and down from the sky swooped a horde of demons in the form of bat-winged lizard-men, to assail the Teeth.

"But, when a demon or other spirit takes material form, it is bound by the laws of matter. The Teeth merely laughed and seized the demons out of the air and tore them to bits like a bad boy dismembering a butterfly. And the survivors of the demons fled back to the Sixth Plane and have refused to be invoked from that day to this.

"Disgusted with Gloé and her spells, Fusinian disappeared again. From time to time he would be seen, in worn, patched garments, in one or another of the Twelve Cities, for he had friends and partisans everywhere. At last, whilst idling in the marketplace at Metouro, he saw a gang of boys raid the stall of a greengrocer, snatching fruit and dashing away ere the wretched merchant could summon aid. The thing that struck him about this incident was the fact that the greengrocer was so enormously fat that he could not even squeeze out of his stall in time to call for assistance.

"That made Fusinian think, and he recalled the tales

he had heard of the monstrous appetites of the Teeth. Soon thereafter, the Faceless Five, who rule Metouro summoned Fusinian to ask his advice about a demand for tribute, which they had received from the Teeth in Kortoli. Fusinian looked at the five black masks and said:

"'Send them not only what they ask, but also twice as much.'

"'You are mad!' cried one of the Five. 'It would beggar us!'

"'Have you had a good harvest?' asked Fusinian.

"'Aye; but so what?'

"'Then pay what I advise in farm produce. Let me explain...'

"Then for a while Fusinian went from city to city, expounding his plan. So food poured into Kortoli in groaning oxcart loads. This continued for six whole months. When one of the Twelve Cities ran short of agricultural produce, it borrowed money to import more from another of the Twelve or even from Shven or Mulvan.

"And at length came the day when King Fusinian rode into Kortoli at the head of his army while the Teeth, now grown so fat they could scarcely move, looked on helplessly and mouthed futile threats. And, whereas the skins of the Teeth were still too tough for ordinary weapons to do more than scratch, the Kortolians bound the giants by massive chains to huge blocks of Othomaean granite, towed them out to the deep sea on rafts, and overturned the rafts. And that was the end of that.

"Or nearly so. Fusinian had an affecting reunion with his queen, the lovely Thanuda. But sometimes, when he had finished making love to her, he would catch her looking at him with a curious expression—a trace of disappointment, or as if she were comparing him unfavorably with someone else. And once during a quarrel she called him 'shrimp.' So his later life was perturbed by the thought that, whatever the faults of the Tooth who had borrowed his wife, the giant must have had certain superhuman capacities that he, Fusinian, lacked. But, being a philosophical man, he made the best of things. And the moral is: Choking a cat with butter may not be the most obvious way of killing it, but sometimes it is the only one that works."

* * *

A moment later, Jorian picked the lock of the door of the cell that held the slave girls. They threw themselves upon him; Mnevis caught him round the neck and smothered him with kisses.

"Na, na, easy all, lassies," he said. "I'll get you out of this, but you must be absolutely quiet. No talking, whispering, laughing, giggling, squealing or other sounds! Now come along. Keep behind me and watch my signals. Softly now."

He led the twelve on tiptoe down the corridor. At the first of the locked doors he halted, picked the padlock, and went in. A quick look showed that the room was full of agricultural implements. The second storeroom proved to be full of heavy winter clothing: felt boots, woolen cloaks, and sheepskin greatcoats.

The third storeroom had shelves on which stood rows of objects that glimmered in the gloom, while on the floor a line of coffers ran around the wall.

"This," said Jorian, "is what I sought. One of you girls fetch that candle in from outside. Careful lest you blow it out. Ah!"

The girls echoed Jorian's ejaculation, for this was the treasury of the Brotherhood. The objects on the shelves were jeweled goblets of gold and silver, pictures in jeweled frames, golden candlesticks and lamps, and similar precious artifacts. The coffers, as Jorian soon discovered by picking the lock on one, contained money and jewels. Some of the Brothers must have saved up tidy fortunes—probably, Jorian suspected, by taking bribes from prisoners not to cause them much pain.

Jorian took out and crammed his money belt full of Mulvanian golden coins; without taking the time to count, he thought he had well over a hundred crowns' worth. He gave handfuls to each of the slave girls, with instructions to stow them as securely as possible. From the shelves and the jewel boxes he selected several handsome gauds, including a jeweled golden cup, a jeweled pendant, and several rings and bracelets. These he likewise gave to the girls to carry.

"Now come," he said. "We're going up yonder stair, but not all the way. Blow out that candle."

At the head of his little procession, Jorian stole up the stair to the main hall, until over the top he could see into the hall. Keeping back out of the lamplight, he silently watched events unfold.

The sound of talk in the hall had risen to a roar. Everywhere the Brothers were engaged in hot disputes, pounding their tables, smiting their fists into their palms, and wagging forefingers under one another's noses. Several more instruments of execution had been brought into the hall. As Jorian watched, two men came in carrying a little portable forge and a set of iron implements. They put the forge down, and one of them set about building a fire in it with stone coals and kindling. The other joined one of the raging arguments.

A louder shout drew Jorian's attention. One Brother had just thrown his beer into another's face. With a scream of rage, the victim hurled his mug at the first man's head and drew his dagger. The other man retreated to the space in the midst of the tables, now occupied by the instruments. He wrenched a beheading ax from its block and, as the other man rushed upon him with uplifted dagger, brought the blade down upon the attacker's head, cleaving his skull to the teeth.

The hall exploded into violent action. Everywhere men madly went for one another with whatever weapon came to hand. All the instruments fit for such use—axes, swords, knives, and the sledge hammer used in breaking prisoners on the wheel—were snatched up. Blood and brains spattered the tables and the floor; bodies fell right and left. Men grappled, rolling over and over on the floor, stabbing with knives and tearing with nails and teeth. The noise rose to a deafening pitch.

Jorian beckoned the girls. Sword out, he led the way to the top of the stair. By skirting the walls of the hall, he kept as much in the shadow as he could. He made the half-circuit to the vestibule that led to the outside. There he paused, waving the girls ahead of him.

As he did so, a figure detached itself from the bloody chaos in the hall and rushed towards him. It was Mehru, his erstwhile guide, waving his two-handed sword. Blood ran down his face from a cut, and his eyes gleamed wildly.

"Get along down to the pier and signal the dinghy," Jorian told the slave girls. "I shall be with you shortly." Then he faced the garrulous Brother.

"You did this, by some sorcery!" screamed Mehru, aiming a slash at Jorian's head.

Jorian parried with a clang, and again and again. The blows came so fast that he had no time for a counterattack. Although Mehru was the smaller man, he wielded his heavy weapon as if it were a lath, and his length of blade kept Jorian beyond the latter's reach. Jorian tried to catch the blows slantwise, so that the headsman's blade glanced off his own, but the force of them numbed his arm.

Step by step, Jorian backed into the vestibule and then into the archway that supported the portcullis. He kept glancing right and left, measuring the distances from side to side of the archway. Now he had backed out on the planks of the drawbridge, which, contrary to the custom of the Brothers, was down despite the darkness.

There he halted his retreat. Mehru, still attacking, was slowing down and panting heavily. Jorian permitted himself a smile, calling out:

"Why do you not fight, sister-impregnator?"

It was the ultimate insult in Mulvani. With a piercing scream, Mehru wound up for a terrific cut intended to shear Jorian in two at the waist.

The archway, however, was a little too narrow for such tactics. As a result, the tip of the long blade hit the masonry, striking sparks. The stonework stopped the blow; Jorian leaping in, sent Randir in a full-arm slash at the executioner's neck. Mehru's head leaped from his shoulders in a shower of blood. The body fell; the head bounced and rolled.

Jorian wiped and sheathed his sword. He sprang to the windlass for manual operation of the drawbridge and heaved. After a couple of turns, something went *clank*, and the wheel began to spin of its own accord from the weight of the unseen barrel of water. Jorian ran up the ever-steepening slope of the rising drawbridge, leaped to the path beyond, and trotted for the pier.

"Ten thousand devils!" growled Captain Strasso. "What means this, Master Maltho?"

"I've told you, sir captain: They refused the shipment. Something about trouble with their wives. We argued for hours. I insisted that a bargain was a bargain, whilst they said they would be damned if they'd pay for merchandise for which they had no use. At last they gave in and paid the amount agreed upon. Here are Belius' ninety-six crowns; pray give them to him when you return to Vindium, as Doctor Karadur and I plan to leave you at Janareth. Since the Brothers averred that they had no use for the lassies, they commissioned me to take them to Janareth to sell, retaining one-fourth of the money thus earned as my commission and returning the rest by your hand."

"Mmp. Be you through with the Castle of the Ax?"

"Aye. Sail when you list."

"Then I'll up-anchor and away. My lads fear the ghosts they say haunt this isle. Besides, there's less chance of meeting pirates in these waters at night. With this moon, we can hold a true course."

Later, in the cabin, Karadur said: "Ah me, I must practice austerities to atone for my craven conduct ashore today."

"You may forgive yourself, Doctor," said Jorian. "As things fell out, you'd only have been in the way when the butchery started."

"What took place, my son?"

Jorian, sitting on his bunk and patiently whetting the edge of Randir where the blows of Mehru's sword had nicked or dulled it, told his tale.

Karadur: "Why, after so deceiving Captain Strasso as to the course of events, did you return Belius' money to him? Why not send the girls back to Vindium and keep the gold, which in the circumstance were scarcely theft?"

"I have other plans for them. Besides, we're rich again. I got more than the price of the wenches out of the Brothers' coffers; here's your share. And I need the girls more than I need the gold."

"How did you ever escape from the castle, with the drawbridge up?"

"It wasn't up. I moved one of the keys of the mechanism that controls it, to make it rise after midnight instead of at sunset. And now to bed; this has been a fatiguing day."

Karadur looked fondly at his young friend. "Do you remember, Jorian, when you told me of the witch's advice to you, to be either a king or a wandering adventurer?"

"Aye. What of it? I have tried the role of king, and once was enough."

"I fear you are not cut out for the adventurer's part, either."

"How so?"

"You are just not ruthlessly selfish enough to succeed at it. A true adventurer—and I have known several of the breed—would have embezzled Belius' gold and would never had tried to rescue those wenches, at least not at any risk to himself. And that brings us to the great moral question that for thousands of years had baffled the keenest minds amongst the philosophers of Mulvan: What is virtue? Some aver..."

But Jorian was already snoring.

V

THE
BUTTERFLY THRONE

DEEP IN ITS WHITECAPPED, EMERALD BAY, AT THE MOUTH
of the mighty Bharma, Janareth lay in the sunshine, with
white, red-roofed houses rising in tiers up the hillside amid
the jade-green palms and dark cypresses, under the blue-
and-white sky-bowl. A pilot boat, with the blue mermaid
flag of Janareth fluttering from its masthead, came bouncing through the chop to guide the *Talaris* through the gap
in the *mole* to the inner harbor.

Ships of many nations were anchored in this harbor or
tied up at the quays. There were trim roundships from
Vindium and Kortoli and Aussar and Tarxia. There were
undecked craft from the Shvenic coast to the north, with
their single square sails and high-pointed ends, like over-
sized canoes. There were several black-hulled war galleys
of Janareth, long, low, and lethal. There was a huge, high-
sided, square-ended three-master, with slatted yellow lug-
sails, from the Salimor Islands, far off in the Eastern Ocean.

Leaning on the rail and staring moodily at the craft, on
the first day of the Month of the Wolf, Jorian gave a gusty
sigh.

"At last we are getting back to a civilized clime!" said Karadur beside him. "Why sigh you?"

"I miss my wives. Nay, I'll take that back. I miss one of them: Estrildis, the little yellow-hair. The others are fine girls and fun in bed, but she is the one I chose for myself."

"How came that to pass?"

"She was the wench I was wooing in Kortoli when Farmer Onnus made the mistake of trying to horsewhip me all day. After I had been king for three years, I learnt that she was yet unwed and got a message to her. I could not ride to Kortoli to claim her, as proper hero of legend ought, because the Royal Guard would not let me over the boundaries of Xylar. But we managed. Some day I'll go back to Xylar and abduct her."

"If the Xylarians have not annulled your marriage and she have not wed some other man."

"I might snatch her anyway, were she willing. She was always my favorite. To preserve domestic harmony, I tried to hide the fact from the others, but I fear without complete success.

"Know, Doctor, that many a man has wished for a seraglio like mine, but I'll tell you how it works in practice. When the dames quarrel—which they do from time to time—the husband must act as judge and conciliator to settle their disputes. When they act in harmony—which occurs betimes—they get whatever they want from the poor wight by working upon him *seriatim*. And he must watch his every act, lest he give any one of them cause to think she has not been entreated so well as some other. If she do, then woe unto him! Scoldings, tears, complaints, and old scores raked up... Nay, if I ever achieve my modest ambitions to be a respectable craftsman earning a decent living, one wife will be plenty for me. But I could use at least one right now."

"Have you not been—ah—amusing yourself with Belius' maidens?"

"No, although how long I shall remain in this unwonted state of virtue is problematical. I haven't known a woman since I parted from that wild wench Vanora in Othomae."

"Your continence does you great spiritual credit, my son."

"Oh, bugger my spiritual credit! I've kept my hands off

110

the poor little dears because it seemed unworthy to take advantage of their servile condition. Since I have, in a manner of speaking, inherited them from the Brotherhood of Rennum Kezymar, they could hardly have refused me."

"What is this mysterious plan you have for them?"

Jorian winked. "For four whole days I've held my flapping tongue, although bursting with my wonderful scheme. I feared that, did I get to talking, Strasso or one of his men might overhear. Once our good captain is on his way back to Vindium, I shall be overjoyed to share the plan with you, Holy Father."

Sailors were furling the sail, whose yard had been lowered into its crutches. Captain Strasso and the skipper of a tugboat exchanged shouts as the tug, propelled by ten brawny oarsmen, pushed against the side of the *Talaris* by means of a cushion of rope draped over the stem, nudging the ship into dock at one of the quays.

As the *Talaris* inched up against the bumpers of rope along the quay and was made fast, a pair of officials climbed aboard. One questioned Captain Strasso, checking the entries of his manifest, while the other scurried about, asking Jorian and Karadur their names, vanishing into the hold and reappearing, and consulting in an undertone with his colleague. By the time the inquisition was over and the officials had departed, a swarm of touts, pimps, peddlers, beggars, porters, donkey boys, and would-be guides had gathered around the shoreward end of the plank, crying:

"Come, my masters, to the tavern with the strongest liquors, the loudest music, and the nakedest dancing girls in Janareth..." "...my nice, clean sister..." "...to view the newly discovered grave of the demigod Pteroun, the ruined Temple of the Serpent Gods, and other fascinating wonders of antiquity..." "Succor the child of misfortune!" "Buy my amulets: sure protection against the pox, the ague, and evil witchcraft..." "Simha's Inn is so clean that not one bug has been seen there since the time of Ghish the Great..."

Wearing his haughtiest royal expression—which he had used as king of Xylar to get rid of bores—Jorian strode down the plank and addressed the tout for Simha's Inn: "My good man, I have with me twelve ladies of quality, traveling *incognito* to Trimandilam. They will remain in

111

Janareth about a fiftnight. Can your inn accommodate them in a style befitting their station?"

"Oh, my lord! But of course, my lord!" The tout bowed over his clasped hands again and again, as if worked by strings. "Do but deign to visit our worthy establishment...."

"Your performance had better match your promises," said Jorian, coldly eyeing the man. "Pick me a few porters of strong back and simple mind—four should do. What is the current porterage fee?..."

The waterfront of Janareth swarmed with the motley, many-tongued crowds of Janareth. Here were Novarians in short tunics and tight breeches; turbaned Mulvanians in skirts or baggy pantaloons of bright-hued silks; cameleers from the desert of Fedirun in brown robes and white head cloths; tall seamen from Shven, with lank, tow-colored hair and garments of sheepskin and coarse brown wool; slant-eyed, flat-faced men from far Salimor. There were semi-human slaves from the jungles of Komilakh, led on leashes. There were men of even more exotic racial types, whom Jorian could not identify.

Although Janreth paid tribute to the king of Mulvan, it retained self-government and still called itself a free city. The ferocious factional conflicts that flared up from time to time gave the Great King ample excuses for meddling, yet King Shaju had so far refrained. For one thing, the factions would instantly unite and fiercely oppose any such attempt. For another, conservative Mulvanians looked upon the great trading port as a necessary evil—a commercial convenience, but a repulsive one because of its mixed population of disgusting foreigners. They were glad it existed but also glad that it did not form part of their vast, orderly, minutely organized empire.

The tout cried back over his shoulder: "Beware! To the wall!"

Jorian and his companions crowded to one side as a cavalcade cantered through. The leader was a Mulvanian in scarlet silken garments, with a jeweled spray of plumes at the front of his turban. A squad of horsemen in spired, silvered steel caps, armed with light lances and little round shields, jingled after him.

"One of our local squires," said the tout after the horsemen had passed. "These landowners are always trying to worm and bluster their way into our governing council and so in time to rule the city—albeit they live out in the hills and come to town only for shopping and whoring." The man spat.

The following day, Jorian was eating his midday meal in the refectory of Simha's Inn when Captain Strasso came in.

"Good Master Maltho!" said the Captain. "The oracle promises fair weather for the next fiftnight, and I've been lucky in finding a good cargo for Vindium, ready to load. So *Talaris* will put out on her last voyage of the season the morn."

"Fine," said Jorian.

"But, there's the matter of the payment to the Brothers. Have you sold the wenches yet, so that I can take the money with me?"

"No, I haven't; nor am I in a hurry to."

Strasso frowned. "How so?"

"Naturally, I crave the highest price; for the higher the price, the larger my commission. Therefore, I've hired a man skilled in such matters to make highly trained ladies' maids out of the girls. This may take a month."

"Then how shall I convey the money?"

"Know you an honest banker in Janareth?"

"Oh, certes. I bank here with Ujjai and Sons. Ujjai seems trustworthy even if a Mulvanian."

"Then present me to him. When I sell, I shall deposit the money with him, and you can pick it up on your first voyage next spring."

Strasso clapped Jorian on the back. "Admirably thought of! But won't the Brothers chafe at the delay?"

"Judging by their actions when last I saw them, I think not. When I finish this narange, I'll forth to Ujjai's stall."

Jorian met the banker Ujjai, bade farewell to Captain Strasso, and returned to Simha's Inn. This time he went upstairs to the suite that had been turned over to the twelve.

Here, a man was coaching the girls in the rôles that Jorian had invented for them. Although slightly stooped with age, the man was even taller than Jorian. He had large, handsome features and flowing white hair. His piercing gray eyes and lordly, carefully mannered gestures instantly caught the vision of anyone in the same room with him. He spoke in a rich, rolling voice to Mnevis, who was walking back and forth in the middle of the room while the other eleven sat about, comparing their fine new clothes.

"Remember!" he said, "you are a queen. You are conscious every instant of status and worth far above those with whom you hold intercourse. At the same time, you wish them well and would not for worlds hurt their feelings—unless they presumed to undue familiarity. To express just that right combination of hauteur and graciousness calls for a veritable triumph of the actor's skill.

"I recall that when I played King Magonius, opposite that great actress Janoria, in Physo's *The Tinsel Crown*, she struck just the right note." He sighed and shook his head. "There will never be another Janoria, even if she *would* throw things at her colleagues off-stage. Greetings, Master Jorian. As you see, I strive to obey your commands. Now come, Mistress Mnevis—Queen Mnevis, I should say—and try that walk once more."

Jorian was watching the work when Karadur knocked and slipped in, saying, "I was searching for you, my son. I was in the library at the Temple of Narzes and—ah—forgot about lunch in my absorption. Then I chanced upon Strasso, who told me you had returned hither. What takes place here?"

Jorian: "Doctor Karadur, allow me to present Master Pselles of Aussar, a leading ornament of the Novarian stage, now fallen upon certain—ah—temporary embarrassments. I've retained him to coach my girls."

"It does not look to me as if they were being trained as ladies' maids, as Strasso said."

Jorian winked. "Na, na, this is the scheme I promised to reveal to you. Know that these are no ladies' maids, but Queen Mnevis of Algarth and her eleven noble ladies-in-waiting."

"But—but you told me in Xylar that Algarth was only a nest of pirates! How can it have a queen?"

"Mnevis, tell the doctor who you are and what you purpose to do."

"My good sage," said Mnevis in a queenly voice, "know that we, Mnevis widow of Serli, are the rightful queen of

Algarth, which is an archipelago off the western coast of Shven, far to the north of the Twelve Cities. A few years ago, these pirates whereof you speak seized our isles for their own fell purposes, slew our husband the king, and kept us captive as a puppet queen, to dance to their strings.

"Lately, with the help of loyal subjects—who have been reduced to serfdom by these bloody corsairs—we escaped from Algarth with these our ladies. Hearing that the mightiest and justest monarch in the entire world was the Great King of Mulvan, we have come hither to pray His Majesty, that he will render us aid in regaining our rightful throne."

Jorian applauded. "Splendid! You should have been an actress in the first place." He turned to Karadur. "Can you think of a better way to ingratiate ourselves into the haughty court at Trimandilam, to whom ordinary foreigners are less than dirt?"

Karadur shook his head sorrowfully. "I know not...I know not. When you get these wild ideas, my son...Will not this imposture be speedily punctured?"

"I think not. They have never even heard of Algarth in Mulvan."

"But what of you?"

"I am now Jorian of Kortoli, their factotum. Since the lassies speak no Mulvani, they will need my constant attendance."

"What if King Shaju says: 'Very good, you shall have the help you require.' What then?"

"We'll make the queen's demands so steep that there shall be no danger of that. How can Shaju send a fleet and an army to Algarth, when Mulvan has no ports on the Western Ocean? They must need cross the desert of Fedirun or the Twelve Cities or the steppes of Shven to come to that sea, and then what should they do for ships to get to Algarth? 'Tis preposterous on the face of it. And a little skillful exaggeration of the rigors of the boreal Algarthian clime will scare off any Mulvanian tempted to join the ladies from motives of knight-errantry."

Karadur shook his head again. "Meseems I spoke in haste when I denigrated your talent for adventurehood, my son. But it is safe to resume your name again so soon?"

"I think so. We shall be far enough from Xylar so that no report of the doings there will circulate. And I weary of being addressed by other names and not recognizing them, so that people get the notion I'm deaf. Besides, since my name is not uncommon, 'Jorian of Kortoli' might be any one of many persons. 'Jorian of Ardamai' would give me away, Ardamai being a mere village."

"Well, may the gods of Novaria and of Mulvan aid you."

The Bharma wound through the Pushkana Gap in the eastern Lograms, which here had dwindled to a mere range of forested hills. Laboring upstream under sail, the river boat *Jhimu* was towed by big, black buffaloes around the great serpentine bends of the river where it traversed the gap, the current here being too swift for the sail alone to make headway against. The steep, dark-green slopes soared into the sky on either hand, with no sign of animal life save a thread of blue smoke from a woodcutter's clearing, or a vulture hanging like a black mote in the blue. At night, however, the *Jhimu's* passengers could sometimes hear the grunt of a tiger or the toot of a wild elephant.

Beyond the bends, the river ran more slowly and comparatively straight between stairlike rises on the east and west to wooded plateaus. Sometimes it widened into marshes where behemoths lay awash, with only their ears, eyes, and nostrils exposed. At night, snorting and grunting, these animals trooped ashore to graze or to raid the Mulvanian peasants' plantings.

From time to time, roads followed the river. On these roads, Mulvanians were always moving, from single wayfarers to parties of fifty to a hundred. There were holy men, religious pilgrims, merchants with laden pack animals, farmers with loads of produce, detachments of jingling soldiery, and miscellaneous travelers of high and low degree. There were people afoot, on asses, in carriages, in oxcarts, on horseback, on camels, and on elephants.

Every league or so, the *Jhimu* passed a temple to one of Mulvan's multifarious gods. The main structure might be shaped like a dome, a cylinder, a cone, a cube, a pyramid, or a tapering spire; each god has his preferred architectural style. All were encrusted with minutely detailed carvings. The erotic statuary that covered a temple of Laxara, the goddess of love and hate, so embarrassed Karadur when they went near it during a stop that the old

116

man kept his face averted. Looking up at the carvings, Jorian stood with fists on hips, grinning through his beard.

"By Imbal's brazen balls!" he cried. "I didn't know one *could* do it in so many positions!"

Some temples were in crumbling ruin; others were active. At night, points of yellow lamplight flickered about these fanes and the sound of music and song came to the travelers, sometimes slow and solemn, sometimes fast and frenzied.

Aboard the *Jhimu*, Karadur studied a magical scroll he had obtained in Janareth, while Jorian rehearsed his girls in their roles. On the sixth day after leaving Janareth, the *Jhimu* neared the confluence of the Bharma and the Pennerath. In the fork rose the vast city of Trimandilam on its nine hills. The massive wall was of black basalt. Over it the travelers could see the hills, topped by gleaming palaces and temples of marble and alabaster, with gilded roof tiles ablaze in the sun. Below these structures spread thousands of the dun-colored, mud-brick houses of the common folk.

As they tied up, the girls, full of giggling excitement, wanted to scramble ashore. But Jorian sternly ordered them back.

"Queens and their ladies do not plunge into a strange city unescorted," he told them. "You shall wait here until I procure an escort suitable to your station."

Away he strode, leaving the captain of the *Jhimu* to dispute with an official from the city and the girls to watch the brown-skinned waterfront crowd. Unlike Janareth, the population of Trimandilam was fairly homogenous. The people were smaller than the Novarians and darker, with straight or wavy black hair. Most went barefoot. The main garment for both sexes was a long skirt, which most of the men tucked up between the legs to make a floppy loincloth. Both sexes left the upper body bare in the balmy air. Outside of the poorest classes, all wore masses of jewelry: necklaces of beads and pearls, bracelets, anklets, fillets, earrings, finger rings, nose rings, and toe rings.

An hour later, Jorian was back on a tall, big-boned chestnut-roan stallion, at the head of a score of lancers in spired helmets and jingling mail. After these followed three immense elephants with gaudily painted heads, howdahs on their backs, and their riders clad in drapes bordered with cloth-of-gold.

Jorian vaulted to the ground and bowed low before Mnevis. When the officer of the troop dismounted more slowly, Jorian said:

"May it please Your Majesty, I would fain present to you the gallant Captain Yaushka, veteran of many fierce battles!" He repeated the sentence in Mulvani.

For an instant, the captain and the queen confronted each other, haughty suspicion on one side and regal self-assurance on the other. Regal self-assurance won. The captain dropped to both knees on the granite blocks of the quay and bent down until his forehead touched the pave. Mnevis allowed herself a tiny nod and a small smile.

"Tell the gallant captain," she said to Jorian, "that if his bravery equals his courtesy, the empire has nought to fear."

Grinning, Captain Yaushka rose and signaled the mahouts. These in turn whacked their elephants over the head with their goads. The blows made hollow sounds, like beating a log drum. The three elephants knelt and then lowered their bellies and elbows to the ground. One mahout produced a small ladder, which he placed against the side of the foremost elephant. Captain Yaushka helped the queen up the ladder into the howdah. The eleven ladies-in-waiting gave a few squeals and giggles at the prospect of riding these beasts, but Jorian scowled at them so fiercely that they quickly fell silent.

When each elephant bore four women, the drivers signaled the beasts to rise. The sudden tilting of the howdahs elicited more squeals. Jorian vaulted back on his horse, while a trooper gave Karadur a leg-up for the latter to climb aboard a big white ass. Captain Yaushka blew a trumpet, and the cavalcade started off.

They jingled through endless, narrow, winding streets, where strange smells hung in the air, the elephants' drapes scraped against the house walls as they rounded corners, and people squeezed into doorways and arcades to let them pass. They passed mansions and hovels, temples and shops, inns and emporia, shacks and tenements, taverns and brothels, all jumbled together.

At last they reached the foot of the hill on which stood the royal palace. A wall ran around the base of the hill, and a massive, fortified gate in this wall gave access to the interior. To one side of the gate stood an inclosure in which an elephant mill operated a huge pump. A pair of elephants, one on each end of a long boom pivoted in the center, walked the boom round and round, while bearings squealed and the pump grumbled in its housing.

At the gate, Jorian and his party were scrutinized, questioned, and passed through the gate while the sentries touched their foreheads to the ground in salute to Queen Mnevis. The horses, the ass, and the elephants plodded up a long, sloping avenue, fifty feet wide, which had been hewn out of a cliff that formed that side of the hill. The cliff had been cut down to form an evenly sloping stone ramp and then roughened by transverse grooves, a finger-breadth apart, to provide traction for the feet of men and animals.

As the avenue rose, the solid stone gave way to a built-up structure of well-fitted stone blocks. The road came up to the level of the main inner fortification wall, of rose-red stone, rising from the top of the cliff and on the right as one ascended the slope. Along the outer side of the avenue, where the cliff fell away, a bronzen pipe, green with verdegris and as thick as a man's leg, passing through holes in stone blocks, carried the water pumped by the elephant mill to the palace and also served as a railing.

The procession reached the gate in the fortification wall and was again passed through. Inside, they faced another gate. Whereas the outer gate was a massive, military structure with arrow-slitted towers, portcullis, murder holes, and other accessories for defense, the inner gate was an ornamental edifice of many-colored stone, with a huge central arch flanked by smaller portals. Under the arch, on the left, a raised platform allowed horsemen easy mounting and dismounting. On the right, a higher platform enabled elephant riders to step on and off their mounts without using a ladder.

As the party gathered afoot under the main arch, a small, wizened brown man came up, bowing repeatedly over clasped hands. "Will Your Highness deign to follow your humble slave?" he said. "I am Harichumbra, your unworthy adviser."

They followed Harichumbra through a series of halls and courts, until Jorian was hopelessly lost. Centuries ago,

119

a king of Mulvan had ordered the entire top of the hill planed off to build this palace, as large in itself as a small city. Hall after hall had been added until the entire hilltop inside the upper wall was now cut up into square and rectangular courts, ranging in size from ball courts to parade grounds.

The halls that divided these courts were long, narrow buildings, mostly of three-story height. They were marvels of Mulvanian architecture. In most of the courts, there had been an effort to give the stonework on all four sides an artistic unity. Thus some courts were walled by white and red stone, some by white and black, some by white and blue, some by white and green, and some by other combinations. Everywhere were arches: plain semicircular arches, pointed arches, segmental arches, baskethandle arches, ogee arches, horseshoe arches, and cusped arches in every possible combination. They topped monumental gates and ordinary doors and windows. Little balconies projected here and there from the upper stories of the halls. Broad eaves extended out from the flat roofs to provide the courts with shadowed spaces against the fierce tropical sun. Domes, spires, and gazebos rose from the roofs.

Everywhere the stonework was enriched by carving and by inlays of mother-of-pearl and stones of contrasting colors, making designs of flowers, beasts, heroes, and gods. Sayings attributed to former kings and holy men were carved in bands of stone or inlaid in polished metal and semiprecious stones in the characters of the Mulvani language.

"These are your apartments," said Harichumbra, indicating a hall whose third story was walled by delicately carved marble screens, so that it was open to the breeze but shielded from the vision of those outside. "Her Majesty will occupy the main chamber at the end of this hall; her ladies, these rooms; my lords, this chamber..."

He showed them the amenities of the place. "This hall is called the Tiger Cub, in case you get lost and have difficulty finding your way back to it. When you have rested and refreshed yourselves, I shall return. Shall we say in one hour? Or two? It shall be as you desire. I shall now summon servants to minister to your wants."

He clapped his hands, and a score of women and several

men appeared through the door at the end of the hall. Harichumbra bowed himself out.

Soon, Jorian and Karadur sat facing each other from the ends of a huge tub, while pretty little brown Mulvanian girls soaped their backs. Speaking Novarian, Karadur said:

"All right so far, my son. You managed the escort very featly."

Jorian grunted. "Save that the damned horse had no stirrups, only a pair of handgrips on the front of the saddle. Not having ridden bareback since I was a stripling on Onnus' farm, I nearly fell off twice. They kindly said I might use the beast during my stay, but I must have stirrups added to the saddle. 'Tis a big, strong beast, though. I think I'll call him 'Oser' after my schoolmaster in Ardamai. Those knobby joints and feet like platters remind me of the old boy. He gives a rough ride, but at least he's willing. Tell me: why don't Mulvanians use stirrups? They've been known in the Twelve Cities for centuries."

"Mulvanians pride themselves on preserving the ancient ways and ignoring the devices dreamt up by barbarians. Did you note that elephant mill outside the palace?"

"I surely did, and an admirable device I thought it."

"Well, that was installed by King Shaju's grandfather, King Sivroka, and it has been a source of contention ever since. Whenever discontent arises against the reigning monarch, those who seek to take advantage of this condition set up the cry: Destroy this unholy foreign contraption, which robs honest water-carriers of their livelihood! When the mill wears out, I do not think it will be repaired or rebuilt."

"And then the Mulvanians wonder why their history is a catalogue of invasions and conquests by loot-hungry barbarians," growled Jorian. "When I was king of Xylar, I tried to keep up with new things."

"And what good did that do you, my son?" asked Karadur gently. Jorian snorted. Karadur continued: "I advise you to get rid of that beard."

"By Zevatas, I've come to like the thing!"

"But in Mulvan it is the badge of either a holy ascetic, an ancient in retirement, or a low-class worker, and you do not wish to pass for any of those."

* * *

Two hours later, the adviser returned. Bathed, shaved, and smelling sweetly of ointments and perfumes, Jorian listened as Harichumbra said:

"Now, my lord, my first task is to instruct you in the rules governing intercourse at the court of the King of Kings. To what class did you belong in your native land?"

"The lesser nobility. So?"

"The manner in which you greet and converse with others depends upon your own rank and that of your interlocutor. In other words, you must use one form of greeting to an equal, another to an inferior, and so on. The same applies to speech. Court Mulvani has eight grades of politeness, depending upon the relative status of the persons speaking. One must master them lest one give unwitting offense—or at least expose onself as an ignorant boor, unworthy of one's own class.

"This applies particularly to your noble self, because their ladyships appear to speak none of our tongue. You must, therefore, interpret for them, using the forms of speech that they would use in addressing Mulvanians of various classes, from the King of Kings down to the lowly classless ones who clean out latrines.

"As one of the lesser nobility of your own country, you will rank below our own nobility but above the official class. You are, of course, aware of the importance of class distinctions in this well-ordered land. Bodily contact between persons of widely separated classes is permitted only in line of duty, as when a barber cuts a nobleman's hair. Otherwise, he of the higher class is religiously polluted and must seek ritual purification. Fraternization is likewise limited, and intermarriage is to us utterly abhorrent.

"Now, let me begin your instructions. First of all, when you approach the Great King—may he reign forever!—the disparity in your ranks requires that you advance no nearer than nine paces from him, and that you touch your forehead to the ground thrice. By the way, that hat you wore upon your arrival would be unsuitable, because of the brim."

"Then I will go bareheaded. This clime is too warm for hats, anyway."

"Oh, sir!" Harichumbra looked shocked. "That were indeed an unseemly act! Respect for the king requires that men remain covered in his presence. Suppose I get you a turban."

"I know not how to wind those cursed things, and I should find them too hot. Is there no small, brimless cap I might wear?"

Harichumbra pondered. "Ah, I have it! I will get you a cap such as members of the Dancing Saints, an ecstatic religious sect, wear. It should meet your requirements.

"And now the grammar. In addressing His Majesty, you will naturally use the politest form. Sentences whereof His Majesty is the subject or the object are put in the third person singular subjunctive...

"In approaching a member of the king's immediate family, or a member of the priesthood in his official capacity, you must halt six paces from the person and touch your forehead to the ground once. In addressing such persons, the third person singular indicative is used with the suffix *ye*.

"In approaching a member of the Mulvanian nobility, you must halt three paces from the person and bow so that your body is parallel to the ground. In addressing such persons, the third person singular indicative is used without the honorific suffix. The nobleman should return your bow, but only by inclining his body at half a right angle to the ground..."

Before taking his leave, Harichumbra informed Jorian that Queen Mnevis would be presented to the king in a public audience the second day after their arrival, that a private audience with the king and his advisers was being set up for the day after that, and that on the tenth day they were all bidden to a court ball.

"Barbarians," said Harichumbra, "sometimes expect to be bidden to feasts, not knowing that amongst us Chosen of the Gods, eating is deemed an unseemly act, to be performed in private or, at most, with one's immediate family. We do, however, have balls—albeit our dancing is much more decorous and decent than in some lands. This ball celebrates the seven hundred and fiftieth anniversary of the Serpent Princess."

"Will the princess attend?"

"I believe she will; it is the only occasion during the year that she leaves her apartment. By the bye, are you an addict of fermented liquors?"

Jorian stared. "I like wine and my ale, but I should hardly term myself an addict. I can do without them if need be. Why?"

"Barbarians oft have a passion for these fluids, which are forbidden to Mulvanians—save the classless, to whom they are allowed to brighten the otherwise cheerless lives they lead as punishment for some sin in an earlier incarnation. If you require these poisons—" (Harichumbra gave a delicate shudder) "—and will write a petition to the effect that you are addicted to them and if deprived of them are liable to go mad and become a danger to the community, I can arrange a regular ration for you."

"I will think about it," said Jorian. After Harichumbra had gone, he asked Karadur: "What sort of man is this King Shaju, as a man and not as a king?"

"Your question, my son, means little, for in Mulvan the role of king is so exacting that the man, as a distinct entity, has little chance of emerging. From morn to night he is busied, if not with state business and the hearing of petitions, then with religious ceremonies. For he is supposed to please both the millions of Mulvanians beneath his sway and, at the same time, the hundreds of gods in the heavens above—a task to daunt the hardiest."

"How is he with his intimates, then?"

"He has no intimates—no friends, as you would use the term. The formality of courtly usage rules every aspect of his life and excludes him from true intimacy. When he summons one of his wives to his bed, she must perform the same prostrations on approaching him that the rest of us do in his throne room. Perhaps, after he has sown the royal seed and ere he goes to sleep, he engages in some small informal talk with the woman—but who would know about that?"

"We managed things better in Xylar; the king was allowed to be halfway human. What sort of man, then, would Shaju be if he weren't king?"

Karadur shrugged. "Who can tell? For the office molds the man as much as the man molds the office—and more so, if the office be so overwhelming as that of Great King. But from what I have seen of King Shaju, I suspect he would be a well-meaning and not unable mediocrity—the kind who, were he your neighbor, you might describe as 'a good fellow but dull.' Of course, he can be cruel and violent as circumstances require, and he showed no qualms about killing off a score of brothers upon his accession. Had he not, one of them would probably have slain him, so he would not be here for us to criticize. But that is kingship for you."

The public audience proved an interesting example of Mulvanian courtly techniques. Every word and gesture had been prescribed by Harichumbra and rehearsed by Jorian and his women. The replies and gestures of the Great King were just as artificial.

Shaju sat on a golden throne at the end of a long hall, whose air was blue with the smoke of incense burners. Behind a screen, musicians twanged and tootled.

Suppressing an urge to cough on the fragrant smoke, Jorian and his girls followed the usher down the hall. At the prescribed distance, Jorian and the eleven ladies-in-waiting prostrated themselves, while queen Mnevis, as a fellow sovran, merely bowed low. While they were in this position, a grinding noise made itself heard. When Jorian looked up from his crouch, the throne bearing King Shaju had risen on a pillar to a fathom above its normal height. With a grinding of gearwheels, the throne sank back to its former level.

This throne was an amazing structure. The back had the form of a gigantic butterfly, as high as a man. The wings of the insect, made of a kind of gold mesh, blazed with jewels, which formed a pattern like that of a real butterfly.

King Shaju was taller than most Mulvanians, albeit shorter by nearly a head than Jorian. He was middle-aged and a little overweight, with a shaven chin and a long, black, drooping mustache. Cosmetics failed to hide a sad, weary expression. In a high-pitched, expressionless voice he said:

"The Great King graciously condescends to receive the homage of the charming queen of Algarth. It pleases the King of Kings to see that other monarchs of the world acknowledge his primacy. My Majesty accepts the gift of Your Majesty with thanks and would have Your Majesty know that you shall not suffer for your generosity." The king turned over the gift—the best of the golden cups from the treasure room of Rennum Kezymar—and said: "This looks like Mulvanian work." He glanced inquiringly at Jorian, who responded:

"May it please Your Majesty, it probably is. Trade has carried the peerless products of Mulvanian handicrafts far and wide, even to distant Algarth."

"I see. Well, for the discussion of matters of state, the Great King will entertain the charming queen in the room of private audience at a time to be fixed by our servants. May the gods of Mulvan and those of Algarth smile upon the gracious queen!"

"Now we back out!" hissed Harichumbra.

The private audience proved more interesting. Besides the ubiquitous guards, there were only five persons: King Shaju, his minister Ishvarnam, Queen Mnevis, Jorian, and Harichumbra. Ishvarnam opened by asking:

"Lord Jorian, one has heard rumors of a king of your name, in one of the more distant Novarian cities. It is called Zy—nay, Xylar. Is your lordship perchance connected with this monarch, who one hears has died, or been slain, or fled the kingdom, or some such thing? The tales contradict one another, and we have no secure source of news from there."

Heart pounding, Jorian answered evenly: "One suspects we are distant cousins, Excellency. One was born in Kortoli City, whereas one believes this other Jorian came from the village of Ardamai, several leagues distant from the capital. One's own forebears moved from Ardamai to Kortoli two generations ago; but there might be a connection, could one take time to trace it down."

"One thanks your lordship for your information," said Ishvarnam. "Now let us to business..."

Translating Mnevis' speech, Jorian made his plea for a vast armed force to recapture the Algarth Archipelago from the freebooters. In actual fact, the pirates had been there since they first appeared in Novarian history. The Twelve Cities knew nothing of any line of legitimate sovrans in those isles. As Jorian expected, however, the Mulvanians had never even heard of Algarth and so were in no position to contradict him.

When he had finished, Ishvarnam and the king exchanged whispers. Then the minister spoke:

"My dear Lord Jorian, much as His Majesty would be

delighted to restore Her charming Majesty to her rightful throne, what she proposes is beyond the powers of even such a world-bestriding realm as Mulvan. What with the pirates of the Inner Sea, and raids by the desert riders of Fedirun, and incursions by the savages of the equatorial jungles of Beraoti, we have all we can do to maintain order in our own realm. One fears Her Majesty asks the impossible."

Jorian and Mnevis put on suitably downcast expressions. Ishvarnam said: "The Great King will, however, see to it that Her Majesty go not hence empty-handed. He will, moreover, provide her with an escort back to Janareth suitable to her rank. Thence she can proceed to places where conditions are more favorable for finding succor. For example, we hear that in the Twelve Cities are many turbulent rogues, always eager for such adventure."

"How shall they reach Vindium, now that shipping on the Inner Sea has closed down for the winter?" asked Jorian.

"The escort will convey Her Majesty and her attendants to Vindium by the land route."

"One has heard—no doubt from some misinformed source—that this route is perilous."

"The escort will be large enough to master such contingencies as arise."

"One sees. It would, in one's humble opinion, be wise for them to set out forthwith, to get through the Lograms before full winter sets in."

"We can speed them on their way tomorrow, if that be Her charming Majesty's wish," said Ishvarnam.

"That will be excellent. One would like, however, to beg His Majesty's indulgence to the extent of allowing one to linger in Trimandilam for a few days after Her Majesty's departure. One would like to see more of His Majesty's world-famous city and to attend the ball to which he was so gracious as to invite one. Since ladies of noble birth and tender upbringing cannot be expected to travel swiftly, one should easily overtake them."

More whispers; then Ishvarnam said: "His Majesty graciously grants the plea of the noble Lord Jorian, in the hope that, by observing the customs and usages of a truly civilized realm, he will be moved to adopt these habits as his own and to spread Mulvanian enlightenment among the backward peoples who dwell beyond our marches. You have His Majesty's gracious leave to withdraw."

The girls left two days later in horse litters, guarded by gleaming cavalry commanded by Captain Yaushka, who had escorted them to the palace upon their arrival. Jorian had lectured Mnevis on the dangers she faced:

"I don't mistrust King Shaju or Captain Yaushka—at least not in this matter. The danger will come when you cross into Vindium. You won't be able to carry on this imposture of being a queen, but you mustn't drop it so suddenly that Yaushka hears about it and carries the word back to Trimandilam. You will have to hire men to tend your gear, guide your animals, and guard your precious persons whilst on your way to your homes. Unless you are both shrewd and lucky, your servants may turn on you, rape you, cut your throats, and make off with your money. Ere you hire anybody, get references to previous employers and follow them through.

"In case a former owner tries to seize you, I've made out documents of manumission for all twelve of you. Some might question whether I was ever your rightful owner, but short of going to Rennum Kezymar to query the people there, there is no way to disprove these documents. If you are serious about a career on the stage, look up my friend Merlois son of Gaus, in Govannian. He taught me such of the actor's tricks as I know.

"Here is the gift from King Shaju to Her charming Majesty, and something over from my own purse. Divide it into twelve equal parts, one for each girl, and give each girl her document. Don't let any of them show their new wealth around, lest its glitter draw evildoers."

"We should be much safer with you," said Mnevis.

"No doubt, and I should be much easier in my mind about you too. But that's impossible, so you must do the best you can and trust to the gods. Now, curse it, Mnevis, don't cry! I have told you why I cannot take wife, concubine, or bondmaid with me."

"B-but l-last night—"

"Na, na, never mind last night. Fun be fun, but a have deadly business before me. Get tha going, lass!"

When the weeping girl had left, Karadur said, "Last night, my son? Methought you had set your feet firmly on the path of virtue."

Jorian sighed and shrugged. "I held out as long as I could; but what is a healthy man of my age to do when a pretty creature like that crawls unasked into bed with him? I may not be the worst man in the world, but I am no saint—dancing or otherwise."

As the time of the ball approached, Jorian and Karadur plotted ways to gain access to the apartment of the Serpent Princess. They had made discreet inquiries here and there, some from Harichumbra, some from other members of the court.

They learnt that the Serpent Princess, Yargali, dwelt in an apartment directly over the ballroom, in a hall called the Green Serpent. Having been an adjunct of the court for many centuries, she stayed in this apartment year in and year out, save on a few special occasions like the forthcoming birthday party. Her function was to guard the Kist of Avlen, which had been brought to Trimandilam from Vindium by the wizard-king Avlen the Fourth, at the time of the Shvenic invasion. The invaders from the northern steppes had overthrown the Three Kingdoms of Old Novaria and brought about the dark age that preceded the rise of the Twelve Cities.

Fleeing these invaders, King Avlen had brought with him a chest of his most precious magical manuscripts, with which he sought to bargain with Ghish the Great of Mulvan for help in recovering his kingdom. Ghish, a nomad from the deserts of Fedirun, had just united by conquest the successor states that had grown up on the ruins of the former kingdom of Tirao. With barbarian practicality, Ghish had strangled Avlen with his own hands and put the Kist under guard, to preserve it for his own use in time of need. None was allowed to read the contents save the chief wizard of Mulvan. A few centuries later, when Yargali arrived at the court of Trimandilam, King Venu had entrusted to her the task of guarding the Kist.

It was said that various noble Mulvanians, from the king on down, visited Yargali late at night, allegedly to seek supernatural wisdom from her lips, although rumor credited her with giving them more tangible favors. There were no recent accounts of her turning into a serpent and devouring her visitors, as tales current in the Twelve Cities credited her with doing.

So Jorian and Karadur plotted and planned but without result. Jorian hurled his embroidered Dancing Saint's cap to the floor with a yell of frustration, saying:

"The curse of Zevatas and Franda and Heryx and all the other deities of the Twelve Cities upon you and your fellow he-witches! I'm minded to walk out and strike for Vindium despite all the aches and pains and nightmares you can send upon me. If your damned princess doesn't turn into a snake and swallow me, Shaju's guardsmen will fill me with arrows until I look like a hedgehog. I should be more usefully employed shepherding those poor girls back to their homes. Why can't you silly Progressives compose your own spells instead of copying those of some ancient wizard—whose magic was evidently not strong enough to keep the barbarians out of his kingdom?"

"Peace, my son, peace. Well you know that you cannot abandon your quest, save at the cost of your life. I would have helped you to escape from Xylar without exacting a price, but my fellow Altruists insisted. Know that at the time of the conquest of Old Novaria, much ancient magical knowledge was lost, and we hope to recover some of it. Perchance some of Avlen's spells have been rediscovered in the centuries since the fall of Old Vindium; but we shall never know until we compare the original documents with those of later times." He sighed. "But things are as they are. Perhaps something will turn up during this ball."

"Will you attend the ball?"

"I had not thought so. I am reading old manuscripts in the royal library and had hoped to spend the evening so occupied."

"But *could* you attend the ball?"

"Surely; as a member of the priestly class I can go anywhere. I outrank every layman in Mulvan, save the king himself."

"Then come to this party. I may want you to distract the king's attention whilst I make friends with the princess."

VI

THE
SERPENT PRINCESS

WEARING A FINE NEW RED SATIN COAT WITH JEWELED buttons, Jorian followed Harichumbra through the maze of courts and halls to the Hall of the Green Serpent. Karadur tottered along behind. As a nobleman and a traveler, Jorian was allowed to wear his sword in Trimandilam, but he had to check it at the entrance to the ballroom. The Mulvanians did not use peace wires. Jorian caught a glimpse of Randir standing in the corner of the cloakroom, the only straight blade in a host of scimitars. The brand was further conspicuous by its plain guard of silvered brass amid the jeweled hilts of the Mulvanians.

The ballroom occupied most of the ground floor of the Hall of the Green Serpent. It had a polished floor of brown marble and long windows, filled with little leaded panes of many shapes, which opened on a terrace. Most of the windows were open to the mild evening air, admitting hosts of insects, which whirled in suicidal circles around the flames of the many lamps and candles. A couple of low-class Mulvanians were kept busy with broom and dustpan, sweeping up little charred corpses from the marble.

The terrace overlooked a large court in the form of a sunken garden, where hedges and bushes loomed dark in the fading twilight and fountains tinkled. On the side of the hall away from the balcony, a huge carpet had been rolled up.

Several score of the nobility of Mulvan and their women were already standing about the ballroom, talking, drinking fruit juice, and nibbling sweetmeats from a long table to one side. The men were gorgeous in silks and satins, plumes and jewels. Lords from the east and south favored skirts, while those from the west and north encased their legs in baggy pantaloons, gathered in at the ankle. Their ladies stood among them, their bangles clashing musically when they moved. The younger ones had flowers, stars, eyes, and other figures painted on their bare breasts.

Harichumbra introduced Jorian to various lords, to whom he bowed deeply until he was dizzy. He sipped fruit juice, wished for something more sustaining, and exchanged words with a young Mulvanian as large as himself. This man, Lord Chavero of Kolkai, wore pantaloons of a brilliant saffron yellow and a spray of peacock plumes in his turban. Jorian said:

"The weather is delightful this time of year in Trimandilam, I find, my lord."

Chavero yawned. "It will do, though you foreigners always complain of the heat in summer. Are you from Novaria or some barbarous place?"

"That is right, although we do not deem it so barbarous as all that."

"Perhaps not, but how would you know, without having visited Mulvan to form a standard of comparison?"

"A good question, but I might ask you the same."

The man pulled a long mustachio. "It stands to reason that, since Mulvan is the center and fount of civilization, all other places must be inferior to it in culture. But you, as a barbarian, cannot be expected to understand logic."

Jorian fought down a temptation to answer back in kind, but temptation won. "It is interesting to hear you speak thus, my lord. For we have a saying in Kortoli, that the most ignorant man is he who thinks he knows it all."

Chavero puzzled over this statement for an instant.

Then his look of perplexity changed to anger as he replied, "And we have a saying, my good man, that the yapping dog must not mind if it get itself kicked. Let us hope it will not be necessary to—"

A trumpet sang, cutting short this speech. A eunuch smote the pave with his staff and cried: "The Great King!"

Shaju, blazing with jewels, stood in the doorway. All the Mulvanians, and Jorian, too, dropped to their knees and touched their foreheads to the ground three times. The king called out:

"Rise, my friends! For the remainder of this even, consider your obeisances to My Majesty as made."

Behind him, Karadur whispered: "That means we can speak to him without prostrating ourselves first." The wizard pulled at Jorian's sleeve. "Come away from that Kolkaian, quickly, ere he embroil you in a quarrel! He is a dangerous man. He would fain be Yargali's next lover, and if he knew of our intentions..."

"Some have thought me a dangerous man, too," muttered Jorian, but he let Karadur lead him off through the crowd. He asked Karadur: "Do His Majesty's wives attend such functions?"

"They used to, but since the distressing affair of the Lady Radmini and Lord Valshaka, he has shut them up, the way they did before the time of King Sivroka. The queens are watching the show now from behind that screened balcony." Karadur nodded his turban towards a marble screen high up at one end of the hall. "And doubtless wishing they could descend to mingle with the rest of us. When—"

Another trumpet interrupted. From the end of the hall opposite to that by which the king had entered, a eunuch struck the marble and called out, "Her Supernatural Highness, the Serpent Princess Yargali!"

Everybody bowed low. In the door stood a woman as tall as Jorian himself—well over six feet—and weighing, as far as he could judge, a good deal more. Her skin, exposed by Mulvanian fashions to just above her delta, was almost black, like that of a Mulvanian peasant. Huge jewels gleamed in her tiara and earrings; a triple rope of pearls ranging up to the size of crabapples hung down between her enormous breasts.

Jorian had never seen so voluptuous a figure; he could

hardly believe his eyes. Those breasts were the most astonishing of his experience. Larger than melons—in fact, as big and round as the udder of a milch cow—they stood out from her massive body without any sag at all. Below them, the body curved in to a waist which, while normal for a small woman, looked impossibly slender on this creature. Then the body widened out to broad, heavy hips and a slightly bulging belly. A cloth-of-gold embroidered skirt hung from her hips, just above groin level, to her ankles, and more gems blazed on the buckles of her slippers. The face beneath the tiara was round and plump, like that of Jorian's Estrildis, but not fat; in fact, if one could ignore her size and tear one's eyes away from her extraordinary bodily development, she was a remarkably beautiful woman.

"By Imbal's iron yard!" breathed Jorian. "With a basin-bone like that, she could bear giants and heroes—"

"Hush!" said Karadur. "The dancing is about to begin. Will you take part?"

"The ladies all seem to be paired off already, so I don't know how to obtain a partner. Anyway, I am not sure I know the steps well enough, for all of Harichumbra's coaching."

The orchestra struck up, and the couples lined up for the grand march. The king and the Serpent Princess led the march, the king holding one arm out so that the tips of his fingers just touched those of the princess. Mulvanian dancing frowned upon any bodily contact other than fingertips. Jorian remained by the fruit-juice table with a few other non-dancers. Karadur said:

"I will present you to Lord Hirayaxa. He has brought both his wives, and I am sure he will let you dance with one—"

"No, no, never mind," said Jorian with a sudden rush of shyness. "I had rather just watch."

The grand march ended, and a eunuch cried: "Take position for the *nriga*!"

The male dancers lined up on one side of the ballroom, the female on the other. The musicians played; the eunuch called the figures. Everybody advanced three steps. The men and the women bowed to each other. They stepped back two steps and bowed. They advanced three steps and bowed. They formed squares and everybody bowed to everybody...

It went on for half an hour at the same slow, stately pace, stepping this way and that and bowing to the eunuch's commands. Compared to the hearty Novarian dances, Jorian found it a tedious performance.

As the music ended and the dance broke up in a frenzy of bows, a startling figure stepped in through one of the long windows opening on the balcony. This was a thin, dark-skinned man, completely naked, with his scrawny body covered with ash. His matted hair streamed down his back, his dirty beard cascaded down his breast, and his white eyeballs rolled wildly. He burst into a tirade in a dialect that Jorian could only half follow.

To Jorian's surprise, nobody moved to suppress or remove the man. Everyone, from the king down, seemed to listen respectfully to the outburst. The naked man raved, foamed at the mouth, and shook his fists. He castigated them all as vile sinners for departing from the ways of their ancestors. He denounced the heathen custom of dancing. He anathematized the elephant mill and demanded that it be broken up. He commanded that all women, and not just those of the king, be shut up in their houses as they were in the days before the wicked innovations of King Sivroka of cursed memory. He called down the wrath of the true gods upon this congregation of sensual sinners. Then he disappeared into the night.

Jorian turned to Harichumbra, who had just bustled up, and asked, "Explain to me, pray, Master Harichumbra, how the king can allow such an affront to his royal dignity?"

"Oh, that is a holy man. He may do as he likes. But come, my lord. The Princess Yargali has expressed the wish to meet you."

Jorian caught Karadur's eye and made a slight but significant jerk of his head. He found the super-voluptuous supernatural being standing beside the fruit-juice table, with the king beside her.

"Your Majesty!" said Jorian, bowing low. "Your radiant Highness! This is indeed a pleasure."

"It iss my pleasure, also," said Yargali, speaking Mulvani with an accent that centuries of dwelling in Trimandilam had not effected. "You are a Novarian, no?"

Karadur materialized like one of his spirits and engaged the king in a low-voiced discussion of the state of organized magic in the empire, while Jorian answered the princess: "Aye, Highness. A subject of the king of Kortoli, to be exact."

"Know you any of those lively Novarian dances? I find the Mulvanian kind all too stately for an active person like myself."

"Permit one to think. One used to be pretty good at our local peasant dance, the *volka*."

"Oh, I know that one! That iss the one that goes *one*—two—*three*—four—*five*—six—*turn*, *one*—two—*three*—four—*five*—six—*turn*, no?"

"Like this?" said Jorian, walking the fingers of his right hand across the palm of his left.

"But yess! In the reign of King Sirvasha, there was an ambassador from Kortoli here, who showed me. Will you ask me to dance the volka with you, my lord Jorian?"

"One wonders if our musicians know any suitable tune?"

"Oh, we can dance it to any tune that iss loud and fast, with a strong one-two beat, no? Come, let us speak to them about it."

Yargali started off across the marble floor towards the orchestra. Jorian followed, feebly protesting: "But, Your Highness! One is sure the king's other guests will not know—"

"Oh, to the next incarnation with them! Thiss will be for just you and me. We will show them barbarians are better dancers than they! We will make them look like the bumps of the logs, no?"

Soon Jorian found himself alone on the dance floor with the princess, the other guests having drawn to the sides. Each placed his hands on the other's shoulders, and off they went in the vigorous, stamping, and whirling steps of the volka. On and on they went, round and round. Having noted that Mulvanian musical compositions were apt to run on for half-hours or even for hours, Jorian feared that he would be compelled to dance until morning.

After a mere quarter-hour, however, the orchestra stopped. Both Jorian and his partner were breathing hard and sweating freely. The noble lords and ladies snapped their fingers by way of applause, while the pair bowed in all directions and Lord Chavero scowled and pulled his long mustache.

"One suggests," said Jorian, "that we could use a bit of that fruit punch."

"An excellent idea, my lord. And you need not use those stilted, ultra-polite forms of speech with me. It iss all very well for these Mulvanians; but my people, who were wise when your forebears were sitting on a bough and scratching, do not bother with such useless refinements. Life iss complicated enough without going out of one's way to make it more so, no?"

A team of sixteen professional dancing girls, wearing a multitude of beads and bangles and nothing else, had come out on the floor and were performing a dance with little, shuffling steps and rhythmic jerkings of their arms and heads. Jorian said:

"How would Your Highness like to step out on the terrace to cool off?"

"By all means."

When they were outside under the stars, Jorian said: "The holy man's outburst does not seem to have discouraged the festivities."

"Oh, these Mulvanians! Always they are talking about their moral purity. No wine, no meat, no fornication, and so on. But when one comes to know them, they are just as sinful in their own little ways as everybody else. Now they will go home feeling very virtuous because they let the holy man harangue them without taking offense, and they will go right on doing the things they always do."

"We had a Mulvanian saint like that in Kortoli once," said Jorian. "He all but ruined the kingdom before they got rid of him."

"Tell me about thiss holy man!"

"Gladly. This took place back in the reign of King Filoman the Well-Meaning—the father of the more famous King Fusinian.

"King Filoman had without doubt the noblest emotions and the best intentions of any king who ever reigned in Novaria. Nor was he stupid; but alas! he had no common sense whatever. One version of the legend says that this was the result of a peculiar planetary conjunction at the time of his birth. Another says that, when the fairies gathered for his naming ceremony, the fairy who was supposed to confer common sense upon him became enraged when she saw that another fairy wore a gown just like her own and left in a huff without bestowing her gift. So Filoman grew up with all the virtues—courage, honesty, diligence, kindliness, and so forth—except common sense.

"It was after the bankruptcy of the kingdom, as a result of the pension scheme of the ghost that Filoman had retained as his minister, that this holy man, Ajimbalin, came to Kortoli. Filoman's new minister, Oinax, had just been promoted from a mere clerk in the Treasury and was too much in awe of the king to tell him aught that Filoman did not wish to hear. So Ajimbalin was soon ensconced in the palace, pouring advice into Filoman's ears.

"Filoman lent these ears willingly enough, for he felt guilty about the collapse of the pension scheme and the hardships that ensued, and even more guilty about his failure to make all the Kortolians as pure and upright and virtuous as himself. 'It is no wonder,' said Ajimbalin, 'when you and your entire people engage in so many vile, sinful habits.'

"'I thought I lived a reasonably virtuous life,' said Filoman. 'But, holy Father, perhaps you can persuade me to the contrary.'

"'To achieve salvation for yourself and your folk,' said the ascetic, 'you must follow the path to moral perfection on which I shall guide you. By setting an example, we may hope to persuade all your subjects to do likewise; and if example and precept avail not, then stronger measures may be needed. First you must give up fermented beverages, your—ugh!—wine and—ugh!—beer.'

"'If you mean drinking to excess,' said Filoman, 'I do not believe I am guilty of that. I have never been drunk in my life.'

"'Nay,' quoth Ajimbalin, 'I mean you must give them up entirely.' So he presently had the court on a regimen of fruit juice, like the punch we have been drinking. Can I get you another?"

"No; please go on with your story."

"Ajimbalin then wished to extend this prohibition to all Kortolians, but Oinax stood up to him and averred that the kingdom needed the tax revenue after its recent disasters. So the general prohibition of wine and beer was put off for the time being.

"Then Ajimbalin told the king: 'You must give up this revolting custom of eating the flesh of slain animals. It shows a lack of proper respect for life. How know you if the cow or pig your servants butcher for your table be not an incarnation of one of your own ancestors?' So the king and the court went on a diet of breadstuffs and green, like that to which I have been subjected during my stay here.

"Then the holy man said: 'Next, my son, you must give up the vile, sensual pleasure of going in unto your wife. Since desire is the source of all sorrow, you can attain happiness and escape sorrow only by extinguishing desire and relinquishing all bonds to earthly things and persons.'

"'But I am chiefly concerned, not with my own happiness, but with my subjects' welfare!' protested Filoman.

"'All the better,' said Ajimbalin. 'By following my rules of life, you will not only achieve a state of indescribable bliss yourself, but also attain such strength and wisdom that you will easily solve your kingdom's problems. You will be able to push over a city wall or pick up an elephant. You will know the secrets of the forty-nine Mulvanian heavens of the gods and of the forty-nine hells of the demons. You will no longer need an army, for you will be able to rout any foe singlehanded. But you cannot have these things and the mingling of your vile flesh with that of a woman, too.'

"'But,' said Filoman, 'if all my subjects gave up conjugal relations, there would soon be no people in Kortoli at all.'

"'All the better,' said the sage. 'If people ceased to be born on this plane, then all the souls would perforce be promoted to the next one, instead of being sent back again and again to this vale of suffering and sorrow. So you and the queen, to set an example, must henceforth live like brother and sister.'

"Filoman gave in. The queen, however, did not take kindly to this scheme. Within the year she had eloped with a sea captain from Salimor, who became a notorious pirate. She left behind her young son, who grew up to be the famous King Fusinian.

"Next, Ajimbalin made Filoman relinquish his fine raiment and wear a piece of sacking pinned about his body, as Ajimbalin himself was wont to do. He made him sleep on the ground in the palace courtyard and spend all his waking hours memorizing Ajimbalin's moral precepts. Filoman's idea of wild revelry had been to sit up till midnight over a flagon of ale and a game of draughts with some crony; but even these simple pleasures were denied him.

"Strangely enough, this regiment did not produce in King Filoman the state of perfect bliss that Ajimbalin had promised. It only made him unhappier than ever. He missed his wife—for all that she had nagged him—and he missed his son, who had been sent off to the court of the Grand Duke of Othomae to serve as a page. He missed his cronies and he missed the hunting and fishing and dancing and the good food and drink he used to enjoy. Instead of the promised strength and wisdom, he found himself enfeebled in body and bewildered in mind. Weeping, he told Ajimbalin that he must be a hopeless sinner, because the life of perfect virtue had not made him happy but the reverse.

"'Then, my son,' said the holy man, 'I see that you are now ready for the final and most drastic step. First you shall make out a document of abdication, naming me king in your room.'

"This startled Filoman, and he argued. But Ajimbalin soon talked him round, for the holy man had so gotten Filoman under his thumb that the king no longer had will of his own. So Filoman wrote out the document.

"'Now,' said Ajimbalin, 'you shall utter a prayer to the true god of Mulvan and slay yourself. Only thus can you promote the welfare of your people and end your own sorrow, for you lack the mettle to impose upon Kortoli the reforms required for its salvation. The gods have therefore chosen me as their humble instrument to effect these improvements. Here is a dagger from your armory; one quick thrust and it is done.'

"Filoman took the dagger, looked dubiously at it, and tried its point on his thumb. Then he pricked his breast a little, said 'Ouch!', and cast the blade from him, for he could not quite summon the courage to thrust it home. Nor could he nerve himself to drink the poison that Ajimbalin thoughtfully proffered him. He broke down into sobs and tears; and indeed he was a pitiful sight, gaunt from starvation, in rags, and covered with sores and dirt from the ascetic life he had led under Ajimbalin's spiritual guidance.

" 'I will get Oinax to do the deed,' he said. So the minister was summoned, and a sword that King Filoman had worn in former days was fetched from the armory.

"Filoman explained the plan to Oinax, who fell on his knees and begged the king to reconsider. But Filoman, to whom death now seemed a welcome relief from his misery, was firm.

" 'I shall kneel here,' he said, 'and when I say, "Strike!", you shall cut off my head. It will be your last act as my loyal subject, and I do but ask that you make the stroke swift and sure. Thenceforth, your loyalty shall be transferred to the future king, the holy father Ajimbalin.'

"So King Filoman knelt and bowed his head, and Oinax, trembling with fear and horror, took up the sword. Being a small man, he had to wield it in both hands. He took his stance, made a practice swing, and glanced at Ajimbalin. The holy man was crouched nearby, glaring at the king with a strange gleam in his eyes and spittle running from his mouth. Now whether this was some form of holy ecstasy, or whether it was a simple, worldly lust for the power he now saw nearly within his grasp, was never known. For Oinax pivoted suddenly on his heel and struck with all his might at the neck of Ajimbalin, whose head went bouncing and rolling across the floor like a football.

"Horrified, Filoman tried to wrest the sword from Oinax, but so weak was he from his austerities that the minister easily frustrated him. Then the king burst into a fit of mad weeping. And when he had finished that, he seemed to come to himself.

" 'How fares the kingdom, Master Oinax?' he said. 'It has been months since I heard aught about it.'

" 'In some ways well, in others not so well,' quoth the minister. 'The leopards, from not being hunted, have become so bold that they snatch children from the streets of the villages. We need to raise the tax on luxurious imports from Mulvan, and we need a new dam on the river Phodon. I have done what I could, but there is much that has necessarily awaited Your Majesty's return from his—ah—quest for spiritual perfection. And I urge that Your Majesty recall his son from Othomae, where I hear he has fallen in with a wild young crowd and bids fair to acquire dissolute habits.'

"So they buried Ajimbalin and tried to pretend he had never existed. And Filoman returned to his former way of life, and Kortoli, to its normal state."

"Did your King Filoman ever get his wife back?"

"No. She preferred to be the mistress of a pirate king. She said that Filoman, though nice in his way, bored her, and she wanted excitement for a change."

"Did he learn common sense from his tribulations?"

"Oh, no, nothing could give him that. Luckily for Kortoli, a few years later he fell from his horse during a hunt and broke his neck. Fusinian—who proved a very different sort—succeeded him."

Yargali: "You tell fascinating tales, Lord Jorian. Do you know many more?"

"Many more indeed. But—" Jorian glanced through the long windows to the interior of the ballroom. "—I fear I should be discourteous to our royal host if I kept you out here for the rest of the ball. Perhaps I might call upon you later...?"

Yargali pointed up to the windows of the upper story of the Hall of the Green Serpent, where lamplights showed through the diamond panes. "Yonder iss my abode, and it would pleasure me to receive you there. But I fear it were impossible."

"Why so?"

"How would you gain access? All the doors and windows leading into this hall are locked after the ball, with armed guards posted at the doors."

"Suppose I could fly and appeared before your window after the ball. Should I be admitted?"

"If you came bearing such tales, aye. But I do not see how you can. You have no wings, and the wall iss without carvings to climb by. You would have to walk up the smooth stone like a fly, no?"

"Leave it to me, Highness. Now, perhaps we had bet—"

"One moment, Master Jorian," said a voice, and a hand was laid, none too gently, on Jorian's arm. It was Lord Chavero, the disagreeable Mulvanian. "I have somewhat to discuss with you."

Jorian twisted his arm free. "I believe I am called Lord Jorian by those would entreat me with courtesy."

"That is one of the things I wish to discuss. But this were a poor place. You will excuse us, Princess? Will you be so good as to descend this stair to the garden, Master Jorian?"

They went down the marble steps at the end of the terrace into the sunken garden, which was six cubits below the level of the terrace. Then Lord Chavero faced Jorian. Although there was no moon—this being the end of the Month of the Wolf—enough light escaped from the ballroom to show each plainly to the other.

"Well?" said Jorian.

"*Master* Jorian," began Chavero, "this ball was to have been for members of the true nobility—that is to say, the nobility of Mulvan, not the self-styled 'nobles' of upstart barbarian realms, who to us of the genuine birth are no more than dirt. We were willing to put up with you as long as it was necessary for you to interpret for Queen Mnevis. Now, however, that condition no longer obtains. Since your presence here is offensive to us of superior blood, you are requested to leave the premises forthwith."

"Quite a speech," said Jorian. "But since I was invited by His Majesty himself, and since His Majesty—may he reign forever!—did not withdraw his invitation upon the queen's departure, I have no intention of complying with your wish. What do you propose to do about it?"

"For the last time, dog, get out!"

"Put me out!"

"I will!" Chavero stooped and fumbled behind a shrub. He straightened up with a naked scimitar in his hand. He stalked towards Jorian on the balls of his feet, blade poised for a quick slash.

Having neither sword, nor cloak, nor dagger to defend himself with, Jorian backed away. As Chavero started a quick rush, Jorian dodged around a fountain. For a few minutes they darted back and forth on opposite sides of the fountain, circumambulating it now clockwise and now contra-clockwise. Although a big, powerful man, the Mulvanian was shorter in the legs and bigger in the belly than Jorian, so the latter managed to keep the fountain between him and his foe.

Then he heard a low call from the balcony: "Lord Jorian! Here!"

A glance showed him Yargali leaning over the marble rail, extending his own sword to him. He left the fountain, bounded over to the foot of the terrace, and caught Randir by the hilt as she tossed it to him.

He spun to face the onrushing Chavero. Their blades met in a whirl of steel; they clashed and sang and struck sparks. Jorian easily parried the whirlwind, slashing attack of the Mulvanian until shortness of breath forced the other to slow down. Then he feinted a backhand cut, reversed it, and slashed diagonally down and to the left, so that the tip of his blade sliced through the sash that upheld the saffron pantaloons.

Jorian then leaped back. Chavero began a quick advance; but what Jorian hoped for happened. Deprived of their support, Chavero's trousers fell down, and Chavero fell prone on the greensward, right at Jorian's feet.

Jorian planted his foot on Chavero's sword. "Now, my lord," he said smoothly, "I think I will carve my name on your pretty little bare, brown arse—"

"Swine!" yelled Chavero, letting go his sword and rolling to his feet. He grabbed for the trousers wound about his ankles and, at the same time, tried to leap back out of reach of Jorian's blade. But he missed the garment and fell into the fountain. He emerged from the water, blowing and coughing, and hauled himself out on the side opposite to Jorian.

The latter darted around the fountain and caught up with Chavero as the latter, now trouserless, gained his feet. Jorian brought the flat of his sword with a loud whack against the Mulvanian's buttocks. Screaming curses and yelling for help, Chavero ran around the paths of the garden with Jorian after him, now and then getting in another blow.

Jorian was almost having too much fun to realize that the noise had aroused the attention of others. Light and motion from the terrace caught his eye. Then he heard the voice of the king, raised in anger:

"Stop this at once!"

Jorian and Chavero stood side by side, looking up at the terrace. Thence the king, surrounded by the plumed and bejeweled nobility of the realm, glared down. Chavero kept pulling down the lower front edge of his shirt to preserve his decency. Shaju pointed to Chavero and barked:

"Explain!"

"This—this b-beastly—(*cough*)—barbarian grossly insulted my honor, sire, and then t-tried to m-m-m-..." Chavero's voice trailed away into spasms of coughing and incoherent stammers and squawks. Between his rage and the water he had taken into his lungs, he could not speak intelligibly. A mutter of anger at the barbarous foreigner ran through the nobles.

While Chavero still sputtered, the king pointed to Jorian. "You, then!"

Jorian gave his best bow. "Your Majesty, since anything one said might be interpreted as self-serving, one prays that you ask the Princess Yargali for an account of this unfortunate event. Having witnessed the whole incident, she can give Your Majesty an objective account."

"Well?" said the king, turning to Yargali, who told a truthful tale of what happened. She explained that, when she saw Chavero chasing Jorian with a scimitar, which he had evidently hidden ahead of time in the shrubbery, she realized that she could not explain to the king or his officials what was happening in time to save Jorian's neck. So she had gone straight to the cloakroom and thence fetched Jorian his sword.

The king's lips twitched, and then he burst into a hearty guffaw, throwing his head back and rocking on his heels. For once he seemed almost human. All the nobles laughed even louder, for it went without saying that a joke by royalty was always ten times as funny as the same joke told by someone else. King Shaju said something to Minister Ishvarnam, turned his back and re-entered the ballroom. Ishvarnam leant over the marble balustrade and called out:

"My lord Chavero! His Majesty instructs me to tell you that you have incurred his august displeasure by your unmannerly conduct. You shall return at once to your estates at Kolkai and remain there until further notice. Lord Jorian, you have His Majesty's forgiveness for any breach of courtly etiquette that you may have committed in defending yourself against Lord Chavero, and His Majesty commands you to remain at the ball as long as you wish and to forget tonight's incident."

Chavero cast one last sneer in Jorian's direction. He muttered, "You shall yet rue your insolence, dog!" before stalking away through the darkened garden.

Jorian joined Karadur on the terrace. The latter said in Novarian: "Lucky for you, my son, that you slew not the miscreant. Had you done so, not even Yargali's tale could have saved you from punishment."

"I figured that out whilst he was chasing me round the fountain. So, when a chance offered to make him ridiculous without killing him, I seized what the gods offered. But by Zevatas's brazen beard, was I frightened!"

"My son!" said Karadur in tones of gentle reproof. "If you would play the role of nobleman, you must not go about telling everybody how terrified you were under this or that circumstance. I know you have more courage in one finger than most of these popinjays have in their whole bodies, but you spoil the impression you make by this harping on your own timidity. Desist!"

"'Tis the simple truth, though, and don't you urge men to utter the simple truth?"

"Mayhap, but in this case we must make an exception. I have known men of many kinds, and I believe that noblemen suffer from fright just as much as the rest. The difference is that their sense of honor forbids them to admit their fear."

"But I am no nobleman, only a—"

"Hush! Whilst you play the part, you must follow the customs, however silly they seem. But now we must beware of Lord Chavero's vengeance. The remaining nobles may befriend you, for that Chavero was much disliked for his quarrelsome and overbearing nature. But he may still hire a poisoner to slip into your soup that which is no elixir of life."

"I hope we can be on our way before the morning's light. Have you that magical rope?"

"Aye, in our quarters."

"Well, fetch it here at midnight. Can you gain access to yon garden without passing the sentries who guard the Hall of the Green Serpent?"

"That were easy; the door in the hall opposite is not guarded."

"So be here with that rope. When I have entered Yargali's lair, go quickly to the stables and take out our mounts. Will the city gates still be open?"

"With luck, since this is a holy day."

"Well then, take the beasts outside the city wall and tether them in some safe place."

"Which gate?"

"Let me think—the East."

"Why not the North or the West? We are going back to Vindium, I trust."

"Fool!" exploded Jorian. "That's the first direction they'll look. We're going up the Pennerath to the first ford or bridge, then east towards Komilakh. Then north across the Fangs of Halgir to Shven and west again to the Twelve Cities."

"You mean to travel right around the Inner Sea? A frightful journey! We shall never get to Metouro in time for the meeting."

"With luck, we shall; I've studied the maps. If we are trampled by King Shaju's elephants, we shall never get there at all."

"But Shaju has elephants trained as trackers, as hounds are employed in other lands. Of all beasts, the elephant has the keenest sense of smell."

"Well, we shall have to chance it. When the beasts are secure, gather our gear and meet me at the Inner Gate of the palace."

"Why not outside the city? Prolonged questioning at the gates is to be avoided."

"I know not my way about this damned monster of a city and should get lost without you as a guide."

"Then let us meet outside the outer palace gate, thus avoiding at least two scrutinies. Use the rope to get over the walls."

"Very well. If they stop you, tell 'em we're on a secret mission for Ishvarnam, or whatever you think they'll believe. Now I'm going in to fraternize with the beauty and chivalry of Mulvan."

Inside, Jorian found that Karadur's prediction had been right. Nobles crowded about him, pressed goblets of fruit juice upon him, and told him that for a barbarian he was indeed a man of parts. One said that Jorian had merely done to Chavero what many others at court had long yearned to do themselves.

147

As he sipped fruit punch, Jorian reflected that at a Novarian ball he would probably have drunk himself dizzy in his triumph and so be useless for the desperate adventure ahead. Even Mulvanian asceticism, he concluded, had its uses.

At midnight, the princess Yargali heard a tap on the window panes of her bedroom. She opened the window to see Jorian, hanging by one hand from a vertical rope, about which his legs were locked, while he tapped with the other hand. As she helped him over the sill and led him into the adjoining living room, she asked:

Good my lord, to what iss the upper end of yonder rope affixed, that it upheld you so firmly?"

"It is affixed to the afterworld, Highness. I do not fully understand the matter myself, although a magician could doubtless tell you. What have we here?" He picked up a pitcher and sniffed. "Tell me not that this is real wine, in this desert of austerity!"

"It iss indeed." She whisked the cover off a pair of golden plates, disclosing steaks. "Real flesh, also."

"By all the gods and demons of Mulvan! How do you manage it?"

She shrugged her huge shoulders, making her great globes quiver. "It iss part of the agreement betwixt myself and the Great Kings. I guard their cursed Kist, whilst they provide me with the meat and drink I wish. I should soon waste away on this Mulvanian diet, which may be good for rabbits but not for me. Now sit and devour, ere your provender cool."

Jorian did so. Between ravenous bites he asked: "How came you by this agreement, Princess?"

"Know that my people are an ancient race, who dwell in the far-off jungles of Beraoti. But, albeit longer-lived than your folk, they beget few offspring. And so they have dwindled during the last myriad of years, until there be but a handful left. As a result of a quarrel—into whose nature I will not go—I wass cast out from amongst them. And I arrived, weary and footsore, in Trimandilam in the reign of King Venu, or Venu the Apprehensive as he was called.

"King Venu greeted me hospitably, but after a while he began to worry over the fact that I ate thrice as much as

148

did he and his better-fed subjects and insisted, moreover, upon forbidden flesh. As his sobriquet implies, he wass one of those who are not happy unless they are unhappy over some impending peril, if you understand me, no? He wass a worrier.

"He also worried about the Kist of Avlen, since there had been two attempts to steal it—one by stealth, the other by bribing those who guarded it. The latter attempt would have succeeded had not one of the bribe-takers suffered a rush of conscience and betrayed the plot. For this, he wass promoted to captain whilst the others were trampled by the king's elephants—an eventuality which hiss so-sensitive conscience had doubtless foreseen.

"So King Venu conceived the idea of skewering two worries with one lance, by making me official guardian of the Kist, in return for which he furnished me with this apartment and with food, drink, and servants to enable me to live in comfort. And that agreement has now been in effect more than five hundred years."

"I should think," said Jorian, "that Your Supernatural Highness would find it oppressive to be cooped up in this one suite, day after day."

"I do not mind, for I do not have the traveler's itching foot, as you men so often have. I have seen Trimandilam and need not refresh my view of it. And I like not the way the Mulvanians of the lower classes stare at me as if I were some sort of monster. My servants bring me news of the outer world, and I am content with this place, which I have redecorated every century to my taste. Now sit beside me on this divan and tell me some of the tales you promised." She refilled the goblets. "For ensample, the tale of the disaster that your King Filoman brought upon Kortoli, when he had a ghost for his minister. I have never heard of putting a ghost to such a use."

Jorian quaffed deeply. "This was early in his reign, when he had occasion to appoint a new minister to replace one who had died. He had reigned for several years in a fair state of justice, order, and prosperity, but it grieved him that some Kortolians still lived lives of vice and crime, for all he had done by precept and example to better things. To remedy this state of affairs, he determined to enlist the services of the wisest man in the Twelve Cities.

"By diligent inquiry, he learnt that the man with the

repute of such wisdom was a philosopher from Govannian, named Tsaidar, who was said to be the most learned man in all Novaria.

"But, when Filoman sent a messenger to Govannian, to tender an offer of honorable employment to this Tsaidar, the messenger learnt that the learned doctor had but lately died. When word of this reached King Filoman, he wept with frustration. But his chamberlain said that all hope had not yet fled. There dwelt in the hills of southern Kortoli a witch hight Gloé, who was an able sorceress and a person of good repute, notwithstanding that she had never been able to obtain a licence as lawful wizardess from Filoman's government. Since Tsaidar had but recently died, his spirit might not yet have passed on to its next incarnation, either on this plane or on the next, and therefore could possibly be raised by Gloé to advise the king.

"So Filoman sent to fetch Gloé to Kortoli City, promising immunity for her illicit practice of magic. And Gloé burnt her powders and stirred her cauldron, and shadows gathered without material objects to cast them, and the flames of the candles flickered although there was no breeze to flutter them, and hideous faces, dissolving into one another, appeared in the smoke, and the palace trembled, and the king was seized with freezing cold. And there in the pentacle stood the ghost of Tsaidar the philosopher.

"'Why disturb you me?' said the ghost in the thin, squeaky voice that ghosts have. 'I was studying a treatise on logic amongst the neglected old manscripts in the library of the Grand Bastard of Othomae and had just come upon a new statement of the law of the excluded middle, when you snatched me hither.'

"Well, Gloé explained King Filoman's purpose. The ghost said: 'Minister, eh? Well, now, that is different. All my life I sought to find a ruler who would accept my advice and run his realm by logic, but I never found one. I gladly accept your offer, sire. What is the first problem I can solve for you?'

"'I would fain put an end to crime and vice amongst the Kortolians,' said the king, and went on to describe conditions in the kingdom and the failure of his previous efforts.

"'Well now, ahem ahem, I have a theory about crime,'

150

quoth the ghost. 'It is obvious to me that criminals are compelled to commit their felonies by want. Men steal to avert starvation. Men rape because they are too poor to afford lawful wives, or even the modest fees of harlots. Remove the cause—namely, the want—and you instantly end the crimes. I wonder that nobody else has thought for so simple a solution.'

"'But how shall I alleviate their want?' asked the King.

"'Simple again; give every convicted criminal a modest but adequate pension and turn him loose. That is logical, now is it not?'

"The king could see no flaw in Tsaidar's reasoning and so permitted Gloé to dismiss him. And he ordered that criminals, instead of being punished, should be given pensions. And so it was done.

"This pension scheme, however, had unexpected results. True, a few of the pensioners reformed, and some even became a credit to the state—like Glous, our leading poet, or Soser the shipping magnate.

"A larger number did nothing either very good or very bad. They settled down to loafing and amusing themselves in more or less harmless ways. What really astonished good King Filoman, however, was that many kept right on committing crimes when, being pensioned, they no longer had to do so.

"Furthermore, the amount of crime actually waxed as Filoman's subjects discovered that to be convicted was the best way to get a regular stipend from the treasury. People robbed and raped and assaulted all over the place and made no attempt to evade capture. Thus, two merchants accused each other of theft; the hatter said the antique dealer had stolen a dozen of his hats, whilst the antique dealer accused the hatter of making off with a costly vase. Even odder, each had his loot in plain sight in his own shop. It was plain to every one save Filoman the Well-Meaning and his ghostly minister that the twain had cooked up this scheme between them, to get on the pension rolls.

"When, during a seance with Gloé, Filoman complained of these unwonted events, Tsaidar's ghost would not admit any flaw in his logic. 'It must,' he said, 'be that the emoluments you pay your felons are not enough to relieve their want. Double all pensions at once, and you shall see.'

"Then so great became the demands on the treasury that Filoman was forced to borrow abroad and then to debase the currency to pay his promised stipends. Soon, Kortolian money contained so much lead and tin mingled with the silver, and copper with the gold, that no knowing person would accept it. The sound money from earlier times went into hiding, whilst all Kortolians sought to rid themselves of Filoman's counterfeits, as they were called. And soon all trade ground to a halt, for none would take the new money and none would part with the old. There were bread riots in Kortoli City and other distressing events.

"At length, King Filoman determined to seek advice from the living to find out what was wrong. He asked many of those arrested for crime why they had so conducted themselves. Some answered with glib lies. Some admitted that they wanted pensions, too. But one scarred old rogue with a missing ear, who had slain and robbed a merchant on the road, at last revealed to the king what was truly in the minds of many of his kind.

"'You see, Your Majesty,' said the robber, 'it is not just the money. To sit at home and live on my pension were too dull to be borne. I should go mad with boredom.'

"'But,' quoth the king, 'there are many worthy occupations, such as soldier or hunter or messenger, which would provide you with healthful activity and enable you to do good at the same time.'

"'You do not understand, sire. I do not want to do good; I want to do bad. I want to rob and hurt and slay people.'

"'Good gods, why should you wish that?' said the king.

"'Well, sire, one of man's deepest desires is to put himself above his fellow men—to compel them to admit his superiority, is it not?'

"'One might say so,' replied the king cautiously. 'But I seek to attain superiority by virtue.'

"'You do, but I do not. Now, a living man is, in general, superior to a dead one, is he not?'

"'Aye, it would seem reasonable to say so.'

"'Then, if I slay a man, and I live whilst he dies, I am obviously his superior by the mere fact of being alive, am I not?'

"'I never thought of that,' said the king, greatly troubled.

"'The same,' said the scoundrel, 'applies to assault, robbery, and other deeds that I delight in. If I give something to a man, or accept a free gift from him, or barter things of equal value with him, that proves nought about who is the better man. But if I take from him that which is his, against his wish, I have proved that my power is greater than his. Every time I make another unhappy, without his being able to retaliate, I have proved my superiority.'

" 'You must be mad!' cried the king. 'Never have I heard so monstrous a philosophy!'

" 'Nay, sire, I do assure you that I am but a normal human being like yourself.'

" 'If you are normal, then I cannot be, and contrariwise,' said the king, 'for our views are as different as day and night.'

" 'Ah, but Your Majesty, I said not that we were alike! People are so various that there is no one normal kind, all others being lunatics and antic characters. And most folk have in them different urges, which pull them now one way and now the other. In you, the urge to do good is so much stronger than the urge to do evil that the latter can be neglected, whereas with me and many like me it is the opposite. But amongst the general, you will find, these motives are more evenly balanced, so that they do now good, now ill. And, when one of your subjects has grown to manhood with these urges in a certain proportion, I do not think you will change this proportion thereafter, no matter what you do to or for him.'

"The king sank back on his throne, aghast. At last he said: 'And where, my good murderer, did you learn to reason so philosophically?'

" 'When I was a boy, I went to school in Metouro under your esteemed minister, Tsaidar of Govannian, who was then not a disembodied spirit but a young schoolmaster. And now, sire, if you will summon your treasurer to put me on his pension roll—'

" 'I cannot,' said the king, 'because you have convinced me of the error of my whole scheme. I cannot call in the headsman to shorten you by the appropriate amount, as you deserve, because you have done me a favor by giving me a deeper insight into my fellow men. On the other hand, I cannot permit you to continue your villainies in Kortoli. So you will be given a horse, a small purse, and twenty-four hours to quit the land, on pain of death if ever you return.'

"And so it was done, not without some soul-searching on the part of Filoman, who felt guilty about turning this rascal loose on one of the neighboring states. He dismissed Tsaidar's ghost and paid off the witch Gloé, whereupon she cried out:

"'Sire! I am bilked! These are those worthless adulterated coins you have been striking lately!'

"'Well, the advice of your ghost proved equally worthless, so we are quits,' said Filoman. 'Now get along back to your cave and bother me no more.'

"And Gloé departed, muttering maledictions, although whether these had aught to do with the king's death in a riding accident some years afterwards is not known. And Filoman appointed Oinax his new minister, and for a while Kortoli returned to its former condition. But then King Filoman fell under the sway of the so-called holy man Ajimbalin, with results whereof I have already told you."

Jorian had inched closer to the princess, and now had an arm about her vast, bare torso. She put up her face to be kissed, then seized him in a grip of pythonic power.

"Gramercy for your story, man," she murmured. "And now we shall see whether you are a better man than those pygmies of Mulvanians, with their tools like toothpicks, no? Come!"

Three hours later, Princess Yargali lay on her side, facing the window by which Jorian had entered and breathing slow, deep breaths. Jorian slid quietly out of the huge bed. He quickly donned his garments, except for his boots, which he thrust into his sash.

Then he searched the bedroom for the Kist of Avlen. The candle in this room had burnt down and gone out, but enough light came through the doorway from the living room, where a pair of butter lamps still burnt, for his purpose. He found that none of the chests ranged around the walls was that which he sought. Nor did there seem to be any closets or secret compartments in the walls. A search of the princess's bathroom proved equally fruitless.

At last Jorian discovered the Kist in the most obvious place: under Yargali's bed. It was a battered little chest, about a cubit and a half long and a cubit in height and depth, with an old leather strap buckled around it to reinforce its brass clasps. It lay under the side of the bed away from the window. Jorian had lain on that side after making love to Yargali. Evidently he would have to pull the chest out from under the bed from that side, tiptoe around the bed to the window, and let himself out.

Moving as if treading on razors, Jorian knelt beside the bed. Slowly he pulled the Kist towards himself by one of the brass handles. It did not prove very heavy. Fingerbreadth by fingerbreadth, almost holding his breath, he teased the chest out from under the bed. At last it lay before him. Grasping the two handles, he stood up and stepped back.

Then, to his utter horror, the princess Yargali muttered in her sleep and rolled over. Her eyes opened. She cast off the coverlet, exposing her huge, brown body with its exaggerated curves.

"Ssssso!" she said.

For an instant, Jorian—still a little drunk from Yargali's wine—was rooted to the spot. In that instant, Yargali changed. Her body elongated; her limbs shrank. The dark-brown skin changed to an epidermis of olive-green scales, with a reticulated pattern of russet and yellow stripes. Her face bulged out and became a long, scaly muzzle. A musky odor filled the bedroom.

She was a serpent—but such a serpent as Jorian had never heard of outside myths and legends. The head, as large as that of a horse, reared up from the pile of coils. A forked tongue flicked out from the jaws. In the middle, the serpent's body was as big around as Jorian's waist.

Sobered abruptly and shaking himself out of his momentary paralysis, Jorian thought with lightning speed. If he tried to run around the bed to get to the window, he would come within easy lunging distance of the head. If he had only caused Karadur to send the rope up to one of the living-room windows, he could have fled that way; but now his retreat was cut off. Too late, he remembered Goania's warning against bedroom windows. If he tried to get out the living-room windows, he would probably give himself a fifteen-cubit fall on the marble of the terrace and break a leg or a neck. The stonework outside was smooth, and there was no ivy to climb by or tree into whose branches to leap.

As the serpent poured off the creaking bed and came for Jorian, he fled into the living room. There were two exits from this parlor. One door, he supposed, opened into the third story of the adjacent hall; there was probably a guard on the far side of it. The other, whose door stood ajar, revealed a descending flight of stairs, down which Yargali had earlier come on her way from her apartment to the ballroom.

Jorian raced across the living room and through the door at the head of the stairs. Down he went; and after him, hissing like a giant's kettle, poured Yargali—all forty cubits of her. The thought crossed Jorian's mind that, in assuming her serpent form, the princess had at least deprived herself of her ability to shout for help.

The ballroom was dark but for one small oil lamp, which burnt on a bracket. The king's servants had unrolled the huge rug that covered the marble when the floor was not being used for balls.

Jorian dashed to the nearest of the long windows opening on the terrace. The window had, however, been not only closed but also locked. The feeble light showed him the keyhole. Yargali's serpent head appeared from the doorway at the foot of the stairs.

Given a few minutes, Jorian was sure he could pick the lock of any of the long windows. Given time and no interference, he could probably batter the glass panes out of the window and burst his way through. But the panes were small and the leads between them were stout and closely set, so that this operation would take many blows with some heavy object, such as a chair, and the noise would fetch the guards who stood outside the big doors at the end of the ballroom.

If he tried to get out one of his pick-locks and pick a window lock, Yargali would seize him from behind, throw a coil around him, smother him in her serpentine embrace, and swallow him little by little, head first like a frog. Now Jorian saw why no one had succeeded for five hundred years in stealing the Kist from her somewhat casual guardianship.

As Yargali's head came towards him, her forked tongue flickering, Jorian set the Kist of Avlen down upon the carpet. Seizing the corner of the rug, he heaved and tugged his way down the side of the ballroom, past the long windows, pulling the carpet with him. It buckled into folds and became frightfully heavy to move, since the whole thing weighed several times as much as Jorian. A smaller or weaker man could not have moved it at all. But, straining and sweating and with muscles cracking with the effort, Jorian hauled the whole carpet down to the far end of the ballroom, where he left it in a crumpled heap.

Then he picked up the Kist—which had come along with the carpet—and went back to one of the long windows. Yargali had now slithered all the way down the stairs and out on the bare, brown marble floor. But here, lacking any roughness or solid objects to exert a horizontal force against, she found herself unable to advance further. Her vast serpentine body rippled; wave after wave flowed from her wedge-shaped head to her tapering tail, but to no avail. Like a flag fluttering in the breeze, she moved but did not progress. Hissing in a fury of frustration, she doubled the speed and violence of her writhings, but her scales slithered futilely back and forth on the polished marble floor.

Meanwhile, Jorian picked the lock of the window at the far end, slipped out with the Kist, and closed the window behind him. He ran to where the magical rope still stood upright on the pave and uttered the simple cantrip that nullified its spell and brought it tumbling down in coils.

A quarter-hour later, Jorian rejoined Karadur outside the main gate, around the elephant mill out of sight of the sentries. He whispered:

"Have you all our gear? My sword? Thanks...Curse it, you forgot my hat! They'll give it to their hound-elephants to smell. Oh, well, no matter; I have this silly cap. Can we make a sling of your magical rope, so I can carry this damned chest on my back?"

Karadur fingered the rope. "Aye, might as well. The rope's magical powers are exhausted, and until it be ensorcelled again it is no more than a common rope."

Another hour saw them riding southward on the road up the left bank of the Pennerath. Jorian told Karadur the essentials of his adventure. The wizard asked:

"How did you ever think of that extraordinary expedient for immobilizing Yargali, my son?"

"I remembered when I was a boy, I caught a harmless little snake and kept it for a few days. Then I went with my father to the house of a squire of Ardamai, where my father was installing a water clock. And whilst I was there, helping my father, the serpent escaped from my purse and fell to the squire's polished hardwood floor. The squire's wife carried on like a crazy woman until I removed the poor little snake, and I was sent to bed that night without my supper. But I remembered that, on this floor, the snake had been unable to move from here to there for want of traction, and so was easily caught. And I thought it might work the same way with the black wench."

"How found you your—ah—sensuous escapade?"

"Bumpy, a little like serving a cow elephant maddened by passion. I could have used stirrups there, too; I was almost thrown out on my head on the floor."

Karadur shuddered. "Was she pleased?"

"She seemed to be, albeit meseems she would have been receptive to more bouts than I was prepared to give. I was but a mere mortal man and a badly frightened one at that."

"Jorian! I have told you not to talk—"

"Oh, very well. But hereafter I'll confine my venery to human women. If I could only get back my little Estrildis..." He wiped away a tear, then turned a startled face to the wizard. "Gods! I just thought: what if the seed take root?"

"Fear not, my son. A hybrid betwixt a man and one of the serpent people were impossible, which is perhaps as well. I tremble to think what a being combining her shape-changing powers and your craft and daring might do to the world!"

VII

THE
RUIN IN THE JUNGLE

IN THE JUNGLES OF KOMILAKH, WHICH STRETCHED FOR MORE than a hundred leagues from the marches of Mulvan to the Eastern Ocean, enormous trees of many species towered over a hundred cubits into the sky. In the upper branches, squirrels and monkeys scrambled and chattered; gaudy birds whirled and flapped and screeched. Lower down, beneath the permanent waves of this green sea of leaves, vines as thick as a man's leg hung in loops and braids and tangles. Along these lianas, hairy spiders as big as crabs, with eyes like octets of little diamonds, crept in search of prey. Parasitic plants with flowers of ghostly colors sprouted from the trunks and branches of the trees.

Still lower, in the permanent gloom of the ground level, an undulating surface of brown leaf mold stretched away among the tree trunks. Here and there this surface was broken by saplings—most of them dead—or clumps of ferns. From the ground, only an occasional fleck of blue sky could be seen through the all-covering ceiling of green; but now and then a golden gleam ahead through the trees gave the direction of the morning sun. Men seldom saw the larger denizens of this level—elephant, buffalo, tiger, rhinoceros, deer, antelope, tapir, and wild pig—because the beasts heard man afar off and made themselves scarce.

Through this somber, silent world, Jorian and Karadur rode, winding among the tree trunks and around the fern clumps, swaying and ducking to avoid the branches of saplings and the dangling loops of lianas. Jorian rode the tall roan, Oser; Karadur, the white ass. Their mounts' heads hung with fatigue, and their riders had to kick and beat them to prevent them from stopping every other step to snatch a mouthful of greenery.

They had been riding since well before dawn. When the brush was thin enough to permit, they forced the animals to a trot. They also kept turning their heads to look back and listen.

For several days they had fled from their pursuers, who consisted of two tracking elephants and ten well-armed mounted soldiers. At the beginning, the fugitives had had a start of several hours, because the first pursuit had been sent in the obvious direction, down the Bharma. But King Shaju had quickly corrected this mistake and dispatched another force up the Pennerath.

Although the pursuers' speed was limited by the elephants, who could not go long distances faster than a horse's trot, nevertheless the pursuers' familiarity with the country and the fact that they led spare horses enabled them to close the gap. When the farmlands of eastern Mulvan turned to isolated clearings and then gave way to roadless jungle, they were only an hour behind.

Since then, the fugitives had fled almost continuously, sleeping in snatches, sometimes on the backs of their animals. Both looked worn and weary. The fine clothes in which Jorian had begun his flight were now dirty, dusty, and stained by rain and sweat. This was the so-called dry season in Komilakh, when rain occurred only every two or three days in place of the continual downpour of summer.

Jorian was stripped to breeches and boots against the damp heat. His left arm was in a crude sling, and he handled the reins with his right hand. Two days earlier, in making camp, he had stepped into a hole, reached out to steady himself, and seized a branch of a small tree covered with long, needle-sharp spines. A few hours later, his left hand had been swollen to twice its normal size and had turned a fiery red. At the moment it was still too painful to use. Any sudden jerk sent sharp pains lancing up Jorian's arm, so that trotting his horse was one long agony. But the thought of being trampled by King Shaju's elephants urged him on.

From time to time he reined in his mount, to breathe the animals and to listen for pursuers. The night before, the rumbling purr of elephants had warned him of their approach. Luckily, this had occurred in a patch of jungle so dense that neither party had sighted the other. Galloping recklessly and riding the animals along a stream bed for several furlongs, Jorian thought they had thrown off the pursuit, but he was taking no chances.

Now, as he halted and let his horse munch ferns, he raised a hand. Karadur froze. To their ears came, far but unmistakable, the squeal of an elephant and the jingle of harness.

"Doctor," said Jorian, "another run, ere our beasts have rested and fed, will kill them. Now's the time for your confusion spell."

"It will be the last time," mumbled Karadur, "for I have materials for but one such spell. Help me down from this ass, and I will do what I can."

Soon the old wizard had a tiny fire going. "Dry twigs, dry twigs!" he muttered. "Nothing wet, for that we want as little smoke as possible. Now, let me see, where did I put the powders for Confusion Number Three?"

He fumbled in his garments and at length produced one of his compartmented purses. When he opened this, however, he exclaimed in horror, "Ah, woe! I have none of the powder of the yellow mushroom of Hroth!" He searched frantically. "I must have forgotten it when I made up this battery of powders. We are lost!"

"Can't you use any old mushroom? Like this one?"

"I know not how it would work. But let us try; it can scarcely put us into a worse predicament."

Karadur crumbled the mushroom into the tiny caldron, added other substances, and stirred. Leaves rustled without any detectable breeze, and the green canopy overhead seemed to press down upon them, closer and darker...

At last Karadur leant back against a tree trunk. "Water!" he croaked in a ghost of a voice. "I am spent."

Jorian passed him the leathern water bottle. As Karadur drank, Jorian sniffed the air.

"What in the name of Zevatas is that stench?" said Jorian. He sniffed again. "It's you—nay, it's both of us! Your spell must have gone awry. We stink like a gymnasium, a slaughter-house, and a dunghill, all rolled into one. The gods grant that a wind carry not this odor to our pursuers...Oh, plague! There it goes!"

A wind had swung up, rustling the leaves of the vast green awning overhead and swaying the smaller branches. Only a light breeze could be felt at ground level, but such as it was, it came from the east and blew towards King Shaju's men.

"Mount! And be yare about it!" snapped Jorian.

"I cannot; I am fordone—"

"You damned old fool, get on that ass or I'll haul you on by your beard! Here they come!"

Through the forest came the loud, brassy cry of an elephant. This was echoed by a trumpet's blast and the sound of voices and movement. Jorian picked up Karadur bodily and set him down on the ass. Then he mounted himself.

"Hold tight!" he said. "They're galloping. They'll probably spread out, thinking to catch us with one quick rush. Off!"

The brief rest had given the animals back some of their strength. Jorian led the way at an easy canter, curving around obstacles, swaying and ducking, while the ass rocked along behind. Groaning, Karadur bounced along on the ass, clutching the saddle. He had little control over the animal; but the ass, being used to following the horse, did so with little guidance.

The sounds of galloping diminished as the pursuers spread out. There were more trumpetings, but farther away, as the elephants were left behind in the pursuit. After Jorian had cantered for some time in silence, he held up an arm and slowed. He led the way to the far side of an enormous tree, whose trunk at the base measured over twenty cubits through.

"There's but one man close behind us," he said. "The others have spread too far and lost touch with each other. They'll have to rally back at the elephants to pick up our trail again. Here, take your cursed Kist!"

"What mean you to do?"

"To await our pursuer behind this tree, whilst you go on. I can't shoot, with this polluted hand, but I can still handle a sword. Not, however, with that thing on my back. Get along!" he snarled as Karadur started to protest.

The ass trotted off, with Karadur bouncing in the saddle and the Kist, slung over one shoulder by its rope sling, bumping against the wizard's back. Unable to grasp the reins firmly enough with his swollen hand, Jorian wound them around his left forearm and drew the sword Randir. Then he waited.

Nearer and nearer came the galloping horse. When it seemed as if Jorian could bear the suspense no longer, the rider appeared: a Mulvanian trooper in scarlet silken pantaloons, hauberk of silvered chain mail, and spired helmet. A quiver of light twirl-spears hung across his back, and he balanced one of these darts in his right hand.

Jorian kicked his horse's flanks. The roan started forward, but not so quickly as Jorian intended, because its rider was not wearing spurs. The delay gave the soldier time to twist about in his saddle and fling his javelin.

Jorian, bouncing in the saddle as Oser broke into his rough gallop, ducked down behind his horse's head. The missile hissed past, missing him by a fingerbreadth.

The soldier made a tentative snatch at his quiver, then changed his mind and reached instead for the scimitar at his hip. But his horse, seeing Oser bearing down upon him, shied a little. Lacking stirrups, the soldier was shaken in his seat. His hand missed the hilt, and he was forced to grab at one of the hand-holds on the saddle to steady himself. He was still fumbling for his sword when Jorian's point took him in the throat. He fell into the leaf mold, while his horse, snorting, galloped off.

When Jorian caught up with Karadur, the wizard looked up at him from under his sweat-stained turban. "Well?"

"Dead," said Jorian, "thanks to the fact that I had stirrups and he did not. The way this nag bounces one, 'tis a wonder I hit the fellow at all. I'll relieve you of that chest now, if you like. Curse it, my hand is hurting again."

"Have you thought of the moral aspects of your slaying that trooper?" said Karadur. "Doubtless he was as good and pious a man as yourself—"

"*Oi!*" cried Jorian. "I save your wretched neck and your box of worthless spells, and you read me a damned sermon!

Dip me in dung, but if you do not agree it was he or us, you can turn back and give yourself up."

"Nay, nay, my son, be not wroth with me for indulging my bent for speculation. The question of what to do when one is confronted by a man no worse than oneself, and whom one must slay to achieve a goal as worthy as his, has long beguiled me. Portentous questions, like that of war and peace, hinge upon it."

"Well," said Jorian, "I don't go out of my way to kill King Shaju's soldiers; but when 'tis a question of him or me, I strike first and argue ethics later. Did I not, I should not be here to discuss the matter. Meseems that, when one takes the king's coin as a soldier, one accepts the risk that, sooner or later, one may suddenly depart this life. None compelled that ill-starred horse-darter to chase and shoot at me. Having done so, he has no legitimate complaint—assuming his spirit will be vouchsafed a chance to protest in one of your multifarious Mulvanian afterworlds."

"The trooper's officer compelled him to pursue and attack you, so he was not a free agent."

"But he put himself under the officer's orders voluntarily, when he joined the army."

"Not so simple, my son. In Mulvan, all must follow their sires' occupations. So this man, born the son of a soldier, had no option but to become a trooper in his turn."

"Then the blame lies, not on me, but on your polluted custom of hereditary occupations."

"But that, in turn, has many advantages. It provides a stable social order, lessens the bitterness of competition for advancement, and furnishes each man with a secure position on the social stair."

"All very well, Doctor, when the sons' natural bent lies in the same channel as their sires'. But when 'tis otherwise? I know from my own life. Esteeming my father as a good and kindly man, I had been well content to follow his trade of clockmaking; but whilst my mind could grasp the principles, my hands proved too clumsy for the practice. In Mulvan, I had been bound to this profession for aye, and starved in consequence."

Karadur: "But even when there's a free choice of livelihood, as in the Twelve Cities, the same dilemma presents itself, when the general levy is called up for war.

Then you will find yourself opposed to another, each of you convinced his cause is just, and no way to settle the question but spear and sword."

"Well, when one fighter is slain, he ceases to have any cause at all, just or otherwise. So justice resides *ipso facto* in the winner."

"A frivolous answer, O Jorian, unworthy of one who has ruled a state! Well you know that, for all your prayers to your various gods, the winner is determined by strength, or skill at arms, or luck—none having aught to do with justice."

"Holy Father," said Jorian, "when you persuade all my quarrelsome fellow-Novarians to submit their disputes to a tribunal of the wisest and most learned minds and to accept without cavil this court's decisions, I will gladly bow to such judgments. But behemoths will fly or ever that happens, and meanwhile I must fend for myself as best I can. But hold! Here's a dingle athwart our path, with a brook running through it. I'll wade the stream for a few furlongs, to see if I can throw them off the scent again. You may follow if you like."

He turned his horse's head downstream and set off at a rapid amble, water splashing in fountains about the roan's fetlocks. Karadur followed.

The stream gathered volume as it flowed, and around noon it joined another. Below this confluence, the united stream formed a small river, a fathom or two in width—small enough for easy fording but too voluminous to use as a path. Because of the density of the vegetation along the banks, Jorian and Karadur followed the stream at some distance, glimpsing the water through the trees.

"Methinks this is an affluent of the Shrindola," said Karadur. "The Shrindola flows into the Inner Sea, they say, albeit no man to my knowledge has ever followed it to its mouth to make sure."

"Then it must curve northward somewhere, in which case we're on the right side to get to Halgir," said Jorian. "Stop and hush for a moment whilst I listen."

There was no sound save the hum of insects and the chatter of birds and monkeys. They rode on. Then Jorian noticed something about his surroundings. Stones or small boulders appeared, scattered about the forest floor. Presently, as these objects became more frequent, he realized that they were too regular in shape and arrangement to be products of nature. Although often half buried and covered with patches of moss, algae, and lichen, they still showed flat faces at right angles, evidently the work of a mason's chisel. Moreover, they lay in lines—wavering, broken lines, but lines nonetheless.

Now the ancient masonry became denser and better preserved. Peering into shadowy, silvan distances, Jorian saw pieces of megalithic wall and the stumps of tumbled towers. Here a structure had been invaded by the roots of a tree growing out of its top, groping downwards between the individual stones and prying them apart, like the tentacles of some vegetable octopus, until the tree supported the remains of the structure rather than the building the tree. There rose a megalithic wall, bedight with sculptured reliefs in riotous profusion. Intricately carven towers of sandstone blocks loomed up through the forest, their tops lost in the masses of greenery overhead. Trees grew out of a monumental staircase, whose massive blocks their roots had heaved and tumbled.

Sinister, scowling stone faces peered out from behind the fronds of palms and ferns. An immense statue, fallen and broken into three pieces, lay among ruined walls and towering tree trunks, its finer details largely hidden by splotches of moss. For a while, the animals walked along a raised causeway paved with large, square slabs of slate and supported on either hand by cyclopean walls made of blocks weighing hundreds of tons.

On either hand stretched endless galleries bounding vast, overgrown courtyards. The entrances to these galleries were stone portals lacking the true arch. Instead, the openings were headed by corbelled arches, each course of masonry overhanging the one beneath until they met at the top, forming tall isosceles triangles. Among the sculptures that decorated the walls of these galleries, Jorian glimpsed scenes of armies on the march, demons and gods in supernatural combat, dancing girls entertaining kings, and workers at their daily tasks.

A flock of small green parrots rose from the ruins and whirred away, screaming. Monkeys scampered over the tottering roofs. Little lizards, some green with purple throats, some yellow, and some of other hues, scuttled

166

over the stones. Huge butterflies came to rest on the tumbled masonry, fanning the air with their gold-and-purple wings before flitting away once more.

"What ruin is this?" Jorian asked.

"Culbagarh," groaned the wizard. "Can we stop here? I shall soon be dead else."

"Methinks we've gained a few hours upon them," said Jorian, dismounting at the base of a headless statue. The head that belonged to the statue lay nearby, but so covered with moss and mold that its precise nature was not evident. As he helped Karadur, groaning, down from the ass, Jorian said: "Tell me about this Culbagarh."

While Jorian staked out the animals where long grass grew in a ruined courtyard and prepared a frugal meal, Karadur told the story:

"This city goes back to the kingdom of Tirao, which preceded the empire of Mulvan. When the last king of Tirao, Vrujja the Fiend, came to the throne, his first concern was to have all his siblings slain, lest any should aspire to usurp his seat. This massacre later became the usual procedure in Mulvan and is now a custom hallowed by time. But in the days of Vrujja—more than a thousand years ago—it caused much comment.

"Hearing of the fate in store for him, one of these brothers, Naharju, gathered his followers and fled eastward into the wilds of Komilakh. They marched eastward for many leagues, until they came to a few scattered ruins, on this very spot. Those ruins were, however, much less extensive than these about us and more dilapidated, because this earlier city had stood abandoned much longer than the mere thousand-odd years since of the fall of Culbagarh.

"None in Prince Naharju's party knew what city those scattered stones were the remains of, although some opined that this had been a city of the serpent people ere they migrated thence into the denser jungles of Beraoti. Amid these scanty ruins stood a worn, moss-grown altar, and beyond the altar the remains of a statue, so weathered that none could be certain what sort of creature it had depicted. Some thought it a figure of an ape-man, like unto the ape-men who are the native inhabitants of Komilakh, and of whom the party had caught glimpses. Others thought the statue not that of one of the higher animals at all, but something nearer to a spider or a cuttlefish.

"Naharju had with him a priest of Kradha the Preserver, to minister to the spiritual needs of his people. It seemed to Naharju that preservation of their lives was the most urgent task confronting the refugees and that, therefore, Kradha were the most suitable god to worship. A modern theologian might argue that Vurnu, Kradha, and Ashaka are all merely aspects or avatars of the same godhead; but in those days thinkers had not yet reached such heights of metaphysical subtlety.

"On the first night they spent in the ruins, the priest, whose name was Ayonar, had a dream. In this dream, he reported, the god whereof the ruined statue had been the image appeared unto him. The folk pressed Ayonar for a description of this god—whether it had the form of a man, an ape, a tiger, a crab, or what; but when Ayonar tried to answer their questions, he turned pale and stuttered so that nothing intelligible came forth. And when they saw that merely to think about the appearance of this god so troubled their holy priest, they left off questioning him and asked instead, what this god demanded of them.

"So Ayonar told the people that the god was named Murugong, and he had indeed been the god of the folk who had dwelt in the city ere it became a ruin, and that he was the chief god of Komilakh and never mind what the priests of Tirao said about their holy trinity's ruling the world. Komilakh was his; other gods, despite their ecumenical pretensions, knew better than to quarrel with him. Therefore Naharju's colonists had better worship him and forget all other gods.

"Then it transpired that Murugong was worshiped with exceedingly barbarous and bloody sacrifices, wherein a chosen victim was flayed alive on his altars. Murugong had explained to Ayonar that, not having tasted the pain of such a sacrifice for thousands of years, he was nigh unto starvation, and they should find a victim to flay right speedily.

"Naharju and his men were troubled, for such usages had long been abandoned in Tirao, and they were not eager to take them up again, let alone to slay one of their own in this uncouth manner. So they took counsel, and whilst they disputed, the priest Ayonar said: 'May it please Your Highness, I have thought how to gratify the mighty Murugong and preserve our own skins intact. Let us go into the forest, seize one of the ape-men, and sacrifice it in the manner prescribed. For, if not so intelligent as a true man, the ape-man stands high enough in the scale of life so that it will suffer quite as acutely as any human being. And, since Murugong thrives on the pain of his victims, he should be just as well satisfied as if one of us had perished in this manner.'

"The men of Naharju's faction agreed that the priest had spoken sound sense, and a hunting party was made up at once. After the ape-man had been devoted to the god, Murugong appeared unto Ayonar in a dream and said he was well pleased with the sacrifice and would adopt the Tiraonian refugees as his chosen people as long as they continued the sacrifices. And so it went for many years. Under Naharju and his son of the same name, the people waxed in numbers and built the city of Culbagarh on the ruins of the older, nameless city.

"Meanwhile the leading men of Tirao, desperate over the enormities of Vrujja the Fiend, sought for a prince to head a rebellion against their sovran. They had trouble in this, for that Vrujja had made a clean sweep of his kinsmen, executing them unto third and fourth cousins and sending men to murder those who had fled to Novaria and other barbarian lands.

"At length, however, the rebels discovered a chief of the desert-dwellers of Fedirun, hight Waqith, who boasted one-thirty-second part of royal Tiraonian blood in his veins. And they invited him to invade Tirao and become king in Vrujja's room. The invasion went briskly, for most of Vrujja's men deserted. Soon Vrujja was slain in an interesting manner that perturbs me too much to describe, and Waqith was crowned king.

"But Waqith did not prove so great an improvement over Vrujja as his supporters had hoped. His first public act was to arrest all the chief nobles of Tirao and have their heads piled in a pyramid in the public square. Having, as he thought, terrified the rest into being docile subjects, he next commanded that the contents of the treasury be dumped on the floor of the throne room. And the sight of so much wealth drove Waqith—who had all his life been a bare-arsed desert thief, to whom one silver mark was a fortune—clean out of his mind. They found him sitting on a heap of coins, tossing jewels in the air and laughing and babbling like an unweaned babe.

"So they slew Waqith and sought for someone to replace him. But now the word of Tirao's troubles had blown hither and yon about the deserts of Fedirun, and other bands of nomads irrupted into the fertile plains of Tirao, where the surviving nobles fought amongst themselves to see who should rule the land. And soon the kingdom went down in blood and fire, and owls and bats and serpents nested in the ruins of the palaces and fortresses of former times. And so things remained until the coming of Ghish the Great.

"Meanwhile, Culbagarh grew and grew, as fugitives from the fall of Tirao sought sanctuary there. But under Naharju's grandson, Darganj, it became even more difficult to catch enough ape-men to keep up the sacrifices to Murugong. For the ape-men had become wary of Culbagarh and gave it a wide berth, so that the Culbagarhis were forced to keep hundreds of men constantly employed on hunts for these beings. And there was talk of choosing victims by lot from amongst the new arrivals in Culbagarh, in case the supply of ape-men failed altogether.

"Amongst the refugees from Tirao was a man named Jainini, who preached a new god, called Yish. This new god, said Jainini, had appeared to him in dreams to expound a religion of love instead of blood and terror. If only everybody, said Jainini, would love everybody else, all their troubles would be over. Furthermore Yish, being a mightier god than Murugong, would protect them more effectively than Murugong ever had.

"The priesthood of Murugong, now grown rich, corrupt, and powerful, sought to sacrifice Jainini on the altar of Murugong as a dangerous heretic. But Jainini had many followers, especially amongst the new immigrants, who had not been pleased to hear of the priests' intention of devoting them to Murugong. And it looked as if the two factions would have to fight it out.

"But then King Darganj went over to the side of Yish and his prophet Jainini. Some said Darganj was interested, not in any religion of love, but in getting his hands on the treasures of the temple of Murugong.

"Be that as it may, Yish became the chief god of Culbagarh, and Murugong was forsaken. And for a while the

170

city enjoyed the benefits of the religion of love. The army was put to such civilian tasks as cleaning the streets of the city. Evildoers, instead of having a hand or a head sliced off by the executioner, were lectured on the virtues of love and turned loose with the admonition to sin no more— although it is said that few of them heeded this advice; the rest continued their careers of robbery, rape, and murder with greater gusto than ever.

"Then, without warning, a horde of ape-men overran and sacked the city and slaughtered its dwellers. For the continued raids of the Culbagarhis for three generations had filled these creatures with hatred, and at last this persecution had driven the many little clans of ape-men to unite against their persecutors. The fact that the hunts for sacrificial victims had been halted made no difference; centuries would have had to pass before the ape-men lost their lust for vengeance.

"'The invaders were armed only with crude wooden spears and clubs and sharpened stones, but they were very many, and the Culbagarhis under the influence of Jainini had put away their arms, melting them up and reforging them into the tools of husbandry. A few, including King Darganj and Jainini, escaped the massacre and fled westward. And the next day, the prophet told the king that the abandoned god Murugong had appeared to him in his sleep. No more than Ayonar, could Jainini describe this god; but natheless he had somewhat to tell of him.

"'He said,' quoth Jainini, 'that it serves us right for deserting him.'

"'Would he take us back under his wing if we resumed his worship?' asked King Darganj.

"'I asked him that,' said Jainini, 'and he said nay; we had proven such faithless and fickle rascals that he would have no more truck with us. The ape-men, on the other hand, would suit him as worshipers very well, being too simple-minded to question his authority by theological theorizing.'

"'What of your mighty god Yish, who was supposed to ward us?'

"'Murugong has trounced Yish and driven him out of Komilakh. I complained that Yish had told me he was the mightier of the two, whereas this did not appear to be the fact. But how could a god lie? Easily, said Murugong, as

171

easily as any mortal. But, I said, I always understood that gods never lied. Who had told me that? said Murugong. The gods themselves, I said. But, said Murugong, if a god be a liar, what hinders him from lying about this as about other matters? Then I was stricken with horror at the thought of living in a universe where not only the men lie, but the gods as well. It was unfair, I protested. Quite true, said Murugong, but then, existence is unfair.

"'Thereupon I fell to cursing the gods and dared Murugong to slay me, but he only laughed and vanished from my dreams. So there we are, sire. And I pray you to flay me forthwith as a sacrifice to Murugong, that some at least of his wrath be turned from this sorry remnant of your people, which my folly had brought to this pass; and that, moreover, that I shall be quit of this dreadful world, where not even the gods are to be trusted.'

"But Darganj told Jainini not to talk rubbish but to flee with the rest of them to the West, in hopes of finding some corner of the former kingdom of Tirao where they could settle without attracting the notice of the barbarians who now fought one another on the ruins of that land. And they had just taken up their march again when a horde of ape-men appeared behind them. Whilst the rest of the Tiraonians fled in terror, Jainini walked boldly into the midst of the pursuers.

"This act so astonished the savages that the other fugitives had time to escape ere the creatures recovered their wits. The last that was seen of Jainini, the ape-men had seized him. It is not known what they did with him, but it is deemed unlikely that he converted them to the worship of Yish. And the city of Culbagarh has lain derelict ever since."

"The moral would seem to be," said Jorian, "to trust nobody—not even a god."

"Nay, that is not quite right, my son. The moral is, rather, to exercise a nice discrimination in all one's dealings, both with gods and with men, and to trust only the trustworthy."

"That's fine, could one only discover which they be. Holla! What's this?"

Jorian's boot struck a half-buried stone. Something about this stone led him to bend over and examine it. He kicked and pulled at it until it came loose in his hand. It was a statuette of a small, rotund, bald, grinning god, seated cross-legged on a plinth. The whole thing was less than half a foot high and weighed about a pound. Being made of an exceedingly hard, translucent green stone, it was in good condition, its outlines only slightly softened by weathering.

Jorian peered at the worn inscription on the plinth. "What's this?" he said, turning the statuette towards Karadur. "I do not recognize the writing; the characters are not those of modern Mulvani."

Karadur, peering through his reading glass, puzzled in his turn. "This," he said at last, "is Tiraonian, from the latter times of that kingdom. Modern Mulvani is derived from Tiraonian, with an admixture of Fediruni words. Evidently, one of the folk of Culbagarh dropped this statue here ere the city fell to the ape-men."

"What says it?"

Karadur traced the characters with his fingers. "It says 'Tvasha,' which I believe to be the name of a very minor god of the Tiraonian pantheon. There were so many that it is hard to remember which was which."

"Well, belike we should worship this Tvasha and ask him for help and guidance. After lying here in the mold for a thousand years, he ought to be glad of a worshiper or two, and I misdoubt the gods of my own Novaria have jurisdiction so far from their own demesne."

"If he have not died from neglect."

"How should we go about it? Catch one of these little green lizards and cut its throat?"

"Not until we know his wishes. Some gods are highly offended by blood sacrifices. Pray that he will appear unto you and advise you."

"He'd better find us something to eat. This is the last of our journey cake. Tomorrow we shall be reduced to catching lizards and serpents for our supper."

Jorian thought he was standing on a black marble pavement in a hall of some kind, although he could not see the walls or the ceiling. Before him in the dimness glimmered the pale-green form of Tvasha, sitting on his plinth in the same attitude as he took in the little statue. The god's head seemed to be on a level with Jorian's own. But, although he tried to focus his eyes, Jorian could never be sure whether the god was the same size as himself at a distance of ten or fifteen paces, or much smaller at arm's length, or much larger and furlongs away. The god's lips moved, and a voice spoke in Jorian's mind:

"Greetings, Jorian son of Evor! If thou but knew how good it is to have a worshiper once again! Before the fall of Culbagarh, I had a worshiper like unto thee; let me think, what was his name? I cannot recall, but he was a big, handsome wight, always in some fantastic scrape, wherefrom he ever expected me to rescue him. I remember one time—"

"Thy pardon, lord!" Jorian, not without trepidation, interrupted the garrulous deity. "We are hotly pursued by men who wish us ill. Canst save us?"

"Let me see..." The god vanished from his plinth, leaving Jorian alone in his dark, misty space. A few heartbeats later, Tvasha was back again. "Fear nought, my son. Though thy ill-wishers are but a bowshot away, they shall do thee no scathe—"

"A bowshot away!" cried Jorian. "I must needs awaken at once, to flee! Let me go, O god!"

"Be not so hasty, dear Jorian," said Tvasha, smiling broadly. "It is so long since I have had a mortal to converse with that I am fain to continue our talk. I will take care of the Mulvanians and their trained elephants. Tell me, how fareth the empire of Mulvan these days?"

"First, lord, tell me how thou wouldst be worshiped."

"An occasional offer of a flower and a nightly prayer suffice me. Tell me how mighty I am. In sooth—betwixt thee and me—I am but a feeble little godlet; but, being like all deities exceedingly vain, I drink flattery as thou drinkest fine wine. Now that—"

The dark, misty hall vanished, and Jorian found himself awake, with Karadur shaking his shoulder. Through the massed leaves overhead, the silver shield of the full moon sent a few ghostly gleams.

"Awaken, my son!" whispered the wizard. "I hear elephants; and if my weak old ears can detect them, they must be close—"

Jorian scrambled up. "Could they be wild elephants? We have seen the signs of many such in this forest...Nay, I hear the jingle of horse trappings. It's the Mulvanians."

He started for the courtyard where the animals were

tethered, then paused. The squeals of the elephants, the creak and jingle of harness, the muffled sound of horses' hooves on the forest floor, and the low-pitched snatches of talk receded. Soon they were so faint that he could barely hear them. Then they died away altogether. Jorian returned to the wizard.

"He's done it," he said.

"Who?"

"Tvasha. He said he would take care of the Mulvanians. I had my doubts, since he seemed a gabby old party and none too sharp. But whatever he did, it seems to have worked. We might as well go back to sleep, for if we go blundering about in the jungle in the dark we may run head-on into our pursuers by sheer mischance."

The air had cooled, so Jorian donned his upper garments, wrapped himself in his cloak, and lay down again. For a long time, however, sleep failed to come. His injured hand throbbed, and he thought about the problem of getting along with one's private god. He was still making up imaginary conversations with the deity when he found himself back in the dark, misty hall, before Tvasha on his pedestal.

"How didst thou do it, lord?" asked Jorian.

"Simply, my son. I cast an illusion upon the tracking elephants, so that they saw and smelt a beautiful cow elephant in heat, beckoning to them with her trunk. They rushed off to take advantage of her offer; and the Mulvanians, thinking their beasts were on a hot trail leading to you and your companion, harkened them on. Now they are leagues hence."

The god smiled smugly. "And now, my dear Jorian, let us resume the discussion we were having when the holy Karadur snatched thee away to thy own plane of existence. How fareth the empire of Mulvan? For the statuette thou foundest in the ruins is the only one of me still in fair enough condition to permit me to use it as a point of intersection between my world and thine. Hence, in my visits to thy plane, I am limited to a short distance from the ruins of Culbagarh. Say one."

Jorian gave the god a brief account of the state and recent history of Mulvan, as far as he knew it. When he told of the death of Shaju's father, King Sirvasha, Tvasha chuckled.

"That reminds me," said the god, "of one of the last kings of Tirao—Vrujja's great-grandfather, but I cannot recall his name. Dear me, what was it? No matter. Anyhow, I will tell thee a very funny story about this king, whose name—bless me, what was that name? It is on the tip of my tongue—anyway, this king..."

Tvasha went off into a rambling tale that seemed to have neither point nor end. Nor could Jorian see anything funny about it. A quarter-hour later, it seemed, he was fidgeting with boredom and impatience while Tvasha rambled on.

Then the god seemed to cast a glance over his shoulder and cry: "Oh, dear me! I have been so absorbed in telling thee this story that I have not noticed the dire peril that creepth upon thee! And, alas, this time I cannot save thee, for they who menace thee are under the protection of the mighty Murugong, whereas I am but a small, weak god..."

Jorian frantically tried to wake himself up. It was like straining at physical bonds. And then a physical shock awoke him all at once. Hairy hands gripped his arms and legs: he yelped as one seized his still tender left hand. A few paces distant, a swarm of the ape-men of Komilakh had likewise pinioned Karadur. To the east, a ruby gleam through the jungle told of the rising sun.

The ape-men were about five feet tall, but very stocky and muscular. Their necks jutted forwards, and their chins and foreheads receded, and their wide, thick lips parted to show rows of large, yellow teeth. They went naked, were almost as hairy as the beasts of the wild, and stank.

Gathering his muscles, Jorian made a furious effort to tear himself loose. But, great as was his strength compared to most men, that of each of his captors was equal to his own. Hairy hands with blackened, broken nails gripped him all the more tightly, and a couple of the ape-men pounded him with their fists until he became quiet. As he lay in the ape-men's grip, he found himself looking at the half-buried head of the nearby headless statue. He suddenly realized that the stone face was that, not of a man, but of a tiger. Goania's warning...

"Resist not!" said Karadur. "It does but madden them the more."

"What are they going to do with us?" said Jorian.

"How should I know? Do you understand aught of their speech?"

"No. Do you?"

"Nay, though I speak five or six tongues besides my own Mulvani."

"Can you cast a spell upon them?"

"Not whilst they hold me, for no spell worthy of the name is effected by a simple babbling of magical words."

Jorian: "Tvasha told me they're under Murugong's protection."

"Ah, woe! Then what Jainini told King Darganj a thousand years ago is still true. I do fear the worst."

"You mean they'll skin—"

Jorian was interrupted by a movement among the apemen. In response to a barked command from one of their number, they heaved Jorian to his feet and half-led, half-dragged him through the overgrown ways of Culbagarh. Others bore Karadur. They zigzagged through ruins until Jorian was lost.

They stopped before some large stones. The nearer and smaller of these was a simple block, two cubits high and twice as wide, weathered until its ancient edges and corners had all been rounded off, so that it might almost be mistaken for a natural boulder.

Beyond the low block rose a large, squat pedestal or plinth, atop which something had once been sculptured; but so worn was this statue that one could no longer tell for sure what it had depicted. Its general shape was that of a seated man, but no definitely human limbs or members could be discerned. It was low and squat and rounded, with here and there a mere suggestion of carving. A large, red-and-black banded snake, lying at the base of the statue, slithered away and vanished into a hole.

"This must be the statue of Murugong, whereof you told me," said Jorian.

"Ah me, I fear you are right. I do blame myself for bringing this doom upon you. Farewell, my son!"

An ape-man appeared, holding a rusty iron knife. This was the only metal tool or weapon in sight, all others being of wood, stone, or bone. The aboriginal whetted the edge on the altar block, *wheep-wheep*.

"Blame not yourself, Doctor," said Jorian. "We must

all take our chances. If they'd only just tie us up and go off and leave us a bit, perchance I could do something..."

Wheep-wheep went the knife. The ape-men had no intention of tying up their captives. Instead, they stood or squatted about them, firmly gripping their arms and legs with ominous patience.

At last the ape-man with the knife completed his whetting, tested the edge with his thumb, and stood up. At a grunted word, the ape-men holding Jorian dragged him to the altar and laid him supine upon it, still holding him firmly. He of the knife, standing before the statue, raised his arms and intoned a speech wherein Jorian caught the word "Murugong."

Then the ape-man turned back to Jorian and bent over the victim. He raised the knife, then drew the blade in a long, deliberate slash along Jorian's breastbone from throat to waist, bearing down hard. Jorian tensed himself to bear the pain manfully.

The knife cut neatly through Jorian's tunic but was stopped by the shirt of fine mesh mail beneath. With a guttural exclamation, the sacrificer bent over, flipping the severed sides of Jorian's tunic aside to examine this garment. Words broke out among the ape-men holding Jorian, and a couple began tugging at the mail shirt to pull it off over his head. While they struggled and argued and got in one another's way, an altercation sprang up out of range of Jorian's vision. Soon all the ape-men were shouting unintelligibly.

Gradually the noise died down. The ape-men holding Jorian pulled him up, so that he was sitting on the altar. He confronted a peculiarly ugly, middle-aged ape-man, who thrust a thick, hairy forefinger at him.

"You Jorian?" said this one in barely comprehensible Novarian.

"Aye. Who are you?"

"Me Zor. You remember? You save my life."

"By Imbal's brazen balls!" cried Jorian. "Of course I remember, O Zor. Tell me not that after you got out of that cage, you marched afoot all the way from the western Lograms to Komilakh!"

"Me strong. Me walk."

"Good for you! How have you fared?"

"Me do well. Me chief."

"And now, what of us?"

"You help me, I help you. Where you go?"

"We should like to get to Halgir, to cross the strait."

"You go."

Zor pushed aside the ape-men holding Jorian and threw a thick, hairy arm around Jorian's shoulders. Jorian winced from the bruises he had received from his captors' fists. Gesticulating with the other arm, Zor made a short but emphatic speech to the other ape-men. Although he could not understand a word, Jorian thought the speech meant that he was Zor's friend, and nobody should harm him on pain of Zor's displeasure.

"How about my friend?" said Jorian.

"You go, he stay. He not help us. We kill him."

"Either let us both go, or neither."

Zor scowled into Jorian's face. "What for you say that?"

"He is my friend. You would do the same for your friend, would you not?"

Zor scratched his head. "You speak good. All right, he go, too."

The next day, having left the banks of the Shrindola, they jogged across country northeast through a thunderstorm, with a squad of ape-men trotting along to show them the way and fetch food for them. Karadur said:

"An I have ever criticized you, my son, I humbly ask forgiveness now."

"What?" shouted Jorian over a roar or thunder. Karadur repeated.

"Why, Doctor?" said Jorian.

"You came within a hairbreadth of letting yourself be sacrificed—in a singularly painful manner—rather than abandon me, when you had an excellent opportunity to escape alone. I humble myself before you."

"Oh, nonsense! It just came out. Had I stopped to think, I should probably not have had the courage. As it was, I was so terrified of that skinning knife—oh, very well, very well, I'll say nought of my own fears aloud."

"Have you our new god with you?"

"'Tis in the pack, though how much good Tvasha will do us is open to question. I think we ought to invent a new religion: the worship of the god of the absurd. If any force rule the universe, it is surely absurdity. Consider:

179

you cast a confusion spell that goes awry and brings the foe right down upon us."

"That was not the fault of the spell. We lacked the proper ingredients."

"Then I stumble upon the statue of Tvasha. The god saves us from the Mulvanians—only to let us fall into the clutches of the ape-men because he's too busy telling me some long, boring tale about a king of olden times to notice them. When he does observe them, he's too fearful of the greater god Murugong to interfere.

"Then we are saved from painful deaths by Zor's happening along, and happening, moreover, to recognize me, when I should never have known him; these aboriginals look all alike to me. Zor believes I purposely released him from the cage of Rhithos' house. Truth to tell, that was a pure accident, resulting from my own stupidity, and for which Rhithos would have slain me had not the wench released me.

"Nor is that all. Were this a tale of some minstrel's fancy, Vanora and I should have been predestined mates and lovers—whereas, after trying me at stud, she finds she can't bear the sight of me and goes off with that halfwit Boso, who would be right at home amongst these escorts of ours. Now try to tell me that the universe makes sense!"

"I am sure it makes most excellent sense, were our puny mortal minds strong enough to grasp its entirety."

"Ha! Howsomever, one more dinner of roots and fungi, served in a sauce made of mashed bugs, and I may tell our friends to take me back to Culbagarh and sacrifice me. From such a diet, death were a welcome relief!"

VIII

THE SEA OF GRASS

IN THE MONTH OF THE RAM, A COLD WIND ROARED ACROSS the steppe of Shven. The gently rolling plain stretched away northward to a flat horizon unbroken by tree, house, or hill. The long grass was a faded yellow-gray, for the new spring crop had not yet come up. When the grass was scanty, it showed the wet, black soil beneath. An occasional water course traced a shallow, winding dale across the plain; here grew small willows and alders along the swollen stream. Snow lingered in patches in the shade of these trees.

Riding the same animals on which they had set out from Trimandilam over three months before, Jorian and Karadur trotted briskly across the steppe. They were coated with mud to their middles, for every *plop* of their animals' hooves sent up a little black fountain of liquid mud.

Arriving at Halgir, at the strait that divided the Inner Sea from the smaller Sea of Sikhon, they had been compelled to waste a month until the weather moderated enough for them to cross the water. The enforced rest, however, had been welcome, for Karadur had been near to death from exhaustion. Even Jorian, whose strength was beyond that of most men, had been badly fatigued, as much from the ape-men's diet as from physical effort.

During this pause, Jorian's injured hand had healed, and they had outfitted themselves for the journey around the northern shores of the Inner Sea. Jorian's boots, which had been falling apart from the dampness of Komilakh, had been repaired. Karadur had obtained a pair of felt boots in place of his sandals. Both had procured knee-length sheepskin coats and fur caps.

Leaving Gilgir, across the strait from Halgir, they had followed the coast, except where they could save distance by cutting across the base or a cape or peninsula. They counted themselves lucky to have seen scarcely another human being for nearly a month.

Once they had passed the burnt-out ruins of a village in a dell. One of the peasants who had dwelt there lived long enough to tell his tale. The village had supposedly been under the protection of Hnidmar, the cham of the Eylings. But they had prospered too obviously, so Hnidmar ordered them destroyed, lest their success draw more settlers to the steppe, which would thus be fenced and plowed and ruined as a grazing ground.

They slept near streams, where they could cut enough brushwood to make beds that at least kept them up out of the mud. Twice, Jorian had supplemented the food they had brought with them by shooting a steppe antelope with his crossbow. Once they sighted a small herd of mammoths, beginning their northward spring migration to the distant forests of Hroth, but they prudently let these animals alone. They also gave a wide berth to the unicorn, a huge, hairy, short-legged, barrel-bodied beast not unlike the nose-horn of the tropics, save that its single horn arose from the middle of its skull, over the eyes.

Few towns arose along the north shore of the Inner Sea. There was Gilgir, at the end of a long, tapering peninsula— one of the "Fangs of Halgir"—facing Halgir across the Strait of Halgir. Gilgir and Halgir were muddy shipping and fishing villages, whose people were mainly of the flat-faced, slant-eyed type found in Ijo and Salimor. Through these settlements passed a small trickle of trade, and ships plying between Salimor and the ports of the Inner Sea often stopped there. But Halgir's trade with the hinterland was

scanty, since the ape-men of Komilakh were hardly profitable customers.

The largest port of the north shore of the Inner Sea was
Istheun, at the head of the Bay of Norli. It was the only
Shvenic city to boast a wall and a fair degree of self-government. This was possible because of the protection of
the cham of the Gendings, the strongest of the Shvenic
hordes. Jorian and Karadur trotted along the coast towards
Istheun in hope of finding a ship for Tarxia there.

They were riding through a depression in the steppe,
when Jorian remarked, "This damned jade's canter is fairly
smooth on the nigh foot but rough on the off. On the latter,
every time the saddle goes up I feel as if I were on my way
to heaven. I'm trying to train the idiot to run only on the
nigh..."

The wind moaned and fluttered the dry grass. Jorian
said: "There is nothing like travel to teach one of the
beauties of home.

"Oh, some like the steaming jungle hot,
Where serpents swarm and the sun shines not,
And sweat runs off and your garments rot;
But I prefer a more temperate spot—
    Novaria, sweet Novaria.

Some yearn for the boundless, grassy plain,
Where rolls the nomad's creaking wain,
And horsemen gallop through wind and rain;
But I love the land of fruit and grain—
    Novaria, sweet Novaria.

And some to the sea with its howling gales,
And mountainous waves and wallowing whales
Where tall ships heel till they dip their rails;
But I'll take the friendly hills and dales
    Of Novaria, my Novaria."

"You have omitted the mountains and deserts," said
Karadur.

"If I ever climb the High Lograms or travel to Fedirun,
I'll add some stanzas..." Jorian paused, reined in, and help
up a hand. "Man ahead," he said in a low voice. "Hold
Oser for a moment."

Slipping off the roan, Jorian handed the reins to Karadur.

Then he took off his cap and ran up the next rise, bending double lest his head show against the skyline. Soon he was back.

"Just a couple of herders, watching horses. We must be getting close to one of the hordes. We'd best double back to the last stream and camp, whilst I ask Tvasha whether to ride in boldly or to slink around their flanks. Dip me in dung, but by all my reckoning we ought to have reached Istheun long since!"

"As Cidam the philosopher said: 'A journey and a sickness always last longer than expected, a purse and a jug of wine shorter,'" said Karadur. "At this pace, we may yet get to Metouro in time for the Conclave. We shall need to stop in Tarxia to draw breath. One of my faction dwells there."

"Who's he?"

"An old magician, hight Valdonius."

"Can he be trusted?"

"Certes; Valdonius is known as a man of strictest integrity."

"Well, let's hope he prove of more probity than Rhithos and Porrex, of whom you were equally confident!"

Karadur was silent for a while, then said: "O Jorian!"

"Yes?"

"Would the magical profession beguile you? I need an apprentice, for that my last one died years ago."

"What did he die of?"

"The poor ninny left a gap in his pentacle when invoking a hostile demon. I am sure you would have better sense. How say you?"

"By Thio's horns, me, a magician? I know not. I've harbored ambitions to be a clockmaster, merchant, farmer, soldier, and poet, but never a spooker."

"Well, you will have a chance to judge my colleagues at the Conclave."

Looking less cheerful than was his wont, the green god Tvasha asked Jorian: "Where are my flowers?"

"Oh lord," said Jorian, "How canst thou expect me to find flowers at this season on this cold prairie? If thou wilt but wait a fiftnight, I will give thee enough flowers to make up for all arrears."

"I still want my posies," said the god pettishly. "In

Tirao there was never any difficulty about offerings of flowers the year round."

"This is not Tirao," said Jorian, trying to stifle his impatience with this childish deity. "Here flowers bloom at certain seasons only."

"Then I hate this place! Take me back to my dear, familiar jungle!"

"Look here, O god," said Jorian, "I dug thee out of the dirt of Culbagarh, and faithfully have I worshiped thee daily ever since. If thou wilt not act thy divine age, I'll tell thee what I shall do. The next time we pass an arm of the Inner Sea, I will fling thee as far out into the waters as I can. Belike thou wilt find the sturgeon and the herring more congenial worshipers."

"Oh, very well, very well," grumbled Tvasha. "I will let thee owe me the flowers. What wouldst thou of me this time?"

"I fain would know about the horde that lieth across our path: who they be and who be their cham."

Tvasha vanished from his plinth, leaving Jorian alone in the dark, misty hall. Then the god reappeared.

"It is the horde of the Gendings, camped about the city of Istheun, and their cham is Vilimir."

"Oh! Is this the same man who was a refugee at the court of Xylar last year?"

"That I know not, albeit I could doubtless find out. Was thy Vilimir a lean man of middling height, clean-shaven, with long, hay-colored hair streaked with gray, and scars on his face and his right hand?"

"That was he. The old cham must have died or been overthrown. Canst thou advise me whether, having once befriended the fellow in his need, to trust myself within his grasp now?"

"Oh, I think thou wilt be safe enough, my dear Jorian. At least, I detected no thoughts of villainy passing through his mind when I looked in upon him just now. I did get the impression of a shrewd, hard-headed wight."

"That was my impression of him, when he visited Xylar. Farewell!"

When Jorian awoke, he told Karadur of his latest interview with Tvasha. "I am still not altogether sure of a friendly welcome," he said. "Vilimir seemed to me too much of a cold-blooded realist to be swayed by gratitude. What would you advise?"

"Oh, Jorian, let us by all means trust ourselves to him! Only thus can we find a ship to Tarxia, and my poor old bones will not endure much more jouncing and shaking across this endless plain. Besides, if we tried to circle about his array, that would delay us for days as well as compelling us to make the journey by land. This in turn might make us late for the Conclave."

"Very well," said Jorian, and saddled up. By noon they had reached the main camp of the Gendings, on a slight rise in the land north of the seaport of Istheun. Beyond Istheun could be seen the steely glitter of the sun on the waters of the Bay of Norli, where several of the undecked, canoelike little ships of this region were setting out on their first voyage of the season under their single brown, square sails. Istheun itself was a crescent-shaped town embracing the end of the bay. A wall of rough fieldstone, atop which a score of windmills whirled merrily in the brisk breeze from the steppe, surrounded the town.

The black tents of the Gendings covered a vast area. Outside this space, troops of nomad soldiery were exercising. They practiced charges, feigned retreats, and shooting from the saddle at full gallop. The bulk of the Gending army was composed of light-armed horse-archers, but the richer among Cham Vilimir's subjects made up squadrons of heavy-armed lancers, covered from head to foot in chain or scale mail and riding big horses, also partly armored. High officers watched the exercises from the backs of tame mammoths.

Nobody paid any special heed to the two nondescript riders, covered with dust and dried mud, who ambled up to the huge red-and-black pavilion in the midst of the array. Jorian and Karadur hitched their beasts to a post, and Jorian told one of the sentries, in Shvenic:

"King Jorian of Xylar is fain to pay his respects to the Grand Cham of the Gendings. He knows us."

"Said you *king*?" replied the sentry, looking Jorian up and down. "I have seen kings ere this, but never one clad as a beggar, with no escort but a diddering ancient on a spavined ass." He was a big young man, almost Jorian's size, with long golden hair in braids and a mustache that hung down to his collar bones on either side. He wore baggy woolens, a mail shirt, a fur cape, and a bronzen helmet with a wheel-shaped crest.

"The fact is as we have stated," said Jorian evenly. "Will you have the goodness to announce us?"

"His Terribility is exercising his troops. Will Your High and Mighty Majesty have a seat in the vestibule until his return?" The sentry gave a low, mocking bow.

"We thank you, soldier. We shall have things to say to you anon."

The sentry turned away with a sneering laugh. After a wait of an hour, a party of Gendings approached the pavilion on mammoths. The drivers made the huge beasts lie down in front of the pavilion, while the riders leaped to the ground. The mammoths rose and moved off while the riders entered the vestibule.

In the lead came Prince Vilimir, wearing a gold-trimmed helmet and closely followed by officers and bodyguards. Knowing at once that narrow, clean-shaven face, Jorian rose. Vilimir paused, then said: "By Greipnek's bowels! Are you not Jorian—" (he pronounced it "Zhorian") "—who was king of Xylar?"

"Quite so, Your Terribility."

Vilimir gave a wolfish smile. "Well, this is a surprise! We beheld your escape from Xylar—an artful feat, that—but never expected to see you here. Come on in."

Presently they were seated on carpets in the main tent, where Jorian received a flagon of ale. His golden ornaments tinkling when he moved, Vilimir said:

"And now, king-that-was, what brings you to Shven?"

"A small errand for the holy father Karadur, here. This is a fine case of turnabout, is it not? How long have you been cham?"

"Three months, since one of our uncle's wives poisoned the old scoundrel. We could never ascertain which one, so we had to kill them all to make sure that justice was done."

"How prospers the horde?"

"Just now, we are preparing for war against the Eylings. Hnidmar needs to be taught a lesson. We sent an envoy to protest a raid into our territory, and he sent the man back without his hands. But tell us of yourself."

"Well, for one thing, your sentry—the young one with

the long-foot mustachios—used me in a most insolent manner when I approached your tent."

Vilimir shrugged. "You cannot expect a simple nomad to treat any sessor as a fellow human being." Jorian looked sharply at Vilimir, wondering if the cham, too, meant to insult him. But Vilimir went smoothly on, "You must have seen some strange sights in your journey through the unknown southern lands."

"That I have!" Jorian began to narrate some of the high spots of his journey, when he became aware of a curious languor creeping over him. He scarcely had the strength to hold up the flagon. Great Zevatas, he thought, surely I haven't drunk *that* much?

He tried to go on, but his tongue seemed reluctant to obey his brain. The hand holding the flagon relaxed, spilling ale. Jorian glanced at Vilimir with sudden suspicion.

The cham snapped his fingers, and a noose dropped over Jorian's shoulders and tightened, pinning his arms. A second snaked out and added its grip to the fist. With a muffled roar, Jorian staggered to his feet. But the Gendings who held the other ends of the lariats were big, powerful men, who easily checked Jorian's befuddled lunges.

"What is this?" he ground out at Vilimir, who sat smiling.

"Why, only that we need money for this war with Hnidmar, and the reward offered by Xylar for your return will serve this purpose."

Jorian's tongue seemed to have swollen to twice its normal size, but he forced it to obey. "You damned treacher! By Imbal's iron yard, I could have sent you back to your uncle likewise, when you came to Xylar."

"No doubt; but, being a silly, sentimental sessor, you missed the chance. It only goes to prove that the greatest sessor is no more than a bug beneath the heel of the lowliest nomad. Put our new fetters on him."

A pair of heavy manacles of shiny new steel, joined by a foot of chain, were snapped on Jorian's wrists and locked with a key.

"The best Tarxian workmanship," said Vilimir. "You should feel complimented, my good Jorian." The cham turned to Karadur, who sat trembling. "And now, O wizard, what of you? The Xylarians would doubtless like to get their hands on the he-witch who compassed their ruler's escape; but, being vile money-grubbers like all sessors, they would probably add nought to the reward. On the other hand, we need a competent wizard. The last one we had, we slew when he could not answer the question of who poisoned our uncle. As a third alternative, we can simply order your head smitten off right now; perhaps that were the simplest solution. Which is your choice?"

"I—I will remain your humble servant."

Jorian cast a bitter look at Karadur, who avoided his eye. The cham said:

"Brakki! Place Master Jorian in the pen and put a trustworthy guard over him. He is, I warn you, skilled at escape from such gyves. Sequester all property of value with him, save his raiment. Make up an escort—ten men should do—to carry him hence to Xylar. Let me think—Xylar is allied with Vindium against Othomae; Othamae is allied with Metouro against Govannian; Metouro is allied with Tarxia against Boaktis; Govannian is allied with Aussar against Metouro. Therefore, Xylar is allied with Vindium, Govannian, and Boaktis against Othomae, Metouro, Assar, and Tarxia, whilst Solymbria, Kortoli, Zolon, and Ir are neutral. The best route were, therefore, through the Ellornas into Boaktis, avoiding Tarxian land, and thence through Solymbria and Ir into Xylar. Is that clear?"

"Aye, Your Terribility," said the man addressed as Brakki.

Then Jorian's legs folded beneath him, and he sank to the carpet unconscious. In his swoon, he found himself again facing the green god Tvasha. Instead of approaching the deity reverently, he roared:

"Why didst thou not warn me this knave lay in wait for me?"

Weeping, the god blubbered, "A thousand pardons, good Jorian! I am but a small, weak god, of limited powers. Do not, I pray thee, think hard of me! I could not bear it. And now farewell, for they are robbing thee of the little green idol, and I must perforce serve this villainous cham henceforth. May stronger gods than I go with thee!"

With Jorian in the middle, the escort wound along trails that snaked up and down the valleys of the eastern Ellornas. Moisture dripped from trees which, just bursting into leaf, loomed up out of the mist. Early wildflowers spangled the wet earth with little stars of yellow and blue and white. When the mist lifted, the higher peaks on either hand were seen to be still covered with snow.

The Ellorna Mountains and the Lograms further south formed twin barriers, walling off the land of Novaria between them. This land formed a broad peninsula, which joined Shven to the north with Fedirun and Mulvan to the south, and which also sundered the Inner Sea from the Western Ocean. Between these two mighty ranges lay the roughly rectangular stretch of hill and plain called Novaria, the Land of the Twelve Cities.

The existence of these ranges had allowed the twelve city-states of Novaria to flourish, constantly squabbling and warring with one another, despite the menace of the nomadic hordes of Shven to the north, the predatory desert-dwellers of Fedirun to the south, and the might of Mulvan to the southeast. The few passes through these mountains were easy to defend.

Since both the fierce steppe-dwellers of Shven and the teeming, docile multitudes of Mulvan looked upon the sea with horror, shipping in the Inner Sea was largely in the hands of Novarians and the mixed folk of Janareth and Istheun. Hence there was little danger of a seaborne invasion of Novaria from the greater powers to north and south—unless one of the Twelve Cities, blinded by hatred of some neighbor, brought in shiploads of these dangerous outsiders to help it in a local quarrel. This possibility kept Novarian chancellors and ministers awake nights, for they knew their own folk. They knew that, when their passions were sufficiently aroused, there was no perfidy they would not commit and no risk they would not run to gain an advantage over the immediate object of their wrath.

Jorian still rode his big chestnut roan, Oser, although his hands were manacled. Another rider led Oser, and the loop of a lariat, in the hands of still another, encircled Jorian's neck. Brakki had wanted to send Jorian on a sorry nag and keep Oser for the cham's herds, since horses big enough to carry a large, armored man were highly valued on the steppe. But the commander of the escort, a Captain Glaum, pointed out that Jorian was the heaviest man in the party. If they mounted him on some worn out little rabbit, the beast would collapse, and they would have to buy or steal another mount along the way. Therefore,

Brakki had sent Jorian on Oser, warning Glaum that he was to defend the life of the horse with his own.

So they wound among the hills. As day succeeded day, the peaks on the right grew taller and more snow-covered. This was the main spine of the Ellornas. The party kept to the southern foothills, skirting the lands of the Twelve Cities. Jorian, glancing to his left at the forested ridges, was sure that if he could only get over a few of them, he would be in Tarxian territory.

And what then? Being allied against Xylar, Tarxia would probably not extradite him. But he had no money and no weapons. The gold he had taken from Rennum Kezymar, his sword, dagger, crossbow, and mailshirt—even his little green god—had all been taken from him. He knew nobody in Tarxia, which stood at the farthest remove from Xylar of any of the Twelve.

Jorian repeated the one Tarxian name he had heard from Karadur—the wizard Valdonius. If the project of fetching the Kist of Avlen to Metouro was now dead, Jorian would presumably be free to go about his business. But he had better make sure that his geas was lifted and that he knew what his business was. In any case, Valdonius of Tarxia seemed as good a person to start with as any.

For the first few days after leaving Istheun, there had been little talk between the Gendings of the escort and their prisoner. They had not treated him badly, but their attitude was that of an unfeeling but practical man towards his domestic animals. They did not wish to injure him, because such hurts might diminish his value; but they did not mean to take any nonsense from him, either.

As the party left the plains of Shven and climbed into the lower Ellornas, relations thawed as Jorian's ebullient spirit asserted itself. The fact that he spoke fairly good Shvenic and could make small jokes helped. And Jorian resorted to crafty tricks to arouse their interest. For instance, while his escort made camp, he remarked:

"These ridges look much like those of the Lograms, a hundred leagues south of here. They remind me of the time that wizard-smith was going to temper his blade by running it red-hot up my—but that would not interest you."

"What mean you?" said Glaum. "Go ahead, tell us."

"Oh, you nomads know all and believe nothing a sessor says. Why should I bore you with my tales?"

"We will not let you arouse our curiosity and then tease us, for one thing," said Glaum. "Now talk, or by Greipnek's prick, I will twist this rope until you do!"

"Oh, very well," and Jorian was off on the tale of his adventure with Rhithos the smith.

By the time they were well into the Ellornas, it had become an evening routine for the Gendings to demand: "Jorian! Tell us a story!"

Glaum made sure that, at any time, at least two men were watching Jorian with weapons ready. He divided the night into watches, during which two watched Jorian while two others stood regular sentry duty.

"We might run across a bear newly emerged from its den," he explained, "and in the higher mountains, the cave men attack small parties. Please Greipnek, neither shall befall us; but we mean to be ready if it come."

One day, Jorian caught snatches of talk that made him suspect that the party would soon turn south, threading its way through the passes into Boaktis. Therefore, he had better escape forthwith if he wished to reach friendly Tarxian territory. That evening he outdid himself as a storyteller.

"If I did but have the wit of King Fusinian of Kortoli," he said, "I should have given you thickheads the slip long since; but alas! I fear I am as stupid as you. You remember my telling you about Fusinian, the son of Filoman the Well-Meaning, a few nights ago? He was a small man, but lively and quick-witted, so that they called him Fusinian the Fox. And I have told you of the time he sowed the Teeth of Grimnor and was driven out of Kortoli.

"After he recovered his kingdom and his lovely queen, Thanuda, all went well for a time. And then one day, the queen vanished, leaving her boudoir in confusion, as if she had been carried off by violence. Naturally, Fusinian was much distressed. Their two children aggravated his grief by tugging at his garments and asking, when was mummy coming home?

"As soon as this disappearance transpired, Fusinian sent out searchers, and issued proclamations, and offered rewards, and consulted knowledgeable persons to try to find out what had become of his beloved. One of the first of whom he inquired was his court wizard, Doctor Aichos, who cast horoscopes and studied the flight of birds and evoked spirits, all to no avail. Then Fusinian consulted with all the other licensed wizards and wizardesses in the kingdom, with no more success.

"At last he resorted to the one person he had sworn he would never hire again: the witch Gloé, who dwelt in a cave in the mountains of southern Kortoli. Gloé had been giving the Kortolian monarchy bad advice for two generations. Moreover, she was determined to make herself the court wizard in place of old Aichos, and this was the price she had exacted from the kings of Kortoli on the previous occasions of her employment by them. As things fell out, her spells had always failed in one respect or another, so the kings had never felt obliged to give her this post.

"Now, rendered desperate, King Fusinian rode south and sought out Gloé's cave. When he asked her what had befallen his consort, she answered readily:

"'Oh, that. A troll, who has lately moved hither from the Ellorna Mountains, has taken up his abode in the Marvelous Caverns. A fiftnight ago, I received word from one of my familiar demons that this troll had brought a woman thither.'

"Now, the Marvelous Caverns were well-known to Fusinian, for his father, Filoman the Well-Meaning, had caused them to be explored and mapped, and Fusinian himself had visited them as a youth. They were a series of limestone caves, opening into a ravine a few leagues from Gloé's cave. Few, however, had visited them, because they were very difficult to get into and had the repute of being haunted by evil spirits. Fusinian asked Gloé:

"'Can you cast a spell upon this troll, to draw him forth from his cave and destroy him?'

"'Alas, nay, sire!' replied the witch. 'Know that, whereas trolls have no inherent supernatural powers, they are singularly proof against spells cast upon them by others. The only spells of mine that might work require lengthy preparations, and also require that the object of the spell hold still during the operation.'

"'Then I suppose I shall have to pursue this monster into its cave myself and seek to slay it,' quoth the king.

"'I advise that not,' said Gloé. 'This is an egregiously

tough old troll, yclept Vuum. Your weapons will glance from his scaly hide as from a granite statue, and such is his strength that he could pick you up and tear you in pieces, limb from limb, and scatter the pieces about his ravine.'

" 'Then I will come with a company of my doughtiest soldiers, and overwhelm him by numbers.'

" 'That will not do either, Your Majesty. For the Marvelous Caverns open out midway up a cliff, and they can be entered only by lowering oneself down by ropes from the top of the cliff. Furthermore, the single entrance to the caverns is narrow, so that your men could come at Vuum only one at a time and thus be destroyed in detail.'

" 'If this is so, then how does Vuum come in and out?'

" 'Because he is a troll, his fingernails and toenails are so thick and talonlike that he can force them into cracks in the rocks that your eye would never notice. Thus he can scale the cliff as easily as a squirrel runs up a tree trunk.'

" 'How about mounting a ballista across the gorge from the cave and skewering him with a dart when he shows his head?'

" 'So keen are his senses and so great his agility that he would see your missile coming and dodge back into the cave.'

" 'Well,' said Fusinian, 'if my time has come, it has come. Whatever the odds, my honor will not permit me to leave this vermin in possession of my dear wife.'

" 'What do you purpose to do?' asked Gloé.

" 'Why, to fare to the Marvelous Caverns, have myself lowered down the cliff, enter the cave, and essay to slay this Vuum.'

" 'Oh, sire! Whatever will Kortoli do without you? We nearly perished under your dear but foolish father. If you die now, we shall face a long regency ere your eldest wean reaches manhood, and you know what perils that entails. Had you any chance at all, I would bless your undertaking. But consider: this troll is half again as tall as you, and twice as wide, and weighs thrice as much. His hide is as hard as that of the crocodiles of Mulvan, and he can crumble rocks with his fingers—'

" 'Wait,' said the king. 'Twice as wide as I, said you?'

" 'Aye, and all made of thews of iron—'

"'Let me think,' said Fusinian. 'I am trying to remember the map of the Marvelous Caverns prepared in my father's reign. Look at you, O Gloé: If I immobilize this Vuum, can you blast him with some spell or other?

"'Well, sire, there is a lightning spell I long ago learnt from a holy man of Mulvan. It is nearly as dangerous to the user as to the victim; but in this case I should be willing to try it. However, I want your word that, if I succeed, I shall be granted my license and made your court magician—'

"'Yes, yes, I knew that was coming,' quoth Fusinian. 'You shall have what you ask if, and only if, your levin bolt perform as you have promised. Now I go to prepare my assault.'

"So the king rode back to his capital, and there he selected his swiftest steed, and his keenest weapons, and a hundred of his most stalwart warriors. And another thing he took with him was a set of bagpipes, such as are used by the shepherds of the hills of Govannian, which the king had been trying to learn to play. The general opinion in Kortoli was that the sound of this instrument was hideous enough when played by a competent piper, but when the king made noises upon it the result was ghastly beyond all description.

"Since Fusinian was king, nobody but Thanuda dared to tell him to his face what they thought of his piping; but from the way they hemmed and hawed when he asked their views, he very soon wist their true opinion. So he took to practicing in a cell of his dungeon, where nobody would be bothered save a prisoner or two. Being a humane man, Fusinian allowed them time off their sentences in return for their having to listen to his playing.

"The king also took the map of the Marvelous Caverns prepared under Filoman and studied it as he traveled. And in due time he came to the ravine whereunto opened the entrance to the Caverns. He took a position on the bluff over against the ravine from the cave entrance and played his bagpipes.

"After he had played for a while, and his hundred stalwart warriors had covered their ears, the troll appeared at the mouth of his cave, roaring: 'What is that hellish racket?'

"'It is no hellish racket, but the sweet strains of my bagpipes,' said Fusinian.

" 'Well, why are you subjecting me to them?' said Vuum.

" 'Because I am King Fusinian, whose queens you have abducted, I want her back, and I want you out of my kingdom.'

" 'Oho!' said the troll. 'So it is our little mouse of a king, is it? Know, worm, that I mean to keep your woman for myself, and if you do not stop pestering me, it will be the worse for you.'

"After they had bandied words thus for a time, Vuum came out of the cave, climbing down the sheer cliff by his nails like a bat, and came roaring up the other side of the gorge to destroy Fusinian and his men. The men loosed a volley of quarrels from their crossbows, but these merely bounced off the scaly hide of the troll. Then Fusinian and his party vaulted into their saddles and galloped off, and the troll could not catch them. But as soon as Vuum returned to his cave, Fusinian was back at his post, serenading him again.

"And so it continued for many days, with the king making both days and nights hideous with his pipes and then fleeing away whenever Vuum sought to retaliate. At length even the iron strength of the troll began to fail, and he contented himself with lurking in the mouth of his cave, hurling stones and insults at his tormentor. Fusinian took cover when the stones came whizzing over, and the insults bothered him not a whit.

"At last the troll called across the ravine: 'O King, if you would fain have your wife again, then agree to fight me man to troll! I will wrastle, or box, or fence, or fight with spears, axes, clubs, or knives, or duel at a distance with the longbow or the crossbow or the sling or the twirl-spear. Can you think of any more ways for us to settle our difference?'

" 'Since I am the challenged party,' quoth Fusinian, 'it is mine to choose the weapons. And I will not wrastle, or box, or fight with swords, spears, et cetera, because I know your strength and hardihood all too well. But I will undertake a fair contest with you.'

" 'And what might that be?'

" 'We shall have a foot race, in your own caverns. We shall start at the entrance, and run back along the main corridor, and around the big loop, and out to the entrance again.'

"After some argument over details, the troll agreed that this was a fair contest. Then Fusinian said: 'Now, as to terms. If you win, I will go away and leave you in undisturbed possession of the Marvelous Caverns and of Thanuda. If I win, you shall yield me Thanuda and depart forthwith from my kingdom.'

"Again they argued, but when Fusinian began to blow up the bag of pipes, Vuum quickly assented. Then Fusinian said: 'Not that I mistrust you, my good troll, but to make sure that there occur no untoward event when I am in your cave, you shall bring Thanuda to the bottom of the ravine and leave her there whilst we stage our contest. My men have orders, in case of treachery on your part, to take the woman and flee, not even trying to rescue me.'

" 'But what about treachery on your part, my lord King?'

" 'The mere fact of my being within your reach takes care of that,' said Fusinian. 'You could squash me like a bug if I played you false.'

"So Fusinian descended to the bottom of the ravine, and Vuum did likewise, carrying Thanuda on his shoulder. And then the troll took Fusinian on his shoulder, and bore him up the cliff again to the mouth of the cave, and Fusinian said afterwards that the journey on this stinking monster's scaly shoulder was the hardest of all his trials to bear. But at last they reached the cave, and the troll gave Fusinian one of the little lanthorns lit by captive glowworms that he used to illumine the darkness, whilst he took another one. Then Fusinian put his head out of the cave and called down to his wife:

" 'All right, dear, you may give the signal.'

"So she called up: 'Ready! Set! Go!' and Vuum and Fusinian were off like the wind, or as nearly like the wind as they could in the darkness of the cave, with its uneven floor and the stalactites and stalagmites to dodge.

"Being a small man and fast on his feet, Fusinian knew he could get off at the very start faster than his lumbering antagonist, who was a fine runner once he got going but slower to reach his best speed. And sure enough, Fusinian found himself bounding along two paces ahead of Vuum. Vuum had the advantage of knowing the Caverns better than Fusinian, who had not been there in a decade, and he began to gain upon Fusinian. But then he ran his head into a stalactite, so that it broke off and huge chunks of limestone rained down upon him. Being a troll, he was not gravely hurt, but the accident threw him off his stride and enabled Fusinian to gain another pace upon him.

"Now, Fusinian knew from his study of the map of the cave that in the main loop, whereof he had spoken, there was a narrow place. And when he got to this strait, he turned his body sideways and nimbly slipped through. But Vuum, following him, got stuck. He must have known about this narrow place, but it would seem that he had never tried to see if he could pass through it. Fusinian paused to call back a few choice insults, whereupon the troll, roaring savagely, tried even harder to push through the strait but only jammed himself in more tightly than ever. As you can see, trolls are not a highly intelligent race, ranking somewhere near the ape-men of Komilakh in this regard.

"And so Fusinian reached the entrance once more and called up to his men—some of whom had come around to the top of the cliff above the cave—to drop a rope down into the ravine. And when Fusinian got his breath back, he let himself down by the rope and seized Thanuda in a loving embrace. Then they climbed to the other side of the gorge, and the king called upon the witch Gloé to perform.

"Gloé had been bringing her cauldron to a boil and putting into it the eye of a newt, and the toe of a frog, and other unwholesome substances. And she uttered a mighty spell and incantation, so that the sky darkened, and a cold wind blew, and rain fell, and the air was filled with the rustle of unseen wings, and a foetor as of the Pit filled the air. And she pointed her wand at the entrance to the cave, and a bolt of lightning flashed from the cloud overhead and struck the side of the mountain—but not the cave entrance. She tried again, and the lightning struck the other side. For an hour she aimed her wand and spoke the words of power, and each time the lightning flashed and the thunder boomed, but never could she seem to hit the mouth of the Marvelous Caverns. When the thunder was not crashing, they could hear the bellows of the trapped troll inside the Caverns.

"Then the thunder cloud wafted away, and Gloé collapsed in exhaustion, without having once struck the target. And whilst Fusinian and Thanuda and the warriors stood about in a daze, half deafened by the thunder and wholly soaked by the shower, a deep rumble was heard. The earth trembled and moved, and the cliff crumbled with a mighty roar, and the entrance to the Marvelous Caverns vanished in a roaring slide of rock and gravel, and the air was filled with choking dust. Some of the other side of the ravine gave way, too, and had not Fusinian snatched his queen away from the brink, they would have fallen with it. As it was, the ravine was now half filled with rubble, and no trace of the Caverns or of the troll could be seen, save a peculiarly sticky green fluid, which oozed out from between the rocks.

"So that was the end of the Caverns and of Vuum, and they returned to Kortoli City rejoicing. Then Gloé demanded the post of court magician, and Fusinian refused on the ground that she had not in fact slain the troll by her levin bolts, which had all gone awry. The coming of the earthquake at that opportune moment, he said, had been a happenstance. Gloé, on the other hand, maintained that, even if her lightnings had not gone into the cave and struck Vuum, they had so disturbed the balance of natural forces as to bring about the earthquake. Hence, she had really performed her part of the bargain, even if not quite the way she had intended.

"The dispute waxed bitter, for Fusinian was too just a king to order Gloé summarily suppressed for dunning him. At last Thanuda suggested that they bring in an impartial outsider to arbitrate. So they put the question to the theocrat of Tarxia, who decided in favor of Gloé. Since Doctor Aichos was ripe for retirement anyway, it looked as if the change could be effected with the least possible disturbance. But Gloé had not enjoyed her new post a fiftnight when she caught a phthisic from some other courtier and died in three days. So Aichos' retirement proved only temporary after all.

"Thanuda assured her consort that Vuum had done nothing worse to her than to make her play draughts with him by the hour. But presently it transpired that she was with child. And when the child was born, it was bigger and more robust than any child ever seen in Kortoli. Moreover, as it grew, its skin developed a rough, scaly appearance, not unlike the hide of a crocodile.

"Happily, the boy was not the heir apparent, having

two older brothers; and, if not especially intelligent, he was good-natured and docile. Named Fusarius, he grew up to be a famous warrior, being twice as strong as the average man, with a hide of such remarkable toughness that he hardly needed armor, although he wore it in battle, disliking the scratches and bruises that would have been mortal wounds had they befallen other men.

"About the paternity of Fusarius, Fusinian doubtless had his own private thoughts. But, being a philosophical man, he made the best of things."

Jorian glanced around. One of his escorts had gone quietly to sleep, curled up against the base of a tree. Of the rest, several should have been sleeping so as to be wide awake when their watches began. Instead, they were all hanging eagerly on his words.

"They tell a tale," he went on, "about this Fusarius and the lonesome lion..."

So he continued for hours, reeling off story after story: some dredged out of his memory, some made up on the spot. Speaking in a low, undramatic voice, he shamelessly padded the tales and strung them out, deliberately keeping them from becoming too exciting. In consequence, by midnight every man of the escort was asleep. Watches had not been posted, because Glaum had dozed off before he thought to do so. The clearing buzzed gently with the snores of the Gendings.

Jorian rose to his feet. He searched inside his waistband for the one possession, besides his clothes, of which he had not been robbed: the little bag of pick-locks. The Gendings had been so elated over his weapons and money belt that they had neglected to search his garments more minutely. Once Jorian had one of the bent wires in his hands, it was only a matter of a few breaths before the manacles opened.

He laid the fetters down carefully to keep the chain from clanking, and picked up the scabbarded sword that one of the escort had laid on the ground beside him. It was a straight, two-edged horseman's blade, even longer than Randir, with a plain cross-hilt. Jorian did not like it so well as the one he had taken from Rhithos the smith; but it would do.

He would like to have stolen one or more purses from

the Gendings. They had, he knew, brought a considerable sum of money wherewith to bribe the officials of Solymbria and Ir if it should prove necessary in order to hustle Jorian through those countries without interference. But, since each man had his purse firmly tied to his girdle, Jorian did not see how he could do this without the risk of awakening somebody.

Oser swiveled his ears and made a small equine sound as Jorian, moving like a shadow, stepped to him, stroked his nose, and untied him. For such nocturnal work, he would have preferred a horse of a darker color than the chestnut roan, but this factor was much outweighed by the fact that this animal knew him, whereas the others did not and might make a row if he tried to lead one of them away.

Holding the reins in one hand and the stolen sword in the other, he quietly led Oser out from among the other animals and up the nearest ridge to the south. Atop the ridge, out of sight of the camp, he paused to study the stars. The crescent moon had set two hours before, but the stars, visible through the branches of trees not yet in leaf, gave him his direction. With a quiet smile to himself, he set off down the further slope towards Tarxia.

IX

THE
SMARAGDINE GOD

THE RIVER SPHERDAR MEANDERED THROUGH THE CENTRAL plain of Tarxia, where teams of buffalos pulled wooden plows through the wet, black earth. The meadows and the borders of roads and fields, where the plow had not trenched, were gay with millions of wildflowers.

Beside the Spherdar, a few leagues from the Inner Sea and at the head of navigation for seagoing ships, stood Tarxia City. Its wall looking imposing from a distance, but a closer view showed that it was out of date and in poor repair. It was made of brick instead of stone and hence would not stand up under the battering of modern seige engines. Many merlons had crumbled away, and here and there a big crack, caused by uneven settling, ran zigzag through the brickwork. For defense, the Tarxians relied more on their god and the supernatural powers of his priesthood than on arms and fortifications. Since the establishment of the theocracy, Tarxia's neighbors had held these powers too much in awe to test them seriously.

The city itself was smaller and shabbier than one would have expected of a major port of the Inner Sea. The streets were narrow, winding, and filthy. Most of the houses were either tall, jam-packed tenements or hovels patched together with odd pieces of brick and board. Even the houses of the richer Tarxians were modest in size and subdued in décor. The streets swarmed with drably clad laymen and black-robed priests of the god Gorgolor.

The city was dominated by one huge, towering structure: the temple of Gorgolor, the patron god of Tarxia and—according to the theocracy—the supreme god of the universe. It was the largest, costliest, and gaudiest temple in all Novaria, not even excepting the splendid fane of Zevatas in Solymbria. The salient feature of this temple was the enormous dome at the center of the cruciform structure.

Supported on a drum and pendentives and braced by half-domes and buttresses, this dome soared over 350 feet into the air. The spring sun blazed blindingly on its gilded tiles. Four slender towers, whence the priests of Gorgolor called the Tarxians to prayer thrice a day, stood in a square at the corners of the structure. Around the temple spread a temenos of park and subsidiary buildings, including the theocrat's palace.

From the temple of Gorgolor, the ground sloped downwards to the waterfront, with its docks and ships and sailors' haunts. Swollen by several tributaries, which joined it above and below Tarxia City, the Spherdar meandered eastward through the great Swamp of Spraa to the sea. Sea cows were strictly protected in Tarxian waters because, by feeding on the swamp plants, the creatures helped to keep them from blocking the river.

On the sloping ground between the temple and the waterfront rose a multitude of dwellings of Tarxia's more prosperous laymen, including that of Valdonius the magician. Around noon on the nineteenth of the Month of the Crow, Jorian knocked on the door of Valdonius' house. When the porter opened the peephole, Jorian said:

"Is Doctor Valdonius at home?"

"What if he is?" said the porter, eyeing Jorian's ragged garments and shaggy hair and beard with distaste. On Jorian's left arm a yellow band was tied, bearing the words, in the archaic characters used in Tarxia:

LICENSED HERETIC—ZEVATIST

"Pray tell him a messenger from Doctor Karadur is without."

The peephole closed, and presently the door opened. As Jorian stepped inside, the porter recoiled with a wrinkled nose. Jorian grumbled:

"If you hadn't a bath in two months, old boy, you'd stink, too!"

When the porter led Jorian down a hall and into a handsome living room, Jorian stopped and stared in amazement. Of the two men seated at lunch, one—a huge, bald, fat man—he took to be Valdonius. The other was Karadur. Valdonius said:

"Greetings, Master Jorian. One need not see a mouse through a millstone to perceive that you somehow gave the barbarians the slip." Then, to Karadur: "You see, old man, my divination worked. Said I not he would be here around midday?"

"Greetings, Doctor Valdonius," said Jorian; then, to Karadur: "What in the forty-nine Mulvanian hells are you doing here? The last I saw of you, you had abandoned me and your mission to become Cham Vilimir's hired spooker!"

A tear rolled down Karadur's wrinkled brown face. "Ah, my son, blame me not over-harshly! It would have availed you nought for me to have been sent back to Xylar with you, or to have been slain on the spot. What else could I—with the most morally upright intentions—have done?"

"You could at least have pleaded with Vilimir, or threatened him with some nameless supernatural doom. All you did was to squeak: 'Aye, aye, sir!' and let me be dragged off to my fate without a word of protest."

"But you escaped your doom!"

"No thanks to you. And now I suppose that, having learnt that Vilimir wanted you to go galloping over the steppe with him in his war with that other horde, you found it better for your health and comfort to slip away and continue your journey, eh?"

"Ah, no indeed, my dear son! I had to say what I did to befool the barbarian, so that I could escape and essay to reach you—"

Valdonius interrupted with a roar of laughter. "Your

young man has grown an old head on his shoulders, Karadur!" he cried jovially. "Master Jorian, I think that shaft went close to the clout. Natheless, if an older if not wiser man may offer a word of advice, assume not that the motive you ascribe to a man, even if your guess be true, is the only one. For men's motives are commonly mixed, with self-interest jostling righteousness and fears mingled with hopes. What if the good Father Karadur allowed self-interest for the moment to overcome all other considerations? Has the same never befallen you? Besides, he is old and infirm, no puissant young hero like yourself. Therefore, the adamantine valor of a Ghish the Great or a Fusinian the Fox should not be expected of him."

"I'm no hero," growled Jorian. "I am only a simple craftsman who would like to settle down and earn a decent living. Natheless, I didn't run off and leave Karadur in the jungles and steppes we have lately traversed, although I could easily have done so. But what's done is done. What is the present state of affairs?"

Valdonius grinned. "Events have taken a most interesting turn. But, my good Jorian, I need hardly summon fell spirits from forbidden planes and unholy dimensions across nighted gulfs of space and time, to discern that you would fain have three things: a solid repast, a bath, and the ministrations of a barber. Is my speculation correct?"

"Eminently, sir. If my hair be allowed to grow any longer, I shall trip on it as I walk. As for the bath, your poor porter wellnigh swooned when he got a close whiff of me. But of all these desiderata, the meal stands foremost, or, I, too, shall swoon."

"How have you subsisted since your escape?"

"When a farmer had firewood to be chopped, I chopped for fodder, for myself and my horse. When he did not, having not the price of a patch for my breeches upon me, I stole one of his fowls. That's an art to which I devoted much study in training for my escape from Xylar. I thank you, fair one," he said as a pretty girl tendered him a goblet of wine and another brought in a hearty meal for him.

"Peradventure you will be known as Jorian the Fox for that accomplishment," said Valdonius with a chuckle.

"Or at least as Jorian the chicken thief."

"What befell you at the Tarxian frontier?"

Between ravenous bites, Jorian said: "I told them I was Maltho of Kortoli, seeking honest employment as a mercenary. They plainly didn't like my looks—or perhaps my smell, or my empty purse—but after some muttering and whispering they let me in on a thirty-day permit. The priest in command of the post tied this damned brassard upon me, as if I carried some fatal and contagious pox."

"From their point of view, you do," said Valdonius. "You bear in your head all sorts of unauthorized thoughts, which if not checked might spread amongst the general populace and imperil that delicate state of mindless acceptance of the True Faith, which the theocracy has so long and so earnestly striven to impose upon the Tarxian populace."

"I know; they made me promise not to discuss religious or philosophical matters with any Tarxian during my sojourn. I trust I have not already violated this injunction?"

"It matters not. For thrice a hundred years, the theocracy succeeded in sealing the borders to such subversive influences. Now, however, the country seethes with restlessness and discontent, for many of the priests have become mere cassocked lechers and grafters, and the benefits they have promised have not come to pass. Ideas have a way of leaking across frontiers despite walls and sentinels. Be reasonably discreet in your subversive utterances and you will have little to fear."

"I wonder they let me in at all?"

"Belike they were impressed despite themselves by that aristocratic manner you learnt as king. They took you for a gentleman fallen upon hard times, who if kindly entreated might be useful to them."

"Which, in a sense, I suppose I am." Jorian finished his plate and sat back with a sigh of repletion. "Zevatas! that was good. There's no sauce like a ravenous appetite. And now, my learned colleagues, pray tell me: How fares the Kist of Avlen and the project concerning it?"

Valdonius chuckled. He seemed to be always laughing or chuckling or smiling, but Jorian found his mirth not especially kindly.

"Well, now," he said, "the Kist of Avlen—" (he pronounced it, "Aulen" in the northern manner) "—is safe and well-guarded in my cellar and shall remain there until you gentlemen have assisted me in a certain enterprise."

Jorian glanced at Karadur, who was shedding another tear. "Fool that I was!" said the Mulvanian. "If ever I survive past the Conclave, I will withdraw from all association with my colleagues and become a hermit, so rare is good faith among them."

"Now, now, old man," said Valdonius, "do not carry on so. After all, what I am doing for the magical profession here in Tarxia is quite as important as what my fellow Altruists propose to do in Metouro."

"And what is it that you would do here?" asked Jorian.

"Ere I go further, let me warn you that this discussion shall not go beyond the three of us, and I have ways of dealing with any who play me false. Karadur tells me you are a bit of a blabbermouth."

"Not when I have a real secret to keep. I will keep yours."

"Very well, then. Have you visited the temple of Gorgolor?"

"Nay; I've only glanced at it in passing on my way hither."

"Well, in this temple stands an altar, and beyond this altar rises a pedestal, and on this pedestal stands one of the wonders of the world."

"The smaragdine statue of Gorgolor? I've heard of it."

"Aye. This statue is in the form of a frog, carved from a single emerald—but this frog is the size of a lion or a bear. It is the largest emerald ever known to have existed, and its value may be greater than that of all the other jewels in the world together. The priests make much of the brilliant radiance of this statue, which they say will blind unbelievers who look upon it. But I have seen it often, and my eyesight is as sound as ever. When Gorgolor manifests himself on this plane, they say, he takes possession of the statue, and to the statue are the prayers of the theocrat and the rest of the hierachy directed. Now, what think you would ensue if this statue vanished?"

Jorian peered out at Valdonius from under his heavy brows. "It would cause much scurry and flurry amongst the priesthood, I should think."

"That, my dear young man, is a magnificent understatement."

"Why make the statue disappear?"

"As you have gathered, many intelligent Tarxians are

less than enchanted by the rule of the theocracy. Look at me, for example. The priests allow only a very limited practice of magic: nought but divination and sympathetic magic. No sorcery or necromancy, no matter how laudable their purposes or beneficial their results. And why? Because their theologians assert, on no scientific basis but solely from their convoluted casuistical reasoning, that any spirits so invoked are by definition evil entities opposed to the good god Gorgolor. Therefore, traffic with such beings is a damnable heresy, to be punished by stake and faggot. So I, who could mightily advance the supernatural sciences if permitted freedom of research, must confine my activities to such trivial pastimes as casting horoscopes and sending my spirit forth in trances to search for my clients' lost bangles.

"Others have other complaints, but they all come to the same thing. We are fettered hand and foot by these obsolete theological gyves. Our polis stagnates, whilst the other Twelve Cities advance in the arts and sciences. I could give you endless instances of the stupid oppressions of literature and the arts, the ban on free discussion, and so on. Why, only last month—"

"Pardon," said Jorian, not wishing to hear all the woes of the Tarxians. "I think I understand your complaints. Let us return to the statue. A carving of that size can't be carried out of the temple in one's pocket; so what will you do?"

"The Kist, which your good colleague has fetched hither so opportunely, contains a useful shrinking spell, which should be applicable in this case. It is better than the modern shrinking spells, which leave the weight of the shrunken object unchanged. If this statue weighs, say, ten talents, to shrink it to pocket size whilst its weight remained constant would leave it as hard to move as it now is. It might even cause it to crack its plinth, because of the concentration of weight in a small space. I must warn you, if you should be called upon to handle the statue, that the lessened weight leaves the mass unchanged."

"What's the difference?"

"Weight is the force wherewith the planet draws objects like yourself and Gorgolor to its bosom. Mass is the quality that makes an object resist a sudden change in motion, as in starting or stopping. The two maintain a constant proportion—save when interfered with by a puissant spell. If you run with the shrunken statue, think not that you can stop it in its flight as readily as you could a simple brick or stone. If you do, its momentum will toss you arse-over-apex."

"What's my part in this escapade?"

"That we must discuss this even, to make sure that every detail has been planned and every contigency anticipated."

"But I," said Jorian, "am weary of this whole business. What makes you think I'll have any part of your scheme?"

"Because, my dear Jorian, you are still subject to the geas that my fellow adepts put upon you. Hence you have really no choice in the matter. Whereas the geas compels you to help, in every way you can, in getting the Kist to Mctouro, and whereas the only way you can do this is to fall in with my wishes, you defy me on pain of those torments of which you have already experienced small samples."

"Not if you no longer live," gritted Jorian, seizing the hilt of his sword and tugging.

As he did so, however, Valdonius shouted words of power, threw a handful of powder towards him, and made some quick passes. The Shvenic sword came out of the scabbard only a few fingerbreadths and then stuck fast. Jorian's powerful arm muscles swelled and knotted, and sweat furrowed the dirt on his forehead, but the blade would not budge. He finally let go with a gasp. The sword snapped back to the bottom of the scabbard with a click.

"You see?" said Valdonius, chuckling. "But come! I am not your foe, so let us make your sojourn here as pleasant as we can. That long-desired bath awaits you. You shall be not only scrubbed but also oiled, massaged, and perfumed like one of the good spirits of the Mulvanian heavens. And I have sent for a washerwoman to cleanse and mend your garments and a barber to give you the look of a civilized mortal and not a club-waving cave man from the Ellornas.

"As for the remaining form of recreation, which I know is in your mind from the glances your gave my maidservants, I fear you must needs wait until you have left Tarxia. Relations between the sexes are governed by strict regulations here, and casual fornication is not permitted even to sailors from the ships that call here. This fact makes Tarxia an unpopular seaport, notwithstanding the profits to be made here."

"Has this government actually succeeded in stopping all lechery and harlotry?"

"Practically speaking, yes. The only ones who get away with such illicit amusements are certain members of the priesthood. Our dear old theocrat is always promising to end this abuse, but somehow he never seems to get around to it."

The following evening, they approached the temple of Gorgolor with Valdonius bearing a lanthorn. In a low voice, the magician explained:

"We are in luck. The theocrat and his hierarchy have been disputing whether to send missionaries to Mulvan or Shven. So, when I told them you had just come from those lands, they arranged an audience at once. You had better review what you know of the religions of those countries."

"I know not much," said Jorian. "Had I been warned that such questions would be asked of me, I could have inquired; but now 'tis too late."

"Well, make up what you do not know, but make it plausible. This audience cost me a pretty penny, and I would have my money's worth."

"They charged for it, even though it's to their advantage?"

"Certes! The first principle of the cult is that every operation shall pay for itself and more. Why else maintain so strict a monopoly in supernatural matters?"

"What's the status of the other gods?"

"At first, after the fall of the Ignadian dynasty, the rule was one of toleration for all faiths. In fact, the promise of such liberty was one tactic whereby the priesthood of Gorgolor—theretofore an obscure minor god—attained power. You have tried kings, they said, and the kings became tyrants; you have tried democracy, and the republic became a cauldron of anarchy and mob rule. There remains but theocracy: rule by the holy gods through their virtuous and moral vicars.

"The Gorgolorians had not long been in power, however, than they began to arrogate unto themselves a monopoly of the supernatural. First they enacted stringent laws against witchcraft. Then a few small, eccentric cults were suppressed. Then the priesthoods of Zevatas and Franda and the other major gods were placed under the orders of the high priest of Gorgolor, who thus became the theocrat.

"Then the theocrat announced a series of revelations from the gods. Each revelation enlarged the power and glory of Gorgolor and shrank those of the other gods. At last the other gods were reduced to mere lackeys of Gorgolor. One by one their temples have been converted to other uses or torn down, and their statues have been destroyed or hidden away on one pretext or another, until they no longer have any separate cults apart from that of Gorgolor."

"I wonder what the gods themselves think of this," said Jorian.

"So do I. Nowadays the other gods are not even named separately in the rites to Gorgolor, but are merely spoken of collectively as Gorgolor's attendant spirits."

"What if a Tarxian tried to revive the worship of Zevatas?"

"They would burn him as a heretic. You as a foreigner are allowed to exist here, but for a limited time only. If you wished to settle permanently, you would have have to accept the True Faith. Now let us see: How shall I introduce you? I told the priests little about you."

"I am calling myself Maltho of Kortoli," said Jorian.

"Not distinguished enough; Maltho is a common name. How about Lord Maltho of Kortoli?"

"Kortoli has no nobility. Save for the king, it is a one-class polis. I persuaded the Mulvanians that I was a Kortolian noble, but that might not work with these priests."

"Well, then, Doctor Maltho?"

"If you like. I did once take a course at the Academy in Othomae, when I soldiered for the Grand Bastard."

"What did you study?"

"Versification. I once harbored an ambition to be a poet."

"Then you shall be Maltho of Kortoli, Doctor of Literature from the Academy of Othomae. Now, we shall arrive just after vespers. As soon as that is over, most of the priests will go about their own business; hence they will not much infest the temple.

"Your audience will be in the theocrat's palace. The theocrat is Kylo of Anneia, who aside from his office is not a bad fellow. I take him for a perfectly sincere and rather simple-minded old man, who believes all the moonshine his priests dole out to the faithful.

"When you have satisfied their curiosity regarding the ripeness of the foreigners for conversion, you might utter some leading remarks about the temple. Hint that you might be ready for conversion yourself, if you could but see its wonders. If I know Kylo, he will insist on showing the edifice to you in person. He redecorated it a few years ago and is monstrously proud of his handiwork.

"Armed guards are posted around the outside of the temple, and inside a couple of priests are supposed to keep a constant vigil, praying to Gorgolor and incidentally watching to see that nobody steals the furnishings. But in these degenerate days, one who suddenly intrudes upon these priests is likely to find them engrossed in dicing or draughts.

"As your party passes near the emerald statue, I wish you to display your storytelling talent. You must so fascinate all within earshot that the priests on watch will leave their posts and follow your party. Dear old Kylo will not, I am sure, rebuke them.

"Meanwhile, Karadur and I will slip behind the pedestal of the statue of Gorgolor. Whilst your party drifts out the main entrance, with you talking your head off, we shall try the shrinking spell. When we rejoin you, it will, the gods permitting, be with a much diminished Gorgolor in our pockets. Even if the theft transpire ere we leave the temenos, it is unlikely that we shall be searched, for the priests will be looking for a crew of twenty to thirty men and a team of oxen, which would be needed to rape away the statue in its present form."

As the party, consisting of Jorian, Karadur, Valdonius, the theocrat, four of his episcopals, and one ordinary priest who was his secretary, approached the main entrance to the temple of Gorgolor, its spear-bearing guards dropped with a clang to one knee. At a word from the high priest, they sprang to the great bronzen doors and pushed them groaningly open.

Kylo of Anneia was a short, stout man with a large,

hooked nose, wearing a white silken robe and a tall head-dress of white felt, trimmed with gold and gleaming with jewels. The episcopals were in crimson; the ordinary priest, in black.

Jorian, now barbered, sweet smelling, and clad in clean garments, was saying "...and so, I cannot extend much hope to Your Holiness in this matter. The nomads of Shven hold all sessors, as they call them, in such contempt that, if you send missionaries thither, they will either laugh at them or slay them out of hand.

"The Mulvanians present no more hope, although their response would be more amiable. They would say: Welcome, O priests; we already have hundreds of gods but are always glad to add another. And they would enroll Gorgolor in their own teeming pantheon, where he would be lost in the throng. When you complained that they had perverted your meticulous theology, they would simply smile and promise to do better—and then go on doing as they have always done."

Jorian paused inside the temple to look around. "Marvelous!" he cried. "Incredible! Such taste! Such artistry! Surely, Your Holiness, your god must be a great and wise god indeed, to inspire men to such an achievement!"

"It is good of you to say so, my son," said Kylo, beaming and speaking with a broad Tarxian peasant accent. "You would be surprised at the trouble I had with some conservative members of my own hierachy, who thought mosaics of mortals and spiritual beings in a state of nudity indecent."

The central portion of the temple was square, with a colossal stone pier at each corner of the square. Huge arches and pendentives sprang from the tops of these piers. From the pendentives a low drum arose, and above the drum, the central dome soared up into dimness. The interior of the dome and its flanking half-domes were covered with gilded, brightly colored mosaics illustrating scenes from Gorgolorian mythology. At the floor level, numerous lamps shed adequate lighting. Further up, the light became fainter, until it picked out only an occasional bit of gilding.

On the floor, an altar stood to one side of the square. From the square, three short arms projected, allowing space for the worshipers to stand; for in Gorgolorism the laymen were allowed inside the temple. On the fourth side of the square, where the altar rested, was the holy of holies to which only the priests had access. This side could be closed off from profane eyes by a sliding screen. This screen was now drawn back, showing the cubical plinth, about six feet on an edge, and on the plinth the image of Gorgolor, carved from a single boulder of emerald.

As the party approached, two black-clad priests hastily rose. One tucked something that might have been a gaming device into his robe. Then they genuflected.

"Incredible!" repeated Jorian, looking up at the lion-sized smaragdine frog, in whose depths green lights seemed to glow and waver. "My only reservation, if Your Holiness will pardon my saying so, is that so much beauty might distract a man from the contemplation of the higher truths."

"True, Doctor Maltho," said Kylo. "With some worshipers, it may have that effect. But with others, it predisposes them all the more to harken unto our edifying homilies. We cannot, alas, divide the faithful into categories and furnish each group with a temple of the most suitable kind. So we seek a moderate approach, which will save the greatest number of faithful souls."

"Ah yes, Holy Father," said Jorian. "In my city, we long ago decided that the best safeguard against such perils was moderation. Even beauty, we found, can be overdone. Know you the tale of King Forimar of Kortoli—Forimar the Esthete?"

"Nay, my son, albeit I recall the name from histories of Novaria. Speak, an you would."

Jorian drew a long breath. Moving a leisurely half-pace at a time towards the main entrance, so as to draw the clerical crowd—including the two priests on vigil—with him, he began:

"This Forimar was a predecessor of Fusinian the Fox, of whom so many tales are told. It seems a rule of royalty that, out of every six kings, a land gets one hero, one scoundrel, one fool, and three mediocrities. Forimar was one of the fools, as his great-grandnephew Filoman the Well-Meaning was after him.

"But Forimar's folly took a special form. State business bored him to distraction. He cared little for law and justice, less for commerce and finance, and nothing at all for war and preparations therefor."

"Would that all sovrans and governments shared your king's distaste for war!" said the theocrat. "Then would men live in peace and devote themselves to leading good lives and worshipping the true god."

"True, Your Holiness; but the problem is, how do you get them all to give up war at once? Especially with so quarrelsome and factious a folk as the Novarians? And if one lay aside his arms before the rest, the rest reward his good example by leaping at his throat.

"Forimar, howsomever, was not a profound thinker about such matters. His passion for art and beauty overpowered all else. When he should have been reading state papers, he was playing the flageolet in the palace sextet. When he ought to have been receiving envoys, he was overseeing the building of a new temple or otherwise beautifying Kortoli City. When he should have been inspecting the troops, he was composing a sonnet to the beauties of the sunset.

"What made such matters more difficult was that he was really competent at all these arts. He was a fair architect, an accomplished musician, a worthy composer, a fine singer, and an excellent painter. Some of his poems are the glories of Kortolian literature to this day. But he could not do all these things and king it, too.

"Hence he left the governance of the polis to a succession of chancellors, chosen neither for probity nor for competence but for their admiration of their sovran's artistic achievements. After the kingdom had long suffered under a series of thieves and bunglers, Forimar's younger brother Fusonio took him to task.

"'My dear brother and sire,' quoth Fusonio, 'this cannot go on.' After he had lectured Forimar on the iniquities of the recent ministers, he added: 'Furthermore, you are nearly thirty but have not yet chosen a queen, to provide legitimate heirs to the throne.'

"'That is my affair!' said Forimar hotly. 'I have long cast an eye upon eligible members of the other sex but have never seen one who qualified. For my sensibilities are so acute that the slightest blemish of mind or of body, which a lesser man could put up with, were to me intolerable. So I am, and shall probably remain, wedded to my art. But fear not the failure of our line, Fusonio. If I die, you will succeed me, and you have already begotten five healthy children upon your spouse.'

"Fusonio argued some more, but Forimar put him off, saying: 'Nay; my only true live is Astis, the goddess of love and beauty, herself. Her I have loved with a consuming passion for many years, and no mere mortal wench can compare with her.'

"'Then,' said Fusonio, 'your duty is to abdicate in my favor, ere your obsession with beauty bring disaster upon us. You would be permitted to pursue your artistic career undisturbed.'

"'I will think upon that,' said Forimar. But the more he thought about it, the less he liked it. Although he and his brother had always gotten along well enough, they had little in common. Fusonio was a bluff, hearty, sensual type, blind to what Forimar deemed the higher things of life. Fusonio's idea of a large evening was to go incognito to some low tavern frequented by the rougher element and spend the even swilling ale and roaring ribald songs with unwashed peasants and ruffianly muleteers.

"Morever, the idea occurred to Forimar that his brother was seeking to oust him from base motives of ambition. Once he resigned, he feared, nought would stop Fusonio from getting rid of him by *force majeure*. On the other hand, as long as he kept the crown, the state's revenues provided him with means of pursuing his arts that he could hardly expect to enjoy as a private person.

"Not wishing to quarrel openly with Fusonio, he devised a scheme to get rid of his brother. He made him admiral of a fleet, to explore the Eastern Ocean as far as the fabled isles of Salimor. Fusonio sailed off without demur, for this kind of adventure appealed to him. And Forimar returned to his arts.

"But the remark he had made to Fusonio, of being in love with the goddess Astis, came little by little to signify a real condition. He could think of little save the goddess. Many an all-night vigil he spent in her temple, praying that she would appear unto him. But the goddess failed to manifest herself.

"In a frantic effort to lure the goddess into his arms, Forimar inaugurated a contest: to sculpture a statue of Astis that should, by its ineffable beauty, overcome the goddess's scruples about mating with a mortal. The treasurer was aghast at the rewards that Forimar offered; but, with Fusonio's influence gone, there was nothing to stop Forimar. He offered not only a huge prize for first place, but also rewards for all the other sculptors, win or lose.

"Consequently, a number of persons entered the contest who had never sculptured anything in their lives, and some very strange works of art were submitted. One was an untrimmed log with the bark on, whose submitter averred that the spirits had told him that this symbolized the true inward nature of the goddess. Another brought a simple boulder, and another a tangle of iron straps riveted together.

"These were too much even for Forimar, who decided that he was being made sport of. He had these self-styled sculptors whipped out of town and their productions thrown into the sea. He did the same with a sculpture showing, with utmost realism, the goddess being impregnated by the war god Heryx, albeit I have seen the like taken for granted in Mulvan. One had, he said, to draw the line somewhere.

"Natheless, many excellent sculptures were made, in bronze and in marble and in pottery. Nearly all showed the goddess in the likeness of a beautiful naked woman, for such had long been the convention of Novarian art. In due course, Forimar awarded the first prize to a certain Lukisto of Zolon, and lesser prizes to the other contestants. And all the hundreds of statues were placed in the temple of Astis, whose priests could scarcely perform their sacred functions, being compelled to worm their way amid masses of statuary.

"Now it happened that, contemporary with the reign of Forimar in Kortoli, Aussar was under the rule of a priest of Selindé, one Doubri. The priest had turned politician to overthrow the hereditary despots who had for a century cruelly oppressed the folk of Aussar. The new ruler called himself Doubri the Faultless, meaning that he had utterly conquered sin and lust in himself.

Doubri did, in fact, make many improvements in affairs in Aussar. But he took what many thought an overly rigid and censorious attitude towards those common human weaknesses that are deemed sins by theologians of the stricter sort. Please understand, Your Holiness, that I imply no criticism of your own regime in Tarxia; I do but strive to relate events as they happened.

"Moreover, this Doubri was not satisfied with 'cleaning up' Aussar, as he called his forceful suppression of drinking, dicing, wenching, and other manifestations of sin. The gods, he averred, had laid upon him the duty of liberating other nations from their slough of sin and error. And, when he looked about him, it seemed that Kortoli was most in need of his virtuous intervention. Its king was wholly absorbed in his pursuit of beauty; its people were sinning on a huge and raffish scale; its army had fallen into decay from neglect.

"So the Aussarians marched into Kortoli to right the wrongs they said were rampant in that kingdom. The Kortolian army fled without striking a blow and sought refuge in the capital, which was presently invested by the forces of Doubri. The Aussarians readied battering rams and wheeled belfries and other engines of war to break down or overswarm the walls. Although these events took place before the invention of the catapult, the besiegers managed natheless to deploy a terrifying array of equipment.

"When it looked as if all were lost, the fleet commanded by Forimar's brother Fusonio sailed into the harbor. Fusonio had gone to fabled Salimor and negotiated a treaty of friendship with the Sophi of that land. When he entered the city, King Forimar ran to him without formality and embraced him, calling upon him to save them all.

"When Fusonio took stock of the situation, he was not encouraged, for the army had become a cowardly rabble, the arsenals contained few usable weapons, the walls were weak and tottery and needed but a few good pokes from a ram to bring them down, and the treasury was all but empty.

"'Wherefore have we no money?' demanded Fusonio. 'There was an adequate balance when I left.'

"So Forimar told of the great sculpture contest. Fusonio refrained from saying what an idiot he thought his brother, although his glance conveyed the message. And he said: 'Before we surrender, let me see that proclamation Doubri issued when he attacked us.' And he read the document, noting the vile acts whereof Doubri the Faultless accused the Kortolians:

218

"'...men, and sometimes women, also, resort to mug-houses, where they consume fermented liquors, instead of drinking healthful boiled water. They waste their substance in games of chance. They indulge in croquet and other frivolous pastimes on the days sacred to gods, instead of spending all their free time in contemplation of their sins and prayers for forgiveness. Men and women openly bathe together in the public bath, which the degenerate King Forimar has erected, exposing their persons not only to those of their own sex, which is bad enough, but even to those of the other, which is an unspeakable abomination. They commit fornication and adultery unpunished. Even when lawfully wedded, they copulate in a state of nudity, for sensual pleasure instead of for the righteous purpose of creating offspring to praise the gods. They wear gaudy raiment and wasteful jewelry instead of the chaste and sober garments that please the gods. They lend money at interest, which is sinful as against nature. They exploit the working class by wringing a profit from the labor of these unfortunates. They sell goods by lying about the virtues of their commodities, excusing this mendacity by calling it "salesmanship"...'

"'Well!' said Fusonio, 'if this priest overcome us, I see we can look forward to a jolly time under his rule. What is this about the bath house? We Kortolians have always bathed together.'

"'Oh,' said Forimar, 'Doubri is an utter fanatic on nudity. To him it is actually worse than fornication. Why, in Aussar, everybody is supposed to bathe in his shirt, even in privacy. Married couples are commanded to wear long gowns to bed, these being furnished with slits in the appropriate places for those who wish to beget children for the glory of the gods.'

"Fusonio thought a while, then said: 'Let me see those statues of Astis, for which you so rashly squandered our treasury.' And the king took his brother to the temple of Astis, where Fusonio spent some time, now and then passing an appreciative hand over a particularly well-rounded curve of one of the statues.

"'All right,' said Fusonio at last. 'I think I know what to do. But lest I merely rescue you from one such predicament, dear brother, only to have you plunge us all into another, I must ask that you abdicate in my favor. Otherwise, I will return to my ships and sail away, for an excellent post as minister for western affairs awaits me in Salimor if I choose to return thither.'

"Forimar pleaded and wept to no avail. He cursed and threatened and stamped and pulled his own hair in rage and frustration. But Fusonio would not bulge a finger-breadth. When Forimar commanded his bodyguards to seize his brother, they suddenly became deaf, saying: 'What is that, sire? I cannot understand you.' So at last Forimar signed the document of abdication, threw the royal seal at his brother, and stamped off to compose a piece of music that is still known as the Angry Sonata.

"King Fusonio then commanded that all the statues of Astis be covered with wrappings and set up on the wall. And when the assault began, the wrappings were pulled off, and there stood those hundreds of statues of the naked Astis.

"Doubri was watching from beyond bowshot. Being near-sighted, he asked his men what was toward. And when he learnt, he was filled with horror. For, plainly, his soldiers could not scale the walls without coming face to face with all these lewd statues. Arrows could indeed be shot at them, but these would merely chip and mar them slightly, and meanwhile the minds of the archers would be filled with unholy sensual thoughts. Since the catapult did not yet exist, he could not smash the statues with stone balls from a distance, as he could today.

"Doubri remained encamped for a few more days. He made a half-hearted attack on the wall, wheeling up a ram tortoise to batter it. But, not needing to take cover from arrow-shot, the defenders easily caught the head of the ram in the bight of a chain and upset the whole engine. Doubri also tried tunnelling, but the defenders flooded the tunnels.

"Doubri knew he could not starve out the defenders, because the Kortolian navy, reinforced by Fusonio's squadron, still commanded the local waters. When a sickness broke out among the Aussarians, Doubri raised the siege and marched away, only to find on his return to Aussar City that his government had fallen, and that one of the more promising younger members of the despot's family had been made ruler in his place.

"And that is the tale of Forimar the Esthete and Doubri

the Faultless. The moral, as we see it in Kortoli, is that both Forimar's artistry and Doubri's morality would have been good things in their way, had they been applied in moderation. But any virtue can be turned into a vice by indulging it with excessive rigor and consistency."

Jorian and his audience now stood in the portico of the temple, outside the great bronze doors. Bit by bit, as he unfolded his tale, he had edged away from the central square, along the nave, and out the main doors. As he did so, he kept an ear cocked towards the holy of holies. At any moment, he expected Karadur and Valdonius to sidle quietly up and rejoin the group. The theocrat was saying:

"A most edifying and amusing tale, Doctor Maltho. Even in our holy cultus, we must sometimes curb the excessive zeal of some of our colleagues. We know that we alone possess the ultimate truth, and that it is incumbent upon us to propagate this verity and to extirpate error; but in this extirpation, excessive violence sometimes defeats its own—"

GLOOP! An extraordinary sound issued from the temple: a sound like a frog's croak, but augmented to the loudness of a lion's roar or a buffalo's bellow.

"Good Gorgolor, what is that?" cried one of the episcopals, turning to look back through the doors. Then the crimson-clad priest staggered back with a shriek, clapping a hand to his forehead. "The Holy Frog save us! The statue has come to life!"

GLOOP! came the bellow, closer, and a squashy, thumping sound accompanied it. Then out through the bronzen doors leaped the emerald god, the same size as he had been on his pedestal but now informed with life. Gorgolor landed among the group outside the doorway. Jorian leaped aside, but several others, including the theocrat, were bowled over. With a final GLOOP, the gigantic frog took off on another soaring leap into the darkness.

Jorian hastily gave Kylo a hand up and picked up the theocrat's battered white felt crown. But Kylo paid no heed, either to Jorian or to his sacerdotal headpiece.

"Send men in pursuit!" he screamed, dancing on the marble. "The god headed for the Swamp of Spraa, and if he gets there we shall never catch him. Turn out the army! Fetch nets! Hurry! Hurry! Are you all turned to stone?

221

You, Eades, send out the pursuit! The rest of you follow me!"

The little fat man set off at a run down the path through the temenos that led eastward, his white robe fluttering. As they ran, others rushed out of the dark to ask the cause of the commotion. When they heard, they joined the pursuit with cries of horror and lamentation. Within a few breaths, a motley throng, many in nightdress, was streaming away eastward along one of Tarxia's winding streets.

Jorian, Karadur, and Valdonius remained alone in the portico. Karadur was weeping again. Beyond the temenos they could glimpse the movement of torches and lanthorns, as the word of the transformation of their god spread swiftly through Tarxia City and hundreds dropped whatever they were doing to run towards the East Gate.

"Well," said Jorian, eyeing his companions, "I suppose your damned spells went agley again?"

"One might say so; one might say so," replied Valdonius, ostentatiously preserving his poise. "Peradventure we mistranslated a word in that old scroll, which is writ in a very archaic form of the language. Natheless, the results will be nearly as satisfactory."

"In any case," said Jorian, "methinks Karadur and I had best flee whilst the Tarxians are preoccupied with catching their god. Where's your ass, Karadur?"

"I abandoned it in the camp of the Gendings, to give myself more time before the barbarians suspected I had left them. I came to Tarxia by a ship from Istheun."

"Do you own a beast of burden, Doctor Valdonius?"

"Why," said Valdonius, "I have a matched pair of whites to draw my chariot. But I cannot break the pair—"

"Oh, yes you can! Either you turn one of those animals over to Karadur to ride, or the theocrat shall hear of your part in this even's events."

"You would not inform on your confederates, would you?"

"Try me and see. I'll talk Kylo into thinking the blame is all yours. Now that I think of it, I'll also tell them you've been practicing sorcery, which is true; I know enough of magic to know that swords do not stick in their scabbards on a word of command, without the aid of a spirit."

"My masters," said Karadur, wiping his eyes on his sleeve, "why does not Doctor Valdonius drive his chariot to Metouro, to attend the Conclave with us? Then he could carry me in his car. The Altruists will need every vote."

"I cannot," said Valdonius. "I must forgather with those of my opinion, to see if we cannot overthrow this priestly tyranny with one sharp blow. Such a chance may not recur during my lifetime. I will lend you the horse; but I expect you to stable it in Metouro until I can send a servant to fetch it back—if I do not end up standing on a pile of faggots."

"Or you may have to flee to Metouro yourself," said Jorian. "When the hierarchy recovers its wits, it will soon infer that you must have had something to do with the theophany of their god. Meanwhile, let's be on our way whilst the gates are still open."

X

THE FACELESS FIVE

JORIAN AND KARADUR RODE DOWN THE VALE OF THE KYA-
mos on the fifth of the Month of the Pike. Spring was in
full tide. Flowers of a hundred hues bloomed everywhere,
every pond resounded to the croaking of frogs, and all the
trees were in leaf. Although the drowsy heat of summer
had not yet arrived, the warmth of the air hinted at its
coming.

The two riders—Jorian on his faithful if bumpy Oser,
Karadur on the white pony borrowed from Valdonius in
Tarxia—no longer wore the heavy sheepskin coats that
had seen them across the steppes of Shven. These garments were rolled up and lashed to their saddles behind
them. The journey had taken them twice as long as it
would have taken Jorian alone, because Karadur did not
dare to move at more than a fast walk. Between fear of
falling and fear of being late for the Conclave, the old
magician was in a constant swivet.

The Kyamos was a small river, which presently widened out into the broad Lake Volkina. On the north shore
of the lake stood Metouro City—or New Metouro as it

was more exactly called. A bowshot from the shore, directly in front of the city, rose an islet, on which stood the Goblin Tower.

Lake Volkina was of relatively recent origin. A landslide in the western part of the valley had blocked the course of the Kyamos a few centuries before, flooding the original Metouro City and creating the lake. In time, the lake had overflowed the natural dam formed by the landslide, and the Kyamos had resumed its course across Ir to the Western Ocean.

At the East Gate, as they dismounted and gave their names to the sentries, a small man in gray appeared. "Doctor Karadur?"

"Aye."

"Drakomas of Phthai, at your service. Our colleague, Doctor Vorko, has asked me to conduct you to your quarters in the Goblin Tower."

"I feared," said Karadur, "that, because of our lateness, all space in the Tower would be taken."

"A thousand nays, fair sir! Knowing the worth of yourself and your companion and the burden you bear, we reserved a suite for you early. Pray come!" To the sentries, Drakomas said: "We vouch for these men."

The sentries waved Jorian and Karadur through. Metouro proved a larger and handsomer city than Tarxia, with straight streets crossing at right angles instead of Tarxia's tangle of winding alleys. While more prosperous-looking than those of Tarxia, the people seemed dour, reserved, and tight-lipped, giving the strangers brief, sidelong glances without any change of expression.

Drakomas led the two travelers, not directly to the boat landing for the Tower, but to an inn. He saw to the stabling of their mounts. In an upstairs room, they found a man and two nonhuman beings. Karadur said:

"Master Vorko, permit me to present my apprentice, Jorian of Ardamai. Jorian, know that this is Vorko of Hendau, the head of our White Faction."

"Your apprentice?" said Vorko, in a voice even deeper than Jorian's. "Is this not the former king of Xylar, who accompanied you as bodyguard and factotum?"

"Aye."

"Has he then determined to enter the profession?" Vorko of Hendau was an extremely tall, lean, knobby man, with a big, hooked nose and a jutting chin. His two attendants were of about human size and shape, but they had scales, tails, muzzles, fangs, talons, pointed ears, and mustaches consisting of a pair of fleshy tendrils, which constantly curled and uncurled and waved about like the tentacles of a small squid. Their big, yellow eyes had slit pupils.

Jorian was staring at the nonhumans as Karadur replied: "Nay, he has not taken the vows. But I hope that, by exposing him to the exoteric side of magic at the Conclave, I shall arouse his curiosity to the point where he will wish to do so. Meanwhile, by your leave, I will continue to call him 'apprentice' to make his admission easy. I trust that none will take technical umbrage at my so doing."

"I think not," said Vorko. "The rules are pretty loose these days. But what of your mission?"

"Esteemed colleague, we are happy to report success. The Kist, Jorian!"

Jorian unslung the little chest from his back and handed it to Vorko by its rope sling. "Here you are, sir," he said. "And now, since I have performed the task for which you laid me under a geas, may I ask that you lift this geas forthwith?"

"Oh, murrain!" said the enchanter. "You're entitled to it, youngling, and you shall have it—but not just now, for want of time. We must needs forth at once to the Tower, without even pausing to wash up. We shall be late as it is. Of course, Master Jorian, you need not attend the Conclave if you do not wish."

"Oh, I will indeed attend, forsooth! 'Tis a small enough reward for the risks and hardships I've undergone for you and your colleagues in the past half-year."

"Very good; off we go. The Kist will be safe here, with my servants to guard it."

"What _are_ they?" asked Jorian.

"Demons from the Twelfth Plane, hight Zoth and Frig, fixed in material form on this plane and bound to my service for nine years. They are good, faithful guardians, albeit not very intelligent. Their main complaint is that I should invoke a demoness or two for them to consort with. But let us hasten; the ferry service is incredible." Vorko spoke a few syllables in an unknown tongue to Zoth and Frig, who bobbed their fanged heads in acknowledgment. Zoth picked up the duffel of the two travelers and silently followed them through the streets to the lake shore.

The lake shore of Metouro had several boathouses for small boats, a stretch of bathing beach, and a few small piers for pleasure craft. Lake Volkina was not large enough to carry commerce. On one pier, scores of men in dark robes and cloaks were lined up. Jorian, Karadur, and Vorko took their places in the line. The pier pointed towards the Goblin Tower, a bowshot away. A pair of rowboats, each pulled by a single rower, plied the water between the pier and the tower, taking passengers across three at a time.

"We've complained of this pediculous ferry service to the Faceless Five," said Vorko in a fretful tone, "but they as much as invited us to move our Conclave elsewhither. They've run the polis so long as they pleased that they are not accustomed to advice or complaints from anybody."

"The Metourians seem a grim lot," said Jorian.

"You would be grim, too, an you had to watch every word lest some nark bear tales to your rulers," said Vorko. "That's what it is to live in a land ruled by a secret society. Suspicion is the way of life here. They would not suffer us to meet in Metouro at all, save that we promised to confine our activities to the Tower. They recall the events that led up to the building of the Tower in the first place."

"I know not that tale," said Jorian.

A magician, robe fluttering, glided in on a broomstick to a landing on the beach. As he approached the shoreward end of the pier, with a carpetbag in one hand and his broomstick in the other, Vorko called out:

"Hail, Sir Fendix! You were asking me, Master Jorian?"

"About the Gob—"

"Certes! I will tell you the whole story—God den, good Doctor Bhulla! How fares the art of Thaumaturgy in Janareth? To resume, Master Jorian: Once upon a time, Metouro was a republic, with a constitution like that of Vindium today. There was an elected archon, and a senate of heads of propertied families, and an assembly of the people. This scheme worked very well for many years, so long as Metouro was poor and backward, having just risen from the dark age that followed the fall of the Three Kingdoms. Ah, greeting, good Master Nors!"

This salutation was addressed to another magician, who

first appeared in the form of a whirlwind of dust. This dust column danced along the beach until it neared the pier, when it collapsed into a brown-robed man.

"The trouble with all these flying spells," said Vorko, "is that they leave the thaumaturge so spent that he can do little for days thereafter. Watch Doctor Nors and Sir Fendix—the latter is an authentic Othomaean knight, turned to magic—and you'll see them dozing through all the sessions—some of which, I confess, are hard enough to wake in anyway.

"As I was saying, the republic flourished until wealth accumulated. Then the leading families gathered more and more land and coin into their hands, until a small clique of the rich ruled the polis, squeezing the much more numerous poor until the latter could barely survive. Behold, here comes Antonerius of Ir on his dragon! He is always fain to make a show of his arrival, but I'll wager he will have trouble stabling his monster."

The magician Antonerius glided into a landing on the back of a wyvern, a flying reptile with a forty-foot wingspread. The wind of the creature's wings fluttered the robes and cloaks of the magicians on the pier. A couple of attendants ran up to take the reptile's reins but shrank back when the beast arched its neck and snapped at them, disclosing fearsome fangs. Its rider whacked it over the head with a goad until it quieted.

"Why do they all land here instead of at the Tower?" asked Jorian.

"Because our good president, Aello of Gortii, has laid a preventive spell upon the Tower, lest in the heat of debate some colleague be tempted to launch a thunderbolt at his opponent or otherwise to wreak magical woe upon him. Hence no spell works in the Tower. If Doctor Sir Fendix, for ensample, were to seek to alight on the battlements, his broom might lose its power just before he touched down and dash him to his death on the rocks below.

"To resume: There arose in Metouro a man named Charens, one of the rich who had lost his wealth. He said the other oligarchs had swindled him out of his property. They said he had lost it by profligacy and dissipation, and we cannot now tell which had the right of it.

"This Charens became a leader of the poor, demanding

reforms: such as compelling the rich to pay taxes, which irksome duty they had thitherto managed most featly to shirk. And he demanded that public moneys be spent on amenities for the poor, such as a public lazaretto and an orphanage, instead of things that benefited the rich only, like hunting lodges and banquet halls. At the next vote, Charens was elected archon despite the efforts of the rich to intimidate the voters and miscount the ballots."

The wyvern had at last been brought under control. While several attendants held its head by ropes, the rider dismounted and tied the animal's wings in the furled position, so that it could no longer flap. Then the attendants dragged away the reptile, hissing and bucking. A huge black vulture now glided in, flopped down on the sand, and changed into another wizard.

"As soon as Charens got power," continued Vorko, "he began to effect his reforms. This so enraged the rich that they hired a gang of bravos to slay Charens as he walked home from the marketplace. Since, under the then constitution, the man having the second largest number of votes became vice-archon, the candidate of the rich became archon and rescinded all of Charens' reforms.

"The oligarchs, howsomever, had not reckoned on Charens' younger brother, Charenzo. This Charenzo had greatly loved and admired his brother, and now he swore to devote his life to vengeance. And soon he had gathered a secret following. One year after the murder of his brother, he led a revolt, which slaughtered many of the rich and forced the rest to flee. This was the first of the great massacres, which for the next few years convulsed the history of Metouro, with heads piled in heaps in the marketplace, and howling mobs cheering on the torture of captives and tearing their opponents' women and children to pieces.

"Charenzo proved a less able and enlightened and much more violent man than his brother. Reforms and public amenities interested him less than vengeance upon his brother's slayers—a class which he little by little expanded to include everybody who opposed him. Hardly a day passed in Metouro but that some unfortunate was led out to death at his command as a suspected oligarch, or at least as a fautor of oligarchy.

"With each execution, Charenzo made more enemies, and even his friends began to be bored and alarmed by the endless charges of treason and oligarchical leanings. When a party of exiled oligarchs appeared with an army of Shvenic mercenaries, they routed Charenzo's armed rabble and seized control of Metouro once more. Then they had their turn at massacre and execution.

"Charenzo escaped from Metouro. Since his people had failed him, he determined to seek supernatural aid. So he sought out the sorcerer Synelius in Govannian. This Synelius was a Metourian, exiled because he was under sentence as a witch. One of Charenzo's own judges had sentenced him in his absence, Synelius having learnt from his spirits what was toward and having prudently fled.

"Now, however, Charenzo made common cause with his former foe. And Synelius said that, yes, he could summon an army of goblins—the vulgar name for demons of the Ninth Plane—to oust the present regime in Metouro. The new oligarchical government, like their predecessors, had learnt nought from experience and were oppressing and exploiting the poor as ruthlessly as ever.

"So Charenzo and Synelius and a host of goblins suddenly appeared amongst the Metourians. Terrified of supernatural beings, the terrible Shvenic mercenaries fled. So did many Metourians, until Charenzo closed the gates and posted goblins as sentinels.

"So began another period of rule by the fierce and implacable Charenzo. Being nocturnal, the goblins were seldom seen in the daytime. But at night everybody cowered behind locked and barred doors, lest one of these bouncing, huge-headed creatures enter to drag him off to some nameless doom.

"Charenzo resumed his reign of terror, until at length Synelius warned him that he was killing off the Metourians faster that they were being born, and that if he continued this process long enough he would have no subjects left to rule. This advice aroused Charenzo's suspicions of his ally, or perhaps he had planned all along to rid himself of Synelius as too dangerous to let live.

"Professing great interest in Synelius' magic, he flattered the old man until the latter revealed the spells and words of power whereby he controlled the goblins. Then Charenzo had Synelius arrested and thrown into a dungeon in the bowels of the citadel, which stood on a hill in the midst of the city. Synelius called upon his goblins to rescue him, but Charenzo countermanded the order. So the goblins did nothing. Not having his magical paraphernalia in his cell, Synelius could not work a spell to free himself by other magical means.

"Meanwhile, a conspiracy had arisen among a group of Metourians, which included representatives of men of all degrees: rich, poor, and intermediate. These people formed a secret society, called simply the Brotherhood, with passwords and oaths and other mummery. They chose a committee of five to command the society, including representatives from Metourians of as many different kinds as possible: rich and poor, young and old, male and female. Thus, if one was a rich old woman, another would be a poor young man to balance her.

"Through one of its members who was also a member of the prison guard, this Brotherhood heard about the imprisonment of Synelius. With the help of this member, they gained access to the dungeon and presented forged documents apparently signed by Charenzo, commanding the warder to deliver Synelius to them. Thus they got the sorcerer out of jail. And when they had taken him to a place of refuge, they urged him to throw in his lot with them. When he agreed to this, they demanded to know if he could get rid of the goblins. Alas no, he said, for that Charenzo now controlled them and could countermand his orders that they return to their own plane.

"Things were not, however, hopeless, for he knew a mighty spell that would turn the goblins to stone. When he said it required human sacrifice, the conspirators drew lots. And when a promising youth drew the fatal lot, the oldest conspirator, who had been an oligarch, insisted on taking his place, saying he was not for many years and was too full of obsolete ideas and prejudices to be useful in the new regime.

"So the spell was cast. There was a mighty flash of lightning, and a deafening roar of thunder, and a shaking of the earth. The citadel collapsed with a frightful crash, burying Charenzo in the ruins, and a landslide blocked the Kyamos below Metouro City. On that instant, every goblin in Metouro was turned into stone. When the conspirators ran to see how Synelius fared, they found the old sorcerer dead with a peaceful look on his face.

"The Brotherhood then reorganized the city according

to their own ideas. They insisted on remaining secret, and this is why Metouro is ruled today by a committee of the Brotherhood called the Faceless Five. These appear in their official capacity wearing black masks, and nobody is supposed to know who they are. When the blocking of the Kyamos created Lake Volkina and flooded the old Metouro City, they built a new one, laid out by an architect with straight, wide streets. Since the citadel was in ruins and the hill whereon it stood was become a mere islet in Lake Volkina, they cleared away the rubbish and built a new stronghold, in which they used not only the unbroken stones from the former citadel but also the hundreds of stones into which the goblins had been turned. Thus this edifice became known as the Goblin Tower.

"Originally, the Faceless Five dwelt in the Goblin Tower. But a century ago they gave up this habit, partly because it made their comings and goings too conspicuous, so that their anonymity was hard to preserve, and partly because the Tower itself was uncomfortable, having been designed more as a fortress than as a human abode."

"How have the Metourians made out under their Faceless Five?" asked Jorian.

"Well in some ways, not so well in others. Like all such self-perpetuating cliques, the main concern of the Five had been to keep all power firmly in their own hands. On the whole, they have given the polis an efficient government, with a fair degree of prosperity. They still have rich and poor, but no industrious man need starve. Not having a glittering court like Mulvan's or an extravagant temple like Tarxia's to keep up, they have not felt the need to squeeze every last farthing out of their subjects. And the custom of choosing members of the Five to represent persons of as many different kinds as possible has made their rule fairly even-handed.

"On the other hand, there is precious little personal freedom in Metouro. The ordinary citizen says little, lest his interlocutor be an informer, and he looks over his shoulder before answering a question about the time of day. Personally I prefer Vindium, with all its disorder and corruption, to quite so oppressively virtuous a regime. Unless—" (the enchanter smiled wryly) "—I myself could be the ruler!"

During this story, Jorian and his companions had inched forward along the pier. As Vorko finished, one of the rowboats drew up, and the three stepped aboard. Zoth dropped Jorian's and Karadur's bundles of gear into the boat, nodded silently to Vorko, and started back for shore.

XI

THE GOBLIN TOWER

As the surly, silent boatman rowed them towards the island, the Goblin Tower loomed up over their bow. It was a simple structure in the form of a narrow ellipse with forty-foot curtain walls. At each end, a single large round tower rose another twenty-odd feet higher. A slender arched stone bridge joined these towers near the summits. The shape of the islet dictated the extreme narrowness of the structure.

The Tower had a drawbridge, which, however, did not join anything at its outer end. It merely hung out over the water and served as a landing pier. Jorian climbed out with his companions and followed them through the gate, under the portcullis, and into a hall. There was no open court inside this tower; the edifice was completely roofed over and built up inside.

In the hall, magicians stood in line before a desk, at which sat a man in a black robe, with a red, conical cap of stiff paper on his head. On the front of this cap was written, in large letters with a broad-pointed pen, the words:

FORCES OF
PROGRESS
SIXTY-FIRST
ANNUAL
CONCLAVE
GNOUX,
RECEPTION

A bulletin board, listing the events of the convention, stood near Receptionist Gnoux.

As Vorko and Karadur reached the desk, the receptionist asked their names, wrote them on a piece of paper, and pasted the slips to the fronts of conical caps like his own but black. He handed them their caps and room keys. When Jorian's turn came, Karadur told Gnoux:

"This is Jorian of Kortoli, my apprentice. I have paid your registration fee, Jorian."

"Welcome, Master Jorian," said Gnoux. "How spell you that?...Here you are." Gnoux handed Jorian a dunce cap like the others, but white to denote Jorian's rank as apprentice, with his name written on the front. "You shall room in twenty-three, with Doctor Karadur."

"Have you an extra key?" asked Jorian. "The good doctor and I may come and go at different times."

"Here you are. Welcome again to this learned assemblage!"

Jorian asked: "Has one Porrex of Vindium registered?"

Gnoux consulted a list. "Nay, though you're the third conventioner to ask me that."

"Peradventure he's swindled the others, too, and they hope to take it out of his hide."

"Well—ah—" said Gnoux, trying to hide a smile, "'tis not my affair, but I did overhear some remarks about red-hot pincers applied to sensitive areas."

Jorian followed Vorko to the ballroom at the end of the hall, which had been turned into an auditorium. It was full of seated male and female magicians, wearing conical caps. When they had found seats, Vorko whispered to Jorian:

"That's President Aello, up there."

The president, wearing a golden dunce cap, was a tall, stooped old man with a long white beard cascading down the front of his black gown. He was introducing celebrities, each of whom received a patter of applause: "...and I am informed that we have with us the distinguished necromancer, Omphes of Thamoe, whose stable of spirits includes some of the most eminent shades not yet reincarnated. Will you stand, Doctor Omphes? Thank you... And we also have the preëminent wizardess, Goania of Othomae; will you take a bow, Mistress Goania?..."

Jorian remembered the gray-haired woman and tried to catch her eyes, but she was too distant. He squirmed on his bench, looking about him. A figure standing against the back wall, near the door, caught his attention. This was a burly, porcine man wearing a red cap. With a shock, Jorian recognized Boso, son of Triis, the ex-gongringer with whom he had fought in Othomae, and whom Goania had taken into her service. Boso not only carried a cudgel but also wore a sword. Jorian wondered if Vanora, too, would be there. Aello of Gortii droned on:

"...the worthy astrologer, Ktessis of Psara; will you stand, Master Ktessis?..."

Increasingly bored and hungry, Jorian wondered if he had been so clever to insist on attending the Conclave after all. He soon lost track of the names. His eyelids became heavy, and twice he caught himself falling forward from his sitting position. He was pinching himself to keep awake when Aello mercifully ended the introductions and announced:

"The first item on the program will be a paper by the learned Bhulla of Janareth on 'Familial Organization and Kinship Nomenclature amongst Demons of the Eighth Plane.' Doctor Bhulla."

Amid scattered applause, a small, potbellied, brown man took Aello's place on the dais and began to read a paper, in a squeaky monotone with a strong Mulvanian accent. Although Jorian, if largely self-educated, was fairly well-read, the discourse was completely unintelligible to him. When he found himself nodding again, he whispered to Karadur:

"I'm going out for a while. Where's our room?"

"One flight up at the west end. I shall accompany you, for the next item is an auction of magical properties, old manuscripts, and historic mementoes of our profession. I think I will absent myself therefrom, also."

"Is there any place to eat in this pile?"

"There will be a dinner here, in this ballroom, one hour ere sunset. A costume ball will follow."

Jorian suppressed a groan. "That's three hours yet! I shall starve meanwhile. Lend me a few pence, will you?"

He followed Karadur out into the main hall but paused to look the company over while the old magician tottered off towards his quarters. In the main hall, Jorian discovered that many others at the Conclave, too, were playing truant from the lecture. Little groups of magicians stood in knots, discussing professional matters with expressive gestures and grimaces. The shrill laughs of women cut the air; there were several such groups, from young to old, some wearing the conical caps of registered magicians and some not. The latter, Jorian supposed, were attached to the magicians in one capacity or another. He wondered about Karadur's insistence that celibacy was an absolute requirement for rising high in the profession.

A small, dimly lit room was filled with magicians sitting at tables, munching dried chick-peas and drinking wine or beer. Jorian squeezed in and took an empty seat. The three men at the table were in the midst of a hot technical discussion. They smiled and nodded to Jorian with absent-minded politeness and went on with their talk:

"...thet astral movement being circular, every azotic or magnetic emission which does not encounter its medium returns with force to its point of departure, does it not?"

"Aye," said another, "but you must admit that the duodenary, being a complete and cyclic number in the universal analogies of nature, invariably attracts and absorbs the thirteenth, which is regarded as a sinister and superfluous number. Hence your cycles will fail to recapitulate their elements in synchronous order—"

"You are both wrong," said the third, "having forgotten that in nature there are two forces producing equilibrium, and these three constitute a single law. Here, then, is the triad resumed in unity, and by adding the conception of unity to that of the triad we are brought to the tetrad, the first square and perfect number, the source of all numerical combinations and the principle of all forms. Hence the astral currents will cycle homogeneously..."

* * *

Jorian became so uncomfortable at being compelled to listen to this incomprehensible talk, while being completely ignored, that he left as soon as he had finished his ale. Outside, he paused before the bulletin board. The board listed the lecture now in progress and the auction to follow it. After that would come a panel discussion on "Invisibility," followed in turn by an informal dinner and a costume ball.

The next morning would be taken up with a debate over the Altruists' proposal to end all secrecy surrounding magic, offering its benefits freely to the general public. There would be a testimonial luncheon to Aello as outgoing president. In the afternoon there would be several learned papers, including a demonstration of evoking a fiend from the thirty-third Mulvanian hell. A small red star after the name of this experiment indicated that it was dangerous.

The evening would see the formal dinner, with awards to deserving magicians and a speech by Doctor Yseldia of Metouro, the guest of honor. Madame Yseldia would talk of recent advances in the enchantment of flying broomsticks. After the banquet would come a series of small closed meetings, to which master magicians only were admitted.

The third and final day would have a couple of papers in the morning and then the business meeting, at which a new president would be elected, the site of the next year's Conclave chosen, and amendments to the constitution of the Forces of Progress considered.

Having absorbed this information, Jorian began to walk away from the board. Then he started and stared as he sighted Vanora, talking with a group of women. The tall, angular girl wore a long gown of emerald-green silk, with a little round cap on her long, black, glossy hair. She was much changed from the bedraggled wench he had left in Othomae. Despite the irregularity of her features, she looked almost pretty and certainly attractive.

"Good morrow, Mistress Vanora!" he said.

"Well, Jorian!" she cried. "Your pardon, girls; here's an old gossip of mine." She took Jorian's arm and walked down the hall. "Did you really rescue that box of moldy screeds from the King of Kings?"

"Aye, that we did and got away with whole skins. How wags thy world?"

She made a face. "That stinkard Boso...But Goania's a dear. I stay with him more for her sake than for his." She pinched a piece of the emerald gown and pulled it out from her body. "She got me this."

"Very pretty. Didn't I see Boso in the ballroom just now?"

"Aye; he's been made sergeant-at-arms, which is to say the same post as ejector that he held at the Silver Dragon in Othomae. But never mind me, who have led a tame enough existence for the past sixmonth. Tell me of your adventures! Rumor has gone out of your hairbreadth escapes."

Jorian grimaced. "Most of these escapades I should have been most heartily glad to be quit of whilst they were happening, I can tell you, however jolly they sound in the later retelling."

"I suppose you'll say you were frightened half to death?"

"'Tis the simple truth. After all, I'm no swaggering gallant, but a simple craftsman who would like to settle— but ere I bore you with a four-hour account of my doings, can you find me something to eat? I have scarcely bared a fang since dawn. We rode from Thamoe to Metouro this morn and then came directly hither without stopping to eat or wash. So I'll not utter another word until I'm fed."

Vanora showed Jorian to the kitchen and wheedled a bun and a flagon of beer from the chief cook. Between bites, Jorian told of some of his experiences in Mulvan and Shven.

Two hours later, he paused to say: "Time is passing, and here I waste our time in self-conceited narration of my own petty affairs! I can resist almost any temptation, save an invitation to talk. Methinks the session nears its end, and I had best rejoin my master."

"Have you become Karadur's apprentice in fact as well as in name?"

"Nay, though a reason for attending this Conclave is to see how I like the profession of magic. But I doubt if the rewards of high magic will persuade me to give up women."

"By giving up all the pleasures of the flesh, Goania tells

me, the most skillful adepts can prolong their lives to twice or thrice that of common mortals."

"Or perhaps it only seems twice or thrice as long, without wine or women."

Vanora looked at Jorian in a marked manner. "Ah— it is about such matters that I would speak to you in conf—"

"Your pardon, Mistress Vanora, but I really must go, instanter!" Jorian handed his empty flagon to a cook. "I'm stinking filthy from travel and must remedy this condition before dinner."

He gave the girl his arm and started briskly for the main hall. There he excused himself and found room twenty-three. He let himself in with his key and found a small sitting room and a small bedroom with two narrow beds. Karadur had been to the suite but had gone out again. Jorian cleaned himself up, trimmed his beard to a dashing point, put on his one clean shirt, tried to shine his battered boots, and returned to the ballroom.

There he found that the auction had ended and the panel discussion on invisibility was in progress. The panelists, who sat in a row on the platform, had finished their prepared statements and were answering questions from the audience. President Aello sat at one end of the row and pointed his wand at auditors he wished to recognize. As Jorian entered, a man stood up, beginning:

"I should like to ask—"

"State your name and speciality, pray," said Aello.

"Merkon of Boaktis, theurgic sorcerer. I should like to ask the honorable members what the advantage would be to making all of themselves but their eyeballs invisible? I should find a pair of disembodied eyeballs following me around quite as obvious as a visible man, and much more disconcerting."

"As I thought I had explained," said one panelist, "total invisibility, while achievable, had the disadvantage of blinding the person employing it, because there is no interaction betwixt the rays of visible light and the substance of human eyes to produce the sensory phenomenon we know as 'sight.' I thought this was known to every apprentice. Hence total invisibility is practical only as a measure for extreme emergencies, when one is hotly pursued. Since the invisible one cannot see until he lifts the spell, he must needs rely upon other senses to warn him of the close approach of his foes—especially his astral sight. But this faculty is poorly developed in most mortals. With visible eyeballs, on the other hand, one can at leisure examine forbidden things, provided one stays far enough from the nearest observor that one's eyes are not noticeable..."

Jorian kept looking for Karadur but could not see him. Hundreds of dunce-capped magicians looked much alike from the back, and Karadur had shifted his place. Jorian began tiptoeing around the aisle at the edge of the hall, in order to see the faces of the audience from the side. In so doing, he came face to face with Boso.

"You!" whispered the sergeant-at-arms, reaching for his sword, "I ought to—"

"Behave yourself, Boso!" said Jorian.

"Futter you! You behave *yourself*, or I'll—"

"Shh!" said several magicians, facing towards the pair and scowling.

Boso quieted, and Jorian continued his search, sweeping his glance back and forth against row after row of faces—pink faces, gray faces, tan faces, brown faces; clean-shaven faces, mustached faces, bearded faces; young faces, middle-aged faces, old faces; male faces and female faces. At last, when he thought he would have to give up, he sighted Karadur across the auditorium, sitting with his conical cap on his head and his turban in his lap. The wizardess Goania sat next to him. Jorian quietly joined them.

The panel discussion was nearly over. When Aello declared the session adjourned, hundreds of magicians rose and stretched.

"Whither now?" said Jorian.

"There will be an apertif in the library," said Karadur, "but I take no fermented beverages. I think I will rest until dinner. Why do you not escort Goania thither?"

"Colossal idea!" said Jorian. "Mistress Goania, may I have the honor?"

"One thing in parting," said Karadur. "Here, of all places, guard that flapping tongue!"

"I'll try," said Jorian.

* * *

In the library, Jorian drank spiced wine and nibbled snacks of salt fish and cookies with Goania, who introduced him to countless wizards, sorcerers, necromancers, diviners, and other practitioners of the magical arts. He soon lost track of names and faces. During a pause, he asked the wizardess:

"How is Vanora making out with Boso?"

"Oh, they had a terrible quarrel yesterday and are not speaking today. But that is how things go with them. Tomorrow they will have forgotten what they were fighting over."

"She gave me the impression she wasn't happy with him. After all, she is a person of some intelligence, if badly organized, whereas he lacks the brains of a polliwog."

"That she is unhappy most of the time I grant. The question is would she be happier with anyone else? I doubt it, for it is her nature to be unhappy and to make those about her unhappy. All of us have some of this in our natures and she, poor girl, has more than most." Goania looked sharply at Jorian. "You and she were close at one time, weren't you?"

"Aye, though it was a painful pleasure."

"Are you nurturing sentimental ideas of 'taking her away from all this,' or otherwise sacrificing yourself to make her happy?"

"No-o," said Jorian hesitantly, because such ideas had in fact been flitting through his mind.

"Well, if any have, dismiss them at once. You cannot change the basic nature of a grown man or woman, even by magical spells. If you took up with her again, you would find you had acquired, not a lover, but a sparring partner— a rôle for which Boso's grossness and stupidity fit him far better than your qualities fit you."

Jorian drew himself up. "You forget, Mistress Goania, that I left five lovely wives behind in Xylar. One of them at least—my little Estrildis—I hope to fetch away some day, to settle down and lead a simple craftsman's uneventful life."

Goania shook her head. "I have cast your nativity and studied your palm, and I fear that a quiet craftsman's life is the one boon the gods do not have in store for you. As for the wenches, I suggest that you adhere to your resolve to regain your Estrildis when you are lured into other bypaths." She glanced across to where Vanora stood, surrounded by young men. "From the way she is guzzling, I suspect we have one of Vanora's lively evenings ahead of us."

"What mean you by that?"

The wizardess sighed. "You shall see."

The library became more and more crowded, as more conventioners drifted in. The noise rose, as each speaker found he needed to raise his voice to make himself heard. Soon the room was packed with magicians and their helpers, all shouting at the tops of their lungs.

Jorian tried to introduce himself and engage those about him in talk but, despite his natural gregariousness and garrulity, with little success. He had to bellow to make himself heard, and the replies, when they came, were mostly unintelligible. He could catch only an occasional word, and that word was often so distorted that he could not tell whether it was a common word misunderstood or some esoteric magical term.

After a while, Jorian became bored by this noncommunication. He tried an experiment. To a long-bearded, dignified wizard, he solemnly shouted:

"Sir, did you know that the ultifang had metisold the otch whangle?"

The wizard's bushy, white eyebrows rose, and he uttered what sounded like: "You do not say so! We mist certimate glasso in the thourimar!"

"Aye, sir, I had it from the bolimbrig gazoo. No doubt abung it. When is the flolling gebisht in vemony?"

"On the fenty-nifth, I shink."

"Perzactly, perzactly. It's been a mosure, sir!"

But even this amusement palled in time. Jorian's feet were tired from standing and his head rang with the uproar when dinner was at long last announced. He took Goania in, but as an apprentice he ate with the others of his rank, while Goania joined Karadur to sup with the other master magicians. Remembering Karadur's last injunction, Jorian refrained from an account of his adventures. Instead, he confined himself to polite replies, leading questions to encourage the others to talk, and occasional quips and humorous verses to turn aside their curiosity about him.

"Are you donning a costume tonight?" asked one of his table mates.

"Alas! My master and I arrived late, without time to gather materials. Now I could only go as one shabby travel-worn apprentice. But tell me how this contest works, since this is my first Conclave."

"We must clear this hall to allow the servitors to remove the tables and push the benches back along the walls," said another apprentice. "A long platform is erected against yonder wall. Then those in costume assemble on the floor, whilst those not so clad sit on the benches. There is always a fuss over folk who stand up, blocking others' view, or inch forward into the press of the costume wearers.

"The master of ceremonies takes the names of all those in costume and calls upon them, one by one, to parade up one end of the platform and down the other, whilst the judges sit, looking judicious and marking their tablets. After all have paraded, the few best are called back to parade again, and from these the judges choose the prize winners."

"We have some comical rules," said another apprentice. "To give an example: human beings may parade in the guise of spirits, but demons, spirits, or other denizens of other planes and dimensions may not enter the contest at all. You'll see old Aello standing at one end of the platform and waving his wand at each contestant as he goes by. His great protective spell is supposed to make disguise by spirits impossible, but he wants to make doubly sure."

"And then," resumed the first apprentice, "there is a rule against complete nudity."

"Why?" said Jorian. "I have always thought that well-formed women looked their best that way."

"So did some of our lady conventioners. It got to be that twenty or thirty of these dames would parade as nude as frogs, so that the event bade fair to degenerate into a body-beauty contest and not a costume contest at all. There was a terrific row, with factions shaking fists and threatening maleficent spells. So a panel of the oldest and wisest magicians was appointed to arbitrate. These decided that a naked person is not, by definition, wearing a costume."

"In other words," said Jorian, "no costume is no costume. A fine philosophical and grammatical point."

"Precisely," beamed the apprentice. "Hence, naked human beings might not enter, not being in costume. But that didn't end the matter. There was a squabble only last year, when Madame Tarlustia, the Kortolian sorceress, paraded with no adornment other than a large jewel pasted into her navel. Did she qualify or didn't she? They ruled that she qualified but won no prizes, her garb displaying neither sufficent ingenuity, nor effort, not esthetic appeal. But 'twas a near thing. Had she been twenty years younger and twenty pounds lighter, the decision might have gone the other way, for she was still a fine figure of a woman."

Two hours after dinner, the company filed back into the ballroom. Jorian noted that most of those in costume— as far as he could see their faces at all—tended to be the younger element at the Conclave: the apprentices and assistants. The older wizards and wizardesses, by and large, preferred to sit sedately on the benches around the walls.

After an hour of milling about and getting the parade organized, the master of ceremonies mounted the platform. On the farther side of this platform, with their backs against the wall, sat the nine judges. President Aello stood at one end of the platform with his wand. The master of ceremonies looked at a list and called:

"Master Teleinos of Tarxia!"

An apprentice, dressed like a demon from the Fourth Plane, climbed the steps at one end of the platform, walked slowly past the judges, and descended the steps at the other end. While he paraded around the hall past the spectators, the master of ceremonies called:

"Masters Annyx and Forion of Solymbria!"

A dragon of cloth and lacquer, borne by two apprentices who represented the monster's legs, mounted the platform.

"Mistress Vanora of Govannian!"

Vanora, flushed but not staggering, marched up the platform in the guise of an undine. This consisted of a knee-length shift of transparent green gauze. Lengths of artificial seaweed were braided into her long black hair. She wore green gloves with webbing between the fingers, and her eyelids, lips, and toenails were painted green.

"Doctor Vingalfi of Istheun!..."

And so it went for three hours. In the end, Vanora won a third prize. Then an orchestra played. Jorian came up to congratulate Vanora, who was again surrounded by apprentices. Boso hovered, glowering unhappily, in the background. She was saying:

"They're playing a Kortolian volka. Which of you knows how to dance it?"

"I was once deemed an expert," said Jorian, extending his elbow for her to take. He nodded politely to Boso, saying: "With your kind permission, sir..."

"Oh, to the next incarnation with him!" said Vanora, seizing Jorian's arm and tugging him out upon the floor. "The witling can't dance a step."

Off they went, stamping and whirling. Although Vanora's breath was heavy with wine, the liquor she had drunk did not seem to have affected her excellent dancing. But the volka is vigorous, and the air was warm and balmy. By the end of the piece, both Jorian and Vanora were bathed in sweat. They found a refreshment table, where Vanora gulped down enough iced wine at one draft to have laid an ordinary drinker flat.

"Jorian dear," she said, "I was a damned fool to carry on about your serpent princess, as I did in Othomae. As if a drunken slut with a hot cleft, like me, should take umbrage at whom you frike on a mattress with! But it's my curse, to rail at every decent man and to bed with swine like Boso."

As she spoke, Jorian's eyes traveled over her body. Vanora wore nothing under the gauzy shift, whose sheerness bent the nudity rule as far as it would bend without snapping. Jorian tried to focus his mind on his lost Estrildis, but the blood poured into his loins.

"Say no more," he said, realizing his voice had thickened. "I'm sure I should have enjoyed it more with you than with her. At least, you wouldn't have tossed a man clear out of bed on the floor!"

"Did she, actually?"

"No, but it was a near thing. And the postures those Mulvanians use! But come, isn't it stuffy in here with all these people?"

"Aye. Have you been up to the battlements?"

"No, I haven't. Let's go."

On the battlements the moon, in its first quarter, was just setting. Stars glowed overhead, while in the south a mass of cloud was fitfully lit by the flicker of distant lightning.

"Isn't it warm for this time of year?" he said, sliding an arm around her waist.

"It is rather. Methinks we shall be in for a rainy spell." She turned slowly towards him and tipped back her head. "What of those Mulvanian postures?"

Soon afterwards, they walked lightly down the corridor leading to room twenty-three. Jorian's pulse pounded in his temples. He whispered:

"I haven't seen old Karadur all evening. If he's in our room, we shall have to try yours. If he's not, I'll lock him out."

"I know where some pallets for late-arriving guests are kept," she whispered. "We could drag one up to the roof."

"We shall see." Jorian tried the door of his suite and found it locked. He inserted the key he had received upon registration and quietly unlocked the door. He pushed it open a crack, then froze, listening. Vanora began:

"What is—"

Jorian made a quick chopping motion with his hand. The look of feral lust on his face had vanished, replaced by a hunter's stealthy alertness.

He pushed the door open a little wider, and a little wider yet, until it was open enough for him to slip through. The sitting room was dark, but a candle was lit in the bedroom. The door between the two was ajar, so that a narrow wedge of light slashed across the sitting room. Voices came from the bedroom, and between the snatches of speech the crackle of old parchment could be heard.

"Here's our scroll," said a voice. "By all the gods and demons! 'Tis a version of the sorcerer Rendivar's great counter-spell, thought to have been lost for aye."

"There's our answer," boomed the deep voice of the magician Vorko. "As I see it, we shall have to proceed by three stages. The first, to be performed tomorrow at the start of the debate, will be to work this counter-spell, thereby opening the way for subsequent actions—"

An old voice with a Mulvanian accent—Karadur's—spoke. In a tone of shocked surprise, this voice said: "You intend to assail our opponents by magic, in despite of all the laws and customs of the Forces of Progress?"

"Certes; what thought you? We've counted noses and

know that our proposal has no chance of passage. We do but lack the votes."

"But—but—you were always such a stickler for ethics—"

"Be no bigger a fool than the gods made you! When it's a question of doing something for the masses of mankind, one quibbles not about rules and ethics."

"But are you not being a little—ah—precipitate?" said Karadur.

Vorko snorted. "If you're concerned about every Maltho, Baltho, and Zaltho getting his hands on all the deadliest spells in the grimoire, you can stop worrying. I am not an utter idiot. I know as well as you that some of the reactionaries' claims—that ignorant men are not to be trusted with such powers—have a mort of truth in them. But offering magic free to all is the way to get power.

"Once we control the Forces of Progress, we can have Altruist governments in every one of the Twelve Cities within a year. I have my plans all laid and agents in those places—"

"But the Forces have always eschewed the politics of laymen!" said Karadur, in a voice that was almost a wail.

"The more fools they. Once we're in power, of course, we must needs proceed with caution, letting the masses in on only the most elemental secrets of magic—which they could learn for themselves in any good library—until they prove themselves worthy of more trust. But getting absolute power is the main thing. Once we have crushed all opposition, we can do whatever seems expedient. And, since I know that my own motives are pure and my plans are logically sound, it is my duty to seek the power to carry them out!

"Now, back to business: The second step will be to collect the names of the leaders of the Benefactors and all those who speak on their side of the question on the morrow. Rheits, you shall perform this task whilst the rest of us work the counter-spell. The session is supposed to last two hours—ample time."

Another voice said: "Are you sure, leader, that the old Rendivar spell will be strong enough? Aello's spell is no petty cantrip."

"As cast by one, belike not," said Vorko; "but by three or four of us simultaneously, I'm sure it will do. Now, as to the third step, if we could collect possessions or parts of the body from all these persons, we could attack them by sympathetic magic: impossible in the time at our disposal. Therefore, Magnas, you shall summon a flight of demons from—"

Jorian, standing in darkness near the connecting door, was horrified to hear a loud hiccup from Vanora behind him. Her consumption of wine had caught up with her. She hiccupped again.

"What's that?" said a voice from the bedroom.

To Jorian's helpless horror, Vanora staggered past him, banged open the connecting door, and cried in a hoarse voice:

"'Tis I, that's who it is! And why don't you impotent old shlobs get to the afterworld out of here, so Jorian and I—*hic*—can use a bed for what a bed's meant for?"

As the door flew open, Jorian had a fleeting impression of several men, besides Karadur, Drakomas, and Vorko, sitting on beds and chairs. Then Vorko's voice spoke a harsh, unintelligible word. Something warned Jorian of danger on his right. As he started to turn, out of the corner of his eye, in the suddenly augmented light, he saw one of Vorko's demons. The demon was stepping towards him and raising a bludgeon. Fast though Jorian's reactions were, the attack came so swiftly that he did not even have time to dodge before the universe exploded.

When Jorian came to, the room was lit by gray daylight through the arrow slit, furnished with a shutter and a casement sash, which served as a window. It took him some time to realize that the flashes and the rumbling were not inside his head but were caused by a violent storm outside. Rain drove against the little diamond panes of the sash and crawled down the glass like tiny, transparent snakes.

Jorian rolled over, wincing at the pain in cramped muscles and at the sharp stab of headache that accompanied each movement. He found that his wrists and ankles were bound and his mouth was full of gag. As his bleary vision adjusted itself, he saw that Vanora and Karadur were likewise trussed.

Vanora, still wearing her shift of green gauze, looked at him from bloodshot eyes over her gag. About Karadur he could not tell; the Mulvanian looked like a heap of old clothes in the corner.

Although Jorian's assailants had done a sound job of tying him up, they had not reckoned on the practice he had had in Xylar at escaping from such gyves. His first step was simply to chew. A few minutes of vigorous chewing parted the rag that held the gag in place and enabled him to spit out the gag.

"Vanora!" he said thickly. "Are you all right?"

"Gmpff, glmpff," she said through her gag.

"Karadur, how fare you?"

A groan answered. Jorian looked across the room, as best he could from his position on the floor. His sword still hung by its baldric from a hatrack by the door.

It is hard for a man whose ankles are tied together and whose wrists have been lashed behind him to rise from the floor, but it can be done. Several times, Jorian almost got to his feet and then crashed down again with bruising force. Little puffs of dust arose from the cracks between the floor boards. At last he made it. He hopped over to the hatrack and butted it over. Then he squatted down and got his hands on the hilt of his sword. A couple of grotesque hops took him to where Vanora lay.

"Seize the sheath with your feet," he growled. When she had done so, he hopped away from her, drawing the sword from its scabbard. Then he thrust the hilt between her feet.

"Now hold that blade steady. If you let go, 'twill skewer me."

He began squatting and rising again, holding the cords that bound his wrists behind him against the blade. When after twenty-odd squats a cord parted, the lashings came quickly off. For a few moments, Jorian stood rubbing his wrists and feeling the lump on his skull. Then he took the sword and quickly severed his and his companions' remaining bonds.

"That's how I once saved my head," he said. "The moral is to keep your sword well honed. These knaves were tyros after all, or they'd never have left aught sharp where we could come upon it."

"Remember, my son," said Karadur, "that they are accustomed to coping with foes, not by such crude devices as swords and cords, but by spirits, spells, and the transcendental wisdom of magic."

"So much the worse for them. What time is it?"

"Good gods!" said Karadur. "It must be after the fourth hour. That means the debate on the Altruist proposal will be under way in the ballroom. Vorko will be working that counter-spell he got from the Kist. Where is the wretched thing? Alas, they have taken it with them. Ah, me, shall I ever cease being a trusting, credulous ninny? But we must hasten to the ballroom to warn the Forces!"

"Gods, what a hangover!" moaned Vanora, holding her head. She did not look at all attractive this morning.

"Are you changing sides, Doctor?" asked Jorian.

"Nay; I have always been on the side of virtue and order. Say rather than Vorko and his minions have deserted me." The old man groaned as he tried to rise. Jorian helped him up. He failed to find his key but got out his pick-locks and went to work on the door, which soon swung open.

"We must lose no time, feeble though I be this morn," said Karadur.

"We?" said Jorian. "Why should I concern myself with the squabbles amongst your spookers? My work for you is done, and I don't intend to join your profession."

"You heard what Vorko said. An you care not for me and other honest magicians, think of Vorko's tyranny, blacker than those of Mulvan, Tarxia, and Metouro combined! But I cannot stop to argue; follow me who will."

The old magician hobbled out the door. After a heartbeat's hesitation, the other two followed him.

The doors of the main ballroom opened to Jorian's vigorous push. Karadur tottered in and down the central aisle between the rows of benches. One of the debaters was on his feet, saying:

"...and if you believe not that the common man be unworthy to be trusted with such fell secrets, let me cite instances of his stupid, swinish conduct from the history of our host country. When the kings of Metouro were overthrown and the Republic established—"

The speaker broke off as he became aware of Karadur, limping down the aisle bareheaded, his eyes glaring.

"Treason!" croaked the old Mulvanian. "A cabal of our members plots to overthrow the governance of this brotherhood and seize all power! Master Rheits, yonder, is gathering the names of the Benefactors, to further this attack! Seize him, an you believe me not—"

As Karadur spoke, Jorian and Vanora started to push through the door after him. As they did so, Boso confronted them. Seeing Jorian first, Boso started to say:

"Apprentices in the balcony for this meeting. Only master magicians down here—"

Then the sergeant-at-arms sighted Vanora. "You!" he barked. His face turned red, and his eyes glared with an insane rage. "You two spend—you spend the night in high diddle, and then you have the nerve—the g-gall—I'll fuff-fix you, strumpet!"

With an inarticulate snarl, he tore out his sword, shouldered Jorian aside, and rushed at Vanora. With a scream, the girl fled back into the main hall.

Torn two ways, Jorian hesitated for a heartbeat. In the ballroom, Karadur seemed to have things well in hand. He poured out his denunciation, while turmoil erupted around him. Several members of the Forces had seized Master Rheits. Jorian turned and ran after Boso.

He came out into the main hall in time to see Vanora vanish up the stair at the end of the hall with Boso in pursuit. After them he went, drawing his own sword—the same long blade he had taken from the sleeping Gending in the Ellornas.

Up he went, flight after flight until he began to pant, at each turn catching a glimpse of those he pursued. Soon he came out on the roof. Low clouds scudded overhead; rain beat slantwise to the flagstones. Lightning flashed, and booms of thunder periodically drowned out the whistle of the wind and the rattle of the rain.

Looking anxiously around, with his left hand up to keep the rain from blinding him, Jorian saw Boso enter the door to one of the two big round towers—the twin keeps—of the castle and slam it behind him. Slipping on the wet flags, Jorian ran to the door and tried it; but Boso had shot the heavy bolt inside.

Boso, thought Jorian, would chase Vanora up to the top of this tower and, if he did not catch her there, out across the bridge that joined the two towers and down the spiral stair in the other tower. So he ran back to the base of the other tower, whose door had not been locked.

Entering the other door, he trotted up the stair. As he came out on the roof, he almost collided with Vanora, who, gasping for breath and with her transparent shift clinging wetly to her, arrived at the same moment on the tower top from the bridge. Behind her came Boso, sword and teeth bared.

"Get back down and get help!" Jorian barked at Vanora over his shoulder as he sprang out on the bridge. The wet, gray stones under Jorian's feet vibrated in the gale like a fiddle string.

The structure was not quite so spidery-slender as it looked from below. The footway was four feet wide, and there was a low, crenelated parapet, a little over waist high, on each side. One was not likely to fall off merely from the effects of wind and rain. On the other hand, it would not be hard to fall out of one of the embrasures during a hand-to-hand fight.

The swords met with a whirl and a multiple clang, which was lost in a roar of thunder. The two powerful men stood on the bridge, still panting from their climb and glaring into each other's eyes, cutting, thrusting, and parrying. For an instant they backed off, breathing heavily; then they were at it again, clang-tzing-zip-clang. There was little footwork, because of the limitations of space and the slipperiness of the wet stones.

Their right arms worked like pistons, until Jorian's began to ache. The wind howled and drove the rain scudding almost horizontally. It staggered both fighters so that they had to clutch at the merlons with their free hands for support, even while they hacked and lunged. Lightning glared and thunder boomed.

Jorian found his horseman's blade a little too long for this kind of work, especially since its hilt was too short for both hands. Boso's blade was of about the same length and weight as the sword Randir, now the loot of the cham of the Gendings. The burly ruffian handled it well, whereas Jorian's parries, doubles, and one-twos were a little slow. Boso easily parried them, no matter how complex an attack Jorian launched. On the other hand, Jorian's extra inches of arm and blade kept Boso a little too far away to take advantage of his greater speed of blade. His stout, short-legged build made him too slow on his feet to slip in by a quick advance-lunge to get inside Jorian's guard.

Moreover, Boso had the bad habit of parrying in the obsolete seconde. Jorian swore that, the next time his foe did it, he would double and skewer him properly...

A new sound and sensation made itself felt. This was neither the crash of thunder, nor the whistle of the wind, nor the humming vibration of the bridge. It was a deep rumble, combined with a heavy shaking as of an earthquake. From below came a rising uproar of thumps, rumbles, rattles, clatters, crashes, shrieks, howls, screams, and bellows. Behind Jorian, Vanora screamed:

"The tower is falling!"

Jorian cast a quick look at Boso, who had withdrawn a couple of paces and stood, clutching a merlon with one hand and his sword with the other. The sergeant-at-arms's face was pale, and his hair was wetly plastered to his low forehead.

Jorian risked a backward glance. Vanora stood a couple of strides from him, clutching the merlons of the parapet of the tower.

"Why didn't you go down—" began Jorian, but then the stones lurched under his feet. With a frightful, grinding roar, both towers and the bridge that joined them began to sway outward, over the rain-lashed water of Lake Volkina.

Jorian sprang to the parapet, where the bridge joined the tower top. "Jump as far out as you can!" he yelled.

As he gathered himself to spring, Jorian took one last look at Boso. The latter was not looking at Jorian at all, but at a being that had appeared behind him. One of the merlons of the bridge parapet had burst into pieces. One stone, falling to the footway of the bridge, had changed into the being. Five feet tall and spindle-legged, it had an enormous head, larger than a pumpkin, and a huge, froglike gash of a mouth. It wore no clothes, and its skin had a moist, froglike appearance. It had no visible organs of sex.

That was all that Jorian saw as the towers leant further and further out over the water. He hurled himself out with a mighty bound, felt the wind whistle in his hair and rain in his face—curious, he thought in a flash, that rain should seem to be falling up; but of course he was overtaking the raindrops on their way down. Then he saw the slate-gray water coming up at him. *Smack!*

He reached the surface, feeling as if a giant had swatted

him with a paddle. On either side of him, someone was splashing. As he got the water out of his eyes and regained his breath, he saw that one of these was Vanora, who, unhampered by her negligible costume, was striking out for shore. The other was Boso, ineffectually wallowing and thrashing and trying to choke out the word: *"Help!"*

Jorian had dropped his sword during his dive. Two strokes took him to where Boso thrashed, bobbing under water and out again with each frantic effort. Jorian hooked an arm under the sergeant-at-arms's chin, secured a crushing hold, and began swimming on his back towards the shore.

A few strokes and he touched down. He dragged Boso to shore and dropped the man on his back in the mud. Boso lay with his eyes closed, coughing, spitting water, and breathing in racking gasps. Then Jorian looked around.

The Goblin Tower had collapsed into a vast heap of stone blocks. From under a few of the nearer blocks, human hands and feet protruded. All around the isle, hundreds of magicians and their helpers stood in the water, up to their ankles, knees, waists, or even chins. Some poked among the ruins of the castle. Injured persons moaned.

The rain had slackened to a steady drizzle. Nearby, Vanora stood naked at the edge of the lake, wringing the water out of her flimsy garment.

"Jorian!" He looked up to see Karadur and Goania wading towards him.

"What in the forty-nine Mulvanian hells happened?" Jorian cried.

Karadur was too winded and frightened to do more than gasp, but Goania explained: "You know how the Goblin Tower got its name? Well, when Vorko worked his counterspell, this nullified not only Aello's protective spell, but also the original spell put upon the goblins by Synelius, back in the days of the tyrant Charenzo. Since the castle had been partly built of these stones, when they were changed back into goblins, the walls collapsed because there were so many gaps in them. Most of the goblin stones seem to have been on the south side, and that is why the towers fell this way."

"I saw one of the things whilst I was up on the bridge, fighting with Boso," said Jorian.

"There must have been many hundreds of them in the lower parts of the castle."

"Where are they now?"

"Karadur released the demon Gorax from his ring and set Gorax on the goblins, whereupon they all whisked back to the Ninth Plane. I think they were worse frightened by awakening from their sleep of enchantment in the midst of the collapsing Tower than we were frightened of them."

"How did you escape?"

"When Karadur told what he knew of Vorko's counter-spell, old Aello instantly knew what was up. He screamed to us to get out of the Tower instanter. Most of us got out, although some were caught, and some were struck by falling stones after they had left the edifice. Luckily, the water on the other side is shallow all the way to shore. Vorko and his minions seem to have been amongst those destroyed; at least, I have seen nought of them."

"And Aello?"

"Dead in the ruins, I fear. He went to the kitchen and the servants' quarters to get those folk out, too, and was last seen poking about there to make sure that none was left behind. But what is this?" She indicated Boso, who was beginning to revive.

"I dragged him out of the lake. He would have slain Vanora up on the roof, out of jealousy. I was fighting with him on the bridge when the castle crumbled."

"Fighting him to death, and then you saved his life?"

Jorian clapped a hand to his forehead. "By Imbal's brazen balls! Why do I *do* these stupid things? Oh, well, I didn't really crave to kill the poor halfwit." Glancing about, he glimpsed a dull, metallic gleam in the shallow water. It was Boso's sword, lying in the mud. Jorian picked it up and shoved it into his own scabbard.

"My own is out in the lake somewhere," he said. "Will you go to law with me about it, Boso, or shall we forget the whole sorry business?"

Boso, now sitting up, shook his head and mumbled: "I hurt my back."

"Well, back or no back, get up! We have work to do." Jorian led the groaning Boso around the isle to where the magicians, standing up to their knees and waists in the water, were loading injured persons into rowboats that had come out to pick them up.

"Vanora!" said Goania severely. "Get some clothes on, child, ere you catch your death of cold."

When evening had fallen on Metouro, Jorian sat in the tavern that Vorko had occupied, with Karadur and Goania. Karadur had lost his turban in the collapse of the Goblin Tower and, feeling uncomfortable without it, had wound a strip of rag around his head as a substitute. Boso and Vanora, the latter wearing a new dress purchased that day by Goania, sat by themselves two tables away. Jorian said:

"Now I've done what your Altruists demanded, Doctor, even if your cursed Kist is buried in the ruins of the Goblin Tower, where at least it won't cause trouble for a long time to come. Since I have performed my part of the bargain, how do I get this geas lifted?"

"It is already lifted, my son. Since Vorko imposed it, his death cancelled it. But we must consider your future. If you would become my apprentice in fact as well as in name, I could make a prime magician out of you in fifteen or twenty years—provided I pass not to my next incarnation in the interim."

"No, thank you. I have my own plans, the first of which is to get back my dear little Estrildis."

"How will you accomplish that, without the help of magic?"

"I know not, old boy, but I shall find a way. During our journey, I observed that when I relied upon my own mundane powers, I usually succeeded; whereas, when I leant on the supernatural, I usually ended up worse off than when I started.

"I used to think that magic was the key to life's
    charade,
And therefore of its learned devotees I sought the aid:
Of necromancers whom the ghosts of men of yore
    obeyed.

Of hoary seers who, they said, the future could
    foretell,
Of sorcerers who to their lairs could summon spirits
    fell,
And wizards who could utter many a dark and deadly
    spell.

257

But when it was all done, I found a better spell was
  made
By counting on my own resource of eye and arm and
  blade,
My native reason, and between my knees a sturdy
  jade.

So now I'm through with horoscopes and pentacles as
  well,
And words to summon spirits who in strange
  dimensions dwell.
To every kind of spookery, I bid a last farewell!

"Horses will play the fiddle before I count on your arcane arts again."

Karadur began to argue: "The most ignorant man is he
who knows it all. Without my arcane arts, you would have
no head on your shoulders to harbor that wit whereof you
boast. An ethical man gives just credit to—"

But Goania cut him off: "Let the lad be, old colleague.
His mind is made up and from his point of view, rightly.
When he attains our age and the blood runs less hotly in
his veins, he may find our mysteries more beguiling. What
shall be your first step, O Jorian? The Faceless Five demand
that we all quit Metouro on the morrow, ere we destroy
the city by another ill-directed enchantment."

Jorian grinned. "I have a horse and a sword—both of
middling quality—but no money. My first task is to get
some of the last-named, and for that I shall need a hat.
My fur cap and my wizard's headpiece are buried in the
ruins of the Tower."

"A hat?" said Karadur vaguely. "I suppose you might
find one in Vorko's room, upstairs. But how can a
hat—"

"You shall see." Jorian rose and started for the stair.

"Jorian!" called Vanora. "Wait." She hurried across the
room and spoke in a low voice. "Leaving us?"

"Soon."

"Well—ah—I am, as you know, a tough and useful
traveling companion—"

Jorian shook his head. "I thank you, Mistress Vanora,
but I have other plans. It has been very interesting to
know you. Na, na, weep not, lass; 'twill but redden thy

nose to none avail. A needs must forth the morn, and ma
nag can bear but one."

He ran up the steps and presently reappeared with Vorko's hat on his head.

"How got you into his room?" asked Goania.

Jorian smiled. "Know you not that I do but make a
mystical pass, and all locks open unto me?"

She glanced over to where Vanora sat beside Boso with
tears running down her face. Vanora and her companion
both stared morosely into space. "I take it she asked to
become your leman again, and you denied her?"

"That's right. Thrice I'd come close to being killed on
that young woman's behalf, and that is twice more than
enough. I'm no hero—merely a simple craftsman—oh, all
right, Father Karadur, I won't say the rest."

The glare that Karadur had given Jorian softened, and
the old magician said: "But the hat—how—"

"Come out into the marketplace in a little while, and
you will see how I do it. Did not the philosopher Achaemo
say that the superior man uses his very faults and weaknesses to advantage? Fare you well!"

Half an hour later, Karadur, Goania, Boso, and Vanora
strolled out to the marketplace. The rain had ceased, although puddles among the cobblestones still reflected the
yellow light of link and lanthorn. A crowd was gathered
around the Fountain of Drexis in the center of the open
space. When the four approached, they saw that the crowd
surrounded Jorian, sitting on the curb of the fountain. As
they came up, he was saying:

"...and so ends the tale of King Fusinian the Fox and
the enchanted shovel. And the moral is, that more woe is
wrought by stupidity than by villainy."

Jorian fanned himself with Vorko's hat, for the night
was warm. "Would you like some more? Let's say, the
tale of ex-king Forimar and the waxen wife? Yes? Then
let us see if you cannot prime the pump a little, to spur
my sluggish memory..."

He passed the hat around the circle, to the clink of
coins. "A little more priming, good gentles; money is the
grease that lubricates the storyteller's clockwork. Ah, better.

"Well, it seems that after King Forimar the Esthete had

259

abdicated in favor of his brother Fusonio, a man set up an exhibition of waxworks in Kortoli City. This man, whose name was Zevager, asked the former king to allow such an effigy to be made of His Highness and displayed with the rest..."

About the Author

L. Sprague de Camp, who has over ninety-five books to his credit, writes in several fields: historicals, SF, fantasy, biography, and popularizations of science. But his favorite genre of literature is fantasy.

De Camp is a master of that rare animal *humorous fantasy*. As a young writer collaborating with the late Fletcher Pratt, he set forth the world-hopping adventures of Harold Shea. These are available today in two books: *The Compleat Enchanter* and *Wall of Serpents*. Together, Pratt and de Camp also wrote the delightfully zany *Tales from Gavagan's Bar*, a book which has remained in print for forty years.

In 1976, at the 34th World Science Fiction Convention, he received *The Gandalf—Grand Master Award for Lifetime Achievement in the Field of Fantasy*. The Science Fiction Writers of America presented him with their *Grand Master Nebula Award of 1978*. Alone, and with his wife and sometime collaborator Catherine, de Camp had been a welcome guest of honor at fan conventions throughout the United States.

The de Camps live in Villanova, Pennsylvania. They have two sons: Lyman Sprague, and Gerard Beekman, both of whom are distinguished engineers.

Enchanting fantasies from

DEL REY BOOKS